DEAD AMERICA
LOWCOUNTRY
BOOKS 1 - 6
BY: DEREK SLATON
© 2021

BOOKS:

Lowcountry - Pt. 1
Lowcountry - Pt. 2
Lowcountry - Pt. 3
Lowcountry - Pt. 4
Lowcountry - Pt. 5
Lowcountry - Pt. 6

FOLLOW NEW RELEASES AT:

www.DeadAmericaBooks.com

DEAD AMERICA
LOWCOUNTRY
PART 1
BY DEREK SLATON
©2021

CHAPTER ONE

Day Zero +1

Grace stared out the passenger window, looking out over the water. The sun was just beginning to rise over their backs, casting a warm glow on the lapping waves. As they crossed the Hilton Head bridge towards Bluffton, she turned to gaze at her brother, Dante, driving the car.

Growing up, nobody had ever believed they were related. Their features weren't terribly similar, and then there was the matter of his ebony hair contrasting her honey blonde. At this point, however, they couldn't look more different.

Her chest constricted as her gaze lingered on his facial scars, scars he had because of her. She traced every dip of his skin, all up his right arm to his neck and face. Her brother didn't have an eye anymore… because of her.

Grace looked down at her left hand, her own scarring much more minor and not noticeable unless one was looking for it.

"You're being quiet this morning," Dante said, side-glancing her.

"What do you expect?" she asked, rolling her eyes. "You drug me out of bed

at seven in the morning to go on a store
run."

He chuckled. "I'm sorry I interrupted
your beauty rest, princess," he drawled.
"But unless I'm mistaken, I'm pretty sure
this Super Center has a coffee shop." The
island was a hotspot for the wealthy elite
to vacation, which meant that they had to
cross to the mainland for something like a
Super Center, lest it blight the landscape
of multi-million dollar homes and resorts.

"Hopefully they have the IV bag
option," Grace groaned, "because if I'm
going to be awake for this funeral I'm
going to need caffeine injected straight
into my veins."

Dante smirked. "Pretty sure that's a
Seattle exclusive."

"Well, sign me up then," she moaned
in excitement. "Only been here three days,
and I'm so ready to get back home. Explain
to me again why we're out here for the
funeral when nobody else is?"

He shook his head. "You know that
Grandma wasn't close to much of anybody
except for us," he replied gently.
"Especially after… you know."

Grace looked down at her hand again.
Fire. Especially after the fire that
disfigured him. She swallowed and nodded.

"Okay, I'll buy that," she said, "but
what I don't understand is why we're

driving off-island to go to the Super Center at seven in the morning."

He shook his head. "The pastor asked if I could pick up a few things at the store for the reception," he explained. "I woke up early and thought it might be good to beat the crowds to the store."

"Well, thank you very much for including me in your little adventure," she said with a sigh. "Glad to know you value my advice on which chips pair well with a wake."

Dante chuckled and reached down, flicking on the radio. "We have a couple more miles to go, why don't you find us a song?" he suggested, and turned up the volume a bit.

"*There have been unconfirmed reports of rioting in Texas,*" a radio announcer said. "*Federal officials have thus far refused comment, saying that they are aware of the situation and are mon—*"

Grace hit the CD button on the dash, and the car filled with crunchy distorted classic rock. She bobbed her head and cranked the volume louder.

"That's better," she declared. "Way too early to be dealing with the woes of the world!"

She unrolled the window and waved her hand in the wind as they drove down the mostly empty road for a few more miles.

There were stretches of apartments and some strip malls, with a whole lot of wetlands in between.

As Dante pulled into the parking lot of the Super Center, there were already a dozen cars sitting out front, as it was the only thing open in the area. It sat in the middle of a long strip mall, stretching for a couple hundred yards in both directions.

"Well brother," Grace said as she turned the volume back down, "your master plan worked perfectly. We successfully beat the rush."

He rolled his eyes. "You joke," he said, "but I'll be willing to bet there isn't going to be a line for the coffee shop."

"You're paying, right?" she asked.

"Depends," he replied with a smirk. "Are you getting coffee, or one of those upscale fancy drinks with forty-seven words in the title that would require me to take out a second mortgage to pay for?"

Grace shrugged. "Well, we are in a resort town," she said. "It would feel wrong to not go fancy with my coffee. And you'll gladly take out that second mortgage because it will mean you won't have to listen to me complain for the rest of the morning that you woke me up before the sun rose."

"Yeah, that's money well spent," he agreed, chuckling.

They got out of the compact sedan, slamming the doors behind them. Dante fumbled around with the key fob, hitting what he thought was the lock, but instead the alarm started blaring, lights flashing on and off.

Grace laughed and shook her head, leaning over and snatching the key from his hand, turning the screeching alarm off.

"Damn rentals," her brother muttered.

"Hey, you're the one that wanted to go budget," she shot back, pointing the key at him. "For an extra ten bucks a day, we could have had a convertible."

He scoffed. "When I reserved the car, I didn't think a convertible in October was the best idea," he explained. "That was before I realized the humidity here is still a hundred and twenty percent, even in the fall."

"Imagine that, other parts of the country have different weather than Seattle," Grace said, gasping dramatically. "It's crazy, I know!"

Dante opened his mouth to respond, but a loud siren cut him off. An ambulance screamed into the lot and screeched to a stop in front of the Super Center.

"That better not be for the barista," Grace joked, shaking her head.

Dante shrugged. "If my experience working retail is any indication," he said, "it's probably for an employee slitting their wrists in the break room because they can't take the customers anymore."

"Did you ever think about seeing a therapist when you were working retail?" she asked, playfully bumping his shoulder.

He barked a laugh. "Guessing you've never seen a retail worker's paycheck."

"Touche," she conceded, and waved for him to follow her. "Come on, let's get that coffee before I'm forced to take a nap in the parking lot."

They headed for the front doors, reaching the sidewalk as two EMTs nearly ran into the store manager exiting the front. He looked frazzled, eyes large and unblinking, a dark crimson stain splashed across his work vest.

"Oh, thank god you're here," he babbled.

"What's the problem?" one paramedic asked.

The manager threw his hands up. "Some homeless guy went crazy!" he exclaimed. "He just came in and started attacking a couple of customers!"

"Is anybody hurt?" the EMT asked.

The older man nodded, jerking his thumb over his shoulder. "Yeah, he bit one of the customers on the shoulder," he said, rubbing his forehead.

"I'm sorry," the paramedic intoned, blinking in shock. "Did you say *bit*? Are you sure?"

The manager raised his palms. "I know, it sounds crazy," he admitted, "but I looked myself. It's definitely a bite mark. Pretty bad one, too."

"Okay," the EMT replied, shaking his head. "Where is the customer now?"

"In my office," the portly man replied.

"And the homeless man?" the paramedic added. "Is he still on site?"

The manager nodded. "Yeah, he just…" He shook his head vigorously. "He just wouldn't calm down. A few customers and I managed to shove him into the handicap bathroom and lock the door. He's still freaking out, banging on the door. He's not saying anything, just screaming or moaning… not sure which."

"Okay, it sounds like he got a hold of some bad drugs," the EMT explained. "These pushers are cutting stuff with some questionable shit. We'll take care of it."

The manager nodded tiredly and stepped aside. He glanced over at the brother and sister standing nearby, and forced a smile. "Don't worry," he blurted, "we're still open. The situation is under control."

"Sounds like it," Dante said wryly.

Grace's eyes softened as she saw the despair on the manager's face and smiled brightly. "Mister manager," she said in an overly bubbly tone, "is the coffee shop open?"

He perked up at the pretty girl, asking for his help, straightening his shoulders. "Yes, ma'am," he replied, smiling and nodding. "Best coffee you're going to find on island or off." He reached into his vest, carefully avoiding the blood, and pulled out a coupon, holding it out to her. "Here you go, this will get you a free pastry with your coffee."

"Well thank you," she replied with a wink, and accepted the coupon.

Dante pouted. "Don't I get a free pastry?"

The manager blanched, patting down his pockets.

"Oh, he's just joking with you," Grace piped up, offering another bright smile, and grabbed her brother's large firm bicep. "And besides, they're just empty calories," she said to her brother. "Can't risk your physique over that. Come on."

She pulled on his arm, and he let her drag him into the store. On the way in, he offered the manager a smile and a nod in thanks for the kindness. The manager returned it and then scrubbed his hands down his face in his panic.

As the duo entered the store, they looked over towards the bathrooms where the banging was coming from. A few employees stood by it, arms crossed, looking concerned but staunchly holding their perimeter to make sure no customers went close.

Dante lingered, listening to the snarling and screaming coming from inside.

"This is my absolute favorite time of year!" Grace gushed as she picked up a sparkly pumpkin decoration. "Can't wait to get back home and decorate the house up right."

Her brother smiled, thinking back to all the years they'd done a big Halloween production, setting up mini haunted houses for the neighborhood kids to come through. It was a big favourite of hers, and he loved to see her so happy.

As she dug through the decorations, he felt eyes on him, and turned to look at the next aisle. Hiding partially behind the end cap display was a young girl, maybe ten years old, peeking out at him, eyes wide with fear.

Dante offered a friendly smile to her, and turned in her direction, kneeling down to get to her level. "It's okay, you don't have to be afraid," he said softly. "I'm not a monster." He reached up and ran his hand up and down his scars. "See, they don't hurt, and they're not going to hurt you. It's just the way I look now."

She swallowed hard, a little more relaxed but still looking afraid.

He stuck his tongue out, making a silly face, and the little girl burst out laughing. An older woman turned around from the vases behind her daughter, and scowled, stepping up and grabbing the girl by the shoulders.

"Just what in the hell do you think you're doing?" she demanded.

Dante stood up, holding up a hand, and the woman recoiled a bit when she looked at his face.

"Your daughter saw me and was scared," he explained gently. "I just showed her that I wasn't a monster, that's all."

She glared at him, grinding her teeth, and then tugged on her daughter's hand. "Come on, it's time to go," she said sharply, turning on her heel.

Dante sighed. He was used to people being difficult about his injuries, but it didn't get any easier. The woman had

looked like she wanted to rip into him,
but likely realized with so many witnesses
she didn't want to become internet famous
for a meltdown in the Super Center.

"Why do you do that?" Grace asked,
stepping away from the decorations.

Dante shook his head. "People
shouldn't be afraid of me because of how I
look," he explained. "I'm just like
anybody else."

"I understand that," she replied,
"but one of these days someone is going to
beat your ass." She crossed her arms.

He winked at her with his good eye.
"There's a reason I took up MMA training,"
he said.

She rolled her eyes. "Grab a cart and
come on," she said. "Let's get what we
need and go find my coffee."

He grabbed a cart from the corral and
they headed for the back of the store
where the grocery aisles were. They headed
down each one, peeking around, but
couldn't find the soft drinks.

"Excuse me, ma'am," Dante said
politely to a young woman in a vest
working an end cap display.

"Yes, si…" she trailed off, jaw
dropping when she looked up at his face.
"Oh my god, I am so sorry sir," she
gushed, waving her hands in front of her
face. "I didn't mean to react that way.

It's just, you caught me off guard, and that's really not an excuse, it's just—"

"It's okay," he assured her, holding up a hand. "My ex had the same reaction when I asked her to marry me."

The woman's mouth stayed open, but no sound came out, her face horrified at how to deal with the situation.

"Don't pay any attention to him," Grace said, stepping forward. "He's just joking." She paused and glanced at her brother, raising an eyebrow. "Wait, you are joking, right?"

He smirked and nodded.

"See?" she said, smacking him lightly on the shoulder. "He's joking."

"I'm sorry…" he trailed off, checking her nametag. "Bailey. Just having a little fun."

She looked relieved, and let out a deep *whoosh* of breath, offering a smile. "I'm so glad," she said, and cleared her throat. "But I mean, what happened?" She clapped her hands over her mouth, eyes widening again, horrified she'd just blurted that out. "Oh my god," she said through her hands, and then moved them to her reddening cheeks. "I am so sorry. I don't know what's wrong with me today. Please, just ignore me!"

"It's really okay," Grace said gently. "My brother Dante here pulled me out of a fire years ago. He's quite the hero."

Bailey nodded, looking grateful that they overlooked her social missteps. "Very brave of you," she said. "Your sister is lucky to have you."

"Any woman would be lucky to have him," Grace said, waggling her eyebrows. "Brave, responsible, extremely fit. He's a catch, my brother."

Before either could respond, somebody barked from behind them, "Hey, if you're done chit-chatting, can I get some help over here?"

Bailey glanced around Dante to see a man in a button-down shirt and shoes that looked more expensive than her car. "Excuse me just a moment," she said, holding up a finger to the duo, and heading over to the impatient customer.

"What in the world are you doing?" Dante hissed to his sister.

Grace shrugged with a smirk. "Just trying to be your wingman."

"Wingman?" he asked, eyebrows reaching his hairline. "I'm old enough to be her father."

She cocked her head. "So?" she shot back. "Maybe she's into older guys. And let's be honest, it's been a while for you."

"How in the hell do you know that?" he demanded.

She crossed her arms. "Am I wrong?"

"Well… no," he admitted through his teeth, and then shook his head. "But still! How the hell do you know that?"

She smirked, but before she could answer, the asshole customer's voice rose.

"You need to learn how to do your job, girl," he declared. "How do you not know if you carry it?"

Bailey wrung her hands in front of her. "Sir, I'm sorry, this isn't my usual store," she stammered. "If you can just give me a minute—"

"Oh, so you're going to waste more of my time?" he snapped. "Fucking worthless kids not caring about their jobs."

Dante clenched his jaw and turned towards the man.

"Just don't hit him," Grace hissed, reaching out to tap her brother on the shoulder.

"No promises," he muttered, and walked over, stepping in front of the young woman. "You really need to learn how to talk to people properly," he said.

The man sneered. "Nice rug burn there Chachi," he mocked, "you must be a hit with the ladies."

"Not the only thing I hit," Dante said, staring him down.

The man glared back at him, fear and tough-guy syndrome warring in his eyes. Before anything could escalate further, a loud scream pierced the air from the front of the store, followed quickly by a second.

"What the hell was that?" Dante asked as all four of them turned towards the source.

The mean customer crossed his arms. "Probably broadcasting your ugly mug on the TVs."

Before Dante could respond, a few gunshots went off rapidly, causing the quartet to flinch. Bailey immediately pulled out her radio, bringing it to her lips.

"Front line, what's going on up there?" she demanded.

There was no response on the radio. Before she could try again, a male employee came tearing down the aisle towards them. Three people ran behind him, gaining on him as he hobbled, one of his legs bleeding crimson all over the tiles.

"Help me!" he screamed, reaching for the stunned group. "Help me!"

They watched in horror as two of the people chasing him tackled him from behind. The kid screamed as they bit into his flesh, one into his thigh, the other for the neck.

Bailey screamed, tears flooding her cheeks, and the asshole customer threw up his palms as one of the EMTs bypassed the tussle on the floor and tore towards him.

"What the fuck?!" he cried, taking a panicked step back, frozen in fear.

Dante lunged forward, grabbing the EMT around the waist and flinging it backwards. The snarling and bloody man hit the ground hard, but immediately scrambled to its feet, rushing him again.

Dante fell into a fighting stance, looking around frantically for something, anything he could use to his advantage. He spotted the next end cap, which was bare, leaving a few metal shelves about chest high. He rushed towards them and grabbed the EMT on the way by, clutching his throat and pushing it away from him.

"You need to calm down!" Dante bellowed, staring into the EMT's glassy eyes as she tried to snap and chomp at him. The dead hunger there made his blood run cold, and he realized there was a massive wound in the man's throat.

This is not a living, breathing human… he thought, his mind reeling. How was this possible? They'd just seen this EMT speaking and walking around normally not ten minutes before.

The dead EMT continued to thrash about, trying to bite at him. Grace screamed something unintelligible behind him, and Dante knew he couldn't let it go and get bitten himself. He grabbed the back of the thing's head and slammed it back towards the metal shelf. He timed it so that when the thing chomped down, he pushed it forward so that its jaws clamped around the metal instead.

"Dante!" Grace screamed as he reared back to deliver a strike, but he ignored her, hitting hard, driving the head partially through the shelf.

Teeth shattered and spewed everywhere, the corpse's mouth hooking on the bottom of the shelf, rendering it stuck. It thrashed violently, limbs everywhere, and Dante backed away from it slowly, standing next to his sister.

"Oh my god, are you okay?!" she cried, gripping his bicep tightly.

He nodded, swallowing hard, not taking his eyes off of the flailing corpse. "Yeah, I'm good," he said absently.

"What the hell is wrong with that guy?" she demanded, voice shrill.

Dante shook his head. "I don't know," he replied, "but I'm not sure he's still a guy."

Bailey screamed, motioning wildly towards the aisle where three more dead-eyed men tore towards them. One was the employee that had fallen and been attacked, and it was clear that something was sinister and unreal about this situation.

"Is there someplace we can hide?" Grace gushed, but Bailey didn't answer, staring wide eyed at the approaching men. She grabbed the employee by the shoulders and turned her away from it, giving her a shake. "Is there someplace we can hide?!"

"The…" Bailey stammered, pointing wildly. "The break room, it's this way!" She took off like a shot, and Grace followed. Dante grabbed the asshole customer by the collar and jerked him along, the man finally snapping out of it enough to follow.

Bailey led them to the back of the store, making a turn down the wall. There was a small room about twenty yards down, and she pulled out a set of keys, fumbling with them to get one into the lock.

Dante glanced down one aisle and saw a young portly couple ducked down behind a cereal display, clutching each other.

"Get over here!" he barked, waving wildly at them.

They scrambled out from cover and he waved even harder for them as a few corpses tore around the corner behind them into the aisle.

"Hurry up!" he bellowed, and Bailey threw the door open so everyone could pile inside.

Dante waited for the couple to fly in past him, and then darted inside, slamming the door just in the nick of time. Bodies thumped against it from the other side, and he threw the deadbolt, backing away from the door, shaking his head.

The group stared in horror as bloodied hands smacked against the small window, gnashing their teeth against the safety glass. A familiar head appeared in the window.

"Jesus fucking christ," the mean customer breathed.

The EMT's bottom jaw was unhinged, missing several teeth, dangling and bouncing against its neck as it tried to smack its way through the door.

Dante clenched his jaw and walked to the door, pulling the shade down over the window to conceal them in the small break room.

Bailey raised a shaky hand to her forehead. "What the hell is going on?"

CHAPTER TWO

The banging on the door continued,
and the group stood silent, trying to make
sense in their heads of what was going on.
The silence broke when the woman from the
cereal aisle began to cough violently. Her
boyfriend wrapped an arm around her,
trying to steady her in her fit.

"Are you okay?" Bailey asked, leaning
over to check on her.

"Yeah, just a cold," the woman
finally gasped, straightening back up.
"Having some issues shaking it the last
couple of days."

Bailey nodded. "We might have some
cold medicine in the cabinets if you think
it would help," she suggested, motioning
to the counter behind her.

"Are you fucking *kidding* me right
now?!" the mean customer bellowed,
throwing up his hands. "We just saw people
get their throats ripped out and you're
talking about cold medicine?! We need to
know what the hell is going on here!"

The girls shared a look that clearly
expressed disdain for his tone.

"On the way up here, we heard on the
news that there were riots breaking out
around the country," the man from the
cereal aisle piped up. "Maybe some of

those rioters have made their way up from
Savannah or down from Charleston?"

"I don't know what kind of riots
you've been in, boy!" the jerk cried. "But
last time I checked, rioters don't
typically eat people!"

"Yelling is getting us nowhere,"
Grace cut in, holding out her hands. "We
need to be productive and figure out how
to get out of this. Now, does anybody have
a cell phone?" As everyone fumbled in
their pockets, she straightened up.

Dante patted his pocket, but shook
his head. "Must have left it at the
hotel," he said, shrugging at Grace.

"I got nothing," the guy from the
cereal aisle said, sighing.

Grace furrowed her brow. "Can't get a
call through?"

"No, I mean I got nothing," he
replied, holding up his phone screen for
her to see. "No service."

The mean customer growled and smacked
his phone before slamming it down on the
lunch table. "You know, I bought this at
your store," he snapped, pointing at
Bailey as she turned around with a bottle
of cough medicine. "Why the hell isn't it
working?"

She stared at him like a deer caught
in the headlights, frozen.

"So that's how you respond to a screwed customer?" he demanded. "Silence? Why isn't this working?"

Grace slammed her hands down on the table. "Hey, dipshit," she snarled, "does she look like a cell phone technician?"

He blinked at her, to in shock the young woman was speaking to him that way.

"Did I fucking stutter?" she snapped. "Does she look like a cell phone technician?"

He shook his head and stammered, "Um… no?"

"No, she doesn't, does she?" she said firmly, standing up. "Now why don't you quit whining like a spoiled five year old and start helping us figure out our next move?"

He lowered his gaze, wilting underneath her tone. Bailey gave her a thankful look, and handed the cough medication to the cereal aisle woman, who offered a smile in response.

"Let's start simple," Grace continued, now in control of the room. "I'm Grace, that's my brother Dante, and this lovely Super Center employee is Bailey."

"I'm Connor," the cereal aisle man piped up as he shoved his useless phone back into his pocket, "and this is my wife June."

She gave a little wave before dissolving into more coughs, fumbling with the package of pills. Everyone else glanced at the asshole customer, who rolled his eyes and crossed his arms.

"Fine," he drawled, "I'm Troy, forty-two, and an investment banker from New York City that makes more in a week than all of you combined in a year. Now if we're done with this first day of kindergarten bullshit, can we kindly figure out what the fuck is going on?"

Dante cocked his head in Bailey's direction. "You've been here all morning, haven't you?" he asked, and when she nodded, he motioned for her to speak. "Do you know what happened with the attack earlier?"

"I was in the back when it happened, so I didn't see it," she admitted, shaking her head. "There was just a scream, and then a panicked call over the radio for security to come up to the front. After a couple of minutes, the manager came on and told everyone to stay in their sections. I just thought another customer was throwing a temper tantrum…" She glanced at Troy, tonguing her cheek. "Which seems to be quite common in these parts."

Before he could get riled up, Dante turned to the young couple. "And you two?"

he asked. "Were you here when it happened?"

"Yeah," June choked out, swallowing two pills dry. "We were near the back when we heard the commotion. We didn't think anything of it and just kept shopping."

Troy rolled his eyes. "Nice situational awareness, there," he scoffed.

"We've both spent time in retail hell," she shot back, narrowing her eyes at him. "We know the kind of shit that goes on. If we had a dollar for every time we've heard someone lose their shit at a cashier, we'd be rich enough to own the place."

Bailey nodded in silent agreement, suddenly looking tired.

Dante peered out the window, pulling back the shade just a hair so he wouldn't give them away. Most of the corpses had moved away from the door, a few of them sprinting up the aisle. He wondered if they'd spotted another poor soul, but couldn't be sure.

A creature staggered towards the door, wearing a bloodied Super Center uniform. He looked closely, seeing it had a bite on the back of its leg and shoulder, as well as a few other places. He shook his head.

"Zombies," he muttered under his breath, disbelieving. "Really?"

"The fuck you just say?" Troy barked.

"Nothing," he said, waving a dismissive hand.

Troy pointed a finger at him angrily. "Bullshit, you said zombies," he declared. "Are you fucking kidding me right now?"

There was a tense silence in the room, as everyone tried to process that information.

"Dante…" Grace said slowly, confused at her normally level-headed brother. "Did you really say zombies?"

He nodded, stepping away from the window. "Yeah, I did," he admitted.

"You sure those burns on your face didn't cook your brain a bit?" June asked dryly.

He ignored her barb, shaking his head. "I know how it sounds," he replied, "but between ripping off that EMT's jaw, and Bailey's coworker who we saw get ripped to shreds running around, I don't know what else to call them. Regardless, it doesn't matter what they are. What matters is that they're fast, vicious, and if we're going to have any chance of getting out of here alive, we're going to need weapons."

Troy stared down his nose at Bailey. "So do you know where the gun section is, sweetheart?" His voice dripped with condescension.

She shook her head. "There is no gun section at this store."

"Are you fucking kidding me?!" He threw up his hands. "This is South Carolina? How in the holy hell is there not a gun section?!"

"Apparently too many rich New Yorkers vacationed on the island and complained to the manager about it," she snapped, putting her hands on her hips, finally having enough of his antics. "Something about offending their *sensibilities*, so he had it removed last year."

He huffed and threw himself down into a chair. "Okay, so what do you have here that we can use to defend ourselves?" he asked petulantly.

"Baseball bats," Dante cut in. When everyone turned to him, eyes wide, he spread his arms. "They're compact, lightweight, and can crush a skull if you hit it just right."

Troy rolled his eyes. "Oh, here we go again with the zombie bullshit," he drawled. "I suppose you think we need to destroy the brain or something?"

"Well…" Dante scratched the back of his head, looking embarrassed. "I already tried ripping the jaw off of one of them, and the thing didn't so much as flinch. Pretty sure whatever these things are, they don't care about pain. So if you want to try and gut punch them, you have at it. I'm aiming straight for the dome. One thing I've learned over my years of training is that if you hit anything in the head hard enough, it goes down, regardless of what it is."

Troy contemplated for a moment, and then begrudgingly nodded.

"Bailey, where is the sporting good section?" Grace asked.

She swallowed hard. "About six aisles down to the left," she said, motioning. "Bats should be in the middle of an aisle, at least they were in my store."

"Okay, Troy," Dante said, rubbing his palms together. "You ready to do this?"

The banker blinked at him incredulously. "Fuck you, if you think I'm going back out there willingly," he scoffed. "I'm content sitting my happy ass here until the cavalry comes."

"This shit just started twenty minutes ago. The EMTs are already wiped out, we're outnumbered, and the cell network has collapsed," Connor said, getting to his feet. "I'm gonna go out on a lib and assume help ain't coming."

Grace nodded. "Connor's right," she agreed. "We gotta go out there and get weapons so we can fight our way out."

"Well, if he's so right, then let him go out there and risk his skin," Troy snapped.

June coughed and shook her head. "My hubby is a lot of things, but a fighter ain't one of 'em," she wheezed. "Hell of a stiff breeze can knock him flat on his ass."

"Well that's obvious if he's letting you do all the fighting for him," Troy said dismissively, waving her off. "What kind of man does that, huh?"

Connor's eyes darkened. "The kind of man that knows she has a bigger dick than anybody in this room," he declared, "and she'll gladly fuck you with it if you don't lay off."

June glared at the banker, and he withered under her intense stare.

"So, what do you say?" Dante asked, regarding Troy. "You wanna man up and help me out? Or do we get to sit back and watch June bend you over a table?"

The banker's eyes flashed, but he bit his tongue and got up from the table. "All right hotshot, let's get this over with so I can go on my way and never have to look at your ugly mug again."

"Fine by me," Dante replied. "You follow my lead, you good with that?" he asked.

"Yeah, whatever," Troy muttered.

Grace reached out and grabbed Dante's hand, drawing her lower lip between her teeth and looking up at him with side eyes. "Brother, you be safe out there," she said.

He winked at her with his good eye and smirked, playfully motioning to his face. "When have you ever known me to play it safe?"

She forced a smile. "Just try," she whispered, "for me."

He nodded and then turned to the group. "Now listen," he said, "there's a good chance we're going to be coming in hot, so you be ready to slam this door as soon as we're through." He looked at June. "Can you be ready to help?" he asked gently.

She coughed, but gave him a thumbs up. "Don't worry," she replied, "my fat ass will make sure that door stays shut."

Dante blushed a little. "My apologies, I wasn't implying—"

"Aw honey," she replied, waving him off. "You ain't got nothing to apologize for. I know what I am, and frankly it's about damn time I put it to good use."

He nodded at her, glad she hadn't taken it personally, especially considering his own physical traits that got addressed all the time. "Okay, we move quick and silent," he said, turning to

Troy. "If there's trouble in the aisle, I'll handle it while you grab the bats. Once they're in hand, we haul ass back here to regroup. You good with that?"

The banker rolled his eyes. "Yeah, yeah," he drawled, "let's get this done."

Dante snapped his fingers. "Hey." He stared him down. "Are you *good* with that?"

"Yes, I'm good," Troy said firmly.

Satisfied, Dante turned to his sister. "You be ready for us," he said, and peeked out the window once more. The immediate coast was clear, so he cracked open the door, and he and Troy slid out of the break room as silently as they could.

CHAPTER THREE

Dante led Troy away from the break
room, taking slow quiet steps towards the
sporting goods aisle. He looked across,
seeing a sign on top of one five aisles
down that read *baseball, basketball,
soccer*. He pointed and looked back at his
companion, who nodded.

He paused at the end cap, peering
down to see if the coast was clear. He
motioned for Troy to follow him and then
darted across to the next end cap. The
next one was clear, and when he stopped at
the third, he spotted three zombies
feasting away on a helpless twitching
victim.

The creatures munched away, tearing
flesh from bone, their meal convulsing as
the last of their life left their body.

Dante turned to Troy and held up
three fingers and then put one to his lips
to signal there were three ghouls and they
needed to be silent. Troy nodded, eyes
wide, and then they moved as quickly as
they could across the way, keeping their
footfalls as silent as possible.

Dante checked the next one, and
glanced back at his companion, who was
checking to make sure the feasting corpses
hadn't noticed them. He gave a thumbs up,
and so they moved up to the final aisle.

Dante looked down and spotted a lone zombie standing near the bats. He turned and nodded to Troy, holding up one finger. They shared a firm nod, and then Dante made the turn, creeping up the aisle.

The zombie stood transfixed by a light glaring off of a metal display, moaning and clawing at it. Dante kept his eye on the ghoul, and the baseball bats on the shelf between them.

If I can reach one of those, then we're in business, he thought. But when he was within five steps of the equipment, the ghoul turned towards him, letting out a growl and sprinting forward.

"Get the bats!" Dante bellowed, and rushed the zombie, lowering his shoulder. He hit it in the gut, and wrapped his arms around its knees, flinging it onto its back. He put his entire weight into his knees, pinning its chest, and held its face down by the throat with his strong hand.

Despite his strength, he was having a hard time holding the thing down. For a corpse it was strong as a bucking bronco.

"Hurry up and brain this thing!" he yelled, and Troy finally reached the rack of bats.

Two more zombies tore around the corner at the top of the aisle towards the main part of the store, and rushed towards them.

The banker's eyes widened, and he stood there for a second with his armload of bats. "Sorry man!" he finally cried, and then turned tail, running back towards the break room.

Dante let out a frustrated growl, looking at the two zombies rushing for him. They were gaining ground quickly, and he knew he wouldn't have time to escape. He pushed off of the zombie's head, giving him an extra second to grab a bright pink baseball bat from the rack.

He whipped around and brought it down vertically, smashing in the top of the ghoul's head as it scrambled to its feet. It collapsed on the ground in a heap, and he turned towards the other two that were within ten yards now.

He darted forward, leaping into the air and delivering a flying knee strike to the lead zombie's chest, sending it crashing to the linoleum. As he landed on his feet, he immediately swung, cracking in the skull of the second zombie.

The fallen ghoul managed to get back to its feet quickly, turning around just in time for Dante to use the bat like a lance, smashing it into its face. The bones in the zombie's face shattered with a *crunch*, its nose completely flattened, and it staggered back a few steps. It moaned and lunged towards him, but he gave it another quick jab to the face.

This time as the zombie tripped backwards, he hit it in the face a third time and then wound up, smacking down on the top of its head.

With the three corpses unmoving on the floor, Dante looked back towards the top of the aisle, seeing no other immediate threat. He rushed to the back wall, heart hammering as he paused at each aisle, looking down to check for enemies. With the amount of noise he'd made, he couldn't get sloppy now.

The first few aisles were still empty, as was the one that had had the feasting zombies in it. Even the corpse they'd been feeding on was gone. When he reached the break room hallway, he peered around the corner at the sound of moaning and banging. Two creatures stood outside the door, which was still open a crack, pounding on it with their bloody hands.

Dante looked both ways, making sure there wasn't anything else waiting to ambush him. When he saw it was clear, he headed for the door, gripping the gaudy baseball bat tightly.

The first zombie didn't see him coming, and he caved in the top of its head from behind. The second one tried to turn, but its arm was caught in between the door and the frame, so it was unable to launch an attack.

The hallway was wide enough that Dante was able to swing the bat normally, the impact forceful enough to crack the creature's skull and snap its neck. Its arm caught in the door with such force that the body just laid there limp, the head slumped to one side.

"Grace," Dante said.

The door flung open, and he stepped over the body. June shoved the dead creature away and slammed the door, throwing the deadbolt and pressing her back up against it.

"Oh my god, are you okay?!" Grace cried, rushing over to him.

Dante's eyes narrowed. "I'm fine," he said flatly, staring at Troy in the corner.

The banker looked ferociously terrified, though seemingly trying to hide to save his macho-man attitude, not wanting to show weakness.

Dante threw the pink aluminum bat on the floor with such force that the *clang* echoed loudly in the small room. He stalked over to Troy, not blinking, not breaking eye contact. He stopped six inches away, but didn't reach out to even lay a finger on him.

"You should know this," he said, voice calm and collected, but injected with venom. "I have broken men in half who have done far less to me than what you just did. As fate would have it, I happen to need you right now." He cocked his head. "However, and you listen to this *good*, if you pull anything even remotely close to what you just did, I won't have a need for you anymore. Do you understand what I'm saying?"

Troy clenched his teeth tightly, and just gave a jerky nod in response.

"What happened out there?" Connor asked, brow furrowing.

Dante continued to stare at Troy, making sure that the man knew he wasn't fucking around. When he was convinced, he gave him a slight nod to remind him who was in charge, and then turned back to the rest of the group.

"What happened, is we got the bats and took down a few zombies," he declared.

Connor shook his head. "No, I mean what happ—"

"That's the only thing that matters," Dante cut in firmly.

"Question is," June piped up, swiping her palms together as she moved away from the door, "now that we got weapons, what in the hell do we do now? I mean, I would say y'all could come over to our place,

but I'm not sure our little trailer is
going to offer much protection from those
things."

Bailey shook her head, wringing her
hands. "I need to get home to my family,"
she said shakily. "My mother is home alone
with my two younger sisters. They've got
to be scared out of their minds right
now."

"Where are they?" Dante asked.

She chewed her lip. "They're in
Beaufort."

"Beaufort?!" Connor howled, shaking
his head. "Hell girl, that's like thirty
miles away, and it's pretty big too, so
there's probably gonna be a ton of those
suckers running around! Gonna be a
madhouse!"

Bailey stepped forward, pressing her
palms together. "But the marine base is
there," she insisted. "They've gotta be
holding things together, don't they?"

"Shit, with as quickly as this stuff
is spreading," Connor replied, "I'm not
sure anybody is going to be able to get a
handle on it."

Bailey swallowed hard, hugging her
arms across her chest, and then burst into
tears.

June pursed her lips and walked over
to the young woman, putting an arm around
her shoulders. "God dammit Connor, cut

that shit out," she snapped, and then turned to Bailey. "Don't worry, I'm sure the marines are getting your mom and sisters right now. It's gonna be okay."

Bailey nodded, sobs subsiding a little as she let the other woman comfort her.

Dante took a deep breath. "I promise we'll get to your family, but right now we need to get someplace safe," he explained. "Thirty miles into a populated area is going to be tough, and staying here certainly isn't an option. If enough of those things realize we're in here, we'll never get out of this room."

"So where can we go?" Grace asked, brow furrowing.

Troy cleared his throat, stepping away from the corner and raising his chin. "You people can do whatever you want," he declared, "but I'm going back to Hilton Head Island."

Dante and his sister shared a glance, surprised that the asshole had actually had a good idea.

"One bridge on and off the island," Grace mused, "should be easily defended."

He cocked his head. "You assume that the interior of the island would be clear."

"Oh, I would wager every dime of my considerable fortune that it is," Troy said, crossing his arms, "or it soon will be."

"Yeah?" June asked, stifling a cough. "What makes you so damn sure?"

"Two words," Troy replied, holding up two fingers. "Theo fucking Atkinson."

There was a moment of silence as everyone thought over the name.

June dissolved into a fit of coughs, wheezing under her breath, "That was three words…"

"Who in the holy hell is Theo," Connor began, and raised his hand into air quotes, "*fucking* Atkinson?"

Grace put a hand to her forehead. "Wait… I know that name," she said, staring at the ceiling to try to remember. "Why do I know that name?"

Everyone thought for another moment, and then finally it clicked for Dante, and he shook his head.

"That's the mercenary guy, isn't it?" he asked slowly, not impressed.

Grace gasped, finally remembering. "That motherfucker is evil as hell!" she cried. "Do you have any idea how many of his mercenaries from QXR Group have committed war crimes while getting paid by *our* tax dollars, no less? I've protested a couple of times outside one of his offices in Seattle. Dude is a prick and a half!"

"I couldn't care less about supposed war crimes in third world shit holes," Troy replied with a shrug. "What I do care about is that his boys kick all kinds of ass, so I can guaran-damn-tee they got that bridge blocked off and have that island under control."

Grace looked helplessly at Dante, who was innately and begrudgingly accepting the plan as the most logical option.

"Dante," she pleaded, pressing her palms together.

He sighed, running his hands over his head. "I know, I know," he groaned. "I'm not exactly thrilled with this plan either. But if this stuff is widespread, it might be our only hope of riding this out."

She shook her head, lowering her hands and clenching her fists at her side.

"So how do we know this Theo dude is on the island?" June asked, finally clearing her throat.

Troy jutted out his chin. "Because I was teeing off on the sixteenth hole when he was flying into the island airport," he explained. "Big ole bitch of a plane. Forget private jets, he was traveling like he was about to invade a small country."

"Guess that's good enough," June replied dryly.

Connor raised his palms. "Having a destination is fine and all, but how in the hell are we getting there?" he demanded. "Weather might be nice, but not sure this is a great day to be going on a five-mile hike."

"We would say you could ride with us," June added, wrinkling her nose, "but our car is kinda trashed."

Her husband nodded. "Plus the starter goes out half the time," he explained, "and with our luck, it would definitely go out when we're feeling zombies… or whatever the hell those things are."

The group turned to Troy, and he shrugged.

"High end sports car," he replied, "so I can fit one."

Grace rolled her eyes. "Least surprising revelation of the day."

"So just by looking at me, you know I like the finer things in life?" he asked, shooting her a smug smile.

June held up a hand. "No, it means one look at you, and we know you have a pecker the size of a lil' smokie."

Troy growled, but Dante stepped forward, speaking loudly to get things back on track.

"Bailey, what about you?" he asked.

She shook her head. "A friend dropped me off," she replied quietly. "My mother needed the car today."

"Well, I guess that leaves us, then," Dante said with a shrug. "We have a sedan. It's going to be a tight fit, but we can all get in."

Troy sneered. "So what's the plan, hotshot?" he asked.

Dante took a deep breath and paced a bit, thinking. "Does the vestibule at the front of the store lock without a key?" he asked.

"Yes, there is a bolt switch that you can hit at the bottom of the doors," Bailey replied, brow furrowing. "Why?"

"Because we don't know what the outside is going to look like," he explained. "If we can get into the vestibule and lock it down, we can catch our breath for a minute before going out."

She nodded, catching his drift. "The interior doors lock from both sides, and the doors to the outside obviously only lock from the inside," she said. "The interior door locks are hidden, so you have to feel along the base for a pop out switch. If you go straight along the panel, straight down from the handle, you can't miss it."

Dante stopped pacing, listening intently. "Good to know," he replied with a nod. "Since you know what you are looking for when we get in there, that's all I want you to focus on. Troy and I will handle any of those things that are inside that area. The rest of you, find locks and flick 'em shut. Everybody good with that?" he asked, and everybody nodded. "Then grab a bat, because it's time to get out of here."

CHAPTER FOUR

Dante looked out the window of the break room, confirming that the hallway was clear. There were no zombies in the aisle directly ahead of them.

"Troy, I want you to take the rear," he instructed. "Everybody else, file in."

The group got into position, with Grace right behind him, the redneck couple behind her, and Bailey in front of troy. Dante threw open the door, bat in hand, and led them down the hallway, carefully and quietly stepping over the corpses still laying there.

They inched their way up to the corner, and he poked his head out, looking both ways. The coast was clear along the back of the store. He led them all the way up the aisle, stopping at the top to peek around.

The main aisle that ran horizontally across the store was just to the left of them. The front aisle was a good fifty or sixty yards to the right, with a whole lot of housewares aisles in between. There would be no easy way for them to cut through the middle of the store, so they'd have to risk going up the main front aisle.

Dante looked further down the left side, seeing a handful of creatures along

the outer wall, a good sixty yards from
them. He motioned to the ground that it
was time to move.

He led them out, darting across the
open area and taking some semblance of
cover against a large shelving unit as
they worked their way up towards the front
of the store. Dante approached a break in
the structure, leading down a small aisle.

He peeked around the corner and found
himself staring at the back of a zombie's
head, not more than an arm's length away.
He reacted on instinct, grabbing it by the
back dollar, spinning it around, and
slamming its face into the ground. As it
thrashed, Grace quickly used the top of
her bat to cave its head in with several
quick blows.

The brother and sister shared a
relieved look, eyes wide at how close that
had been. THe rest of the group held their
collective breath, listening intently for
any noise.

There was moaning coming from a few
side aisles down, where some of the things
had caught on to their position. Dante and
Grace quickly slid back behind cover, and
he peered down the row.

Three zombies emerged, jerking their
heads around in an attempt to figure out
where the food was. After several tense
moments, two of them wandered back down

where they'd come from, but one remained, about ten yards away. Dante held up a finger to let the group know that there was still one ghoul there and then waved for them to follow.

He led them across the opening, moving quickly and quietly. As Connor stepped over the corpse, he was more concerned with the zombie ahead, and his foot caught the dead one's wrist. As he shook it free, the watch adorning its wrist blinked on the ground.

The tiny noise was enough to catch the attention of the zombie, and it turned, moaned, and ran towards him. June threw up her hands, but he shoved her aside, out of harm's way. He tried to lift the bat to strike, but the creature hit him too quickly, tackling him and driving them both into the grocery section across the main aisle.

They hit the floor hard, and the ghoul latched onto his cheek, ripping it clean off. He screamed in pain, and June shrieked his name, lunging towards him.

Troy caught her waist and shoved her after Grace. "He's gone, move!" he yelled, giving her another shove. The other two zombies that had deserted were back, and he spotted them as they closed in. "Fuck," he muttered.

Bailey raised her bat, but she could barely hold it steady, eyes wide with fear. In a split second decision, Troy grabbed her and pulled her away from the opening, heading in the opposite direction of the other three in the group.

"Bailey!" Grace shrieked, but Troy dragged her to safety, moving down the center main aisle and vanishing around the corner.

The two zombies rushed out for food, and Dante grabbed June and jerked her after him and his sister. In a matter of seconds, the two creatures spotted their buddy feasting on Connor, who twitched on the floor, whimpering and losing life fast with each bite and tear.

June clamped her hands over her mouth, tears streaming down her face, but not making a noise.

Dante motioned that they needed to keep moving, so Grace grabbed the heartbroken woman's arm and pulled her along after them. June shook her off and readied her bat, giving a firm nod.

The trio moved up the side aisle, running parallel with the aisle running to the front of the store. There were signs of struggle and death, various housewares scattered about the ground, resting in pools of fresh blood.

Dante worked the group up to the front, stopping them at the top of an aisle just off to the side of the front registers. Past those, about twenty yards away, was the vestibule, which had a few zombies in it. There were four ghouls also scattered about the checkout line, with a few more milling about in the clothing section directly across from the registers.

The vestibule itself was small, with four doors on the exterior leading to four interior doors straight ahead. Two on the smaller interior wall were for people to exit after completing their purchases. Dante studied everything thoroughly before whispering to his companions.

"We're going for the side doors," he said quietly. "I'll take out the two zombies inside, you two get it locked up."

Grace gave him a thumbs up, and he looked back out, taking a deep breath, ready to make his move. Before he could step out, however, his sister grabbed his arm, stopping him. He spun around and saw she was holding up a solid metal garlic press. He furrowed his brow, not understanding what she wanted him to do with it.

She leaned in and whispered, "Throw it into the clothing section. It might draw some of the ones away from the register."

He nodded, impressed with her idea, and took the handheld press. He reared back and then flung it as hard as he could over the shelving. A few seconds later, there was a loud *clang* as it bounced off one of the metal display racks.

He watched as most of the zombies in the register area immediately rushed off towards the noise, moaning and thrashing as they went. This left only two in the register area, and two in the vestibule. Dante led them out, the three of them running hard.

They reached the register area, and one of the zombies spotted them. It moaned and started rushing, but Dante didn't stop moving at full speed. As they prepared to crash into each other, he ducked down, planting his shoulder into its gut, picking it up and throwing it onto one of the checkout baggage areas. It hit hard, before sliding off into the area where the cashier would have stood.

While this happened, June ran forward, straight at a zombie near the double vestibule doors. It turned and started to come at her, but she managed to crack it on the head with her bat, dropping it to the ground. She swung several times, sending blood splatter onto herself and everywhere else.

Grace and Dante caught up to her, with Grace touching her shoulder to get her to calm down and focus. She nodded, and they continued on to the vestibule about ten yards away.

Dante flew through the doors first, immediately heading towards the two zombies at the far end. They quickly turned when the door opened, and rushed at him, so he lowered his shoulder and slammed into the lead ghoul's chest, driving it back into the other.

They crashed into the back wall and flopped to the ground, giving Dante a brief moment to deliver strikes with his bat. He swung swiftly and violently, giving half a dozen strikes in rapid succession. With them thrashing on the ground, it was hard to see if he was making clean hits or not, so he kept going until they stopped moving. As soon as they were down, he turned his attention to the outer doors, finding the locks and getting them shut tight.

While he was battling, June focused on the doors they'd just come through, finally getting them locked. Grace rushed over to the two sets of double doors leaning into the store, frantically running her hand down the panel and trying

to find the secret release. When she
finally found it, she popped it out and
secured it.

When she moved over to the second
one, she popped it out, but then froze at
the sight of Troy and Bailey running
towards her, several zombies hot on their
heels. As they blew through the clothing
section, several more corpses darted out
and joined the pursuit.

Grace's eyes widened. She didn't want
to lock the door in case they could make
it. She held steady, watching as they ran
hard towards her. To the left she spotted
one of the zombies from the register area
running on an intercept course, and threw
open the door, darting out.

"Grace!" Dante screamed, but she
ignored him, taking a few steps away from
the door and swinging her bat hard,
catching the ghoul in the torso and
sending it staggering back.

Troy and Bailey flew through the
door.

"Hurry up, girl!" Troy barked, and
Grace quickly leapt back inside the
vestibule, pulling the door shut just in
time.

A dozen zombies smacked into the
glass, and Troy and Grace struggled to
keep it shut as Bailey fumbled for the
lock.

"Hold it steady!" she screamed.

"We're fucking trying!" Troy bellowed back.

The door shook violently, and she tried to time the lock turn just right so that the bolt would slide into place. Finally there was a satisfying *click* of metal on metal, and the door was secure.

The duo tentatively let go of the door, taking a step back to make sure it was going to hold against the smacking angry monsters on the other side.

It did, and the three of them breathed a sigh of relief. Troy patted Grace on the back.

"That was one hell of an assist, there," he said, sounding genuine for the first time since they'd met.

Dante crossed his arms. "And one major heart attack on my part," he added darkly.

"Sorry," Grace said, avoiding his gaze. "I saw that thing was going to take them out, and I just reacted. Didn't have time to think, just went into action."

Bailey ran her hands over her disheveled ponytail. "I didn't even see it."

"Only reason I did was because she took it out," Troy replied.

Dante took his sister's arm, turning her to face him. "Are you okay?"

"I'm fine," she said firmly, jutting out her chin and finally looking up at him. "I am capable of fighting, you know."

He took a deep breath. "I know… it's just…" He sighed. "I know." He didn't have the words to put the situation in perspective, so he dropped it. With the sudden silence, June's racking sobs in the corner overtook the space, and the girls rushed over to her for comfort.

"Good job keeping her safe," Dante said quietly to Troy.

The banker forced a smirk. "See, I'm not a total asshole."

"Come on, we're not out of this yet," Dante said, chuckling, and gave him a playful punch in the arm. They joined the others by the front window, and the sight of the parking lot took their breath away.

It looked apocalyptic outside. There was an overturned car at the top of the parking lot, with several zombies crowded around it. There were also a handful of ghouls mingling in between the cars, though thankfully none had come up to the front of the store.

"So, which car is yours?" Bailey asked.

Grace inclined her head. "The shitty grey sedan on the right side, there," she said.

"It doesn't look so bad," June said through her sniffles, voice thick.

Dante rolled his eyes. "She wanted the convertible," he teased.

"That would have been perfect for this time of year," Troy pointed out. "You know, without the whole end of the world thing."

Grace glanced at her brother with a sly smile, her eyes saying *see, I told you so!*

"Yeah, yeah, I know," he groaned, "weather is different in other parts of the country."

June got to her feet, straightening her shoulders and wiping her eyes. "So, how are we doing this?" she asked.

They studied the soon-to-be battlefield, scanning the several zombies by the cars. Grace angled her view out the front windows to see the left and right. "I'm not seeing anything to the sides, but I can't get a great angle," she said. "There may be some by the front walls, but I can't be sure."

"We'll just have to check when we exit," Dante replied. "Grace, you and June handle our flanks. If it's one, take it out. If it's more, call for help."

They nodded firmly, tightening their grips around their bats.

"Troy, you and I are going straight for the car," Dante continued. "We need some time to get everybody in, so we're probably going to have to take those things down."

The banker nodded. "All right," he agreed. "You lead the way, I'll brain whatever you don't."

Dante offered him a smile, thankful that the asshole finally seemed to be on board. "Okay, let's do this."

CHAPTER FIVE

Dante and Troy stood by the front doors, ready to do battle to get them to the cars. Bailey knelt down beside them, reaching over with her hand on the lock.

"Just tell me when," she said.

"You ready?" Dante asked, turning to his partner.

"Ready as I'm ever going to be," Troy replied.

Dante nodded. "Unlock it," he said, and Bailey complied.

It clinked open, and as soon as she moved her arm, the two men burst out of the store, sprinting towards the cars.

The others piled out next, June and Grace checking the flanks. One ghoul on June's side spotted them and came forward at a run. She stopped dead in her tracks, raised the bat above her head, and jutted out her chin.

"Come on, motherfucker!" she yelled, and then cracked it over the top of the head, dropping it in a single blow. She didn't hesitate after killing it, rushing after the rest of the group.

There were about a dozen cars in the parking lot, Dante's vehicle at the far end on the right side. As the two men grew close, their footsteps attracted the ghouls in their direction.

Troy swung at a young-looking zombie, no more than twenty, missing several chunks of flesh from its neck and face. The bat caught it in the side of the head, sending the frail creature tumbling head over heels.

Dante saw two zombies running towards him from the next aisle, but kept rushing to the sedan. He hopped up onto the trunk and clambered over the top to the hood. The zombies reached him, but he was able to keep enough distance that they couldn't bite him. From this vantage point, he smacked down the ghouls one after the other, cracking their skulls.

Dante looked over and saw Troy confronting another zombie. It ran up on him quick, and he couldn't get a clean swing at it, so he used his large frame to pick the smaller corpse up and pile drive it into the pavement face first. Even at ten yards away, Dante heard the telltale *crack* of the neck snapping.

He watched the trio of women getting closer and then looked over at the road. Some of the car crash crowd had broken away from the wreck and sprinted across the lot towards them.

"We got incoming!" he bellowed.

Troy glanced over, seeing the new threat about forty yards away. "Well come

the fuck on, then!" he yelled, raising his
bat.

Dante hopped down from the car and
rushed over, pulling out the keys and
hitting the unlock button correctly this
time. Everybody reached the vehicle, with
Troy hopping in the front seat and the
girls clambering into the back. They
slammed the doors shut, and a few seconds
later, rotted hands smacked into the
glass.

Bailey jumped, afraid of the zombies
that smeared crimson all across the back
window, teeth gnashing at the glass,
trying in vain to get through.

"Sometime today, Dante!" Troy cried,
flinching away from the window.

Dante finally got the keys in the
ignition and started up the car. He
flipped it into gear and floored it. The
tires squealed as much as they could on a
late model sedan and then lurched forwards
out of the space. There were a few zombies
on the hood, and he swerved back and forth
to throw them off.

When he reached the driveway, he
stopped, looking both ways.

"What the hell are you waiting on?"
Troy demanded, throwing his hands up.
"Pretty sure you aren't going to get a
ticket if you blow through the stop sign!"

Dante didn't respond, simply looking to the west, away from the island. There were zombies everywhere, congregating around a multi-car pileup near another of the shopping center exits. He finally snapped back to it and made the turn.

He picked up a bit of speed, but kept it manageable, about thirty miles an hour. As he focused solely on driving, the others watched the landscape roll by in horror.

There was a wreck on the side of the road with two zombies actively pulling a driver out of the car. He thrashed and screamed while being eaten alive. Down the street a little further, a pack of zombies chased a poor soul, frantically firing a handgun back in his pursuers' direction, missing badly.

"Isn't there anything we can do?!" Bailey moaned through her fingers.

"Yeah, we can survive," Troy replied flatly.

She fell silent, overwhelmed with helplessness, fear for the victims, and for her family.

When they were within a couple miles of the bridge, Troy yelled, "Watch it!"

A small pack of zombies darted out from the side of the road, smacking into the vehicle. Dante wasn't able to get it out of the way in time, so one of them flipped over the passenger side bumper, crashing into the windshield and cracking it, leaving a blood-stained spider web behind.

"Doesn't look like you're getting your deposit back," Troy muttered, uncurling his fingers from the handle above his head.

Dante shook his head. "That's why I always pay for the extra insurance."

Troy chuckled, trying to diffuse his tension as they continued down the road.

One mile from the bridge, they hit trouble. There was a moderate pileup on the road, half a dozen cars with one flipped completely over. Dante slammed on the breaks and a pack of ten zombies turned towards them, tearing their way.

"Just plow through them!" Troy declared.

Dante shook his head firmly. "And then what?" he asked. "This car isn't making it through that wreck." He looked to the median, seeing that there was a metal barrier, so they couldn't cross over. He threw the car into reverse.

"What are you doing?!" Troy cried.

"There was a crossover a mile back," Dante grunted, "we'll get on the other side and make our way up."

"Wait!" June cried, and he stopped the car.

"What do you see?" he asked, brow furrowing.

June tapped on the window. "Apartment complex on the right," she said. "They have to have multiple exits, right?" she asked.

The men shared a glance and shrugged.

"Good enough for me," Dante said, and threw the car back into drive, quickly speeding into the complex. The parking lot was a bigger mess than the highway, carnage everywhere, zombies running around, bodies scattered everywhere. Just a bad day.

He drove fast, treating the speed bumps like ramps, flying through the air a bit. As they came around a corner, he was forced to slam on the brakes when another car appeared from one of the side alcoves.

The other driver didn't slow down, smashing into the front of the car hard, spinning them around and sending shattered glass everywhere.

Dante was stunned for a moment, before snapping back to it. He looked around, checking out his passengers.

"Is everybody okay?" he asked.

There was a chorus in the affirmative, and then he unclipped his seatbelt, staggering out of the car. He shook his head to regain his wits and looked at the other car. The driver wasn't

wearing a seatbelt and was halfway out of
the windshield, a massive pool of blood
forming on the hood.

He didn't spend long focused on that,
as he heard moaning and loud footsteps
coming from behind him. He looked down the
complex, spotting a couple dozen zombies
rushing towards them, about fifty yards
away and closing.

"Coe on, we gotta move!" he barked.
"We gotta move!"

The urgency in his voice got the
group moving, quickly getting out of the
car and to their feet. They saw the threat
quickly closing in on them, and panicked,
frantically looking around for options.

"Got an open door over here!" Grace
cried.

"Go, now!" Dante yelled, and they
took off towards the open apartment door
as quickly as they could. When they
reached it, he went first, raising his bat
cautiously, unsure of what would be
waiting inside.

The small one-bedroom apartment was a
mess, a clear struggling having taken
place. The dining room table was knocked
on its side, pans strewn all over the
kitchen floor, the stove still on. The
rest bustled in and quickly shut the door,
locking it at Troy and Dante inched their
way towards the bedroom. There were

distinct munching and smacking sounds coming from there, and the sickening noises made them tense as they approached.

Inside, they found a young woman in her twenties, her blonde hair perfectly coiffed, munching away at a young man on the bed.

When they entered the room, the feasting zombie growled and rushed them. Troy didn't waste time delivering a solid strike to the head. Dante walked over to the victim, eyes widening when he realized he was still alive, though barely.

The Man was covered in bite marks, missing huge chunks of flesh, bleeding out quickly. "What do you think?" he asked as Troy came over.

"I think he needs to be put down before he starts chasing us around in here," the banker replied.

Dante gave a solemn nod, knowing he was right. He took a deep breath, hesitating.

"I can do it if you want," Troy offered softly.

Dante shook his head. "No, just make sure the others don't come in," he muttered. "They don't need to see me do this."

Troy nodded and headed out into the hallway.

Dante swallowed hard, staring at the man's wide eyes, terrified, knowing that this was the end. "I'm sorry man," he said, shaking his head as he raised his bat. "I really am."

He drove the bat straight down into the man's forehead, wincing at the *crack* of his skull as the body went limp. Dante hit him a few more times, just to be sure. When he was satisfied, he turned away with a sick feeling in his stomach, and headed out of the room of death.

CHAPTER SIX

Grace sat by the window, looking back at the wreck and watching as a dozen zombies continued to congregate around the other driver. She stayed out of sight, not wanting to draw them over.

"How's it looking out there?" June asked quietly, coming up beside her.

"They all seem distracted by the other driver," Grace murmured. "I don't think they saw us come in here. Or if they did, they've already forgotten about it."

June nodded. "Are you hungry?" she asked.

Grace's eyes nearly popped out of her head. *How can you eat at a time like this…* she thought, but then shook her head, realizing that it would be a good idea to eat while they had the chance. She patted her stomach.

"Amazingly enough, I think I am," she said.

June nodded and gave her shoulder a squeeze. "I'll whip you up something good, then," she said. "Assuming they weren't new age health freaks, in which case I'll do my best to make something edible out of soy sausage." She dissolved into a coughing fit, and then put a hand to her forehead, straightening up. "I'll… put a mask on, too."

Grace smiled appreciatively, though her eyes were tired.

As June went to the kitchen, Bailey fiddled around with the remote control, finally clicking it on. There was an old rerun of an 80s sitcom, complete with a laugh track.

"That hardly seems appropriate," she muttered, "given the situation." She clicked around to several different cable stations, all of them showing their regular programming, which made her brow furrow. "What is going on?" she murmured to herself. "Why are they ignoring this?"

Grace crossed over to her. "Most of the cable stations are automated," she suggested, "so they have their programming set up in advance. Chances are, nobody is at the controls."

"Try channel twelve," June suggested, "pretty sure it's local. Well, Beaufort, so local enough."

Bailey nodded and punched in channel twelve. The screen displayed an empty news studio. There were some scattered papers on the desk, and one of the chairs was missing, but nobody was on the screen. There was no sound coming from the studio either.

"Maybe they're on a break?" she asked, though her voice was shrill and uneasy.

A few moments later, one of the anchors, a middle-aged white woman with perfectly styled hair, wandered by the camera.

She turned jerkily, revealing dark blood all down the front of her, eyes glassy and milky white, mouth open in a hungry snarl.

Bailey dropped the remote. "We have no news," she said hoarsely.

Grace swallowed hard as she stared at the news anchor, and then squinted when she noticed small words scrolling across the bottom of the small tv screen. "Wait a second," she said, pointing. "Look at the bottom of the screen."

She and Bailey moved in closer, reading the white scrolling words.

I need help! My name is Katie McClure and I am trapped in the control room of the TV station! The address is 427 Maple Lane in Beaufort! Please, someone, help me, I'm all alone in here and there are so many of those things outside the door!

"That poor woman," Grace breathed, sitting back as the message repeated itself.

Bailey clenched her jaw, staring at the screen as if she were looking through it into space.

Grace cocked her head. "Are you okay?"

"Yeah, just thinking," the younger woman replied, and chewed her lip for a moment. Finally she snapped her fingers, eyes brightening as she turned to Grace. "Wait! I know exactly where that station is! There's not a sign out front anymore, but it's only a few blocks away from my house! If we get to my family, we can get to her as well."

Grace didn't want to dampen her spirits, so she just smiled and nodded, sitting back on the couch. Dante and Troy came out of the bedroom after ransacking it.

"What's going on?" Troy asked.

Grace simply motioned to the tv, where the zombie tv anchor thrashed and moaned about.

He sighed. "Guess that means we're not getting the Knicks score, are we?" he asked wryly.

"It's the Knicks," she replied breezily, "they probably lost."

His brow furrowed, and he looked like he was going to retort something, but then shrugged. "Yeah, that's fair."

"That's not all though," Bailey piped up, pointing to the message, "look at the bottom of the screen."

Dante tucked a small plastic package he'd brought under his arm and leaned over to look.

"Man, sucks to be her," Troy murmured, standing back up after reading.

Bailey crossed her arms. "Wow, such compassion," she snapped, sarcasm evident in her tone.

"What? I said sucks to be her," Troy replied, shaking his head. "I thought that was compassion."

Bailey scowled and opened her mouth, but Dante held up a hand.

"We'll add her to the list," he said, "but it's way down there."

Grace cocked her head, pointing to the plastic package under his arm. "What you got there, brother?"

"A gift," he replied, and handed it over.

She opened it, eyes widening at the handgun inside. It was loaded with a spare magazine, and she picked it up, inspecting it like an old friend.

"I mean, if you don't want it," Troy said sheepishly, "I'll take it."

Dante shook his head. "No, Grace is going to be best with it," he said firmly.

Troy jutted out his chin. "How do *you* know that?"

"Because I target shoot twice a week," Grace spoke up, checking the chamber expertly. "For the last five years. I may not be the best shot, but I'm good enough."

Troy chuckled.

"What's so funny?" she challenged.

He held up his palms. "Just find it ironic that someone that would protest outside of Theo Atkinson's QXR Group offices would spend so much time firing a weapon," he said.

"Nothing ironic about it," Grace replied easily. "Guns are fantastic, but it all depends on what you shoot. I fire at paper targets, his people fire at civilians. Not that difficult to see the difference."

He shrugged, avoiding her gaze, and then sniffed, noticing pleasant smells from the kitchen. "Are you cooking?" he asked, shock in his eyes as June slid a large portion of scrambled eggs onto a plate.

"Just because the world is ending doesn't mean we get to stop eating," she quipped, and tossed a few forks onto the counter. "Grab you a fork and dive in. Might be awhile before you get fresh eggs again. Same with bacon, which will be coming up in a minute."

Nobody waited to be asked twice, congregating around the counter and diving in.

"So what's the plan now?" Bailey asked after swallowing her mouthful.

Dante smacked his lips, giving June a thumbs up before replying, "Depends on how it looks outside."

"They're still feeding," Grace said, "but I can't imagine it will last much longer."

Her brother nodded. "Well, when they disperse, we're going to make a break for it," he said. "The bridge can't be too much further up. Half a mile or so once we get to the other side of the complex."

"Are we sure there's another exit?" Troy asked through a mouthful of egg.

Dante shrugged. "We didn't pass the front office, and the driveway keeps going up," he explained. "Can't imagine they'd have the only entrance so far away from it."

"Solid enough logic," the banker admitted.

"Then what are we doing?" June asked, putting a hand on her hip as she set down a plate of bacon.

Dante took a big bite of his eggs before grabbing a slice of bacon. He pointed at Troy with the fried meat. "We pray that he's right and that Theo *fucking* Atkinson has done his job and blocked off the bridge."

He bit into the bacon, chewing it slowly and savoring the flavor as they all

ate in silence, contemplating what would
happen if the bridge *wasn't* blocked off.

CHAPTER SEVEN

Half an hour later, Grace stood guard at the window, looking out at the wreck. Only a couple of zombies remained, hanging out around the cars while the others had wandered off. It was difficult to see from her vantage point, but she could see that the driver had started thrashing about, still trapped in the windshield.

Dante sidled up next to her, bumping her shoulder playfully with his own. "Don't focus too much on the horror, sis," he said softly. "Just keep an eye out for an opening to move."

"Easier said than done," she replied flatly.

He nodded, giving her shoulder a reassuring squeeze, and headed back to join the others sitting around the television. After tiring of the news feed, Bailey had changed the channel to a rerun of an 80s sitcom. The group chuckled as one of the characters fell face first into a cake.

"What are you watching?" Dante asked, raising an eyebrow.

"No clue," Troy admitted. "Just something from a simpler time. Not sure when exactly, just know it is older than four hours."

Dante shook his head, chuckling at the lighthearted barb from the surly New Yorker. Before he could sit down to join them, Grace clucked her tongue.

"I think we can move," she said.

Her brother hurried back to the window, looking out to see the zombies by the cars were rushing off in the direction away from the bridge.

"I don't know what distracted them," he said, "but we're going to take advantage of it." He looked to the group as they all stood up and got ready to go. "We stay close, kill what we have to, but the goal is to move as quickly as we can. So if you have to knock them down and keep moving, do that." He turned to his sister. "Don't fire that gun unless it's absolutely necessary. One shot from that, and we're going to be on every one of those things radar."

She nodded firmly, tightening her grip around the weapon and patting her pocket where the spare mag fit snugly.

"Troy, I want you up front with me," Dante said, turning to the New Yorker. "We may have to plow through these things." He waited for his companion to join him at the door, and then he threw it open.

The five of them poured out of the apartment and immediately ran up the main driveway. They reached the wreck, finding

the driver that had been shredded by both
the windshield and the zombie bites
thrashing about. It tried to moan, but it
just came out as a gurgle, as it was
missing the majority of its neck.

Dante motioned for the group to
follow him, and they moved up about fifty
yards to the next apartment alcove. As
they crossed the driveway opening, a trio
of zombies spotted them and rushed at
them.

Dante and Troy stepped up, quickly
bashing the first two down, and the latter
grabbed the last one by the shirt collar
to hold it at bay for Dante to deliver a
kill strike.

The group continued running, and
spotted the front office, with the
entrance to the complex fifty yards past
that. They moved quickly, but when they
reached the office, a dozen zombies
congregated around the side door and
turned towards them.

As soon as the first ghoul noticed
them, it let out a loud dead scream and
sprinted towards the group. The noise
attracted the rest, and within seconds the
entire dozen came at them, mouths open in
excitement.

"Grace, shoot!" Dante cried.

His sister didn't hesitate, taking
aim at the leader and pulling the trigger.

The bullet ripped through the forehead of the ghoul, blowing out the back of its skull and dropping it to the asphalt. The others lined up, readying their bats.

"How do you want to do this?!" Troy demanded, panic in his voice.

Dante inclined his head. "We knock em down, they bash their heads," he said quickly. "You ladies hear that?"

June and Bailey echoed a chorus of "Yeah," and raised their bats.

As Grace continued to fire at the back, Dante and Troy lunged at the first few ghouls, swinging their bats at chest level, sending the zombies tumbling to the sides. June and Bailey rushed over to the fallen zombies and smashed with everything they had, June delivering a kill shot on her second swing, but Bailey having a little more trouble.

She kept hitting hers in the head, but all it did was knock the corpse back down, not killing it. Finally she let out a scream and swung with all of her might and adrenaline, cracking the skull and ending its undead life.

Grace stepped to the side, aiming carefully and pulling the trigger. With the zombies distracted by the two men, they were easy pickings, not flailing around too much. One by one, she dropped five of them rapidly.

There were still four ghouls pressed up against Dante and Troy, who held their bats horizontally and at arm's length to keep them at bay. The creatures thrashed about, smacking them in the face with their wet gooey hands as they tried to get a bite.

"On three, push hard and up," Dante grunted, "try to hook them under the arms."

Troy nodded, catching exactly what his companion wanted to do.

"One, two, *three*!" Dante cried, and they managed to hook the ghouls and drive them back, sending them crashing to the ground. They immediately began smashing down, cracking the skulls of the zombies as they scrambled to get back to their feet. Within seconds, the immediate threat had ended.

The group of five stood there, breathing heavily, spent from the culmination of the morning and this epic battle. Dante looked around at the shocked faces of his companions.

"Is everyone okay?" he asked.

One by one, they all sounded off that they were okay.

It didn't take long, however, for more moaning and footsteps to echo at them from the complex.

"Quick, this way!" Dante cried, and led the group over to the pool by the front office. He deftly hopped over the four foot high fence, and went over to the gate release, hitting it so the others could get in. They quickly took cover behind the building, staying quiet.

Dante looked out and waited, trying to control his breathing. In thirty seconds or so, a group of twenty to thirty creatures sprinted by the front office, heading off towards a small business park on the other side of the street. When they were clear, he took a knee, relieved.

"So are we good?" Troy murmured.

Dante nodded. "Yeah, I think so," he said quietly. "They just kept running. I lost sight of them when they crossed over into that business park. Hopefully they keep going so we can get up to the highway."

"Why the hell didn't they come after us?" Troy hissed.

Dante shrugged. "Maybe they just heard the gunshots and followed it, but without something to hold their attention they just kept going, trying to find it," he replied softly. "Whatever the reason, they're not here, and that's all I really care about at the moment."

June wheezed and then clapped her hands over her mouth as she started to have a coughing fit. Bailey and Grace huddled around her, trying to muffle the noise, and soon they subsided, and she took a deep, ragged breath.

Dante looked back out at the road, but the noise thankfully hadn't attracted anything.

"Come on," he whispered, "the bridge can't be too much further up."

CHAPTER EIGHT

Dante led the group out of the pool area, with Grace gently shutting the metal gate behind them. As they reached the driveway, he looked towards the business park and his brow furrowed when he saw that the zombies had completely vanished.

He motioned for the group to follow him, but Troy grabbed him by the arm. He pointed out a little trail through the woods about ten yards off of the driveway. Dante nodded and led them to it, figuring that a little bit of cover would be better than none.

They reached the side street, hiding behind some trees. Dante scanned the park, finally catching a glimpse of some ghouls. They were at the far end, banging on the door of a small office. Dante had no idea if there was anybody inside, but even if there had been, they wouldn't be able to do anything about it.

The side street up to the highway was clear, so he led them out. They walked on the grass to muffle their footsteps, not wanting to take any chances. As they grew closer to the highway, they heard gunshots. It wasn't panic fire, but slow, deliberate shots, one right after the other.

"Sounds like I was right about Theo Atkinson and his boys," Troy whispered, smirking.

Dante pursed his lips. "Maybe," he murmured.

He led them the rest of the way up the road, stopping at the top of it. They looked towards the bridge, and saw that it was fortified. There was a string of cars stretching from one side of the bridge to the other, with several armed men set up along it, all about a quarter mile from where they were. A few dozen bodies lay scattered on the pavement leading up to it.

"Just follow my lead," Dante whispered.

The group nodded in agreement and began to move.

Dante stopped short and glanced back at his sister. "Grace, holster that," he instructed. "We don't want them to think we're hostile."

She nodded, putting the handgun in her back waistband and covering it up with her shirt.

He raised his hands high, bat in the air, leading them out slowly. The zombies moved fast, and he assumed that if they moved slowly they'd look as different from the ghouls as possible.

They walked up about halfway to the
barricade, and one of the shooters boomed
out, "Don't move, we aren't shooting at
you!"

The group froze, and several shots
cracked from the barricade. Most of the
group flinched, and Baile screamed. Dante
glanced over his shoulder and saw that a
few zombies had just been dropped twenty
yards behind them.

"It's okay," he said quietly,
"they're covering us."

"Make your way to the checkpoint!"
the man from the barricade bellowed. "Far
left of the bridge. Move now and move
quickly!"

Dante picked up the pace, leading the
group over to a makeshift checkpoint on
the side of the bridge. The car barricade
was a little wonky there, with the final
car pushed forward about five feet away
from the line, creating a bit of an
opening.

As he went through, he was greeted by
four men in black combat gear, holding
high-powered assault rifles, battle
hardened and ready to rumble. They were no
nonsense and didn't use kid gloves as they
grabbed the bats away from the group,
tossing them to the ground before shoving
all five of them against the concrete
barrier.

Dante glanced over the edge, seeing deep water below. He studied the area behind the barricade, which was set up like a small campground. There were crates of material stacked behind the line, and a smaller makeshift barricade on the opposite side of the road to prevent a rear attack. All told, there were about twenty men stationed there, keeping a close eye on everything.

The four main guards stood a few yards away from the group as the occasional gunshot went off in the distance, taking out yet another zombie. A few tense moments passed before a smarmy looking twenty-something sauntered up.

"Well well well," he drawled, raising his chin. "Some more survivors. Didn't think anybody else was going to make it here today."

Dante took a deep breath. "It wasn't easy, I'll tell you that."

The guy looked them up and down, noting that they were coated in blood and looked exhausted. "It wouldn't appear so," he said with a sneer. "But hey, not everybody can be as well-trained as we are." He glanced over at the other three men, who were simply standing there. "Well, are you going to get them processed, or not?" he snapped, waving his hand at them. "This island isn't going to clear itself. Get moving."

Each of the men pointed at a different person and motioned for them to step up. The fourth guard stepped next to Dante and Bailey, guarding them with his hand on his weapon. They moved slowly, and one of the mercenaries grabbed Grace by the arm and shoved her behind the line.

"Hey, take it easy," Dante protested.

The lead guy whipped around, glaring at him. "You stay right there, cowboy," he snarled. "You'll have your chance to get felt up in a minute." He looked him up and down. "Oh yea, you look big and strong, you're going to be put to good use."

Bailey and Dante exchanged a concerned look at his choice of words, and the pretentious guy sauntered over to the three about to have their pat down.

"Okay, listen up," he barked. "Bites will turn you into one of those things, so we need to make sure you're not bitten. That means a forceful pat down. If you refuse, then you're free to leave."

Grace looked at Dante with a questioning gaze, but he nodded at her, hoping she'd understand to just roll with it.

Before they could start their inspection, June dissolved into a massive coughing fit. All the mercenaries took a step back in shock.

The leader held out his palms. "What is your blood type?!" he yelled.

She shook her head in confusion as she stifled her coughs, finally calming down. "What in the hell are you talking about?" she wheezed as she caught her breath.

"I said, what is your fucking blood type, bitch?!" the guy barked.

June coughed again, putting a fist to her mouth. "What the fuck did you just call me?"

"Tell me your fucking blood type, *now!*" he demanded.

She straightened up finally, glaring at him. "It's A-positive motherfucker, what the—"

The mercenary pulled his handgun and shot her in the face.

As she slumped to the ground, her quartet of friends left behind blinking in shock. Grace let out a scream of rage, drawing the handgun from the back of her pants.

"No!" Dante yelled, and the second that the lead mercenary turned to look at him, his face exploded as Grace shot him in the back of the head.

The other three raised their weapons, all aiming at Grace, screaming at her to drop the gun. She couldn't do anything, however, because she was frozen with shock, the moment overwhelming her.

"Everybody calm the fuck down!" somebody boomed, and a large man stalked over to the standoff. He stopped five yards away, unarmed. "Somebody want to tell me what the hell is going on?"

"Your boy there shot our friend in the face for no reason!" Troy yelled, voice shrill.

The tall man crossed his arms. "No reason, huh?" he drawled. "Somebody want to expand on that?"

"She had A-type blood," one of the guards said.

The man cocked his head. "Is that so, huh?" he asked, running his tongue over his teeth. "And even so, he thought it was a good idea to execute her in front of her friends? I know we have orders to kill, but goddamn, show some fucking common sense, or else you may end up like Zack here." He kicked the dead man's leg.

"Orders to kill?!" Troy demanded. "Why?"

The man shook his head. "Whatever this virus is, targets people with A-type blood," he explained. "All we know is that they get sick, die, and then come back as those things. So our orders are to kill on sight, which this dead dumbass took a little to literally." He glanced at Grace, who still stood holding the gun, breaths coming out in panicked pants. "Ma'am, I'm sorry about your friend, I really am," he said, tone considerate and gentle. "But she was not going to last longer than a day. Now, I can't excuse what this man did, but it would appear as though I don't have to, since you dealt with him appropriately. We don't have a wish for more bloodshed, so please, but down the gun."

"Grace, listen to him," Dante said carefully. "These boys mean business, and you're not shooting your way out of this. Please, put it down."

She looked at her brother, tears filling her eyes as the gravity of what she'd done took root. She lowered her arm, and then, as if in slow motion, laid the gun down on the ground, covering her face with her hands.

The man walked over and gently picked up the weapon, tucking it into his belt. "Thank you, ma'am," he said, as she scrubbed her hands down her cheeks. "You can call me No Name. May I ask who you are?"

Her brow furrowed as she stifled her tears. "I'm Grace," she said shakily. "But you really don't have a name?"

"When you are asked to do the things I've been asked to do, it's best not to have an identity," he replied. "Especially when there are people I still care about in the world… or at least there were, before today."

Before he could continue, a grizzled thirty something man stormed over to them. "Goddamn, what the fuck happened to Zach?!" he barked. "He seems to have misplaced his fucking face!"

"He did something stupid, and paid for it," No Name replied.

The angry man planted his hands on his hips. "Oh, he did something stupid, did he? What would that be, huh?" he demanded, and then spotted June's dead body on the ground. "Let me guess, he shot that fat bitch because she was sick and one of these fuckers took offense. That sound about right?"

"Close enough," No Name replied.

"Then why the fuck haven't these people been put down yet, huh?" the angry man bellowed, throwing up his hands. "Or are you sweet on this one, you no-named motherfucker? They won't let you have a name, but you think they'll let you have a piece of pussy? Is that it?"

No Name glared at him, jaw tight.

"Oh yeah, get pissed, big fella," the angry man snarled, smirking. "Okay, if that's the way you want it, then so be it. Fuck it, we aren't going to put them down, we're gonna put them to work. Boys, slap some cuffs on 'em and let's get them processed. Lots of buildings to get cleared."

"Dante, go!" Grace screamed.

He didn't want to leave her, but he knew he didn't have a choice. If he wanted to save his friends, he had to be alive and get help. He struck the throat of the guard next to him, causing him to double over and gasp for air. Before the other guards could turn in his direction, he grabbed Bailey and leapt over the edge of the bridge.

The young woman screamed the whole way down, and Dante kept a tight hold of her, positioning them so that they'd hit feet first. They splashed down, vanishing underneath the murky waves. Safe, at least for the moment.

CHAPTER NINE

Dante and Bailey tread water, bruised
from their fall from the bridge. He
spotted a small island just off of the
shore of the main Hilton Head Island.
There were several small personal boats
that ran up on the shore, a few hundred
yards away.

"Are you going to make it?" he
sputtered.

Bailey struggled a bit, trying to
keep her head above the cold water. "Yeah,
I think so," she huffed.

He shook his head and grabbed her,
flipping her onto her back. He held her
arms as she flailed in a panic.

"Don't move," he said gently, "just
do your best to float on your back. I'm
going to pull you for a bit, okay?"

She stopped fighting him, just went
with it. She did her best to stay above
the water, and he grabbed the back of her
shirt collar, pulling her alone while
swimming with one arm. This tired him out
more than the swimming, but he was bound
and determined not to lose another person
today.

When he started to get tired, still a
hundred yards away from the island, he
thought about Grace, who was stuck on the
bridge with those maniacs. Rage flowed

through him, white hot fire that he'd let Troy convince him it was a good idea.

Troy, who was in the same situation as his sister now.

You'd better watch over her, he thought bitterly. *God help you if you don't.*

He kept going, his splashes attracting the attention of a young man on the shoreline about fifty yards away from the boat.

"Lily, Phillip, get over here!" he cried. "We have some company!"

Dante watched a young couple join the man, the trio standing on the shore as he found his footing in the soil below. Bailey touched down and then helped him to shore, the two of them collapsing in the sand.

"Holy shit, are you two okay?" the woman, apparently Lily, asked. "Where in the hell did you come from?"

Bailey pointed vaguely back the way they'd come, her arm like lead. "We… jumped off the bridge," she huffed.

"Nothing like a little daredevil action to get the blood pumping," Phillip quipped.

"What did you go and do that for?" the first young man demanded.

"Armed assholes tried to shoot us," Dante said through his heaving chest.

The trio exchanged concerned looks.

"God, have they taken the bridge already?" Phillip asked.

Lily rubbed her forehead. "It makes sense, given what they're doing on the island."

"There's more of those guys?" Bailey shivered, more from fear than from cold.

"A lot more," Phillip confirmed. "At least we think there are."

Dante sat up, rage flowing through him even harder than before. The trio stared at him, eyes wide at either his anger or his facial injuries, he couldn't be sure.

"Did…" the third guy trailed off. "Did they do that to you?"

Dante's brow furrowed, and he shot an indignant look at him.

Lilya smacked her companion hard on the arm. "Man, what the hell is wrong with you?" she snapped. "No, they didn't just do that to him, that's just the way he looks. And if you had any common fucking sense, you'd look in the mirror and realize you're in no position to be commenting on appearance."

"Yeah, what she said," Dante said tiredly.

"Forgive him, he's an idiot," she continued, turning to the duo. "I'm Lily."

Bailey offered a tentative smile. "I'm Bailey and this is Dante."

"The short one over here is Phillip," Lily said. "The tall moron is Cam. Nice to meet y'all."

Bailey nodded and then hugged her knees to her chest. "If you don't mind me asking," she said slowly, "what are you three doing here?"

"We're from the hotel just across the water," Lily replied. "When the shit hit the fan this morning, a group of us got out along with some of the hotel guests."

Phillip took a deep breath. "We thought those things running around were bad," he said, shaking his head, "but they were nothing compared to whoever those armed assholes are."

"They're mercenaries," Dante said flatly.

"*Mercenaries*?" Cam blurted. "On Hilton Head?"

"Long story, that doesn't really matter at the moment," Dante replied, waving him off. "What matters is, can I use one of your boats?"

Lily's brow furrowed. "For what?"

"No no no," Bailey croaked, grabbing his arm, tears swelling up in her eyes. "You are not going to the island."

"I have to get Grace," he said firmly.

She clutched him harder. "Dante!" she pleaded. "You are *not* going to the island!"

"Listen to your girl here," Phillip said, pointing at her, "you really don't want to go to the island."

Dante growled. "I don't care how many of them there are," he snapped, "I'm going to get over there and find my sister."

"I hate to be the bearer of bad news," Lily said slowly, "but you wouldn't make it within fifty yards of the docks."

"She's right," Cam added. "We barely made it out before those assholes started shooting the place up. Even shot at our boats as we got out."

Dante clenched his fists and tore away from Bailey, peeling himself off of the ground and beginning to pace back and forth.

She followed him, walking alongside him, trying to catch his eye with her pleading gaze. "I know you're upset," she said. "We'll get Grae. But right now, we need to find someplace safe to get to."

He stopped moving, screwing his fists into his eyes for a moment, hating that he felt so helpless.

"Where is that hotel employee with my lunch?!" a shrill woman squawked. "I was told that there would be lunch on this little unscheduled trip that I was so rudely forced upon!"

They glanced over at a middle-aged woman sitting on a log in expensive clothes and oversized sunglasses, fiddling with her phone.

"And why can't I get any service in this godforsaken place?" she demanded, voice like nails on a chalkboard. "I thought you people would have made sure I could get cell phone service!"

Dante blinked at her. "Is this bitch for real?" he asked.

"Unfortunately, she is," Lily muttered.

"Spoiled trust fund kid who never had to work in her life," Cam quipped, "so she spends months down here making our lives a living hell."

"Phillip!" the woman barked. "That's your name, Phillip! Where is Phillip! I demand to be helped!"

He shook his head. "I'd better go calm her ass down," he said with a sigh. "With our manager out of commission, she's just going to carry on until someone appeases her."

"What happened to your manager?" Bailey asked.

Cam swallowed hard. "One of those crazy people bit him."

"Is he on the island?" Dante demanded, Bailey stiffening beside him.

Lily nodded, brow furrowing. "Yeah, he came over on one of the boats with us," she replied, jerking a thumb over her shoulder. "He was just hurt, but we weren't going to leave him behind."

"Pretty sure a few of the others were bitten, too," Phillip added.

"We can't stay here," Dante said quickly.

Cam shook his head. "What? Why?"

"Because those bites are infectious as hell," Dante explained. "They're deadly and they turn the people who are bitten into those zombie things, whatever they are."

The shrill woman continued to scream for Phillip. He finally threw up his hands. "I'm going to go calm her ass down," he said, turning away. "When you figure out where we're going, come get me."

"Are there any other islands out here?" Dante asked.

Cam nodded. "Yeah, but chances are they're going to be in the same position we are."

Bailey opened her mouth, but Dante put up a hand to silence her.

"I know you want to go home to Beaufort," he cut in, "but we need sparsely populated. I promise I'll get you there. Just not right now."

She closed her mouth and nodded, sighing but trusting him to keep his word.

"Sparsely populated, huh?" Lily asked. "We can go to my cousin's house up in Tillman."

Dante shrugged. "I'm from Seattle," he said flatly, "I have no idea where that is."

"Hell, I'm from here, and have no idea where that is," Bailey added.

"Not surprising," Lily replied, "it's a one stop-sign town with about twelve houses and a gas station." She motioned vaguely with her hands as she spoke. "It's on highway three-twenty-one on the other side of the interstate. Can't be more than twenty, twenty-five miles from here."

Dante sighed. "Sounds great, except for the fact that my rental car got totaled," he replied with a shrug. "And going back to the hotel for yours isn't exactly an option."

Lily shook her head and smirked. "Ironic, entitled bitches like that are actually going to be useful for once," she said.

"I don't follow," he admitted, brow furrowing.

"A few months ago, some bridezilla came in with her entourage and started throwing a level five bitch-fit about how there wasn't enough parking in the lot for her limo and all her friend's cars," Cam explained. "She chewed our limp dick manager's ear off for twenty minutes, and instead of explaining to her there was a major conference going on at the hotel, he promised to handle it."

Lily raised a finger. "And by handle it," she declared, "he meant make the staff park offsite and carpool in one vehicle."

"And that offsite lot?" Dante asked, a smile beginning to form on his face.

"It's off-island, just across the water there," Lily replied, pointing.

Bailey wrung her hands. "Won't that take us too close to the bridge?" she asked, worry evident in her tone. "I don't really want to get shot at."

Cam shook his head. "Not only is our manager limp-dicked, he's also a cheapskate," he explained. "The lot he rented for us is a mile down a gravel road running alongside a swamp. Those assholes will never know we're there."

"I like it," Dante replied, pointing at him. "Let's get Phillip and anybody else you want to bring along, and get out of here before things start getting real bad."

Lily lowered her gaze. "None of our other friends made it," she said hoarsely. "And unless you want to listen to that while we escape," she continued, motioning to the shrill woman, "I would recommend leaving everyone behind, because they're all just like her."

"Not that they would listen to us anyway," Cam muttered.

"Okay then," Dante agreed with a nod, "let's move."

The four of them marched over to where Phillip stood in front of the entitled customer.

"Now you'd better be remembering all of this," she squawked, "because if you don't and my room isn't refunded in full and my next stay comped, then I'm going to have you fired! You understand me, little man? You don't know who you're dealing with, my father is—"

Lily tugged on Phillip's arm. "We're out," she said.

The woman gaped at them, eyes wide with fury. "Excuse me, did you just—"

"Ma'am," Phillip interrupted with his best customer service smile, "if you would be so kind as to go fuck yourself, I would be forever in your debt." He raised both of his middle fingers and backed away.

"Bye bitch," Lily said, giving a playful wave. The woman leapt up and

grabbed her arm, and Lily's eyes blazed.
"Oh hell no," she snarled, and her inner
redneck flared. She swung hard, catching
the woman on the bridge of her nose,
shattering her designer glasses and
sending her tumbling into the sand.

"I'm going to have you all fired!"
she screeched through the blood pouring
down her face. "Every last one of you! And
my daddy is going to sue you for
everything you got!"

The group clambered up into the boat,
a smallish single engine vessel, ignoring
the angry woman's wails. Cam was about to
start it up, but Bailey glanced at Dante
with a wide-eyed look.

He understood what she was getting at
and put a hand on Cam's shoulder. "Hold up
a second," he said. "This isn't right."

He stood up at the back of the boat
and let out a loud whistle to get
everyone's attention. "Okay, everyone,
listen up!" he bellowed. "Those things on
the island running around, their bites are
infectious. Those injured people are going
to turn into those things soon. If you're
smart, you'll get off this island and get
someplace safe."

After a brief moment of silence,
somebody yelled out from the grass, "Blow
it out your ass, Frankenstein!"

A smattering of laughter rippled through the hotel guests, and Dante parked his ass, turning to Cam and motioning for him to go.

"Told you they wouldn't listen to us," he said apologetically.

Dante shrugged. "Well, my conscience is clear," he replied, "which is all I really care about." He glanced at Bailey, who gave him a thankful smile for doing the right thing.

Cam pulled the boat out onto the water, leaving the ignorant hotel guests on their own.

CHAPTER TEN

Cam guided the boat onto shore, which was more rock than sand. Dante got out and helped pull it up a bit more as the others jumped down to land. When they were all ready, Lily took the lead.

"It should be just through the woods up here," she said, and headed through some dense brush.

They came through the other side to a small lot. There were a dozen cars, but also a few zombies. Dante saw movement and grabbed Lily, pulling her back behind cover. She glared at him for a moment, but then saw what he'd focused on, and realized he'd just saved her ass.

She gave him a pat on the arm to silently thank him.

The group watched the zombies milling about. A few of them wore hotel outfits like the three employees hiding in the brush. Dante waved for the group to follow him back a bit so they could talk quietly.

"Friends of yours?" he whispered.

Lily shook her head. "Not really, we just know them in passing," she said.

"Second shift coming in," Cam added.

"Which car is yours?' Dante asked.

Lily motioned vaguely. "The sporty yellow one at the far end of the lot, sitting by itself so nobody scratches it up."

"God, are we all going to fit in that thing?" Cam moaned.

She smirked. "You may have to sit in Phillip's lap," she teased, "but knowing him, he'll probably like it."

Dane held up his hand. "Does your car have a sunroof?" he asked.

"Yeah, why?" she replied, brow furrowing in confusion.

"Because we don't have weapons," he explained, "which means we're going to have to get creative."

Bailey swallowed hard. "Dante," she warned.

"It is amazing that you just met my sister this morning, and already you have that concerned tone down just like her," he muttered, chuckling. "Don't worry, I'll be fine."

"So how do you want to do this?" Lily asked.

Dante held up his hands, motioning as he spoke. "I'm going to come out running and get on top of a car, pulling all those things my way," he explained. "As I'm doing that, I want the rest of you to stay in the bushes and get to your car. When you get piled in, open up the sunroof and come pick me up. Just make sure you get close enough for me to make the jump."

"I can handle that," Lily replied, with a firm nod.

"Here goes nothing," Dante said with a sigh, and got in position. He waited for the others to work their way around and took a few deep breaths.

He knew this was far from his best idea. But they had to get out, get safe, and figure out how to get Grace back. He sprinted out from cover, running towards the first car he saw, a large family sedan that looked like it could fit half a dozen people comfortably.

He jumped up on the truck, and then effortlessly hopped up onto the roof. He smacked the hood a few times, letting out some whistles and yells, gaining the attention of every zombie in the parking lot.

"Yeah! Come and get me!" he bellowed.

As he kept them occupied, Lily led the others through the dense brush to her car. She quickly unlocked the door, and the others piled into the back seat so that Dante would have a place to land. It was tight, but they managed to fit.

As soon as she started up the car, some of the zombies headed her way. Dante was concerned for a moment, but it subsided as he saw the car moving, his companions safely inside.

Lily did a few cycles around the lot, trying to peel off a few of the ghouls from where Dante was so she could get close enough for him to make a jump. Finally, on the third pass, she drove in, stopping about six feet from the other car.

He stepped back as far as he could, took a step and leapt, landing flat on his stomach on the roof of Lily's bright yellow car. The wind knocked out of him, he gasped for air, but managed to scrabble his way into the passenger seat, head first.

Once he was inside, Lily punched the gas, kicking up gravel into the faces of the zombies as she left them behind. She sped down the lot, finally hitting pavement before making the turnoff to the main highway.

She looked both ways, seeing that the way out of town was clear. No mercenaries in sight.

Dante finally managed to get himself situated in the passenger seat and regain his breath.

"You gonna make it there, cowboy?" Lily asked, grinning.

He nodded as he fastened his seatbelt. "Yeah, just a little winded," he huffed. "Your roof packs quite a punch."

She chuckled, petting the steering wheel. "Yeah, my baby is tough," she cooed.

They drove out of Bluffton, and there were signs of struggle everywhere. Abandoned blood-stained cars, zombies running through the neighborhoods. As they slowed down to make their way through a wreck, Dante spotted a dozen zombies clustered around a house.

In the window, a middle-aged man sat, cradling a shotgun. He waved to Dante, who waved back with a sad smile. As much as he wanted to help him, he knew he didn't have the means to.

Instead, the group did the only thing they could do. Get to safety in Tillman and figure out what to do next.

CHAPTER ELEVEN

The group drove through Tillman, South Carolina, which was exactly as described. Lily stopped at the stop sign, just to point out that she wasn't exaggerating.

"Told you," she declared, "one stop sign. There's the gas station slash restaurant slash emergency clinic on the right. And that's about it."

Dante raised an eyebrow. "Emergency clinic?"

"Don't let the name fool you," Lily drawled, rolling her eyes. "It's just a toothless sixty-year-old named Gator who gives you a shot of whiskey and a bandaid. If you're pretty, he'll even give your boo-boo a kiss."

Dante touched his face. "Finally, something going my way today."

The group chuckled at his self-deprecating humor.

They drove a mile up the road, making the turn into the lot of a rundown single story brick home. There was a broken-down car on blocks on the far end of the lot, and various car parts scattered about. As she put the car in park, her cousin burst out of the house brandishing an AK-47. He was short but jacked, with a black mullet and insane eyes.

Lily honked her horn and stuck her head out the window. "Put that thing down, Ace," she drawled, "nobody is here to rob you."

"Lil? Is that you?" he asked, squinting at her as he let his guard down. "What in the hell are you doing here?"

She got out of the car and put her hands on her hips. "What the fuck do you think I'm doing here?" she scoffed. "The whole world has gone crazy, and you're all the family I got nearby. Of course I'm coming here."

"And you felt like you needed to bring you friends," he replied dryly, rolling his eyes. "Even better."

She pointed a finger at him. "Hey, when you and your dumbass friends got high and needed a place to crash, where did they do it at?" she demanded.

Ace wrinkled his nose, lowering his gaze petulantly. "At your place," he admitted.

"And when you and your daddy threw that molotov cocktail at the police car," Lily continued, "whose basement did you hide in?"

He toed the dirt beneath his feet like a toddler. "Yours," he muttered.

"Goddamn right," she replied, raising her chin. "Now show some hospitality!"

Ace strolled up to the group, staying focused on his cousin and then moving down the line of her companions standing with her.

"To you, absolutely, but what the hell am I supposed to do with a couple of hotel losers…" He paused in front of Bailey, and gave her a wink. "Okay, you're cute, I can work with that," he continued, and then stopped in front of Dante, eyes widening. "And holy fuck…" He trailed off, staring intently at the bigger man's face.

"Ace!" Lily snapped at her cousin's ignorance.

"I mean, Jesus Christ, what the fuck happened to you?" Ace drawled, eyes wide. "Did you lose a fight with a belt sander?" He chuckled to himself.

Dante stared him down, speaking confidently. "No Ace, I just made the mistake of going down on your sister the other night," he drawled. "Next time you see her, can you tell her to shave? Because as you can see she really leaves a mark. I mean, I would say you'd see for yourself the next time you fuck her, but you strike me as the type to just pump and dump rather than showing one iota of interesting in getting your partner off, you inbred, sister-fucking, backwoods mullet-wearing hillbilly."

The silence was so thick, nobody moved an inch. Lily stared at the two men, face pale.

And then Ace burst out laughing, leaning over and slapping his thighs. "Holy fucking shit, I fucking love this dude!" he bellowed and pointed at his cousin. "Lily, you gotta marry this guy, I need to be related to him. That was fucking gold, man!" He threw an arm around Dante's shoulders, leading him back towards the house. "Come on, let's get you a beer, it looks like you could use one."

Dante looked back at Lily, bewildered, and she laughed, giving him a thumbs up.

"Rest of you come on too," Ace continued over his shoulder, "there's something you need to see."

The group hustled into the house, which was just as much of a crap heap as the outside.

"Y'all excuse the mess," Ace called. "If you don't like it, feel free to sleep on the lawn!" He plopped himself down on the couch and smacked the grimy cushions.

"What do you want to show us?" Lily asked, taking a seat next to him. The rest of the group took their seats, Bailey perching half on the arm of the couch, looking more than a little uncomfortable at a large stain in the last empty spot.

"Just give me a second," Ace replied, pulling up the DVR. He scrolled through a bunch of his recordings, all clearly porn he'd ordered from pay-per-view.

Lily groaned, shielding her eyes. "Ace, really?" she groaned.

"Don't judge," he said brightly, "internet's been down this week." He clicked through several programs, stopping on a wrestling show.

Lily furrowed her brow, opening her mouth.

"Just shut your pie hole and watch," Ace said, flapping a hand at her.

The intro to the program started, but about forty-five seconds into it, the news came on. It was channel twelve in Bluffton. The female anchor with the big hair was there, along with a snappy-dressed male co-anchor.

"This shit came on in the middle of the night," Ace gushed, "totally saw this in the morning and freaked out!"

Lily shushed him, leaning over and poking the volume button to turn it up.

"*Our top story, reports of rioting in Charleston and Savannah are coming in,*" the female anchor was saying. "*It appears to be in different parts of both cities, and we have a camera crew on location in north Savannah. Lets go to them now.*"

The feed changed, showing a young female reporter standing in the street. A fire raged behind her, and there were silhouettes of people running amok in the background.

"*As you can see, the situation here is getting tense,*" the reporter began, motioning over her shoulder. "*Several people are rampaging for no apparent reason, and one local restaurant is currently ablaze. On our way here, we saw several other places like this, and—*" She stopped short, looking off screen, and somebody screamed right close to the camera, likely the cameraman himself.

The view turned as the camera tipped over, hitting the ground and showing their feet. The reporter shrieked and ran towards the fire, several sets of feet chasing after her. The feed turned back to the newsroom.

"*Well, let's hope she's okay,*" the female anchor continued, as if nothing terrifying were happening, "*and we'll check back in with her later. Now let's go up to Charleston.*"

Ace hit pause on the DVR. The room was silent, everyone dealing with the idea that this issue was spreading around the region, not just near them.

"Man, Charleston *and* Savannah," Cam finally said, scrubbing his hands down his face. "We're not going to be able to get away from this, are we?"

Phillip took a deep breath. "I mean, this stuff can't be everywhere, can it?" he asked shrilly.

Dante and Bailey shared a concerned look, both thinking about what the mercenary had said about A-type blood. Before he could speak up, however, Ace leaned forward, hitting fast forward on the newscast.

"Hate to burst your bubble there bubba," he drawled, "but we're all kinds of fucked here." He hit play on the newsroom again.

"*And now we have some dramatic footage coming in from Austin, Texas,*" the female anchor continued, "*where it appears as though some sort of major bomb has gone off.*"

The live feed showed huge plumes of smoke coming from downtown, filling the night sky with the glow of flames. The anchor's voice came through overtop of the video, "*We don't have all the details, but when we do, we will bring them to you. And now—*"

There was a commotion and the feed came back to the newsroom, both anchors looking off screen with panic in their eyes.

"Oh god, oh god!" she screamed, throwing up her hands, and a zombie practically flew at her, tackling her to the floor. The male anchor scrambled away, but his screams soon filled the space.

"I think we get the point, Ace," Lily muttered.

He quickly turned the TV off. "So yeah," he said, leaning back and scratching his head. "This stuff is everywhere."

"It's worse than that," Dante piped up.

Ace gaped at him. "How in the hell can it be worse than that?!" he demanded.

"We don't have proof," Dante admitted, raising his palms, "just going off of what one of those mercenaries said on the bridge today. The virus targets anyone with the A-blood type. So if you have A-type blood, you turn into one of those things."

There was a long pause, and then Phillip asked hoarsely, "How many people have that?"

"Little less than half the population," Ace replied. When everyone turned to stare at him in shock, he shrugged sheepishly. "What? They covered it in Basic when I went through it."

Bailey blinked at him. "You're military?" she asked.

"Kind of…" he trailed off, tilting his hand back and forth in the air. "Dislocated my hip and destroyed my knee six months out of Basic during a training jump." He slapped his leg for effect. "Military decided it was cheaper for them to cut their losses than keep pouring money into me. So I was discharged. But still, that information stuck."

Lily put a hand to her forehead. "Holy fuck," she breathed, "forty percent of the country are going to become those things?"

"More, when you factor in bites turning them," Dante added.

Ace shook his head. "This shit is going to get real ugly *real* fast if that's the case," he said.

"Do me a favor," Dante said, inclining his head towards the TV, "turn it onto the live feed for channel twelve, will you?"

The redneck raised an eyebrow. "Why?" he asked. "It's just dead air."

"Just humor me, please," Dante replied.

Ace shrugged and changed the channel, which still showed an empty studio. "See, nothing," he said.

"Check the bottom of the screen," Dante prompted, and the group, minus Bailey, leaned in to read it.

"Well I'll be damned," Ace breathed. "I guess I should pay closer attention to things."

Dante cocked his head. "We could use some help going to go get her," he said.

"Whoa now," the redneck drawled, raising his hands. "You're cool and all, and I'm a-okay with you crashing at my pad as long as you need to, but there ain't no way in hell my happy ass is willingly going out there."

Dante crossed his arms. "She might have information on what is going on," he insisted, "and about Theo Atkinson."

"Who the fuck is that?" Ace asked.

"The leader of the mercenary group on the island," Dante explained, clenching a fist. "His men kidnapped my sister Grace, and another one of our friends, Troy."

The redneck shook his head slowly, spreading his arms. "Man, I'm sorry for your loss and all," he said, eyes sincere, "but I really don't see how going into Beaufort is gonna help things."

Dante glanced at Bailey, and she sat up straight, eyes widening into pleading orbs, pressing her palms together.

"But my mother and sisters are in Beaufort," she said, "really close to the station. If you could help us out, I would be awful happy about it."

The redneck withered a bit and then looked at his cousin.

Lily put up her hands. "Don't look at me," she drawled, "you're the one trying to puss out in front of a pretty girl."

Ace sighed. "Okay, fine, we'll go into Beaufort," he said petulantly. "But we ain't going today. It's going to be dark soon, and this doesn't seem like the kind of situation we want to be caught outside in without the sun."

The group nodded approvingly, the mood brightening at the prospect of a plan.

"So, what you got in the fridge, cuz?" Lily asked, slapping her knee and getting to her feet. "We got a house full of hungry people, and I'm cooking."

Ace pointed a finger at her. "Just don't burn my kitchen down," he warned.

"That was one time!" she scoffed, rolling her eyes. The duo led Cam and Phillip into the kitchen, leaving Dante and Bailey on the couch alone.

They stared at the TV, reading the scrolling message over and over. Finally he looked over at the young woman, studying the concern on her face.

"Your family is fine," he assured her. "They're probably more worried about you than you are for them. We'll get them tomorrow."

She smiled, drawing her knees up to her chin. "Thank you," she said quietly. "You don't have a reason to do all this for me, but you still do. So, thank you."

He didn't say anything, just smiled, and she returned it, leaning her head on his shoulder for a time.

"Yo, Scarface, heads up!" Ace bellowed, entering the living room and tossing a cold beer.

Dante caught it, and Bailey laughed, getting up and heading into the kitchen to join the friendly argument inside about what to eat for dinner.

Ace plopped down onto the cough next to him as he cracked open the can.

"Scarface, huh?" Dante asked, and took a long gulp.

Ace shrugged. "Well, I was gonna go with Leatherface," he drawled, "but that would imply that you know how to use a chainsaw. And I can't in good conscience be making assumptions like that."

Dante chuckled and raised his can. "Cheers."

They clinked their cans and took long gulps.

"Really do appreciate the hospitality," Dante said sincerely.

"It's my pleasure, man," Ace replied with a grin. "My cousin told me how you washed up on shore and saved her life. I got mad respect for you doing that. Whatever you need from me, I'm game."

Dante nodded thoughtfully. "Good to know, man, good to know."

"Now, for the most important question of the day," the redneck declared, pointing a finger at him. "How do you like your steak?"

Dante grinned. "Just run it through a warm room, and it should be good," he replied.

Ace grinned, rubbing his palms together. "Oh, this is gonna be fun," he said conspiratorially. "Been a long time since I Had a running partner. Yo Lil! Your new man is fucking awesome!"

Dante sat quietly as the cousins playfully bickered, everything else tuned out as he nursed his beer. Too many things ran through his head, but all of them revolved around one thing.

Saving Grace.

END

Up Next: Grace and Troy fight for their survival against foes living and undead in Lowcountry - Pt. 2

DEAD AMERICA
LOWCOUNTRY
PART 2
BY DEREK SLATON
© 2021

CHAPTER ONE

Day Zero +1

"Dante, go!" Grace screamed, and watched as he throat-punched the guard next to him. Her heart leapt into her mouth as he grabbed Bailey and leapt over the side of the bridge. Moments later, there was a loud splash, and her heart skipped a beat.

Please make it… please be alive… she thought, closing her eyes.

The rest of the men on the bridge were stunned into silence. The only sound amongst the group was the struck guard, who leaned over, gasping for air.

Mosley barked a laugh, heading to the edge of the bridge and looking down at the water a good fifty feet below. "Well holy fucking shit," he drawled, "I had no idea that messed-up looking dude had that in him." He turned back to his prisoners, Grace and Troy, as the mercenaries cuffed their wrists in front of them. "Your man there is quite the daredevil, sweetheart. It's a shame he's a pussy, leaving you and big fella up here all alone."

"Don't worry," she replied, forcing her voice to stay steady, "he'll be back."

Mosley shook his head, chuckling to himself. "Sweetheart, this ain't the movies," he said, spreading his arms for effect. "Your man isn't going to find a shiny set of armor out there and come riding in on a fucking white horse to save the day. No, if he's smart, he'll forget all about you and move on, find himself another woman, and get as far away from here as possible."

"He's not my man," she snapped, jutting out her chin, "he's my brother."

Mosley grinned. "Well hell, we're in the deep south," he drawled, "could be both."

Despite the situation, Grace found it impossible not to roll her eyes.

"Oh, not a fan of my humor, huh?" he asked, clucking his tongue. "Well no matter, if you didn't find that funny, you're sure as shit not going to find what happens next funny." He pulled out a walkie talkie, raising it to his lips. "Valentine, it's Mosley. I'm on the bridge and have a couple more volunteers for the meat grinder. Where you want them?" There was no response, and he growled. "Well hell, Valentine, didn't realize it was break time already. Guess what boys, we're taking five!"

"In case you haven't noticed," a forceful but calm voice drawled through the speaker, "there's a lot going on today, and quite frankly you're not at the top of my priority list. So unless you want to volunteer yourself for the meat grinder, I suggest you remember that."

Mosley sighed, his swagger dropping a notch. "I hear you," he replied into the walkie talkie. "Now where do you want these volunteers at? They are just eager little beavers to get into the fight."

"Take them to the main resort at the northwest corner of the island," Valentine replied. "It's about two miles north of the main road once you clear the bridge. There's a lot of activity in the area, so it'll be easy to spot when you get close."

Mosley nodded. "They're on the way." The line clicked, and he wrinkled his nose as he pocketed the radio. "Well, looks like you two get to live the resort life, at least for an afternoon. Get them loaded up."

Two of the guards escorted the prisoners over to a van and shoved them roughly inside. As they left, Mosley approached No Name, who looked after the duo with his brow furrowed.

"Quit your pouting," the former quipped, "it doesn't suit you at all, you no-named bastard."

The tall bald man crossed his arms. "Not sure I'm a fan of this."

"Bullshit," Mosley spat, "I know for a fact you've done far worse than this in your life."

No Name glared down at him, his biceps bulging as he flexed his arms. "You don't know a damn thing about what I've done," he said.

Mosley just chuckled, smacking him on the back and sauntering off to the firing line. No Name watched the van drive away, uneasy in the pit of his stomach.

CHAPTER TWO

The van sped along the highway, leading towards the main part of the island. Hilton Head was a popular destination for the wealthy elite to visit throughout the year, with a fluctuation population of forty thousand or so. This time of year, however, the number of residents was significantly less outside of the resorts at least.

With the weather cooling in the northern parts of the country, the weather in the Lowcountry was still warm and humid, perfect for the city dwellers to get away and be pampered by underpaid staff.

Grace could only hope that most of the vacationers had been planning to visit later in the year, seeing as how they were about to fight those that had chosen to come down early.

"Not wanting to sound like Captain Obvious here," Troy drawled, "but we're in some trouble here."

She glanced to the front of the van where a metal partition separated the back from the cab. There was a small grate at the top in the center, so that the driver could look back, but it didn't seem as if anyone was listening in on them.

"Gee, you think?" she said, rolling her eyes. "Whatever gave you that idea?"

"I'm serious," he hissed. "Mercenaries are executing civilians in broad daylight and kidnapping others to do god only knows what. Whatever is happening out there just isn't happening here. This shit has to be national, or more likely, global. These boys wouldn't risk this unless they know there aren't going to be any repercussions."

Grace pursed her lips, contemplating his words, but realized he was right. QXR group was known for committing war crimes overseas in war zones, this being the whole reason she'd protested their offices in the past.

But for them to do this on American soil… that was a risky move even for them, at least in normal times. If they were doing this, then it was sure they could get away with it.

"From what I understand," she said quietly, "your boy Theo Atkinson and his QXR Group receives military briefings. If what you say is right, and they know the world is fucked, there's no telling what they might do."

Troy nodded like a bobblehead. "Question is," he continued, "what do *we* do?"

She took a deep breath. "We bide our time," she said.

"I was kind of hoping for something more substantial than just sitting around and waiting," he said dryly.

She shook her head. "Didn't say sit around and wait," she replied. "I said bide our time. Dante is out there, and he's going to come get us. We just have to do everything we can to stay alive and wait for him."

"Why in the world do you think he's coming for us?" Troy asked, blinking at her incredulously. "Assuming he survived the fall and got somewhere safe, which is a *big* if, why would he risk it?"

Grace crossed her arms. "Because he's already given so much of himself to protect me," she replied, "he's not going to let anything happen to me now."

He paused, contemplating. "His… his face?" he asked quietly.

She nodded, avoiding his gaze. "It was about fifteen years ago," she began. "I was home with my parents when the fire broke out. It was the middle of the night, and I don't even know what happened, just woke up and there was smoke in my room. I tried to get out, but the flames were right outside my door." She held up her hand, showing the burn marks on her palm. "The pain woke me up fully, but the smoke was just too much. Ended up collapsing while trying to get my bedroom window open. A few moments later, I heard someone crashing through my door. It was Dante. He got me outside, but he paid a big price for it."

Troy swallowed hard. "And your parents?" he asked.

"Didn't make it," Grace replied hoarsely, shaking her head. "He tried, but their room was blocked off by the fire. He took me in after that, did everything he could to take care of me. Even though I'm twenty-eight and fully capable of taking care of myself, he's still always there for me."

He nodded. "Good to have people out there to watch your back," he said quietly.

"Especially someone as determined as my brother," she added.

The van started to slow down, and the sounds of gunfire cracked outside. The passenger in the front seat turned around, banging on the back wall.

"Hope you two are ready to fight!" he called.

Grace leaned in, whispering into Troy's ear, "Remember, we stay alive and bide our time, no matter what."

He nodded in response as the vehicle came to a halt. A few moments later, the back doors opened, two mercenaries standing there and waving them forward.

"Come on, let's move," one of them demanded.

Grace and Troy climbed out of the back, stepping down onto the parking lot of the gigantic all-inclusive resort. The main hotel was large, eight stories tall, and stretching for a couple hundred yards. There were a few dozen cars in the parking lot which had been moved to the outer edge of the lot to act as a makeshift barricade, however it only covered about half of the lot edge.

A handful of mercenaries had set up along the line, occasionally firing off a few shots into the distance. In the center portion of the lot were a trio of black pickup trucks, set a few yards apart, with a tent to the right.

"Wait here," the mercenary said, and walked towards the line of civilians standing outside of the tent. It was about a dozen deep, with a middle-aged white woman at the front with dyed hair wearing expensive clothes.

As she reached the entrance to the tent, one of the mercenaries patted her down, and she jerked her arm away as they touched it. She tried to pull away, but he took a fistful of her shirt, ripping the sleeve away. Her arm beneath was bandaged, but blood seeped through the fabric.

She screamed as two other mercenaries gripped her body, dragging her off to the side. About twenty yards away, they held her in front of a dumpster, and her screams turned to unintelligible pleading sobs.

Unfazed, one of the mercenaries pulled out a handgun and shot her in the head. Some of the people in the lineup screamed, some already sobbing, as the mercenaries lifted the now-dead woman and tossed her body in the dumpster.

"Looks like they know the bites are deadly, too," Troy murmured.

Grace swallowed hard. "And really not taking any chances, either."

The mercenary that had told them to stay blew out a sharp whistle, motioning for them to come over.

"Let's move," their guard snapped, and gave Troy a shove to get them headed towards the tent.

"No need to shove asshole," he muttered, "just tell me where to go."

The mercenary raised his hand to shove him again, but stopped at the glare coming from his prisoner. "Just keep moving," he snapped. "Head to the lobby."

Grace and Troy walked into the building, entering the marble-floored lobby. There was a small coffee shop in the corner, a piano in the corner tinkling out an automatic tune, and a long stretch of sofas and recliners along the far wall, which was floor-to-ceiling glass overlooking the water.

The mercenary looked around, spotting someone waving them in next to a group of five civilians sitting on the floor. He led Grace and Troy over, and pointed to the floor, where they sat next to the five males nervously perched there.

A mercenary headed out of a back room carrying a cardboard box, and walked into the center of the group, dropping the box on the floor. There was a metallic clinking as it settled, and then the man gave it a kick, sending it toppling over onto its side.

Heavy duty cutlery skittered across the floor, and he glared at the silent and still civilians beneath him. "I suggest you find a weapon in there you feel comfortable using," he demanded. "Because in two minutes you're being marched up to the third floor conference room to clear it out."

An older gentleman dressed in a high-end bright green golfing ensemble got to his feet, pointing a finger at their captor. "I don't know who the fuck you think you are, coming in here and barking out orders," he snarled, "but we're not playing your little game."

The mercenary stared at him for a moment, blinking with almost an impressed look on his face. "Is that a fact, now?" he finally asked.

"Oh you bet it is," the golfer replied, squaring his shoulders. "I may not know what's going on, but I know I'm not taking orders from some lowlife like you. In fact, I think—"

His tirade cut short as the mercenary shot him in the head, dropping his body to the ground. He turned to the rest of the wide-eyed group, waving the weapon around and raising his voice.

"Let me be very fucking clear with all of you," he declared loudly. "In one minute and fifteen seconds, you are going to be marching up to the third floor to clear out a room full of whatever those things are. If you don't want a weapon, that's your business, but you *will* be marching or else you'll end up like your friend there. Now, if you want to take the easy way out, it's no skin off my back, because I have a bullet for each of you." He wiggled the gun in the air. "So make your decision."

The group sat for several seconds in shocked silence. Finally, Grace got up and walked over to the box, picking through a few of the chef's grade cutlery before deciding on a meat cleaver. She picked it up, and gave it a few practice swings before turning to Troy, who was still sitting on the ground.

"What the hell are you waiting on?" she snapped. "Get off your ass and grab something."

As if snapping out of a trance, he nodded jerkily and scrambled over, grabbing a large butcher knife. He stood next to her and gave her a nod.

Grace looked around at the rest of the group, all of whom were dressed in fancy clothes, clearly staying at the hotel rather than working there.

"Well, what are the rest of you waiting on?" she demanded. "An invitation? Get to your feet and grab something, now!"

They scrambled to their feet, faces pale and scared, and picked up weapons, holding them nervously. She wondered if any of them had ever even held a kitchen utensil in their life.

The mercenary who'd given them their pep talk let out a whistle, and then pointed at Grace when she looked at him, motioning for her to come over. "Yeah, come here a second," he said.

She squared her shoulders and approached him, careful to let her cleaver hand hang next to her side to make sure he

didn't get trigger-happy thinking she was
going to use it.

"What's your name, girl?" he asked.

She gritted her teeth, but replied
calmly, "Grace."

"Grace, huh?" He nodded. "Okay, I'm
Dodson. I'm going to go out on a lib and
say you aren't one of these pampered fucks
who still thinks they're on holiday," he
said, motioning to the rest of the group.

"Quite the intuition there, Dodson,"
she snapped, before she could stop
herself, tone laced with mocking.

He smirked. "Forceful and has balls,
I can work with that," he said, pointing
at her. "You're going to be my go-to
person on this."

"My day is now complete," she replied
dryly.

"Not yet it isn't," he said brightly,
and pulled out a military-grade
switchblade. He hit the button and the
six-inch blade rocketed straight up. He
held it up in front of her face. "This
blade is no joke," he said. "Little work,
and you can cut through bone." He flicked
the knife closed and handed it to her.
"Just to show you I'm serious about you
being my go-to person, I'm giving this to
you. There's bound to be close encounters
up there, so this might help."

She flicked it open, inspecting the blade, and then closed it, shoving it into her pocket. "Thanks," she muttered, and then turned on her heel, heading back to Troy.

Dodson smirked at her back, checking out her bottom half and then let out another whistle. "All right, listen up," he bellowed. "This is Grace, and she's the only one of you that's shown any initiative, and frankly, any willingness to live through the next half hour. I strongly suggest you listen to her, and follow her lead."

Everyone turned to her, but she didn't look anyone in the eye, unfazed by the praise.

"Third floor, let's move," Dodson continued, motioning to a stairwell door about twenty yards away. "Cortez, you're with me. The rest of you stay back and wait for more volunteers."

Volunteers, my ass, Grace thought bitterly as she followed Dodson to the stairs and up towards the third floor.

Another tall and muscular mercenary, who must be Cortez, followed, bringing up the rear.

Nobody spoke as they marched up the stairs, the only noise footfalls echoing on concrete, muffled gunshots coming from outside.

They reached the door on the third floor, and Dodson held up a hand, pulling out a keycard. He held it out to Grace.

"Your main target is the conference room at the center of the hallway," he said. "However, my men have identified room three-twelve as an infected room. I would suggest you tackle that one first, so you get a good sense of what you are up against."

She took the keycard, still emotionless as she wrapped her hand around the door lock bar.

He reached out and held it shut, stopping her. "And one more thing," he drawled. "We're on a tight timetable here, so you have twenty minutes to get this done. If you don't, then Cortez and I are going to use you as human shields to keep them occupied while we take them out." He winked at her glare. "Happy hunting!"

He backed up and waved them in with a flourish.

Grace opened the door and led the group into the hallway, which looked surprisingly clean given the events of the morning. There was nothing between them and the conference room, with the exception of a single luggage cart with several bags scattered on the floor.

She glanced up at the numbers on the closest door, reading *320*. "A few more doors down," she muttered.

They reached the door, and she turned to face the group. There was movement inside, clear bumping and moaning and shuffling emanating from the room.

"Okay," she said quietly, taking a deep breath, "these things are fast and vicious. I think our best chance at taking this thing out is to… who are you?" she asked, pointing to a forty-something man in moderately decent shape to her left.

"Charles," he replied.

She nodded. "Okay, I want you and Troy here to go low and hold this thing in place while—"

"You're being way too dramatic about this," one of the other men snapped, and snatched the keycard from her hand, swiping it on the door. He grabbed the door handle before anyone could stop him, and turned it, pushing it open. "Let me show you how it's—"

His speech dissolved into screams as a small female zombie flew through the door, tackling him. It immediately latched onto his nose, biting down hard and pulling back, taking most of the skin and the tip of it clean off, chowing happily.

Before it could go in for a second bite, Grace swung the cleaver, the sharp blade going through the skull like butter and dropping the ghoul.

The man pressed frantically at his face, screaming in agony. "Don't just stand there!" he yelled as blood poured down his face. "Help me! Get me a towel!"

Charles moved towards the open door, but Grace put out a hand to stop him.

"One thing you have to realize about these things," she said, "is that the bites are deadly. You get bitten, there's no coming back from it. Well… there is." She pointed to the dead zombie on the floor. "But as one of them."

Troy chewed his lip. "So what do you want to do with him?" he asked.

"Do you want him chasing after us?" she replied.

He shook his head. "Not particularly."

"Then you know what to do," she said, her eyes cold and emotionless.

Troy nodded and looked down at the man on the floor. "Sorry man," he said, "but we have to protect ourselves."

The man held out his hands. "No, no, I'll be fine, it's okay, please—" His pleading cut short as Troy took his butcher knife and went in for the kill.

He plunged it into the man's forehead, ending his suffering, and stood up, glancing at Grace, who had a fire in her eyes. He couldn't deny it terrified him a little to see this sweet girl flipping so quickly into survival mode.

"Now are you rich fucks going to start taking this seriously?" she snapped. "Or do you want to end up like him?" She pointed to the dead man, and the others nodded, unable to speak. "Good, now let's get to the conference room before those assholes use us as bait."

CHAPTER THREE

Grace stopped the group just outside of the conference room. There was a lot of noise inside, and the double doors leading in had a makeshift barricade holding them shut with heavy potted plants moved over to hold it.

One of the doors was partially open, not more than a foot wide. It butted up against the giant potted plant, and Grace tried to shove it back against the door, but it wouldn't budge.

"I can see why they used these," she muttered. "Sturdy."

As soon as she finished talking, a couple of zombies smashed into the door, startling the group, and they all jumped back. A trio of arms jetted out from the opening, clawing frantically at the fresh meal, thankfully unable to fully make it through the gap.

Grace turned back to the others and shrugged. "I'm open to ideas."

"Yeah, I got one," one of the men drawled, raising a hand. "Why don't we hide from these people?"

"Or better yet," another added, "try to escape?"

Troy shook his head. "Man, you saw what they did to that dude in the lobby," he said. "As soon as he started to act out, they just shot him in the face. What do you think is going to happen if we try to escape, or they find us hiding?"

"We gotta try *something*," the first man argued.

"Fine," Grace snapped, waving a flippant hand at him, "if you want to run away or find a hiding spot, you have at it. We won't give you away. We also won't mourn you when they gun you down." She checked her watch. "Now, we have sixteen minutes to clear this room or they are going to kill us. So if you aren't in this fight, get the fuck out now, because I need to know what I have."

The group all shared nervous looks, but nobody made a run for it or tried to hide.

"Okay," she said with a nod, "let's figure out how to get this done."

She turned back towards the door, angling herself so she could see into the room. It was difficult to see anything, with the zombie arms flailing about, but she caught glimpses of the far wall.

"It's not much, but it looks like there's a decently sized buffet line on the left side," she mused. "About four tables long, still has most of the silver serving dishes on it."

"How much resistance?" Troy asked.

She shook her head. "Not sure," she admitted. "I count eight, not including the three by the door. So that's eleven, just on one side of the room."

"And we're armed with knives," one of the men scoffed. "Yeah, this is gonna go *great*."

"It will, if we work together," Grace said firmly, and looked down the hallway. There was a rolling food trolley used to deliver room service parked outside one of the doors. She strode over and grabbed it, rolling it back to the door.

Troy lifted the silver dome on top and peeked into the plate beneath. "I ordered the omelette," he said snootily, "not the benedict."

Grace rolled her eyes and then turned to the group. "Okay, here's how we're doing this," she said firmly. She pointed to the two men to her left. "One of you is going to brace the door, while the other pulls that giant potted plant away from it. Those things are putting up a hell of a fight, so it's not going to take long for that door to come open. I just need you to hold it long enough for this cart to fit through. Once it is, Troy and I are going to shove it through them so we can get into the room."

Charles raised a tentative hand. "Why not just block up the door and fight them off here?" he asked. "Wouldn't that be safer?"

Grace motioned to the door, at the still maniacal flailing arms. "The zombie heads are a foot behind the door, and there are at least three of them," she said. "If you want to reach in there to try to stab one, you be my guest."

"No, I mean, what if we open the door wider and use the cart to block them off?" he replied, a little frustrated she wasn't getting his point while they were running down the clock. "We would have easy access to their heads."

She cocked her head back and forth. "True," she admitted, "but the noise would bring in the rest of the room. It would take everything we have just to hold the cart in place, and unless you want to hop on Troy's back, I doubt you'd be able to reach them."

"And already saying no to the back thing," Troy added, raising his hand. "But that does beg the question, what are we doing if we somehow get inside?"

Grace jerked a thumb over her shoulder. "The buffet line," she replied. "It's close to the wall, so it's going to be close quarters, but we can use that to our advantage. I'll plow through to the other side and block off that side, but

Troy, you're going to have to get creative to hold them off on the other side."

He peeked through the crack in the door, focusing on the buffet. He focused in on one of the large silver domed food serving containers.

"I'm pretty sure I can use that serving dish to hold them off," he said. "If I can get one of them hung up on it, it should work."

One of the men shook his head, pressing his palms to his temples. "So great," he moaned, "instead of having a breakfast buffet, we become a meal? They're just going to jump over the tables and get us!"

"Show of hands," Grace declared, "has anybody seen any of these things jump?" When nobody moved, she shook her head. "Me either. Not saying they can't, not saying they won't, but I haven't seen it. And with…" She checked her watch again. "With fourteen minutes to do this, I vote we assume that they can't and proceed."

The man wrung his hands, looking uneasily at the knife handle in his fist.

Troy reached over and put a hand on his shoulder. "Hey, big guy, you need to get in the game, here," he said, firm but not unkindly. "Judging by your appearance, I'm assuming you've always looked down on the hired help, so look at this as your long awaited opportunity to finally reach out and hit them instead of just making their lives a living hell by yelling at them."

The man furrowed his brow, scowling at the insinuation.

"And he's back," Troy declared with a grin, patting him on the shoulder. "Let's get this show on the road." He gave the guy a push towards the door, and then joined Grace behind the pushcart, which was just big enough for both of them to get a good grip on it.

The two men set up by the door, one on the plant and the other wedging himself against the door. He leaned back to avoid getting caught by the still-flailing zombie arms.

"You ready?" Grace asked.

Troy nodded. "As ready as I'm going to be," he replied.

She glanced back at Charles, standing right behind her, and he nodded as well, mouth set in a thin line. She turned back to the door. "Do it," she said.

The two men made eye contact, sharing their fear and determination.

Grace lowered her knees into a stance ready to spring and began to count. "Three… two… one!" she cried, and the man by the plant began to heave.

It took a moment, but he managed to slide it by yanking as hard as he could, getting it out of the way, and then darted back beside Charles. As soon as the pressure on the door was relieved, the zombies pushed harder, and the man at the door struggled to keep it from opening.

His feet began to slide on the carpet, and he quickly lost ground, straining, the door inching open more and more. When a zombie head managed to poke through the gap, he panicked, grabbing the knife from his belt and jabbing wildly.

With the angle he was at, there wasn't enough force behind the blows, and the blade glanced off the size of the ghoul waiter's head. It cut deeply, but the wounds were superficial, not stopping the corpse in any way.

After a couple of quick strikes, Grace barked, "Stop stabbing at it!" She waved wildly. "We need these things on their feet so we can push through!"

The man nodded, his panic subsiding a bit, trusting her and her plan for the time being. He stuck the knife back in his belt, and refocused on the door, pushing as hard as he could to keep it in place.

The gap was now a foot wide, the zombies frantic now that they'd figured out there was fresh meat on the other side. Troy looked over their heads, spotting a few more rushing towards the door, attracted by the frantic, excited moaning of their brethren.

"We gotta go now!" he cried. "Open the door!"

Grace startled, but didn't question him—there was no time for it. She readied herself for the big push, tightening her grip on the handle. The doorman jumped back, allowing the door to open, and then ducking behind it as a shield from the ghouls who were incredibly interested in him.

He didn't jump back far enough, however, and the heavy wood smacked hard into his face, stunning him. He snapped out of it, however, screaming as a zombie reached back behind the door and caught a hold of his arm.

With the door clear, Troy and Grace ran at the opening, taking four large strides to build up a head of steam. They smacked into the trio of ghouls in the entryway, shoving them back into the room.

They didn't stop to look around, instead pumping their legs towards the buffet line on the far edge of the wall. The room was fairly large, with the makeshift barricade about thirty yards away. As they ran, a few corpses from the buffet tables turned and rushed at them.

"Keep pushing!" Troy screamed, and Grace didn't need to be told twice.

They raced forward, picking up speed and slamming into the ghouls. The two corpses tumbled to the ground, and they turned the pushcart to the back side of the buffet line. They ran behind it, thankful that it was empty between the tables and the walls.

Troy let go so that Grace could push it to the other side and block it off. He turned back to the rest of their team and saw they were having some issues.

"Move your fucking asses!" he barked, cupping his hands around his mouth.

Charles and his partner were about fifteen yards behind them, but struggled with a couple of zombies. One creature had the latter by the arm and he struggled to break free, swinging around and jerking his limb up and down. He finally remembered his knife and pulled it out, stabbing the zombie in the eye socket. Crimson goo splashed out onto his face, and he recoiled, but managed to disengage his arm from the corpse's death grip.

Charles fought against another ghoul, what had once been a young waitress, and he thankfully had quite a bit of body weight on her. He pressed against her chest to keep her snapping jaws away from his face and then spotted movement in his periphery. Swinging her around, he spotted more zombies rushing his way.

Letting out a primal yell all the way from his bowels, he shoved the zombie back with all his might, sending it careening into the others and knocking them to the ground.

Both men finally free, they tore for the buffet line, rushing past Troy who stood guard on the one end with one of the giant serving dishes as a shield. They were heavy duty, weighing about ten pounds and stretching nearly a yard in length.

As soon as the men were clear, Troy got into position, waiting for the ghouls to rush him, which didn't take long.

Within seconds, four zombies crashed into him. He extended his arms as far as he could, while holding the container up. Rotted arms flailed everywhere, smacking into his body and uncomfortably close to his face. But he steeled himself, managing to hold them at bay.

Grace secured the cart by locking down the wheels, which were close to the back wall, before turning around to survey the room. There were about fifteen ghouls in total, all rushing towards the table.

Charles and his partner had their knives ready, but they stood shoulder to shoulder, shaking with fear, the glittering blades quivering as the enemies got closer.

"Spread out!" Grace yelled. "We gotta thin 'em out!"

The two men took several steps away from each other, putting about five yards between them, and also her. She readied her cleaver before realizing they were missing a person—the man from the door.

"Where the hell is the other guy?" she demanded.

Everyone looked towards the door, which didn't have any zombies within ten yards of it. The man peeked his head into the hall, watching as the zombies reached the buffet line. His eyes were side, and he didn't make any move to join the fight.

One of the running zombies caught sight of him and immediately changed course, shrieking. He froze like a deer in the headlights, and when the zombie was within a few yards, he finally turned tail and ran away.

The ghoul was fast, however, and within two steps it tackled him from behind, sending him face first into the floor. As soon as he hit the carpet, the corpse latched its teeth into his shoulder, tearing out a huge chunk.

He screamed and thrashed about, reacting violently to the sudden injury. He bucked like a wild bronco, trying to

shake the ghoul, but it was no use. The
zombie chewed its foot before going in for
another bite, this time on his arm.

Adrenaline kicked in as pain shot
through the man's body like electricity,
and he managed to flip over. He faced his
attacker, what had once been a teenage boy
of no more than seventeen. He had a slight
frame with bite marks on several parts of
his torso, and chewed hungrily on the bit
of bicep still in his putrid maw.

The wounded man's head swam, pain and
blood loss mingling in a heady mix as he
stared up at the zombie in cold fear. He
had trouble processing the moment, not
able to wrap his brain around the fact
that his life was very quickly coming to
an end.

When the zombie lunged back in for
another bite, he lifted his arm to catch
its mouth before it reached his face. On
instinct, he reached down to his belt,
pulling out his knife and stabbing up into
the ghoul's face. The corpse went limp on
top of him, twitching a bit, and he simply
laid there, too weak to move.

Back at the buffet line, the bulk of
the zombies had reached the tables,
slamming into them and bushing them back
into the others. The three defenders
planted their legs against the edges to

keep the tables in place, the wood digging
into their thighs.

Grace raised her cleaver as two
zombies reached over the serving dishes
and knocked one to the ground in a
clatter. She buried it into the ghouls'
head, but was unable to jerk it free
before the corpse fell to the ground,
taking the cleaver with it.

She made a mad grab, but the other
zombie lunged at her arm, and she pulled
her hand back quickly. Now weaponless, she
looked around the table for something she
could use to kill the ghouls with.

She spotted a small plate filled with
metal skewers, each about a foot long. She
reached for one, but the zombie lunged for
her arm. She smacked its hand away,
jerking back to avoid its gnashing teeth.

She took a deep breath and lashed
out, managing to snatch one of the
skewers, and readied it for a strike. The
ghoul toppled during another bite attempt,
and as it thrashed back to its feet, she
didn't waste the opportunity, jamming the
skewer forward into its eye.

The first one glanced off of the side
of its face, and she screamed, jamming
again, this time finding her mark. She
kept a good grip of the skewer, yanking it
back out before the zombie flopped down
onto the floor.

Grace looked over at her team, noting the seven ghouls between the other two who were flailing wildly to try to take them out. The closer man continued to flinch as he tried to slash forward, but the three zombies grasping at him had him so spooked he could barely reach forward to do any damage.

Not wanting to draw attention to herself, she ducked down and pushed the long tablecloth out of the way, crawling underneath the buffet tables. She peeked out of the front, making sure that the zombies were still focused on the man behind.

She pulled herself out, grabbing her cleaver from the fallen ghoul, and wrenched it free of the skull with a sickening slick noise. She moved slowly, staying on the ground and crawling to a nearby table that was about five yards away from the buffet line. She got up on one knee and peered over the table.

The zombies were all engaged with the men, not paying her any attention, so she slowly stood up, gripping the cleaver tightly. She walked cautiously and quietly towards the line, staying just to the right of the creatures. When she reached striking distance, she lunged forward, swinging hard and catching the rightmost ghoul in the side of the head.

The force of the blow sent the professional grade cutting utensil right through the back half of the skull, clipping enough of the brain to drop the zombie. The falling corpse generated enough of a ruckus to alert the ghoul next to it, so she didn't hesitate, using the momentum from her swing to bring the cleaver around, embedding it into the face of the turning corpse.

The third and final ghoul attacking the man broke away from him and darted towards her. In a panic, she dropped the weapon and shoved her hands out to grab it by the chest. The creature growled and snarled at her, and she struggled to hold it at bay.

A second later, the man jumped over the table and jammed his knife into the side of its head, dropping it. His eyes wide in shock, as if he hadn't thought he was capable, he turned to Grace and gave her a nod.

She responded in kind and then bent down to retrieve her cleaver.

The duo turned to the four zombies that were focused on Charles. He'd managed to ding one of the creatures, and it lay face down on one of the tables, shaking from side to side as its brethren continued to ram into it to get at their meal.

Grace and her partner took a few steps back before beginning their approach from behind. She took the one on the right, and he went for the middle. When they reached striking distance, she brought her cleaver down in a rough overhead strike, in a fruitful killing blow. He jammed his knife into the base of one ghoul's skull and grabbed the back of its shirt to slam it into the other one.

He managed to use the weight of the dead zombie to pin down the other creature to the table. He held it in place as best he could, and Charles drove his knife into the back of the flailing creature's head. With the immediate threat gone, he stepped back with a huff, rubbing at his face.

"Uh, are you okay, man?" Grace's partner asked, motioning to the blood all over his hand.

Charles looked confused for a second, and then looked at his palm, eyes widening with panic at the blood coating it. He carefully inspected himself for a bite, but couldn't find one. He pulled a length of tablecloth from the buffet line, and wiped his hand, finding nothing.

He held up his hand and turned it this way and that, to show he was clean. "Must have been one of theirs," he said.

"Could you people give me a hand before taking a fucking smoke break?!"

Troy bellowed, and the trio startled, immediately leaping into action.

Charles stayed behind the buffet line, rushing over and throwing his weight behind the serving dish to help hold the ghouls at bay.

Grace and her partner rushed along the tables, staying close. As they came within a few yards of the edge, a couple of the ghouls in the back broke off and came around towards them. They readied themselves, extending a free arm to hold back chests, and striking with the other.

Grace nodded at her partner, once a reluctant man, now delivering kill strikes with no hesitation.

Troy, faced with only one remaining zombie, was fed up. He let out a grunt before giving the serving tray a heave, sending the ghoul back onto the floor. As it tried to get back up, he raised the heavy metal platter up over his head and drove it down, cracking the corpse's skull.

Unsatisfied, he brought it down a few more times, despite the zombie no longer moving, obliterating its head until there was nothing left but goo. He finally tossed the tray to the side, causing a racket as it clattered to the floor.

The quartet stood silently for a moment, chests heaving, hearts hammering, each reflecting on how they'd survived the fight.

Grace looked down at her watch. "Four minutes to spare," she said.

"I don't know about the rest of you," Troy declared, holding up a hand, "but I vote we use every last second of our allotted time. I could use a breather." He massaged his arms, sore from having held the thrashing zombies at bay for so long. He headed over to a seat in front of a plate of now-cold food, plonking down and putting his feet up on the table.

"I agree," Grace said, heading for the table. "Not only do we need the rest, but we need to see just how strict these assholes are on timing."

CHAPTER FOUR

Exactly four minutes later, Dodson
and Cortez walked down the hallway towards
the conference room. Rifles raised, they
moved soundlessly down the carpet, ready
to throw down at a moment's notice.

They stepped over the bodies of one
of the group sprawled beneath a zombie
from the room. Dodson cocked his head,
noticing the stab wound as well as the
missing nose, nodding in appreciation that
they'd put him down after being bitten.

They approached the conference room,
spotting a zombified civilian pinned
underneath a dead waiter. It flailed
around, snarling at the sight of fresh
food.

Cortez didn't hesitate, aiming for a
clean headshot and taking it to silence
the noise. The duo stood fast, weapons
raised at the door, in case anything was
going to come barreling out to meet them.

When nothing did, they nodded at each
other and leapt forward, bursting into the
conference room. They lowered their guns
and relaxed as soon as they spotted the
quartet sitting around a dining table.

"I have to admit, I'm impressed,"
Dodson drawled as they approached the
table, waving his hand at the pile of

corpses by the buffet line. "Only two casualties in clearing out this room."

She swallowed a big bite of blueberry muffin before replying dryly, "Guess I owe you five bucks."

"You oughta be giving that money to us," Troy declared, linking his fingers across his chest, still lounging. "Since we're doing your job for you."

Cortez narrowed his eyes and opened his mouth to speak, but Dodson raised a hand to cut him off.

"Don't worry," he said, "you keep doing work like this, and then Atkinson will certainly see fit to reward you."

Troy shook his head. "Yeah, with a bullet to the back of the head," he muttered under his breath.

Dodson furrowed his brow, not having heard the utterance, but assumed it wasn't favorable. He pulled out his walkie talkie with a shrug, raising it to his lips. "Need cleaners on three," he said. "Conference room just down from the elevators."

"Copy that," somebody said on the other end.

"Cleaners, huh?" Troy piped up. "Kind of surprised you aren't making us clean this mess up."

Cortez sneered. "Keep it up and we just might," he snapped.

Dodson raised his hand again, shooting his subordinate a pointed look. "No sir, you see, you are now a victim of your own success," he said, smiling at Troy. "Now that we know you can deliver, you get to keep moving up the floors, clearing them one by one. We have a whole list of rooms, both small and large, that have unwanted occupants that need to be evicted."

The group shared concerned, defeated looks, save for Grace who simply continued eating her muffin.

"But, I know that nobody can work non-stop," Dodson continued. "So why don't you take five, help yourselves to whatever food you can find. You've earned it."

Troy glanced at the plates on the table, wrinkling his nose at the blood splatter across them. He lowered his feet, poking at a miraculously blood-free omelette. It was cold and rubbery, and he grimaced.

"There goes their five-star review," he joked.

The elevators along the far wall gave a cheerful *ding*, and they all turned to look as the doors slid open. Four people exited, each pushing a luggage cart. They were older, easily late fifties or early sixties, two men and two women. None of them appeared to be in terrible shape, but they moved slowly, clearly not up to be fighting.

One of the women in the back took in the sight of corpses and burst into tears, prompting the man beside her to put an arm around her shoulders for comfort.

The other two looked to Dodson for instructions, though they stayed stiff and nervous.

"One of you get the duo by the front entrance," he said, snapping his fingers. "The rest of you get started on the buffet line."

They started moving, albeit slowly, walking over to the corpses and loading them onto the luggage carts.

Troy stared in open-mouthed horror. "Jesus Christ, that's all kinds of fucked up," he breathed, watching the retirees lug dead bodies.

Dodson strolled over to the table, and grabbed one of the prepackaged muffins that Grace had torn into, cracking open the plastic. He tore off a piece and popped it into his mouth.

"Admittedly that's not my proudest moment," he said through blueberry dough, "but if you are not going to be a part of the team you gotta be useful."

"And if they're not?" Charles asked.

Troy snorted. "Always a dumpster out back," he said dryly.

Dodson smirked, taking another bite of his muffin. He looked around the table as Grace finished hers, noticing that nobody else was eating.

"Well, if none of you want breakfast, I guess we should make our way up to the fourth floor," he said with fake sympathy. "Hope you are ready for a challenge, because there is a party ro—"

A torrent of gunfire erupted from outside, and his brow furrowed. He and Cortez shared a concerned look, and the four civilians stiffened, unsure if the mercenaries being on edge was a good thing or not.

"That doesn't sound good," Cortez said.

Dodson shook his head. "We got some real badasses down there," he said, but his tone sounded like he was more trying to convince himself than his partner. "They should be able to handle anything thrown at them."

As soon as he finished speaking, his radio crackled to life. "Fall back! Fall back!" somebody yelled in a panic. "Get to the lobby!"

There was screaming before the walkie talkie cut out, and the gunfire continued at an alarming pace. The two mercenaries rushed to the windows overlooking the parking lot of the hotel. The four civilians ran over as well, hearts pounding.

The six of them stared out at a veritable war being waved below. Dozens of zombies flooded the area, rampaging throughout the lot. The processing tent had been abandoned, with the exception of a trio of zombies feasting on some poor soul.

There were patches of ghouls scattered about, digging into still living people, who struggled to break free from their grasp. Four soldiers backpedaled towards the entrance, laying down suppressing fire towards the creatures racing towards them.

They managed to put down most of them, with only four still running when they came within five yards. One of the soldiers stepped up, using his rifle as a bludgeon to try to take them out at close range. He cracked one in the face successfully, but was quickly overwhelmed by the other three.

The other soldiers fired into the mass as it consumed their comrade, but had to abandon their position as more zombies tore towards them at a dead sprint.

More gunfire echoed through the building, and the six at the window turned around, almost able to trace the path through the floor. Finally, after what felt like an eternity, the gunfire came to a stop.

They stood in silence for a moment, straining their ears, but there was nothing.

Dodson pulled out his radio, hesitating with it to his mouth for a moment, tense and afraid of what the response would be. "This is Dodson," he finally said. "Does anybody copy?"

There was nothing, and the civilians looked at each other. There was obviously no love lost between them and the mercenaries, but being trapped in the hotel with a bunch of flesh-eating monsters was not exactly high on their priority list either.

"This is Dodson," he tried again, "does anybody copy?"

"This is Stanton." The voice sounded frantic with heavy breathing.

Dodson let out a sigh of relief and asked, "What's your status?"

"Situation is fucked down here," Stanton replied. "We were completely overrun in the staging area."

Dodson nodded. "We're on the third floor, so we had a bird's-eye view of the carnage," he replied.

"Are there any survivors out there, or are we it?" Stanton asked, and the grimace was evident in his voice.

Dodson turned back to the window, seeing nothing but zombies roaming around. They didn't seem attracted to any area, and he peered carefully to see if he could spot anyone hiding, but there was nothing.

He raised the walkie talkie to his lips. "I'm afraid you're it," he said.

"Fuck!" Staton cried. "Mother fucking fuck!"

"Settle down," Dodson replied, keeping his voice level and calm. "I had some men in the lobby before all this went down. Did you see them?"

"Negative," came the shaky reply. "Only thing we saw were those things. If it's any consolation, I didn't see any feeding, so they could still be out there."

Dodson nodded. "Good to know," he said. "Now, are you secure?"

His comrade was silent for a few moments, presumably to take the time to calm himself down and check his surroundings. "Yeah, we are," he finally replied. "There are three of us in some small office just behind the front desk."

"Is the door secure?" Dodson asked.

"Yeah, we got it locked and have a desk in front of it," Stanton explained. "It took three of us to move that big bastard, so I don't think they'll be able to get through."

"Okay, that's good," Dodson said with a nod. "Tell me what you can see."

"Not much, unfortunately," Stanton admitted. "There's only a small window looking out to the front, and there are zombies everywhere."

Dodson took a deep breath. "How many are we talking?"

"Fuck man, too many to count," came the frantic reply. "A few dozen at least."

Dodson grimaced, and Cortez shook his head, pressing his palms to his temples.

"Okay, hang tight," Dodson said, taking a deep breath, "I'll get back to you as soon as I know something."

"We ain't going anywhere, that's for damn sure," Stanton said.

Dodson fiddled with the dial on the radio.

"So what now?" Cortez blurted, lowering his hands but clenching his fists at his sides.

His companion shook his head as he dialed in a frequency. "Going to call Valentine," he said.

"Who in the hell is Valentine?" Troy demanded, throwing up his hands.

Dodson cocked his head. "He's our second in command."

"He handles the operational side of things," Cortez added, taking a deep breath to steady himself, "so that

Atkinson can focus on the big picture stuff."

Troy shook his head. "Hope he knows what he's doing, because if not, we're fucked."

Cortez nodded in agreement, and for a moment, they weren't mercenary and civilian, just two men stuck in the same deadly situation.

"Command, this is Dodson at the northern resort," he began. "Do you copy?"

There was a moment, and then the line clicked open. "We have you Dodson, what's the situation?" a voice asked.

"Catastrophic containment failure," Dodson replied. "Need to speak to Valentine."

"Hold, please," dispatch said.

Cortez clenched his jaw and raised an eyebrow. "That's not a good sign if they're patching you right through," he said. "They usually ask a few followup questions to see if it's worth his time."

"Guess we should take notes and add catastrophic to every report we file," Dodson said dryly. "Might get more done that way."

The radio chirped back to life, and then a no-nonsense voice came on, "Dodson, report."

"The outside command center has been completely overrun," he replied, quick and to the point. "Entire lobby is infested as well."

"Survivors?" Valentine asked.

Dodson took a deep breath. "We have three in an office in the lobby, and six up on the third floor," he explained. "Might have a few more in house, but they're off com and no confirmation."

"Enemy numbers?" came the reply.

Dodson wrinkled his nose. "Two to three dozen in the lobby," he replied, looking out the window, "maybe another fifteen or so in the front parking lot."

There was a moment of silence, and then Valentine said, "I need you to secure your position and stay put. I'll get back to you as soon as I have new information."

The line went dead, and Dodson hooked the radio to his belt, crossing his arms and staring out the window.

"He seems friendly," Troy muttered.

Dodson shook his head. "Lot on his plate today," he explained, "doesn't have tie to fuck around."

Cortez headed for the double doors leading to the conference room. "I'm going to get the doors secure," he called over his shoulder. "You two, help."

Charles and Troy didn't waste any time following. The dangerous situation called for banding together, at least at this moment.

"So, what now?" Grace asked, sidling up next to Dodson.

He took a deep breath. "We do as Valentine says," he replied. "We wait."

CHAPTER FIVE

Twenty minutes later, the retirees had finished loading the corpses onto the luggage carts, and shoved them over into the far corner away from everyone. They sat around a table by themselves near the window, nursing some lukewarm coffee from a dispenser.

The rest of the group sat at a table near the doors, waiting not only for a response from Valentine but also on guard in case they had unwanted visitors attempting to get through the doors.

"Does it usually take this long to hear back in a life or death situation?" Troy finally broke the silence. "Or is he just shitty at his job?"

Cortez narrowed his eyes. "He knows what he's doing," he snapped. "This shit came out of nowhere, and he's managing a whole island response."

"What *is* going on, anyway?" Charles piped up. "You boys seem to be clued in. Why not share with the rest of the class?"

The two mercenaries shared a pointed look, and then Dodson shrugged, waving for Cortez to give him the go-ahead.

"Information isn't exactly flowing freely, but this is what we know," the latter began, leaning back in his seat. "Last night, we got a call from one of our military contacts, saying that there was a shitstorm headed our way. Some virus was spreading out of Texas and it was infecting people with A-type blood. Within seventy-two hours of being exposed, they fell ill and died, only to come back as those zombie-like things. Apparently it's been spreading around the country for days, and nobody noticed until it was already too late."

The man next to Charles, who they'd discovered was named Karl, raised his hand. "And given what you guys are currently doing," he said, "I think it's safe to assume this stuff is everywhere."

Cortez nodded. "The country is done for," he replied, "and most of the world is probably in the same boat as well. Maybe some isolated countries like Australia might be able to catch most of the cases in time… not that we'll ever know, or care, really." He shrugged. "So Atkinson and the rest of the higher-ups decided to take matters into their own hands and secure a safe space."

"Well, safe for y'all," Charles scoffed.

Cortez jutted out his chin. "*And* for those who help us secure it," he replied, pointing a finger at the older man. "I know it may seem harsh what we're doing, but it's necessary not just to rid the island of those things, but to also figure out who is going to contribute going forward."

"Oh, bullshit," Charles snapped. "The bottom line is that you are more powerful than us, and you're doing what you're doing to save your own asses without a care in the world for us."

Cortez bristled, but Dodson raised a hand to calm him down. The rest of the table remained silent, letting the confirmation of the country being gone settle over them.

"Just a damn shame," Troy murmured.

Karl cocked his head. "What's that?"

"Always thought the world was going to go out with a giant meteor or nuclear holocaust," he admitted. "Something with a clock on it so that we could have one hell of a final party. Kind of sucks to wake up and find out that everything is already over."

Karl raised an eyebrow. "I'm guessing these boys still have a key to some of the rooms," he suggested. "You can always raid the mini-bar."

"And pay twenty-three dollars for a shot of whiskey?" Troy snorted. "I'll pass."

"Dodson, do you copy?" Valente's voice came through the radio, and the mercenary quickly grabbed it, turning the volume all the way up.

"Copy," he said.

"After careful consideration," Valentine continued, "it's been determined that the only viable course of action is to liquidate the asset. It's not strategic, and we can't afford to spend more resources to secure it."

Dodson nodded, though his jaw set tight. "Understood," he replied. "Timeline?"

"Drone liftoff is in twenty," Valentine replied, "with a seven-minute flight time."

He checked his watch. "Understood," he said. "Will contact in thirty."

The mercenaries shared a defeated look, and Dodson tossed the radio on the table with a clatter. Grace raised her arm and set a timer on her watch for twenty-seven minutes.

"A drone, huh?" Karl asked brightly. "They doing some recon to figure out how to get us out?"

Dodson and Cortez stared at him with incredulous faces.

"What?" he demanded.

Troy sighed. "They're liquidating us, dipshit," he snapped. "That drone isn't to take pictures, it's to launch a missile at the building."

His face went ghost white, and he squeaked for a moment before spitting out, "What the hell? How?" He shook his head, running his hands through his greying hair. "Why?!"

"Because our forces are spread thin," Dodson replied tersely, "and other teams must be encountering stiff resistance. Not worth the risk to life to save ours."

Charles threw his hands up. "How in the holy hell do you guys have access to a missile launching drone?" he demanded.

"We have a permanent residence on the marine base in Beaufort," Cortez replied.

Charles crossed his arms. "Still doesn't explain how you have access to a drone."

Grace growled, leaning forward and resting her arm on the table. "It doesn't matter how they have it, only that they do," she snapped. "Now, we need to talk about how we're getting out of here."

Troy took a deep breath as everyone turned to her. "Assuming we can get down to the second floor," he began, "there has to be a window we can get out of. With any luck, there won't be too many of those things on one side of the building."

"We're not going without our boys in the lobby," Dodson declared, shaking his head.

Troy blinked at him. "We don't have time to clear out a room that size."

Dodson pulled out his handgun and slammed it on the table. "You're going to help us get them," he warned, "or you're not leaving this room."

Troy glared at him, and then crossed his arms, letting out a frustrated grunt.

"One thing is for damn sure," Charles piped up, "you aren't using me as a human shield. You try that shit, and I'll latch on and pull you down with me."

Dodson nodded and shoved his gun back in the holster. "Fair enough," he said.

"Still…" Cortez said slowly, scratching the back of his head. "There's no way we can clear out the lobby with two gunmen and four people with knives."

Grace shrugged. "Then give us guns."

"Oh, hell, no." Cortez shook his head, waving his arms back and forth in front of his face. "I don't even feel comfortable with you across the table with me, and all you have is a cleaver. No way in shit you should have a gun."

Dodson shot her a sympathetic look. "I'm afraid he's right, Grace."

She leaned in, voice low and forceful. "You've already been written off by your commanding officer," she said. "Left to die, because your life isn't worth saving. You have to fight your way out, and you only have…" She checked her watch. "…Twenty-five minutes to get out. Now, what do you think is a bigger risk? Giving me a handgun, or trying to fight an army of those things with only Cortez by your side?"

Dodson sat back in his chair, chewing his lip for a moment. Finally he nodded, slowly, as if the thought was slowly seeping in. He drew the handgun and set it back on the table, sliding it over to her.

He held up a finger. "If you do shoot me in the back, please have the decency to shoot me in the head," he declared. "I'd rather not have to think about the colossal fuckup that led to my demise."

"Deal," she replied, snatching up the gun and checking the chamber.

"Whoa, what the fuck are you doing?" Cortez demanded.

Dodson shot him a stern look. "Giving us a better chance of walking out of here," he replied. "Now take your sidearm out, and give it to one of them."

His companion didn't move, simply scowling at him.

"Do it *now*," Dodson demanded. "That's an order."

Cortez stared at him in disbelief, before finally pulling his handgun from its holster and slamming it on the table. Before any of the others could react,

Charles grabbed it, pulling it into his lap before the other two could take it.

"Is there another stairwell to the lobby?" Grace asked. "Because the one we came up in is way too close to the front desk."

Dodson nodded, pulling out a sleep black tactical pen from his vest. He clicked it once and moved the plate in front of him, drawing directly on the cream tablecloth. He made a big square, and then drew an x.

"Okay, this is the lobby," he said, and then tapped his finger on the x, "and this is the front desk. I'm assuming the office door is right behind it. About twenty yards this way is the front door, and there's a secondary set of doors at the far end which are exit only. If we go out that way, there's a good chance there won't be too many of those things outside." He pursed his lips. "At least until they follow us out."

She leaned over, watching as he drew. "What about stairs?" she asked.

He thought for a moment, before drawing another x on the opposite side of the lobby across from the front desk on the far end of the room. "I'm fairly confident that the stairs are in this corner," he said. "With any luck, there won't be too many of those things near it, so we should be able to slip in undetected. What we do then…" He shrugged. "Well, that's anybody's guess, because I have no idea what's around there for cover."

"One problem at a time," Grace said with a sigh, and stood up. "Let's get down there."

The others got up too, save for Charles, who raised his hand.

"Aren't you all forgetting something?" he demanded.

The mercenaries shared a confused look and didn't respond.

Charls growled and motioned to the retirees in the corner. "What about them?" he demanded.

"You have a gun now," Cortez said coldly. "You can put them down if you want."

Charles's eyes widened, his face growing red with rage. "Are… did…" he stammered and then slammed a hand down on the table. "Are you serious right now?!"

"You saw them," Cortez replied flippantly. "They can barely walk. There's no way they're going to be able to get out of that lobby. And we don't have the manpower to protect them. Hell, I'm going to be shocked if we get out of this."

Charles growled, pointing a finger at the mercenary, but Grace reached out and put a hand on the older man's shoulder.

"You need to calm down," she said.

Charles gaped at her. "But—"

"Let me speak," she said forcefully, but with a hint of compassion in her voice. "I think we all understand that we can't protect them and make it out of here in one piece, which is why Dodson here is going to tell them in ten minutes they're free to go. We'll tell them about Troy's second floor escape idea and wish them the best. Doesn't that sound good?"

She glanced at Dodson, giving him a pointed look that dared him to disagree with her.

The mercenary nodded jerkily. "Cortez, go tell them what's up," he said.

His partner swept off and headed across the conference room to the retiree's table.

Grace turned back to Charles. "Are you good?"

He didn't answer right away, and she tapped her watch to remind him they were on a time limit. He clenched his jaw and shook his head, finally backing down.

"They know what's up," Cortez announced as he headed back over.

Dodson nodded. "Good, let's get moving," he declared, and led the group of

six out of the conference room and down
the hallway to the target stairwell door.
The two mercenaries stood on either side
of the door, and then Dodson nodded with a
quick hand gesture, and Cortez burst
inside.

They each took a side, one aiming up,
and one aiming down.

"Clear up here," Cortez said,
lowering his weapon.

Dodson nodded. "Same here," he said.
"Still, cover our six."

The four civilians moved into the
stairwell after him, with Cortez bringing
up the rear. They stopped at the ground
floor.

Dodson readied his rifle. "I want
everybody back up on the landing," he said
quietly.

"What?" Cortez asked, raising an
eyebrow.

"If it doesn't look good, we may have
to backtrack," Dodson explained. "If it
really doesn't look good, that might
happen quickly. I want you to be ready at
the second floor door, and I would rather
not have to shove anybody out of the way
to get there."

Everyone moved up except for Grace,
who stayed next to him. He didn't argue,
knowing there was no time to defy the
determination in her eyes. He readied

himself by the door which would open in towards the lobby, gripping the release bar tightly.

"I'll take care of the door," he whispered, "you just be ready with that gun."

She nodded as she readied her gun, taking a step back.

Dodson took a beat, holding his rifle in one hand and the release bar in the other. Finally, he pushed gently on the release, and it pinged loudly despite his best efforts.

He opened it a couple of feet wide and poked his head out, but the noise had attracted several nearby zombies who rushed the door. Dodson jerked back on the release, wedging two ghouls in the door. He braced his foot against the doorframe, holding it as tight as he could to keep them from pushing inside.

Grace didn't wait for instructions, carefully taking aim and firing at point blank range into a few skulls. They slid down a little, limp, but still held fast by the door.

"We got more incoming!" she cried, looking past the corpses to the lobby.

"Get that second-floor door open!" Dodson bellowed up the stairs.

Cortez didn't waste any time, immediately rushing up to the second floor landing and opening the doors with the others in tow. He looked both ways down the hallway and then ducked back into the stairwell.

"We're clear!" he called.

Dodson turned to Grace. "You a good shot?" he asked.

"Better than most," she replied.

"Good enough for me," he said, and pointed up the stairs. "Get up on that landing and be ready to cover me. I'm going to hug the railing."

She nodded and sprinted up the stairs, taking up position on the landing. She aimed towards the door, waiting for him to make his move.

Once she was in position, he let go of the door and tore up the stairs, staying against the railing all the way up. Grace immediately started firing, sending half a dozen rounds towards the door.

She hit one of the zombies in the head, dropping it, but the rest of the bullets found torsos, which didn't do much. The single kill caused some of them to stumble, buying Dodson enough time to get up to her.

As soon as he rushed by, she followed him up to the second floor door, the ghouls in hot pursuit. Troy waited for them, and he immediately slammed it as soon as they flew into the hallway, cutting off the pursuing zombies.

They stepped back from the door, breathing heavy, as the creatures smashed into it, smacking and moaning at their lost meal.

"You two okay?" Troy asked.

The two breathed heavily, bent over, and gave him a thumbs up. After a moment, they finally caught their breaths, and Dodson turned to Grace.

"Not bad for a civilian," he said, raising an eyebrow.

She shrugged. "Told you I was better than most."

He cracked a smile as he motioned for them to go up and join the others, who were about ten yards down the hallway.

Dodson approached Cortez, whose brows were furrowed in concern. "What is it?" he asked.

"There's noise up ahead," Cortez replied.

Dodson raised his rifle. "Well, let's go find out what it is, then," he said, waving for everyone to start moving."

The two mercenaries led the group up the hallway, the faint sounds of gnawing and moaning growing louder as they approached the center elevator lobby area. They came around the corner and spotted fifteen zombies stretching down the hallway to the left, past the elevators, most of which a good thirty yards down the hall.

Several of them knelt down beside a badly mangled corpse that wore the same type of combat gear Dodson and Cortez wore, about five yards down the hall from the elevator lobby.

Dodson quickly turned to the others and put his fingers to his lips to signify to be quiet. He then turned to his partner and motioned up the hallway straight ahead of them, using his fingers to signal *stairs*. They snuck across the opening, trying to stay unnoticed, but they had no such luck.

One of the creatures gnawing on a mercenary corpse looked up and saw the group going across. It let out a groan, dropping a chewed a hunk of flesh on the ground before sprinting towards them.

Charles panicked, took quick aim, and fired, hitting it in the chest but not slowing it down at all. He fired again, hitting nothing but air.

As it closed in, Cortez blew back around the corner and fired, hitting it in the forehead. The lifeless body slid across the marble floor, however the immediate threat wasn't over as the nose had attracted every zombie on the floor.

They came running down the hallway leading to the other set of stairs, as well as the opposite hall of munching zombies.

Dodson opened fire at the half dozen rushing down the hall, pouring out of a room towards the end. They moved so quickly that he only managed to hit two of them.

"Back up, back up!" he bellowed.

The bulk of the fifteen zombies on the other side of the lobby started rushing towards them, and Troy leapt into action. He shoved through a couple to get to the luggage cart, flipping it over in front of the opening to create a slight barricade.

Grace followed him into battle, shooting the first zombie he tossed aside in the head, while grabbing the other by the shirt and holding it at bay as it flailed around. Karl rushed up, jamming his knife into its head.

Cortez turned his attention towards the ten or so zombies that came down the opposite hallway, firing several times into the crowd and dropping a few. The two mercenaries retreated to the elevator area, laying down suppressing fire towards the coming horde. They managed to drop half of the combined horde, but at the expense of their magazines.

"I'm out!" Cortez barked.

Dodson shook his head. "Same!"

Rather than try and reload, which they didn't have time to do, they braced themselves for the coming horde. They used their guns as blocking tools, catching a couple of ghouls in the chest and using their bodies to hold the others off.

Meanwhile, Troy did everything he could to shove creatures back as they tried to overcome the toppled luggage cart, but it was a losing battle. Grace stood beside him, popping off shots where she could, but with so much movement it was difficult for her to get a clean shot.

When her gun clicked empty, she growled and broke from the line. "I gotta reload!" she cried.

Charles took her place. As she headed for Dodson to get another mag, she spotted the mercenaries having trouble as well. Karl stood off to the side, frozen in fear, looking unsure of what to do.

Grae looked past him at the elevators, and she grabbed his arm. "Help me get these open!" she barked.

It took him a moment to snap back into the moment, but he finally joined her, and they jammed their blades into the seam, prying open the doors. She peeked through to see the empty shaft, relieved

that it wasn't an elevator full of
zombies.

"Dodson, let one through!" she
yelled, and he peeked over his shoulder at
her.

He nodded and then looked at Cortez,
who was also struggling to hold the
zombies at bay, using the ones hooked on
their guns to keep the others back.

"Take a step to the right," he
barked, "go!"

Both of them moved to the right,
creating a narrow pathway past them. One
of the ghouls at the back slithered by,
and Grace jumped up and down.

"Over here, over here!" she screamed,
flailing wildly to get its attention.

The creature made a beeline for her,
and she positioned herself right in front
of the door, waiting on the ghoul to get
close. As it approached, she swung her
arms to the side, catching it in the torso
and shoving it.

The uncoordinated zombie tumbled,
falling head first into the open elevator
shaft. A moment later, a satisfying thud
echoed up to them.

"Send another!" she yelled.

Dodson nodded. "Move over another
step!" he instructed.

They took another, making the opening
larger. Grace whistled, trying to get

another one's attention. Finally, one
locked onto her and broke away from the
pack, rushing forward.

Karl stepped forward. "I got this
one," he said.

He readied himself by the door just
like Grace had, repeating the same
swinging motion that she did. He caught
the zombie in the same spot, shoving it
into the shaft.

Unfortunately for Karl, the zombie
managed to grab onto his wrist, and yanked
the flailing man down with it.

"Karl!" Grace screamed, lunging
forward and grasping at air. She watched
helplessly as he disappeared down the
shaft, screaming all the way down, cutting
short as he hit the bottom.

She swallowed hard, but shook herself
from it—there was no time to mourn or try
to see if he was okay. He was gone.

"Grace, get behind us!" Dodson cried.

She rushed over to the two of them,
still struggling with the five remaining
zombies. She stood between them, pushing
on their backs to help steady them.

"Okay, we gotta shift them towards
the shaft," Dodson instructed. "Let's go,
your way," he said to Cortez, and his
partner nodded.

They took small steps in unison,
moving to the right and twisting around to

angle the creatures towards the elevators. It took a solid minute to get them properly lined up, but once they were, it was time to act.

"PUSH!" Dodson yelled, and the trio shoved with everything they had, inching the creatures backwards.

All five of them remained fully engaged and hungry, trying to get to their meal. The creatures were forceful, but not very coordinated, so they finally managed to drive them to the edge.

After the first zombie fell, the load was lighter, and it made it easier for the trio to keep pushing. Thirty seconds later, the last zombie finally fell, splattering to the bottom of the shaft.

Dodson glanced down, pulling out a flashlight and shining it in. There was a mangled mass of bodies on the ground, with some still writhing about, not quite dead but too broken to be a threat.

"I'm out!" Charles cried, his gunfire ceasing.

Dodson pulled out a handgun magazine and handed it over to Grace. "Why don't you go finish them off?" he suggested. "We'll cover you and make sure nothing sneaks up on us."

She nodded and took it, reloading her gun and darting over to the luggage cart barricade.

There were several bodies on the floor, unmoving, but Troy still worked at shoving several back as they tried to get over the barrier. Grace stepped up and took aim, firing at the ghouls as Troy knocked them down.

With the numbers thinned, they were far easier to pick off.

Charles watched as she killed the last ghouls, gripping his gun tightly with a nervous look on his face. He looked back at the two mercenaries, who had their backs to them, keeping a watch down the other hallway.

Grace took out the last zombie with her last bullet, ending the threat. "Okay, that's the last of them," she finally said, letting out a deep sigh of relief as Troy got to his feet.

"Okay, let's take them," Charles said quietly.

"What are you talking about?" Troy asked.

The older man gestured wildly to the mercenaries. "Their backs are to us, and we have guns," he hissed. "Let's finish them and get out of here!"

Before the other two could respond, he raised his gun and took aim. He quickly fired, having bluffed about his mag being empty.

His aim was poor, hitting Dodson in the back with a shot. The impact on his vest sent him tumbling to the ground.

Cortez immediately turned around and raised his rifle as Troy dove out of the way, wanting no part of the firefight.

Grace dropped her empty gun and snatched the switchblade that Dodson had given her. She quickly popped it open and jammed it into the side of Charles' neck, causing him to fire his next shot into the wall.

He dropped the gun and turned to her, eyes wide with confusion and betrayal as he tried in vain to stop the bleeding from his throat.

Within seconds he was on the ground, twitching and gargling for air, and Grace immediately raised her hands, bloody knife still in her fist.

Dodson grunted as he got to his feet, rage blazing in his eyes. "Fucking hell that hurts!" he spat and turned around. "Who the fuck did that?" He stared at Grace standing there with the bloody knife over Charles' body. He cocked his head. "Cortez?"

His partner motioned to the dead man. "That cowardly piece of shit shot you in the back," he snapped. "Before he could shoot me, the girl took him out."

Dodson's gaze softened, and he walked over to Grace, motioning for her to put her hands down. "So, you like the knife, huh?" he asked.

"That blade is no joke," she replied, lowering her arms. "Just as advertised."

He smirked and inclined his head to the stairwell. "Come on, time's running out, let's move."

They headed off towards the stairs, and Troy darted out of hiding, sidling up to Grace as she wiped the blood from her hand and stuck the knife in her pocket.

"What did you do that for?" he hissed.

"We're not getting out of this building without these guys," she replied coldly. "And even if we did, it's highly unlikely we would be able to get off the island."

He took a deep breath, and then finally nodded. The situation was dire, and he knew she'd gone with the best option to keep them alive.

She looked at her watch. "Fourteen minutes," she said, and clapped him on the back. "Come on, we gotta move."

CHAPTER SIX

The quartet stopped by the stairwell to plot their next move.

"It's going to be a bitch getting into the lobby from this side," Cortez said. "Especially being this close to the front desk."

Troy jerked a thumb over his shoulder. "You're more than welcome to try the other route."

"Time?" Dodson asked.

Grace checked her watch. "Thirteen and change," she replied.

"We may not have a choice but to go for the lobby," he said, taking a deep breath. "Grace, ammo?" he asked.

"Out," she replied.

Dodson motioned to Cortez, and he pulled out one more handgun mag, holding it out to her. "Last one, so make it count," he said.

"Rifle ammo?" Dodson asked.

Cortez popped in a fresh mag on his rifle. "Last one on this, too," he said.

"Same here," his companion replied, reloading his own. "So as long as we don't miss, we should be okay."

"I'm sorry to say," Troy said tentatively, "but we might have to leave your boys behind."

Cortez stepped up to him, pointing a finger in his face. "We are NOT leaving them behind," he snarled. "You understand me? Either we all go or none of us do. You understand me?"

Troy raised his palms and nodded, backing down.

"Good," Cortez snapped. "Now, let's figure this shit out."

Grace pointed to the ceiling. "Somebody needs to go up," she said.

The other three looked at her, eyebrows raised.

"You know we're trying to get *out* of the building, right?" Troy drawled, sarcasm evident in his tone.

Grace put a hand on her hip. "And going up is the only way," she replied. "Are the upper floors clear?"

"Hallways should be," Dodson replied with a shrug. "The only reason this one wasn't, was because those things followed up my men as they escaped the lobby."

She nodded. "Okay, so we sent one person up to the fifth floor," she explained. "They get into the stairwell across the way, which is the one we need to take to breach the lobby safely. They cause a ruckus, get those things moving up and out of our way. That gives us a chance to get to the lobby without them knowing."

"And what about the runner?" Troy asked, crossing his arms. "What are they supposed to do?"

Grace whirled a hand around her head. "Double back to the stairwell, and get down to the lobby," she replied. "We'll pull the zombies away from the front desk, giving them a chance to get the others out. Then we run like hell and hope we get far enough away before the drone strike."

The mercenaries exchanged a look and then shrugged.

"Fuck it, better plan than I got," Dodson admitted. "Let's do it."

Cortez nodded. "I'll go high."

"No, you won't," Troy cut in. "You got a gun, so they're going to need you on that side of the lobby. I might not be fast, but I'm fast enough. I'll get your boys out."

Cortez nodded.

"Get moving, we're on the clock," Dodson said, and Troy took off like a shot.

He ran to the stairwell, running up the stairs two at a time. When he reached the fifth floor, he paused before opening the door.

"Be empty, be empty, be empty," he prayed, and then pushed into the hallway.

He checked both ways, relieved to see nothing there. He immediately raced down, pausing only at the elevator lobby to look both ways and make doubly sure he was alone.

The only sounds were his footsteps and the occasional banging on some of the hotel's doors from dead inhabitants wanting out.

When he reached the stairwell, he paused again, psyching himself up before opening the door. He peeked in and saw one ghoul on the landing with its back to him. It looked down the stairs at nothing in particular, seeming lost in space.

Troy carefully pushed the door open as silently as he could, and then lunged forward, giving it a forceful two-handed shove in the back. The zombie flew through the air, landing head first on the stairs below. The snap of its neck echoed on the concrete.

"Come and get me, assholes!" Troy bellowed.

Almost immediately, the sound was deafening. Moans and footsteps ricocheted off the walls as the zombies congregating on the second floor landing raced up the stairs.

He let out a few more yells, hooting and hollering curses at them, watching through the center gap at the flailing limbs ascending the stairs.

When the first zombie reached the fourth floor landing, Troy ducked back into the safety of the hallway. He slammed the door shut, sealing them inside, and gave the door a couple of smacks for good measure.

"Okay, Grace, it's your show, now," he muttered, and then tore back down the hallway to the other stairwell.

Meanwhile, Dodson, Cortez, and Grace stood by the second floor stairwell, listening to Troy yell from above. They stayed silent as they listened to the horde on the other side race up towards him, abandoning their post.

After several seconds, Cortez started to reach for the door, but Dodson held out a hand to stop him. A few seconds later, another set of footsteps raced by the door on their way up.

They waited a few more seconds to be sure, and then Dodson cracked the door, peering down to make sure there were no more coming up. With the coast seemingly clear, they inched into the stairwell, staying as quiet as possible.

Dodson looked up, aiming and making sure that nothing was going to come back their way, while Cortez aimed down, leading them down towards the lobby. When they reached the bottom landing, the door was still open, resting on the couple of zombies that Grace had put down earlier.

They moved to the door, and Cortez opened it a little more, quietly, so they could see the entire lobby floor.

There were still about fifteen to twenty ghouls spread out around the lobby proper, with the bulk of them over by the front desk. About seven of them were several yards apart, stretching from the desk to the nearby furniture that looked out towards the water through the windows.

"So what are we doing?" Cortez whispered. "Guns a blazing?"

Dodson shook his head. "Too risky," he replied quietly. "We have to get inside and secure this door before we start shooting, or else we're going to be fighting on two fronts."

"Then what the hell is the plan?" his partner asked.

Grace looked out, studying the lobby, and spotted the auto-playing piano close to the set of exit-only double doors. "The piano," she murmured.

"What about it?" Cortez asked.

Dodson smiled. "There's a button on the side to get it to play on its own," he whispered, catching her drift. "If somebody can get to it, the noise will draw those things to it, giving us a chance to get out."

"And it shouldn't be loud enough to draw the zombies from upstairs back this way," she added.

Cortez surveyed the area, the piano and the exit doors. "So a hit and run out the doors," he mused quietly, "I like it. But after one of us is outside, then what?"

"Those pickup trucks are still in the parking lot, right?" Grace asked.

Dodson shrugged. "Unless those things learned how to drive," he replied.

"I can get into the bed of it," she explained. "Should provide enough cover until you can get out there and clear them out."

He raised an eyebrow. "So you're volunteering, huh?" he asked.

"I'm a better shot than most," she replied with a shrug, "but I'm pretty sure you guys are better than me. Plus, since I saved your life, I'm going to assume you'll pay me the same courtesy."

He simply nodded at her, and she checked her watch. Seven minutes left.

"See you boys on the other side," she said, and gripped her handgun tightly before darting out of the stairwell.

She sprinted across the marble floor and fell into a slide, skidding behind one of the sofas. She carefully peeked over the edge of it to get a lay of the land.

There were a couple of zombies about ten
yards away on the other side of the
furniture, which had an almost complete
line of coverage all the way down to the
piano.

She crawled on the floor, staying low
and silent, making her way to the piano.
When she was halfway there, she stopped at
a gap in the furniture where a walkway cut
through. She peeked out, and saw the
closest zombie was only about five yards
away, and turning towards her.

She jerked back behind cover, staying
out of sight. She chewed her lip as she
tried to figure out what to do next. The
piano was still about twenty yards away,
and if she was spotted it would be a
struggle to get there.

She carefully pulled the slide back
on her handgun, popping out a single
bullet, before gently putting it back in
place. She peeked out again, relief
flooding her that the zombie hadn't caught
on to her.

She reared back and tossed the bullet
over the couch. It pinged a few times off
of the marble floor, drawing the attention
of the ghoul.

As it rushed over to investigate the
noise, she slipped across the gap before
another could take its place. She stayed
low and moved as quickly as she could.

When she was ten yards away from the piano, there was an excited moan and footsteps raced towards her.

"Shit," she muttered, and sprung to her feet. She sprinted for the piano, several zombies in her periphery racing towards her. The closest was ten yards away, and on an intercepting course.

Rather than fire her handgun and alert the ghouls in the stairwell, she readied herself for a shoulder strike. As the corpse approached, she adjusted her speed, slowing for a brief second to get into position to level the zombie.

She timed it perfectly, hitting it in the side and sending it careening to the ground. It slid on the marble floor on its back, safely out of her path.

Grace reached the piano and hit the play button as she flew by towards the doors. The instrument fired up, playing a jubilant tune that resonated happily throughout the lobby. The tinkling music was loud enough that every ghoul inside immediately turned its attention towards the source, tearing for it with their arms outstretched.

Grace didn't waste any time admiring her handiwork of freeing up the area by the front desk, slamming into the exit-only doors, flinging them open and tearing into the parking lot.

There were still a dozen or so zombies in the lot, spread out all over the place, and the truck bed was a good thirty yards away. It was a few feet off of the ground, not exactly a full lift kit, but substantially higher than a run-of-the-ill vehicle.

A few ghouls in her path turned and rushed her as she approached. With more hot on her tail, Grace knew there wasn't time to fight, only time to run.

The first one that approached, she sidestepped it, deftly moving out of the way, its rotted hands grasping nothing but air. The next one closed in fast on her without much tie for her to prepare. She lowered her shoulder and hoped for the best.

Grace plowed over the zombie like a running back taking out a defender, sending it to the ground. She staggered over it, stumbling as its flailing arm clipped her leg.

She got a hand down on the hot asphalt to steady herself, barely staying on her feet. She pushed hard, leaping back up onto her feet, propelling herself forward with only one more zombie to go. It was a smaller creature, likely having been a teenager just a few short hours ago.

She had the weight advantage, and she used it, lowering her shoulder and slamming into the center of the ghoul's chest, sending it flying back.

Grace reached the truck and leapt, putting her foot onto the bumper and diving headfirst into the bed. She landed with a thud, knocking a bit of her breath out, but forced herself to roll over, readying her handgun just in case any of the zombies managed to clamber up somehow.

Within seconds, she was surrounded by corpses, arms flailing up over the sides of the truck bed. The top of the railing was chest high on an average sized zombie, which thankfully made it difficult for them to reach inside.

Grace inched herself to the center, putting as much distance from them as possible, laying flat on her back as she steadied her breath.

"Okay Dodson," she muttered to herself, "don't fuck me over."

Inside, the mercenaries watched as Grace hit the piano button and raced out the doors. Several zombies followed her, however the majority of them converged on the piano.

"We gotta stay quiet," Dodson murmured, and his partner nodded.

They broke from cover in the stairwell door and moved across the lobby as lightly as they could. Dodson covered from the front, while Cortez kept tabs on the ghouls by the piano in case they lost interest in the concert.

As the duo approached the front desk, Troy came out of the other stairwell door. Dodson aimed at him, nearly firing, but when he realized who it was, he gave the man a thumbs up.

The trio reunited and headed for the front desk office. As they stood outside of the door, they heard the telltale scrape of a desk against a floor. A moment later, the door opened, revealing three mercenaries.

Dodson held a finger to his lips, and then leaned in, speaking softly. "We got a friendly in a truck bed outside," he said. "Let's go get her."

"Her?" Stanton asked, raising a skeptical brow.

Dodson jutted out his chin. "Yes," he said firmly. "Now follow me."

Stanton and his team fell into line with Dodson leading the way across the lobby, silent and quick. They blew outside and spotted fifteen to twenty zombies around the truck. He motioned for the men to spread out and form a firing line.

Dodson took aim at the back of a ghoul near the truck hitch. As soon as he fired, the rest of his team opened up as well. The five mercenaries made short work of the corpses, preventing them from even turning in their direction, let alone running towards them.

Their fire attracted the attention of several ghouls inside, however, and Troy pointed wildly.

"Behind us!" he cried.

Cortez and Staton turned, popping off a few shots and taking out the zombies tearing through the doors. They remained engaged, staring down their sights to make sure no others came out.

As they stood guard, Dodson walked towards the truck. "Grace, you good?" he asked.

She extended one of her arms up, giving him a thumbs up. She sat up, wiping some blood splatter from her face as she approached the railing.

"Hell of a job in there," Dodson commended as he reached the truck bed, offering her a smile.

She shrugged. "Just doing my part to live," she replied, hitting the safety on the gun and holding it out to him. "Here, you're probably going to want this back. Don't want you getting in trouble for giving a *volunteer* a gun."

He took it, nodding, appreciation in his eyes.

Grace's watch beeped, and she looked down, seeing the one minute warning on her timer. "One minute," she said flatly.

Dodson's eyes widened, and he threw open the driver's side door of the truck. "We got one minute!" he barked at the others. "Everybody in!" He jumped into the driver's seat, feeling to make sure the key was still in the ignition, which it was.

The men broke away from the lobby and leapt up into the truck bed with Grace. Cortez was the last one in, and smacked the side of the vehicle, prompting Dodson to punch the gas pedal. They sped off just as the roar of the drone echoed through the air.

He drove several blocks away before skidding around a building for cover.

"Everybody down!" Cortez screamed, and everyone ducked down against the floor of the truck bed, covering their heads.

The missile whistled and then there was a deafening blast that rattled the vehicle, but thankfully didn't shatter the windows. The group stayed still for a moment, and then slowly sat up, hair askew with looks of pale relief on their faces.

Stanton reached over and clapped Cortez on the back. "Really appreciate you coming and getting us," he huffed.

Cortez shook his head and motioned to the two civilians. "Don't thank me," he said, "thank them. Without their help, none of us would have made it out of there alive."

Stanton and his team nodded at Grace and Troy.

The latter rolled his eyes. "I mean, if you really wanted to thank us, you could drop us off at the docks with the keys to a boat," he drawled. "Also wouldn't turn down a six-pack."

Cortez winced and offered a halfhearted smile. Troy simply shook his head—he knew that plan wasn't in the cars for them.

Dodson got out of the driver's seat and strolled back to them. "Everybody okay back here?"

"Oh, just peachy," Troy said dryly.

Grace leaned on the railing. "So, now what?" she asked.

He pulled out his walkie talkie, holding it up and wiggling it in the air. "Let's find out," he said, and dialed up the command center. "This is Dodson, do you copy?" he asked.

"Yes, we copy," somebody replied. "Please hold."

A moment later, Valentine came in, "Glad to hear you made it out, Dodson."

"Thank you, sir," Dodson replied stiffly.

"What's your situation?" Valentine asked.

Dodson looked up, glancing down to the street he'd turned off of. "We're a few blocks south of the resort," he reported. "Two of us are in desperate need of a resupply. Have three others ready to rejoin the fight."

"Good," Valentine replied. "There is a hot zone three quarters of a mile to the east. Have the ones ready for a fight head that way. It's one of the schools, so they won't be able to miss it. As for your resupply, head to the airport in the northeast. We have a plane coming in. Load up and then head to the school."

Dodson nodded. "Understood, sir," he said, and then took a deep breath. "But there's one more thing."

"Yes?" came the terse reply.

Dodson rubbed his forehead. "Sir, I have two civilians with us."

There was a long pause, and then finally Valentine said, "I'll be blunt, our supplies are limited. Are they worth keeping?"

Dodson looked over at Grace and Troy, chewing his lip. "Yes sir, they are," he said firmly. "I wouldn't be talking to you without their help."

"Very well," Valentine replied. "Instead of going for a resupply, bring them down to Harbor Town."

Dodson let out a sigh of relief. "Yes, sir." The line went dead, and he put the radio away. He looked over to Stanton and his team as they clambered out of the truck bed. "You boys okay on foot?" he asked.

"Yeah, we could use the exercise after being holed up in that office," Stanton replied.

Dodson nodded. "Be safe, those things are still roaming the streets," he instructed. "That bomb going off will surely agitate them."

Stanton gave him a thumbs up and glanced back at the two civilians. He gave them a nod as well, and then the trio took off, running down the road towards the school.

Before Dodson could get back in the truck, a loud engine roared overhead. Everyone looked up at the big military transport plane flying low, headed to the airport just a couple of miles away.

"Mother of god, that's a big ass plane," Troy breathed.

Cortez nodded. "Big enough to hold a hundred men and enough ammo to conquer…" He paused. "Well… a small island."

Grace and Troy shared a look, wide-eyed at the fact that Theo Atkinson really wasn't messing around.

"Get comfortable," Dodson announced, "it's a bit of a haul down to Harbor Town." He smacked the side of the truck and got inside, firing it up. They pulled out from behind the building and headed south.

On the southwestern tip of Hilton Head Island rested the community of Harbor Town. The extremely high-end mixed-use burg stood alone as the premier destination on the island. While the resort to the north had been reserved for the wealthy, Harbor Town was reserved for the super wealthy.

As they approached, Grace and Troy looked around at the several layers of roadblocks, stretching out from the road into the yards. Two heavy machine gun nests were set up on the main road in, with a guard motioning to Dodson to pull over.

When he did, the guard climbed down and walked up to the truck.

"Sir, this area is off limits," the guard said, a hint of regret in his tone.

Dodson motioned to the back of the truck. "Valentine ordered us to bring in these two civilians," he said firmly.

The guard took a look at Grace and Troy, dirty and bloodied, and pulled out his radio, wandering away to speak out of earshot.

The duo scanned the area, watching a couple dozen guards roaming about behind the barricades. Corpses littered the road and grass in front of the wall.

"Impressive setup," Troy said with a sigh, "especially given that this whole shitshow just started ten hours ago."

Cortez shrugged sheepishly. "There's a reason the military spent billions hiring us out."

"Bet with that kind of bankroll you could afford a huge roster of talent," Troy replied.

"Oh, no doubt," Cortez agreed. "Ten thousand strong, spread out around the globe. Highly trained and well equipped. We might not have the firepower to conquer a nation, but by god we could put a hurtin on anybody."

The guard headed back over to the truck. "Okay sir, you're cleared to go to the command center," he said. "Do you know where it is?"

"Yes, I do," Dodson replied.

The guard waved him through. "Carry on, then." He motioned to the crew by the blockade, and they cleared a path for the truck to drive through.

The activity within Harbor Town was a hive, civilians moving about everywhere alongside dozens of heavily armed mercenaries. A group of soldiers piled up into a pickup truck and sped off.

"They're off to throw down," Troy said, shaking his head.

After a few moments, they pulled up
to the command center. Dodson got out of
the truck and waved for the trio to come
down.

"Cortez, I'll take them inside," he
said. "You go see if you can get us a
resupply."

His partner nodded and turned to walk
off, but then paused for a moment. "You
two did alright back there," he said,
giving the civilians a nod. "You keep it
up." He sauntered off, and Dodson motioned
for the duo to follow him.

They headed into the command center,
which was fairly sophisticated inside. The
mercenaries had taken over a small
restaurant, with monitors set up around
the outer edges of the room. In the center
stood Carter Valentine, a beast of a man
that looked to be in his early forties. As
they approached him, he glanced up from a
folder of papers.

"You must be Dodson," he said, in a
terse, no-nonsense tone.

"Yes sir," came the reply, "I have
the civilians from the resort."

Valentine set down his folder and
approached them, giving them a once over.
"I'll be honest," he said, crossing his
arms, "I have no doubt this man can hold
his own. But I'm curious as to why you
think this woman is capable."

Grace clenched her jaw, stifling the glare she wanted to shoot him for the sexist nature of his words. She didn't want to risk being executed without mercy.

"Sir, she's smart, a heck of a shot, and as cold-blooded as they come," Dodson explained. "She slit a man's throat and saved my life in the process."

Valentine pursed his lips for a moment, staring her down. "I'll take your word for it," he finally said.

A short man with glasses came rushing over, holding a clipboard.

Valentine turned to him. "What is it?" he asked.

"Sir, base commander wants to know what the orders are," the man replied quickly. "The hundred reinforcements you requested just landed at the airport."

Valentine checked his watch. "Not much daylight left today," he mused. "Have him fortify their position on base, and make preparations to raid every local food source starting at first light. Tell him to prepare to take everything that will keep."

"He also requested guidance on civilian encounters," the man continued.

His superior shrugged. "If they look capable, bring them in," he said. "If they don't, instruct them to shelter in place."

"And if they're hostile?" the man asked.

"Respond in kind," Valentine said simply.

"Yes, sir," the man replied, and hurried off, scribbling on his clipboard.

Valentine turned back to the two civilians standing nervously in his space. "Apologies for the interruption," he said tersely. "Dodson here says you're capable, so I'm going to assign you to a special civilian task force that we've assembled here. I'm not going to bullshit you. Your life expectancy on this detail will most likely be measured in hours. However, if you listen to the specialists in charge, you just might live to see another day. Do you have any questions?"

"Yeah, I got a question!" a shrill voice echoed from the back of the room. A man emerged from behind a stack of boxes and crossed his arms. "Why isn't this bitch dead yet?"

Grace rolled her eyes, recognizing him as one of the brutes from the bridge.

"Something you'd like to add, Mosley?" Valentine drawled.

"Yeah, this trigger-happy bitch shot Zach in the face!" Mosley snarled, pointing a finger at her. "Isn't that right, sweetheart?"

She forced herself not to flinch away from him, despite his nasty breath.

"Care to explain yourself?" Valentine asked, raising an eyebrow.

Grace cocked her head. "He shot my friend in the face," she drawled, keeping her voice level. "Figured an eye for an eye was warranted."

"So even though you were surrounded by heavily armed men," Valentine said, "you still felt compelled to shoot?"

She shrugged. "Didn't think about it like that," she admitted. "Just reacted to the moment."

Valentine smirked, staring at her with something akin to admiration. "You're right, Dodson, this one is capable," he said. "Quick acting and cold-blooded, I can use that."

"Well hell," Mosley said, throwing up his hands, "if you're going to use her, then you might as well go ahead and send her over to Beach Park. That place is a clusterfuck."

Valentine shook his head. "It's getting late," he said, "but that will be their target at first light."

"What's this first light bullshit?!" Mosley bellowed, face growing red. "Who gives a shit about these civies? Send 'em in already."

Valentine turned to him, gaze darkening. "I don't recall asking for your opinion on this matter," he said, voice low. "So unless you are volunteering to lead this operation, I suggest you shut the fuck up and walk away. Because I don't care about your personal vendettas, I care about securing this island." He raised his chin. "So what's it going to be?"

Mosley stared at him for a moment, and then swallowed, clenching his fists and walking away in a huff.

"Dodson, I believe that is all I need from you," Valentine said, turning back to his subordinate. "Please resupply and link up with a team. I have a feeling it's going to be a bumpy night out on the island."

"Yes, sir," Dodson replied, and headed to Grace and Troy, shaking each of their hands in turn. "I know when you first met me, you probably wanted to put a bullet in my head." He chuckled. "Hell, you probably still do." He shook his head. "Even so, I'm grateful for what you did today."

They didn't respond, simply giving him a slight nod, and he headed off.

"Looks like you made quite the impression on him," Valentine declared.

Troy shrugged. "Bonds of combat," he said, waving a hand. "Or something like that."

Valentine smirked and then leaned over to tap one of the working mercenaries on the shoulder. "I'll be back in ten," he said, and then waved for the civilians to follow him. He led them out of the command center and into the heart of Harbor Town.

The middle of the burg was an actual harbor, a series of docks with several vessels floating and bobbing on the water.

"I've spent a lot of time here during the last few months," he said as they walked, "being the point man on the military base installation and all. A lot of the wealthy locals didn't take too kindly to a military grunt like myself invading their safe haven, but once word got around to who I worked for…" He paused, tilting his head back and forth. "Well, their attitudes changed a bit."

Troy snorted. "Given what's happened today, I'm guessing their attitudes changed *quite* a bit," he said.

"That they have, sir," Valentine replied, "that they have."

He led them onto a dock in front of a massive yacht, easily fifty yards long and three stories high. They walked up a large ramp to reach the deck, and he turned around, spreading his arms.

"This vessel is Molly's Recompense, named in honor of Theo Atkinson's late daughter," he said.

Troy looked around the massive boat, taking in the luxury of it. "What happened to her?" he asked.

"Cancer," Valentine replied, shaking his head. "Took her when she was seven. Atkinson was just an enlisted man at that point, and couldn't afford any of the experimental treatments that may have saved her life. Shortly after that, he was discharged and made it his mission in life to make sure he was never that helpless again." He turned towards a staircase. "Ten years later, he delivered on that." He motioned for them to follow him into the hold. "This way."

The duo followed him down several flights of stairs, glancing down hallways at every floor. There were workers and mercenaries wandering about, busy as bees. When they reached the bottom, they found several jail cells, however they'd been made to be very homey looking, with full-sized beds, televisions, and a small kitchen area in each cell.

"Looks like Martha Stewart was housed here," Troy said dryly.

Valentine patted the bars on the nearest cell. "We can't have you roaming around freely," he said, with a hint of sympathy in his voice. "However, I felt as though you needed a little comfort. Especially given what you are tasked to do."

A couple of the cells on the left housed some rough-and-tumble looking men. One lounged on his bed, reading a book, and another wore headphones plugged into his television. None of them even bothered to look up at the newcomers.

Valentine punched a code into a keypad on the wall, and the two cells on the right opened up. "Please, if you wouldn't mind," he said.

Grace and Troy looked at each other, and then each picked a cell, walking inside.

"Dinner should be served within the hour," Valentine said as he punched another code to close the doors tight. "It should be nice, as we have one of the island's best chefs on staff here."

Troy raised an eyebrow. "How long has that been the case?" he asked dryly.

Valentine checked his watch. "Oh, about ten hours now," he said with a smirk.

Troy shook his head, chuckling darkly.

"If you are hungry in the meantime," Valentine continued, "there should be some

snacks by the mini-fridge there." He
motioned to the appliance in the corner.

Troy headed over and opened it up,
finding a six-pack of beer alongside water
and soda. "And beer, too!" he declared,
picking up a bottle and checking the
label. "Good stuff, too."

"I think you'll find that the QXR
Group takes care of those who can
contribute to its goals," Valentine said,
and then turned to the stairwell. "Now if
you'll excuse me, I have to get back to
the command center." He didn't wait for a
response, simply headed up the stairs.

Troy popped open his beer and downed
half of it in a single gulp before
plonking himself down on his bed. It stood
against the bars, separating him from
Grace's bed. She simply sat on hers,
staring off into space.

"You okay?" he asked gently.

She swallowed hard, and then blinked
a few times before nodding. "Yeah, I'm
fine," she said, her voice cold and level.

He sighed, throwing up his free hand.
"Okay, what the fuck is going on with
you?" he demanded.

"What do you mean?" she asked, her
face betraying no emotion.

"I mean this morning, when we're at
the store, you're acting almost like a
helpless little puppy following Dante

around," he drawled, shaking his head, "then two seconds after he hits the water, you turn into Sarah fucking Connor. What gives?"

Grace lowered her gaze to the floor. "Not sure you'd understand," she said quietly.

"Well hell," he said, taking a swig of beer, "it's not like we have a whole lot else to do. Try me."

She sighed. "Okay." She fiddled with a loose thread on her pants, still not looking at him. "Do you have any idea what my brother gave up for me?"

"Yeah, his face," Troy replied, waving his hand around his own face.

She shook her head. "No, he gave up a normal life for me," she said, chewing her lip. "Do you think it's easy walking around like that? I can tell you that just based on people's reactions that I've seen, it's not. Yet my brother carries himself with dignity every single day, even though it's not easy." She swallowed hard. "He doesn't complain. Even though I know it pains him that he can't have a normal life. And he's like that because of me, because I wasn't strong enough to take care of myself."

"It's not your fault," he said gently, wrapping both of his hands around the bottle. "You were young."

Grace sighed. "I appreciate it, but it's really easy to say that when it's not you," she explained. "But ever since the fire, I've dedicated myself to learning how to take care of me. Learning to shoot, learning to fight, staying fit. Partially because I want Dante to be proud of me, but also because of guilt." She clenched her fists. "Guilt because I wasn't strong enough to get out of the fire myself, and it cost him everything as a result." She looked up at the ceiling, blinking back tears. "And you know what he's done since the fire? Taken care of *me*. So when a situation comes up where he can take charge, I let him. Because unless I have a damn good reason to take that away from him, I'm not going to do it."

Troy took a thoughtful swig of beer, and then slowly nodded. "Well, I can tell you this with certainty," he finally drawled, "you definitely know how to take care of yourself. So on that point, you've done your brother proud."

She nodded, and then got up, opening up her own fridge and pulling out a cold beer. She cracked it open and sat sideways on the bed, holding the bottle through the bars. "Here's to living through the first day of the apocalypse," she said.

He smiled and clinked his bottle against hers, and they took a sip,

finishing their brews in silence. Quiet
contemplation with the anxiety over what
the next day would bring.

     END
     Up Next: Left to fend for
themselves, Grace and Troy are at the
mercy of QXR Group and their mission to
secure the island from the undead threat.
They quickly learn that the flesh eating
zombies aren't the biggest threat to their
survival in Lowcountry - Pt. 3

DEAD AMERICA
LOWCOUNTRY
PART 3
BY DEREK SLATON
© 2021

CHAPTER ONE

Day Zero +2

Dante laid on his makeshift cot that consisted of a beaten down comforter with some questionable stains on it and a musty knitted blanket that barely covered half of his body. Even though this was far from the Ritz Carlton, he was happy to have it.

He rolled onto his back and stared up at the ceiling, his muscles still sore from the chaos of the previous day. Fighting, running, a high dive off of a perfectly good bridge. As he ran through the events in his head, rubbing his biceps to soothe them, he could see Grace's terrified face as he grabbed Bailey and leapt from that bridge.

Just hang in there, he thought, prayed. *I'm going to figure out how to get to you.*

He gazed around the living room, where most of the crew slept soundly, or at least as soundly as they could given the accommodations. Lily sprawled on the couch, her shoulder length bleach blonde hair splayed across her face in an epic tangle. Bailey was tucked away in the corner, still wearing her vest from her work at the superstore. Cam and Phillip shared a blanket in the middle of the floor, occasionally tugging it back and forth to try and get some more coverage.

He ran a hand down the puckered skin of his face, thinking darkly of the last time he'd seen Grace so terrified. The first time he'd thought he was going to lose her. He'd risked everything for her then, and he would do it again, a million times, to keep her safe.

There was a shuffle on the front porch, and he sat up straight, heart pounding a mile a minute. He caught the shadow of someone outside and let out a deep breath of relief when he spotted an arm bringing a cigarette up to a face.

Looks like Ace is up early, he thought, and pulled himself from the small mattress with a groan. He stretched his arms above his head, reveling in the crackle of his back as he relieved some of the tension in his muscles. He moved softly to the front door so he wouldn't disturb anyone, and slipped out onto the porch, closing the door silently behind him.

As he stepped forward, Ace jumped, nearly fumbling with his cigarette.

"Goddamn Scarface," he blurted, "you part ninja or something?"

Dante cracked a smile. "I was the neighborhood hide and go seek champion four years running," he said. "So I guess that counts."

"It must, because you quiet as hell," Ace replied, and motioned for his companion to join him on the stairs. He moved his hunting rifle from the step next to him to make a spot.

The sun had barely risen above the trees, painting the sprawling yard in a beautiful golden glow. Dante took a deep breath of the nice and crisp fall air, the light breeze hitting his face as he sidled up on the stairs.

Ace pulled out his pack of cigarettes and flipped the top, holding it out to him, but he shook his head, politely holding up a hand.

"So you sleep all right?" Ace asked, stuffing the pack back into his shirt pocket. "I know my place ain't exactly set up to be a hotel, after all."

Dante chuckled. "Believe it or not, I've stayed in worse," he admitted. "Learned the hard way hotels are like tattoos, you shouldn't go for the budget option."

Ace laughed and shook his head, but sobered quickly at a rustle in the bushes. He tensed and put his hand on his rifle, eyes widening, but then a squirrel darted out from the leaves and he let out a deep breath of relief.

"Man, we're gonna be on edge for a while, aren't we?" he asked, rubbing his forehead as he took a deep drag of his smoke.

Dante nodded slowly, offering him a sad smile. "Afraid so," he replied. "Still trying to process everything."

"You ain't kidding," Ace agreed. "When my neighbors would get drunk and start yelling at each other all hours of the night, I'd lay in bed swearing to myself that one of these days I was going to shoot those fuckers." He clucked his tongue with a wet smack. "Kind of crazy I had to do that yesterday."

Dante clasped his hands together, leaning his elbows on his knees. "Amazing how quickly this illness spreads and turns people."

"Oh, they hadn't turned into those things," his companion drawled. "I just saw on the news that the world was going to shit and decided to take my shot."

Dante blinked at him with concern, his mouth slightly agape in shock.

After a beat, Ace dissolved into laughter, shaking his head and slapping his thigh. "Holy shit Scarface, you thought I was serious?" he gasped through a gale of giggles. "Come on man, I got a mirror, I know damn well I don't look that trustworthy!"

His new friend joined in the contagious laughter, relief washing over him. "Man, I may be part ninja just rolling out of bed," he said, "but my brain definitely needs coffee."

"Well, we'll run up to the store here in a bit," Ace replied. "But I want to ask you something first."

Dante's brow furrowed. "Have at it," he said.

"You know I'm just fucking with you, right?" his companion asked, the smile gone from his face.

Dante raised his eyebrow. "About shooting the neighbors?" he asked. "Yeah, I gathered that."

"Nah, I mean about calling you Scarface," Ace replied, waving his hand in front of his face before taking another drag of his cigarette.

The bigger man shrugged. "I mean, I don't take any offense to it," he assured him. "People handle the way I look differently, I don't let it get to me."

"Nah man, it's not like that. I don't give a shit how you look," Ace replied through a lungful of smoke, and then exhaled before flicking the butt into the yard. "I had this buddy from school, Scotty Sterling. We came up together from first grade with a few other boys. Just a bunch of holy terrors causing teachers to drink and rethink their life choices." A ghost of a smile crossed his face at the memory, and then disappeared. "Well, as hard as we were on them, we were a lot harder on each other. Calling each other every name under the sun, pulling pranks, I mean you name it and we did it to each other. I swear, if I had a dollar for every time I've shit in a bag and threw it at a moving car, well, let's just say I wouldn't be living in *this* place."

Dante smirked. "Nothing like the charm of that small town life," he said.

"You ain't kidding," Ace agreed with a chuckle. "Anyway, after high school, Scotty decided to join up and serve his country. That lasted all of about eighteen months. Guy got deployed and sent home after an IED fucked him up good. He was so bad he made you look like a beauty queen."

Dante spread his arms, motioning to his chest. "I mean, I do have a hell of a swimsuit body," he joked.

"As long as it ain't a speedo," Ace quipped.

The bigger man grimaced and shook his head. "I think we have enough horror going on without that," he replied, and then motioned for Ace to continue.

"So Scotty gets back and me and the boys don't really know how to act around him," he said, leaning back on his hands.

"I mean, we tried to be supportive and
friendly, and definitely no bag bombs.
Finally after about two weeks he snapped
and laid into us. Turns out, ever since
the attack, people had been treating him
with kid gloves. Doctors, nurses, his
family, and he was pissed that we were
doing it too." He shook his head. "Only
thing he wanted was to be treated
normally." He held up a finger. "So, from
that moment on, we mocked the hell out of
him. Pulled pranks, called him shit, you
name it. There was this one time about six
months after he got back, he managed to
snag a date." He snickered before
continuing, "He had just had another
surgery on his leg and was in a wheelchair
for a bit. Well, he made the mistake of
telling us what restaurant he was taking
this pretty little thing to, so we took it
upon ourselves to support him."

Dante put a hand over his eyes. "I'm
guessing that doesn't mean sending them a
bottle of wine?" he asked.

"No sir, it did not," Ace said
through a shit-eating grin. "We got one of
those steering wheel club things that
little old ladies would put on their cars,
so if someone tried to steal it, they
wouldn't be able to drive it. Well, we
rushed in, and attached it to one of his
wheels, and ran out." He let out a big

belly laugh, and then through his mirth added, "I still remember his parting words, *This isn't what I meant, you assholes!*"

Dante barked a laugh, shaking his head. "I get where you're coming from," he finally said, offering his new friend a smile. "So you feel free to lay into me all you want."

"Oh, it's going to happen," Ace replied, pointing a warning finger at him.

"And on that note," Dante replied, all trace of humor gone from his face, "I just want to say about the sister fucking comment from yesterday. I meant every single word of it."

Ace guffawed at his companion's serious tone, and Dante couldn't keep a straight face for long before joining in.

"Oh, we're gonna have some fun, Scarface," he said, clapping him on the back.

"You boys are in a good mood today," Lily said as she stepped out of the house.

Ace and Dante both startled at her voice, the former turning around to bark at her, "Goddamn, don't do that!" He gave Dante's shoulder a playful punch. "See, what's the shit you did to me."

The bigger man shrugged sheepishly before moving over so Lily could take a seat between them.

"So, what has you in such a good mood today?" she asked.

Ace sighed wistfully. "Just telling Scarface here about ole Scotty."

"Oh, I haven't thought about him in years," she said with a smile. "Whatever happened to him?"

Her cousin motioned vaguely before pulling out his pack of cigarettes. "Moved up to Columbia about a year ago," he replied, shoving a smoke between his lips. "His wife got a job or something up there, so they headed out."

"I hope they're all right," Lily said quietly.

Ace lit his cigarette and blew out a long stream of smoke. "Eh, he's a tough bastard," he said flippantly, "I'm sure he's laughing his ass off wondering how we're faring down here in the middle of nowhere."

"Yeah, that wouldn't surprise me," she agreed, though she didn't sound convinced. She glanced down at his offered cigarette pack and shook her head. "Quit a few months back," she said.

Ace shrugged and stuck the pack back in his pocket. "Works for me," he declared, "gonna be a shortage of these, so glad to know I have dibs when we come across 'em."

"Hopefully we're going to find more than just smokes," Dante piped up. "I'm pretty sure food is going to become an issue sooner rather than later."

Ace nodded, taking a thoughtful drag. "Yeah, I barely had enough in the cupboard to keep me going for the week, let alone everybody else."

"Looks like we're going to have to do a store run," Lily said, clapping her hands together.

Her cousin leaned back on one hand. "We can hit the gas station up the road," he said, pointing with his cigarette hand. "There's about half a dozen houses nearby too that we can take from."

"What if there are people still there?" she asked.

Ace shook his head. "Ain't nobody left," he drawled. "Had to put a few of them down myself, and the rest of them just fled when the news started going south."

"Fled?" she asked, furrowing her brow. "To where?"

Her cousin shrugged. "Didn't ask, didn't care," he replied. "This shit is everywhere, so the more people who get away from me, the better."

"Even so," Lily said slowly, "I doubt there's going to be enough food to keep us all fed for very long."

"Just means we'll have to add a grocery store stop when we go into Beaufort today," Dante piped up, and the two cousins blinked at him in shock.

"I'm sorry, what?" Ace asked, cigarette forgotten in his hand.

Dante raised his chin. "We're going to Beaufort today," he repeated. "We gotta get Bailey's family, and since we'll be in the neighborhood, we can save whoever is trapped in the TV station. Just doesn't feel right to leave someone to die when there's something we can do about it."

The cousins shared a pointed look with each other.

"Ain't you been complaining how the men you meet are lazy and good for nothing?" Ace drawled, poking her in the shoulder. "There you go Lil, man of action right there."

Ignoring him, she leaned forward on her knees, regarding the larger man to her left. "I know you want to help," she said softly, "but what about those things?"

"We're just going to have to deal with them," he replied firmly. "While they are fast and do doubt vicious, they're dumb, and we can use that to our advantage." His eyes darkened. "Plus, we need information about those goons on the island. Grace was taken by them, and if

I'm going to get her back, I need to know what I'm up against."

Lily straightened. "We," she corrected, putting a hand on his arm. "You aren't doing anything alone out here."

Ace patted his rifle lovingly. "Damn straight," he added. "And don't worry, I got a few toys that can help us out, too."

"I appreciate it," Dante said, sincerity in his eyes. The expression broke when he couldn't fight out a violent yawn, and he covered his mouth before composing himself. "Unless I'm mistaken, didn't you say something about coffee?"

Ace smacked his thighs and stood up, flicking his butt into the grass. "You are absolutely right, Scarface," he said, and pulled out his keys. "Come on, let's head up to the gas station." He locked the front door of the house, and then snatched up his rifle, strolling down the driveway to the road. When he didn't hear footsteps behind him, he turned around and spread his arms. "Well come on now, it's only about a half a mile up. Walk will do us some good."

Dante chuckled and nodded, motioning with a flourish for Lily to go first.

She smirked as she got to her feet, planting her hands on her hips. "You just want to check out my ass, don't you?" she teased.

"Well, if you insist," he drawled, winking at her with his one eye.

She laughed and grabbed his hand, pulling him up off of the steps. They joined Ace, and the trio headed up the road towards the gas station.

It was empty of cars, and thankfully, of zombies. Birds chirped in the distance, as if it were just a normal fall day. It was almost eerie.

"So man, I don't think you ever said where you're from," Ace said, resting the barrel of his rifle on his shoulder.

Dante cocked his head. "Is it that obvious I'm not from around here?" he asked.

"Yeah, just a bit," Ace agreed, holding up two fingers just a hair's breadth apart.

"I'm from Seattle," Dante replied with a chuckle.

Ace let out a low whistle. "Seattle?" he repeated, shaking his head. "Holy shit, there you go Lil, you always said you wanted a big city boy."

She smirked. "No, I said I wanted a *big* city boy," she said.

Ace wrinkled his nose, waving his hand back and forth in front of his face at the innuendo. "Yeah, we ain't going there."

The other two laughed at his discomfort, and then Lily cocked her head. "So, how did you end up down here?" she asked. "Seattle isn't exactly just around the corner."

"We were in town for a funeral," Dante explained with a sigh. "Just so happened this hit while we were here. Probably a good thing, too, because I can't imagine what's going on in a city that size."

Silence descended on the trio as they contemplated the horror of that.

Dante took a deep breath and then spotted the gas station about seventy yards ahead. Ace stopped and held up a hand, motioning for them to follow him as he knelt on the asphalt. He pointed to two zombies roaming around the parking lot, moving slowly and aimlessly without a target to focus on.

He readied his rifle, adjusting the scope on the top, and then took a breath, squeezing the trigger. The gun fired, and a split second later, a zombie's head exploded, the rest of it crumpling to the ground.

The other ghoul whipped around, frantically searching for the source of the noise before spotting them. It let out a screech and sprinted towards them.

Ace calmly chambered another round, taking aim and firing at forty yards. The running zombie didn't fare any better than its partner, its head blowing off with an impressive spray of blood and brain.

"Nice shooting," Dante said, nodding appreciatively.

Ace threw him a wink. "Years of hunting combined with a father yelling at me for not being a good enough shot finally paying off," he said.

Dante patted him on the back, and they continued their walk towards the store. When they reached the doors, Ace drew a knife from his belt and handed it to Dante. He then raised his rifle like a baseball bat and nodded that he was ready.

Lily threw open the door and then followed the duo as they burst inside. The trio spread out, quickly clearing the small space, relieved to find it empty.

The store had a few rows of goods, candy and snacks mostly, but there was a single shelf of non-perishable items like canned soups and ramen noodles. In the back there was a small grilling area that still had some charred food on the heated top.

Ace hopped behind the counter as the others checked the meager offerings on the shelves.

"Well, this might feed the crew for a day or so," Lily lamented.

Dante nodded with a sigh. "Even if we ration we wouldn't be able to stretch it to the end of the week."

"Who wants an omelette?" Ace exclaimed as he scraped the burnt food from the grill with a spatula.

The others wandered over, confused, then spotted him kneeling down in front of a mini fridge full of eggs and other perishable ingredients like cheese and cubed ham.

"Three egg ham and cheese omelette?" Ace asked, buzzing like a kid at Christmas. "Who's in?"

Dante shrugged. "Might as well," he replied. "Probably going to be awhile before we can have another one."

"Lil?" Ace asked, pointing at her with the egg carton.

She nodded. "Yeah, I'll have one." She looked around, spotting the large coffee maker against the wall. "I'll get us some coffee going, too," she said. "What kind do you want?"

"Whatever sounds good to you," Dante replied with a smile. "As long as it's hot and full of cream, I'm good."

Ace clapped his hands. "He likes his coffee like I like my women!" he cried. "Hey-oh!"

Lily rolled her eyes and headed for the coffee maker as her boisterous cousin cracked open eggs with flair, dropping them onto the hot plate and mixing in ingredients like a seasoned pro.

"Looks like you've done that before," Dante said, leaning against the counter and crossing his arms.

Ace grinned and saluted him with the spatula. "Worked at my uncle's restaurant through high school," he explained. "A few things stuck with me."

"Lucky for us," Dante replied.

"Coffee will be ready in five minutes or so," Lily said as she headed back over to them.

Dante nodded at her gratefully, and then Ace inclined his head to him as he fussed over the omelettes.

"Okay Scarface," he began, "how are we doing this today?"

"Figured we'd take your truck into Beaufort," Dante replied with a shrug, "and get what we need to get. Then hit the store on the way out."

Lily nodded, leaning against the counter next to him. "If things don't look too bad, we may want to check out the Marine base," she suggested. "It's on the north side of town."

"I suppose so," Ace replied, drawing out his words. "If anybody is going to have their shit together, it's going to be those boys."

Dante nodded. "We can certainly do that," he agreed. "So who do we want to take with us?"

"I love Cam and Phillip to death," Lily said with a wince, "but I could kick both their asses at the same tie. Not sure they're going to be much use out there."

Dante frowned. "Same thing with Bailey," he admitted. "Don't know what we're going to be running into out there, but she's going to be more of a liability than an asset in a fight."

"We can still put 'em to work, though," Ace cut in. "Sooner or later some of those things might work their way through here, so we're gonna want to get the house fortified."

Lily nodded. "It should be safe enough for them to clear this place out, too," she suggested.

"But not any of the houses," Dante added, putting up a hand. "Could still have those zombies, or whatever they are, locked up in there. They don't need to be dealing with that."

Ace barked a laugh. "Holy shit, *zombies*?" he asked incredulously.

"You got a better name for them?" Dante challenged, raising his eyebrow.

The shorter man pursed his lips for a moment in thought and then shook his head as he flipped the omelettes. "Well… not really," he admitted. "Guess that'll work." He checked the food and then snapped his fingers in victory before grabbing three plates and dishing up breakfast. "Alright y'all, eat up! Looks like we got a long one ahead of us."

The trio took the plates, savoring the fresh hot meal that was surely to be one of the last they'd be having for a long while.

The trio headed down the street, bellies full from their big breakfast. They sipped at their large paper to-go cups of coffee, Lily carrying a tray of three more for the others.

As they approached the house, they spotted Bailey on the front steps, hugging her knees. When she saw them she leapt up and ran over to them.

"Are you okay?" Dante asked when he noticed her red-rimmed eyes.

She nodded jerkily, forcing a smile. "Yeah, I am," she said shakily. "Just… had a bad dream, and when I woke up, you guys were gone. I just… freaked out a little."

Guilt washed over him for having left without telling the others, and he put his arm around her to calm her down. She leaned into him, letting out a deep sigh of relief, and he gave her shoulder a reassuring squeeze as they headed back to the house.

"Are the others up?" he asked.

She nodded. "Yeah, they were flipping through channels when I went outside," she said.

"Let's go see if they found anything good," he suggested, and they walked up the stairs and back inside.

Cam and Phillip were sprawled on the couch, watching an old black and white gangster movie. They both looked up, eyes lighting up at the tray in Lily's hand.

Ace glanced at the TV and then back to the guys. "You boys know I have movies, don't you?" he drawled.

"Just trying to enjoy the thrill of finding something while flipping through channels," Phillip replied with a shrug.

Lily laughed and held out a cup of coffee to Bailey. "Slim pickings, I take it?" she asked, setting the tray with the other two on the coffee table.

Cam held up the remote and started flicking through channels as Phillip dove for one of the coffees. Virtually every one was either a blue screen or a static *Please stand by* image.

"Guessing the news networks are out of commission?" Dante asked, letting go of Bailey to sit on the arm of the couch.

Cam nodded. "All of the cable ones are gone," he explained, "which isn't surprising since they're either in New York or L.A."

"What about the local one?" Lily asked.

He flipped it over and the scrolling message at the bottom of the screen was still there, but was different.

Day two… still locked inside. Whatever those things are, several of them are in the control room. Please, if anybody is out there, come get me.

"We'd better get to it," Dante said, taking a deep breath. "You want to get our gear?"

Ace nodded, chugging the last of his coffee and vanishing into his bedroom.

Bailey wrapped her hands around her cup, but didn't take a sip. "Are we going to get my family?" she asked, eyes hopeful.

"We are, but you're not," Dante replied gently.

Her brow furrowed. "But… why?" she asked.

"Because we need people who can fight," Lily cut in, and glanced at the couch. "Same goes for you two losers."

The boys flipped her off in unison, but relaxed, used to her good-natured abuse. Bailey looked dejected, chewing her lip, but nodded in agreement.

"Don't worry," Dante assured her, "we'll get your family. You just need to show us where they are." He spotted a notebook laying on a shelf by the door, and grabbed it along with a pen, holding it out to her. "Can you draw us a map? Give us anything that might help us?"

She nodded vigorously, and took the supplies, plonking herself down on the couch and setting her cup on the coffee table.

"Hey, y'all come get your stuff," Ace called from the bedroom.

Dante and Lily headed inside, where their host had stuck a crate on the bed. He cracked open the lid, revealing several weapons. There was a shotgun, a hunting rifle, and a few handguns. Several large knives in sheaths were piled up along the one side.

"It ain't much, but should give us a fighting chance when we run into these…" Ace paused, wrinkling his nose. "Zombies."

Dante reached in and plucked out a handgun, an extra mag, and a knife. Lily snatched the shotgun, grinning.

"That's pretty big Lil," her cousin teased, "you think you can handle it?"

She glared at him and loaded up a few shells, forcefully cocking it. Ace playfully held up his palms in surrender.

Dante picked through the rest of the crate, only spotting two extra handgun mags. "You have any more of these hiding somewhere?" he asked.

Ace shook his head. "That shit was expensive, man," he drawled. "Decided to spend the money on more ammo so I could shoot more."

"Hard to argue with that logic,"
Dante admitted, and handed one of the mags
over to the shorter man, pocketing the
other one. Each of them attached a knife
holster to their belts, and then headed
back out to the living room where Bailey
sat, clutching her finished map in her
hands.

"Here you go," she said, standing up
and holding the paper out to Dante.

He stared at it, running his finger
along her crude drawing. "So if I'm
reading this right," he said as he traced
the lines, "we get across this big bridge
and then head south? And it's what, a mile
down or so before turning?"

"Yeah," she replied, nodding as she
sidled up next to him to point it out.
"It's the first main turnoff after the
bridge, and it connects to my street."

Lily regarded the paper from the
other side. "And the TV station?" she
asked.

"Oh yeah," Bailey replied, and took
the map out of Dante's hands, studying it
for a moment before clicking the pen open
and drawing a side road off of her street.
She put a big *X* where the studio was.
"Just go up about three more blocks and
hang a right, you'll see it." She handed
the map back over and then snapped her
fingers. "Oh, and one more thing." She

headed over to the corner where she'd left her work vest after waking up and plucked her name tag off of it. "My mother is a lot of things, but trusting isn't exactly one of them," she said as she headed back over and extended the tag to Dante. "She might freak out when you come knocking, especially since my sisters are in there. Just show her this and she'll come around."

He nodded, pocketing the tag. "Don't worry," he said, "we'll bring 'em back safe."

She smiled thinly and then sat back down on the couch.

"So what do you want us to do in the meantime?" Cam piped up, taking a noisy sip from his cup.

Ace jerked a thumb over his shoulder. "I got some wood out back by the shed," he drawled. "Find you's some hammer and nails, and start fortifying this place."

"You can also go up to the gas station and start clearing out anything that might be useful," Lily added. "Food, drinks, medicine, whatever you can find."

Dante held up a hand. "Just don't go into any of the houses," he said firmly. "We'll clear them as a group once we get back."

"Get a couple gas cans too and fill 'em up," Ace added. "I got a generator out back for when the power goes out."

There was a long stretch of silence as the thought of having no power settled over each of them. The world was crumbling to the ground around them, and it was only a matter of time before the power was all gone.

"We'd better get moving," Dante finally said.

They headed outside, and the three travelers got into the large black pickup as the three staying stood on the porch to watch them go. Lily sat in the middle, wriggling to get comfortable as Ace fired up the beastly vehicle.

"Hold on to your butts," he declared, and peeled out of the driveway, fishtailing a bit as he squealed towards Beaufort.

CHAPTER THREE

Ace pulled the truck to a stop just shy of the highway 170 bridge. The three of them looked out over the bridge spanning the massive inlet, trying to take it all in.

The two-lane sides of the bridge had a large gap in between. To the left side was a massive pileup, with a transfer truck jackknifed and several smaller vehicles pinned beneath it. Just behind that, several cars and trucks were in a massive pileup, apparently unable to stop. Then the original wreck happened.

Even though they were a hundred yards away from the cars, they could still see movement inside. Trapped zombies flailed at the glass, trying to escape their metal tombs.

The right road was completely clear, with the exception of a lone abandoned vehicle on the far side of the road. As they peered into the distance, there were a few zombies outside of the pileup wandering around, emerging from behind the wreckage.

"You think there's anybody alive in there?" Lily asked.

Dante shook his head. "Looks like there was a violent crash," he replied. "If they did survive, I doubt we're going to have a way to get them out. Still, we'll have a look as we go by."

"Guess that's my cue," Ace said brightly, and hit the gas, though he drove at a far slower pace than he had been before.

When they came up alongside the wreckage, he all but stopped the truck. A few of the zombies by the crash rushed towards them, but hit the concrete barrier. One smacked into it with so much force that it toppled over, careening down to the water below.

Ace barked a laugh. "Ain't the brightest bulbs, are they?" he asked.

"Be thankful for that," Dante replied dryly.

"Oh, I am," Ace assured him. "That shit was just funny as hell."

Lily smacked his arm, and he groaned playfully as if it had hurt terribly.

"Come on, cuz," she said, motioning him forward, "let's get going. I don't see anybody alive in there."

The trio sat silently as they moved up the road, pausing at the car on their side. There were bloody handprints on the driver's side windows, the back just completely smeared with gunk and gore. They peered closer, and saw the passenger window wide open against the far side of the bridge, leaving the vehicle empty.

"Whoever was in there must have taken a swan dive," Ace said, brow furrowing.

Dante nodded. "Let me tell you, that's a hell of a fall," he said.

"Especially in these waters," Ace agreed, nodding. "May not look like it, but that current is strong. Unless he got lucky, he's now in the middle of the Atlantic."

Lily shook her head. "From the looks of things, he's in a better place than he was," she murmured.

Her cousin hit the gas and continued up the road. When they approached the end of the bridge, Dante unfolded the map Bailey had drawn for them.

"Okay, according to this," he said as he traced his finger along their route, "we need to take the highway coming up on the right."

Ace nodded and made the turn. "Yeah, this cuts through to the other bridge in a few miles," he said. "Where am I turning?"

"About a mile and a half up on the left," Dante replied, pointing. "Sandy Cove Lane."

Ace continued, looking intently out the window for the road so that he didn't miss it. The other two gazed around at the neighborhood. The side streets were full of signs of struggle, although the outdoor zombie population was somewhat smaller than they'd expected, only a dozen or so over the course of three blocks.

"I would have thought there would be more," he murmured.

Lily shrugged. "The Marine base is up north, and there's a lot of shopping areas up there too," she pointed out. "These things like noise, and they're probably causing a hell of a ruckus up there."

"Whatever it is, I'm all for it," Ace declared, and finally found the target road, making his turn.

"Bailey said her house was a block down on the left," Dante instructed, and they crept down along the row of houses, looking at each one.

Some of them appeared to have been broken into by zombies, and there were a couple of corpses on the front lawns. Most of the cars in the driveways were gone, with one sitting in a driveway with the driver's side door open.

"There it is," Dante said, pointing to a small brick house on the corner. The front door was closed tight, and the car was still in the driveway.

Ace idled for a moment as they looked for any signs that the house had been breached, and then put the truck into gear, driving on.

"What are you doing?" Lily asked, blinking at him.

"I was just thinking," he drawled, "we're going to have a tough enough time at the TV station without having to babysit. They look like they're just fine, so they can wait a little longer, don't you think?"

Lily glanced at Dante, and he nodded.

"Good point," he agreed, and inclined his head forward. "Three blocks up on the right."

Ace paused at the last intersection before the station so they could scope it out. There were four ghouls in the parking lot, mostly by the back door.

"Any ideas, Scarface?" he asked, leaning his head against the headrest. "Or you just want me to start picking them off?"

Dante pursed his lips for a moment, contemplating. "We need to limit gunshots," he reminded them, "because the last thing we want to do is draw a crowd. You got a crowbar?" he asked.

Ace reached behind the front seat into the tiny space between the seats and the back. He pulled out a large crowbar and handed it across to Lily. "What you planning on doing with that?" he asked.

Dante just smiled and opened the door, jumping down. He moved to the bed and clambered up into the bed of the truck.

As he did that, Ace grinned as it dawned on him what his plan was, and he reached back to slide open the small window panel behind him. "You hang on tight," he instructed. "I'll do my best not to fling you out when I spin it around."

"That would be appreciated," Dante replied, taking a knee. He hooked his arm into the window, holding on as Ace hit the gas.

The truck sped towards the TV station, squealing into the parking lot. He cut the wheel hard, doing a 180 as the tires shrieked across the pavement. The noise attracted all four zombies by the door. They rushed towards the truck, smacking into the side of it. Thanks to the lift kit, they struggled to reach over the side.

Dante stood up, and casually walked to the edge of the bed, looking down at the four ghouls trying to grab at him. They were a mix of ages from twenty to sixty, all with various wounds marring their bodies. He took a deep breath, reminding himself that they weren't people anymore.

He swung down hard, cracking a skull, and built up his momentum. In a manner of seconds, his assault was over, a quick game of whack-a-mole complete with carnage. Four corpses lay on the ground, and he stared at them for a tense moment to make sure they were truly dead and not about to get back up again.

"We're good," he finally said, turning back to the window. He climbed down as the others got out of the truck, walking around to survey the pile of bodies.

Ace let out a low whistle. "You got a mean swing, brother," he drawled.

"If it's all right," Dante said, holding up the crowbar, "I'm going to hang on to this."

The shorter man grinned. "Consider it yours," he said.

Dante nodded and headed for the door. He paused in front of it as they clustered around and turned to his companions.

"Melee as much as you can," he said quietly. "The building is going to muffle the sound somewhat, but with our luck, they'll be a mob within earshot. Ace and I will go in first. Once we're through, I'll need you to secure the door." He put up a hand as Lily began to protest. "I know you're capable," he assured her. "But we don't know what we're up against in there. If we start getting overrun, Ace and I are going to have an easier chance of holding them at bay while you get the door open. That's all."

He held up his palms, and she nodded begrudgingly.

"I'm ready when you are," she said firmly.

Dante and Ace got into position to storm the building as she put her hand on the door. She did a quiet countdown and then jerked it open, allowing the boys to rush inside. She slammed it shut behind them and threw the deadbolt, waiting with her hand on it just in case they had to make a hasty exit.

The entry hallway looked like a battle zone, blood coating everything. As soon as the trio stepped forward, a zombie about fifteen yards away at the far end turned and rushed towards them. Dante lashed forward, holding up the crowbar with the pointy tip outwards.

When the ghoul came within range, he shoved it forward, combining the creature's momentum with his own force, driving the metal right into the bridge of its nose. The corpse crumpled to the ground, and Dante shook its face loose from his weapon, quickly raising it again just in case something else was nearby.

All was quiet, and he motioned for his companions to join him. The trio moved cautiously towards the door at the end of the hall. They looked through the small window into the newsroom.

Four zombies stood off to the right, and somewhere out of sight there was a chorus of banging on the far side. As they scanned, they spotted a zombie off to the left, standing in front of another door, all by itself.

"I can take out that one on the left," Ace murmured. "You just cover me in case the others see me."

Dante nodded and quietly opened the door. He and Lily knelt down next to it, staying out of sight in the darkness, with most of the light focused on the news set.

Ace drew his hunting knife and crept along the shadows as he approached the lone zombie. It stood there, virtually motionless, staring at the door as if it had given up trying to get in. Ace reached striking distance, studying the ghoul to make sure it hadn't seen him. He readied his knife before stepping out of the shadows, darting forward silently.

He closed the five yard gap, managing to plant the blade in the back of the monster's skull before it even knew he was there. He did his best to catch it as it fell, but the corpse was a little too heavy, falling into the door.

Its head smacked against the wood with a light *thud*, but thankfully not causing enough of a sound to alert the ghouls on the other side of the room. It was, however, loud enough to draw the attention of a zombie on the other side of the door.

Ace jumped back, startled by the sound of a ghoul smacking into the door, moaning and scratching against it in hungry fury. He was frozen for a moment, but then looked back frantically, seeing the other four zombies turning to rush him.

"Fucking hell," he breathed, and when they were halfway across the room, he broke to the left and raced towards the news desk. He managed to dart behind it, grabbing one of the padded swiveling chairs and tossing it back hard enough to knock one ghoul to the ground.

The other three bunched up, tearing for him. He quickly grabbed the other chair and held it out in front of him to brace himself. He cracked one ghoul in the ribs with the wheels before flattening his back against the wall for extra support to hold them at bay.

The ghouls pushed against it, but he managed to stack them up safely behind the flimsy barrier.

Dante appeared then, immediately swinging. He cracked one creature in the back of the head, dropping it, and the sound made a second zombie whip around. He stabbed it in the face as it turned to him, and then Ace used the distraction to slam the knife into the skull of the third ghoul.

A gunshot went off, and the two men startled, turning to stare open mouthed at Lily, who stood in the middle of the newsroom, lowering her handgun.

"What the hell you do that for?" Ace demanded, setting down his chair barrier.

She didn't respond, just pointed to their left. Both men looked over to see the fourth zombie only a few yards away from Dante, its arms outstretched even as it lay on the floor dead.

His breath hitched, realizing he'd almost been blindsided. "Thank you," he said sincerely, turning to her.

"Anytime," she replied with a shrug.

Dante nodded and then turned back to Ace. "What the hell caused them to rush you like that?" he asked.

"Something is behind that door, and really wants to get out," the shorter man explained, pointing back to the door in question.

Lily shook her head. "It can keep wanting," she declared, "cause I'm not going near it."

"Come on, let's go see if our new friend is still alive and kicking," Dante said, and led the trio across the newsroom to the control room door. It was slick with bloody splotches from the ghouls bashing at it.

He stepped aside and motioned for Ace to knock, and the redneck gave an excited *shave and a haircut* rap on the wood.

"Kind of predictable, don't you think?" Lily asked, raising an eyebrow.

Her cousin shrugged. "Just paying respect to the classics."

A few moments later, the door unlatched, and a dark-haired woman opened it. "Hi there," she said, as casually as if they weren't in the middle of an apocalypse. "I'm guessing you saw my message?"

"Nah, we're just looters who have a hard-on for high end camera equipment," Ace drawled with a smirk.

Lily smacked him on the arm, rolling her eyes. "Ignore him," she said, "his favourite snack as a kid was lead paint chips."

The girl chuckled and slipped through the door, quickly shutting it behind her.

Ace's brow furrowed. "That wasn't suspicious at all," he said, cocking his head. "You, uh… hiding something in there?"

"Nothing you would want to see," she replied sharply.

He crossed his arms. "Oh, really?" He stepped past her and opened the door, a putrid stench immediately hitting him in the face. He gagged and slammed the door shut, gasping for air. "What the fuck is that?!"

"I've been locked in that room for thirty hours without air conditioning," she replied, crossing her arms. "Or a bathroom."

Ace held up his hands in surrender. "Yep, that's it," he choked out.

"You got a name?" Dante asked.

"Katie McClure," she replied.

He nodded. "Okay, Katie McClure," he said, and put a hand to his chest. "I'm Dante, and this is Lily and Ace."

She nodded, regarding everyone, and he watched her glance quickly over his face before focusing on his good eye. "I can't thank you enough for risking your lives to come rescue me," she said.

"It's our pleasure," he assured her. "Just didn't feel right knowing someone was in danger and not doing anything about it. Even if it meant risking our wellbeing."

She took a deep breath. "So is it bad out there?" she asked.

"Shit's spreading faster than STDs at an unregulated strip club," Ace said, and his cousin looked at the ceiling, shaking her head at his example.

"Yeah, it's pretty bad out there," she added.

Katie pursed her lips for a moment and clasped her hands in front of her. "I hope this doesn't come off as a callous transition," she said slowly, "but do you happen to have any food or water? There was a strict no food policy in the control room, so my stomach is rumbling, to say the least."

"We… kind of neglected to bring anything with us," Lily said with a wince. "Not that we had a whole lot going around to begin with."

Katie nodded in understanding. "No worries," she replied, "the break room over there was set up for a party before… well. Food should still be good though, as it was in the fridge."

"Where's the break room?" Dante asked, looking around.

She pointed to the door that Ace had declared a zombie on the other side, and he grimaced.

"I'm afraid one of those things is in there," he said apologetically.

"Wait, wait, you said party," Ace piped up before anyone else could react. "Is there cake?"

Katie nodded. "I brought ice cream cake," she said.

Ace turned to Dante, pressing his palms together, eyes wide and pleading. "Come on, man," he whined, "this is probably the last chance we'll ever have to eat one of these! And besides, we could use the practice going through doors."

The bigger man chuckled and shook his head before looking around the newsroom. He focused on a giant camera, and headed over, pulling the cables off of it.

"If we're going to do this," he declared, "we're going to do it safely."

"Yes!" Ace hissed, fist pumping the air, and trotted over to follow Dante as he rolled the camera towards the door.

He adjusted the stand so that it was as low as it could go, resting about waist high. He placed it in the middle of the doorway, and the beastly machine was large and wide enough to cover the majority of the opening.

"Lily, if you'd do the honors," Dante invited, getting a good grip on the camera.

She nodded and turned the knob, pushing the door open before leaping back out of the way. The lone zombie inside immediately rushed them, and Dante shoved the camera forward, holding it at bay with the giant lens. Ace lunged forward, lashing his arm over the threshold to stab the ghoul in the face.

Dante nodded and pulled the camera back, letting the corpse fall to the floor. He grabbed it by the collar and dragged it out of the way, then motioned for the others to enter the break room with a flourish.

"Looks like it's party time," he said.

Katie entered first, looking around the break room that was a huge mess. The corner had a giant pool of blood, where it appeared the zombie had bled out as a human after being bitten, escaping the newsroom carnage.

She raised her chin and headed for the fridge, opening the door and pulling out trays of snacks, bottles of soft drinks, and finally the ice cream cake from the freezer, setting it all on the table. She removed the plastic coverings and then sat down before grabbing a handful of pasta salad and shoving it into her mouth like an animal.

The trio stared at her, stuffing her face for a few moments, amusement on their faces, before she finally noticed and swallowed a mouthful, face going red.

"Sorry… I was just…" she trailed off helplessly.

Lily shook her head, taking a seat next to her. "Honey, you should see these two," she drawled. "You never apologize to them, or me."

Katie gave her a relieved smile, and continued to eat, albeit slower than before. The others joined the table and started dishing up food for themselves.

"So what is it that you do here at the station?" Dante asked as he grabbed a few mystery meat triangle sandwiches.

She swallowed her current mouthful and inclined her head to him. "Little bit of everything really," she replied. "Sometimes work the teleprompter, sometimes in charge of party planning. But mostly I was our field reporter coordinator."

"What's that?" Lily asked as she scooped some potato salad onto a plate.

Katie took a sip of cola. "I was in charge of setting up interviews and basic facts of a story so that our reporter knew exactly what was going on," she explained.

"Did you ever do a story on Theo Atkinson?" Dante asked, leaning forward.

She nodded, swallowing another mouthful of food. "Of QXR Group, oh yeah," she replied. "He was quite the target in recent months with the controversy up at the Marine base."

"Controversy?" Lily asked, raising an eyebrow. "What was going on?"

Katie shook her head. "Some of the military brass wasn't happy with the QXR Group being given space on the base," she explained. "A couple, like the base commander General Whitley was particularly vocal about it."

"Must have been a big deal if the base commander was making a public stink about it," Ace put in, his chin already covered in ice cream. "That kind of shit can get you removed from your post."

Katie shook her head again. "He was an anonymous source feeding us information about how someone higher up the food chain okayed the move," she said. "He never went on camera or on the record, but the General and I spoke quite often about it. He was hoping to raise enough public awareness about it that the pressure would get them removed from base."

"What were they even doing there, anyway?" Lily wondered.

Katie wrinkled her nose. "Officially? They were there to help train the marines in hostile suburban combat scenarios," she said dryly. "Unofficially? They were using the base as a launching pad for covert operations, or at least that's what the rumor was."

"I can see what that would be controversial and put a General on edge,"

Ace agreed through a mouthful of cold dessert.

Dante chewed thoughtfully and then set down his sandwich. "So I'm guessing they're well trained?"

"Oh, without a doubt," Katie replied, chasing her pasta with more cola. "They not only recruited from our military, but from special ops around the world. These guys were some of the best in their field, and commanded top dollar, which was what Theo Atkinson was happy to pay."

Dante leaned his arms on the table. "How big is their force?" he asked.

"They had a thousand men stationed there," Katie replied. She furrowed her brow as the others all shared concerned glances and motioned around at them with a fork. "But why all these questions about Theo Atkinson?"

Dante let out a sigh. "Because his men took over Hilton Head Island," he said.

Katie stopped chewing, blinking at him rapidly. She almost choked as she swallowed her mouthful, shaking her head. "I'm sorry," she croaked, "did you just say they took over Hilton Head?"

"Took it over," Dante confirmed, nodding. "They're executing people they think are infected with the virus causing all this, and…" He lowered his gaze.

"Kidnapping," Lily spoke up. "They took his sister yesterday."

Katie set down her fork, shaking her head. "Unbelievable," she breathed, putting a hand to her forehead. "They're executing civilians? If they're that brazen, then it doesn't bode well for anyone, or the world as a whole." She lowered her arms and picked up her cola, swirling it for a moment before regarding Dante. "You said *virus* that's causing this. What did you mean by that?"

"One of the people with us was sick," he explained. "They demanded to know her blood type, and when she said A-positive, they shot her down like a dog."

"A blood type?" Katie mused thoughtfully. "A blood type… and you said she was sick?"

Dante nodded, raising an eyebrow in question. "Yeah, flu-like symptoms."

She took out her phone and started flipping through screens.

"Whoa," Ace said between scooping more ice cream into his mouth, "didn't realize that the phone service was still up and running."

Katie shook her head. "It's not, however, my notes from upcoming stories are on here and…" she said, and then straightened up. "Bingo. Two days ago, one of my contacts at the hospital said they were getting a huge influx of people with a mysterious virus showing up to the ER. The doctors were dismissing it as the flu, but my contact wasn't convinced. We were preparing to do a story on it later this week, but it turns out we don't need to." She chewed her lip as she scrolled through her notes, and then her eyes widened. "Holy shit."

"What is it?" Dante asked, leaning forward.

"My source at the hospital said that every patient had the same blood type," she replied. "Which is what made her think this wasn't the flu."

Ace pointed his spoon at her. "Let me guess, A positive?" he asked.

She shook her head, swallowing hard. "*All* A-type blood," she said. "Which if true, explains why this stuff got completely out of control seemingly overnight."

"I don't follow," Ace admitted.

"Roughly forty percent of the population has A-type blood," Katie explained. "If most… or all of them are affected by whatever this virus is…"

"It would mean between that and the bites being infectious that in the span of a day, we pretty much became outnumbered by zombies." Dante finished.

She raised an eyebrow. "*Zombies*?"

"Yeah, it's crazy," Lily cut in, waving her off, "but just roll with it."

Katie nodded slowly. "Okay then."

"So what's our next move?" Ace asked, serving himself up a third slice of ice cream cake.

"I say we get Bailey's family," Dante put in, "pick up some food, and get back home." His brow furrowed, and he turned to Katie. "I'm sorry, do we need to go by your place? Anybody there we need to get?"

She shook her head. "No, I'm all alone down here," she replied. "However, based on what you've told me about what QXR is doing on Hilton Head, we should go to the Marine base. If General Whitley finds out what they're doing, he'll put a quick end to it."

Dante glanced at Ace and then nodded, laying his hands flat on the table. "Okay, new plan," he said. "We're going to go get Bailey's family. Lily, I'm going to have you escort them back to Ace's while we go to the base."

She jutted out her chin, eyes narrowing, but he held up a hand before she could argue.

"And I'm having you do this because I know you'll get them safely back to Bailey without scarring them for life with an inappropriate story from your wild youth." He gave Ace the side-eye, and the redneck raised an eyebrow as he stuffed his fourth piece of ice cream cake into his mouth.

"What?" he asked through a mouthful, a stream of chocolate melting out of the corner of his mouth.

Lily laughed and shook her head. "Okay, I'll buy that," she finally said, and then pointed a finger at Dante. "But this is the last pass you're getting on that, mister."

He smiled and got to his feet, the rest following suit. Ace snatched up a handful of napkins and cleaned his face, smacking his lips and patting his belly as they headed back out into the newsroom.

"Sorry, I have to do one more thing before we go," Katie said, and rushed back into the control room. A few moments later, she emerged, coughing under her breath at the stench.

"What was that all about?" Ace asked as he checked his rifle.

Katie pointed to the TV monitor to their left that showed the live feed. Along the bottom, the scrolling message read, *I've been saved. People with A-type blood and bites are infectious. Take caution and good luck.*

"Good call," Dante said with a nod.

Katie shrugged. "I have them, every now and then," she quipped. "Come on, let's get going."

CHAPTER FOUR

Ace stopped the truck a block from Bailey's house, which now had a couple of zombies clustered by the front door.

"Shit man," he breathed, "they must have heard us rumble by and ran up there."

Dante lifted the crowbar and wiggled it. "Let's clear them out, then," he said, and opened the door to clamber up into the back.

Katie furrowed her brow, but moved over a little, enjoying not being so squished in the seats.

"Don't worry, this works like a charm," Lily assured her as Ace hit the gas.

He rolled up to the house and reversed into the driveway. Just like the TV station lot, the ghouls rushed over and Dante put them down with well-placed strikes to the head. As soon as they crumpled to the ground, he hopped down and walked over to the passenger's side.

"Why don't you stay in the truck?" he asked as Katie opened the door. He held out the crowbar, and Lily reached across to take it. "Might go a little easier in coaxing them out."

They nodded, and he shut the door, heading up to the house. He approached slowly and then knocked as gently as he could on the front door.

"Hello?" he called. "Is anybody home?"

"I don't know who you are, but I got a gun and I swear to christ I'll blow your dick off!" a shrill voice shrieked from inside.

Dante blinked, shaking his head at how specific the threat had been. He put his hands up just in case she was watching him from a window or through the peephole.

"Ma'am," he said gently, "your daughter Bailey sent us to get you and her sisters."

"Bullshit!" the woman barked. "You're just trying to get in here!"

Dante shook his head. "I have proof, I just need to reach into my pocket," he called. "I'm going to move slowly." True to his word, he reached down as slowly as he could and pulled out the name tag, holding it up to the peephole. "Ma'am, Bailey is safe, and she wants you to be safe too, which is why she sent us."

There was a moment of silence, and then the deadbolt clicked. A woman in her forties with deep bags under her eyes opened it, a shotgun gripped in her hands.

"Where did you get my angel's name tag?" she demanded.

Dante held it out. "She gave it to me before we came out to get you," he explained. "Said you would recognize it."

She took it, the shotgun falling to the floor as she ran her fingers over the raised lettering. "I didn't think I'd see my baby again," she said, voice thick. "You're not lying to me, are you?" She looked at him with wide, watery eyes. "She really is safe?"

"Yes, and we're going to take you to her," Dante replied firmly.

The woman swallowed hard and then turned back into the house. "Hazel, Violet!" she yelled. "We're going!"

A moment later, two young girls no older than ten appeared, each holding a small backpack.

Lily jumped down from the truck, heading over slowly.

"Ma'am, this is Lily," Dante said gently. "She's going to be taking you to Bailey."

Lily smiled and gave a little wave. "Do you have a car?"

The woman nodded, pointing to the minivan in the driveway. "It's a little bit of a rough ride, but it'll get us there," she said hoarsely.

"If you like, I can drive so you can attend to the girls," Lily offered.

The woman nodded and stepped inside to grab her keys off of the wall, handing them over to her new companion.

"Scarface!" Ace yelled from the driver's side window, and Dante turned to see two zombies tearing towards them from the house next door.

He didn't hesitate, full reflex kicking in, and jumped forward so he was in their direct path as he drew his knife. The ghouls were eight yards apart, with one running faster than the other. He stood his ground, waiting on the first one to arrive. Just before it did, a shot rang out, clipping it in the head to drop it. A few seconds later, another went off, hitting the other ghoul between the eyes and sending it to the grass right beside the other one.

Dante turned and appraised Lily, who playfully blew on the end of her handgun barrel.

"See, this is what you're missing by not bringing me along," she teased with a smirk.

He laughed. "Duly noted," he promised. "Now, you should get a move on before more of these things show up." He took a deep breath. "And Lily?"

She cocked her head. "Yes, Dante?" she asked playfully.

"Be careful," he said. "You still got a lot more to show me."

She winked at him. "You know, somebody with a dirty mind might take that statement in a way you didn't mean," she purred, and then trilled a laugh as he blushed.

Once the girls pulled out of the driveway in the van, Dante got into the truck and closed the door.

"I see you flirtin' with my cousin," Ace quipped with a smirk.

Dante didn't respond to that, simply shrugging his shoulders. "Come on, let's get moving," he urged.

Ace followed the van back out to the highway and then made the turn towards the base. Dante watched Lily drive over the bridge until she vanished on the horizon.

"Okay, so where is this base at?" Ace asked, inclining his head to Katie, who sat between them.

She motioned as she spoke. "It's about four miles up the highway, then a left on the twenty-one," she explained. "Straight shot from there."

"Let's get this over with, then," he drawled, but couldn't speed up to accentuate his point due to the cars and zombies on the road. It wasn't anything too major. The debris and bodies spread out fairly well, but he didn't want to

smack anything while going too fast and
end up stuck.

About half a mile up from the bridge,
Dante spotted a grocery store on the left
side of the road. There were a dozen or so
zombies in the parking lot milling about,
with several more banging on one of the
small shop windows.

"Looks like a stop on the way out of
town," he said.

Katie chewed her bottom lip. "There's
a lot of those things there," she said.

"Aw, don't worry hon," Ace said, "we
can handle it."

Dante nodded in agreement. "And we
don't really have a choice," he added,
"unless starving seems like a viable
option to you."

Katie nodded, though her gaze seemed
far away as she contemplated just how
difficult of a situation they were in.

Dante scanned the neighborhoods as
they continued up the highway, inspecting
shopping areas as they went. Zombies were
everywhere. There were no massive hordes,
but packs easily as large as twenty or
twenty-five running around.

Signs of struggles were rampant—car
wrecks, homes with busted windows and wide
open front doors, and bloodstains all over
the sidewalks missing the bodies that
usually would come with them.

"How could this happen?" Katie moaned, pressing her hands to her temples.

Dante shook his head. "Don't know," he admitted, "but at the end of the day, it doesn't really matter."

"How can you say that?" she gasped, gaping at him.

He sighed. "Because even if we knew what was causing this, we aren't in a position to do anything about it," he explained. "The only thing I care about is how we survive this."

She swallowed hard, and then lowered her hands, nodding in silent agreement.

Ace pulled up at the highway twenty-one intersection. They looked around, and the immediate area was eerily deserted. The only signs that something had happened recently was a pileup to their right, with about twenty corpses scattered across the road.

"Looks like your Marine buddies paid a visit to these assholes," Ace said.

"Or QXR," Dante murmured.

The other two paused with concern as the realization settled over him that he could be right. But there was no point in dwelling on the implications of that.

"Hang a left," Katie said, letting out a deep breath. "The base is a couple miles up on the right."

Ace hit the gas, and they started the final stretch to the base. The side of the road was littered with zombie corpses.

As they crested a hill, the base loomed in the distance, and Katie smacked the dashboard.

"Stop!" she barked.

Ace slammed on the brakes, startled by her outburst. "What the hell?!" he demanded.

"There's a side road just up ahead on the right," she said, motioning. "Turn down it."

"Why?" he asked.

She sighed. "Because there's a delivery entrance near the back of the base that's right beside the General's office," she explained, the words tumbling out of her mouth quickly.

"You're concerned about the QXR, aren't you?" Dante asked gently.

She nodded. "Based on what you've told me," she replied, "I think we all should be."

"Ace, hang a right," Dante said, and the redneck did as he was asked, turning down the small access road running alongside the base. On the left, they peered through the chain-link fence, but didn't see any movement of any kind.

"I'm not a military expert or anything," Ace drawled, "but shouldn't there be some people or something?"

Katie clasped her hands in her lap tightly. "Yeah, there should," she murmured. "Lots of them, actually."

Dante didn't say anything, simply pulled out his handgun and checked the ammo, making sure there was a round chambered.

Katie furrowed her brow in concern, looking at the gun and then glancing at him, but he avoided her gaze and she didn't press the issue.

As they continued along the fence, Ace stopped just outside of the side gate. There was an opening large enough for a transfer truck to drive through, with the only thing blocking the road being a large metal crossbar stretching across.

They sat there, idling for several moments, waiting on someone to come out to greet them, but nobody did.

"This isn't right," Katie said, her knuckles white.

Ace shook his head. "Where are the guards?" he asked. "Shouldn't there be guards?"

"If we did this on a random Tuesday afternoon, we'd have four people with machine guns staring us down," she said.

"With everything that's going on, how is nobody here?"

"How far up is the General's office?" Dante asked.

She pried her hands apart and pointed to a building about fifty yards up on the right. It was a two-story building, small and standing alone from everything else.

"That small one on the right," she said. "His office is on the second floor overlooking the base."

Dante nodded. "Ace, pull this thing to the side of the road," he instructed. "That fence isn't going to provide much cover, but it won't be standing out like a sore thumb, either."

"We're going on foot?" the redneck asked.

Dante took a deep breath. "I don't like the way this looks," he admitted, "and we need to keep a low profile."

Ace nodded and backed the truck up, parking it on the road. The three of them got out of the vehicle and stood together on the shoulder, listening and hearing nothing.

"Just… silence," Katie whispered.

Ace shrugged. "Look at the bright side," he drawled, "at least we aren't hearing those moans and thundering footsteps headed our way."

"Thank god for small miracles," she muttered.

"Come on," Dante said, "stay close and quiet." He led them to the entrance, and they slipped under the metal bar. There was a building just to their left, and they jogged over to it.

Dante pressed himself against the wall, inching up towards the corner so he could look out over the base. As he peeked around, he pursed his lips at the sight of the vast, empty space. The center portion was nothing but asphalt, with a string of buildings and hangars on the far side, more buildings running down the line from where they were hiding.

He pulled back and turned to Katie. "Is this the only portion of the base?" he asked.

She shook her head. "No, there's a huge airstrip about half a mile long on the other side of those buildings," she replied.

"There more buildings out that way?" he asked.

She nodded. "Some hangars and barracks."

Ace slipped by Dante and peered out, and then popped back, shrugging. "If there is anybody here, that's probably where they're at," he suggested. "Maybe we should head that way?"

"I wouldn't," Katie replied.

"Why not?" Ace asked.

She crossed her arms. "Because that's where QXR was stationed."

"Fuck me sideways, man," Ace growled. "Are you telling me that if somebody is here, that it's the assholes killing everybody?"

Dante held up a hand. "Let's not give up hope, yet," he said. "Come on, let's pay the General a visit." He led the way across the open area quickly to the small outbuilding. They stood by the door, and he listened closely for a sound inside, hearing nothing. He held a finger to his lips and spoke quietly. "Follow me in, stay close to the door in case there's company," he whispered. "If things get bad, make a run for the truck."

The other two nodded as he took a deep breath, steading himself before turning the knob. He inched the door open slowly, hoping to catch a glimpse of danger if it were to come at him.

As he pushed it wider, there was no movement inside whatsoever. By the time it was halfway open, he simply flung it the rest of the way, bathing the interior of the room in sunlight.

The trio stood in the doorway, looking over an office area that looked frozen in time. There were a dozen or so desks spread out in the room that looked like they hadn't been disturbed at all. Computers were still functioning, stuck on whatever report that was being worked on. Papers remained stacked, and some cups of now-cold coffee sat on coasters.

They filed inside, and Katie shut the door behind them as they fanned out around the room.

"Everybody else is getting turned into zombies, and these people just got straight raptured," Ace drawled as they moved. "What the fuck is going on?"

Dante leaned over a nearby desk, inspecting the computer monitor. The report on the screen had directions to Edisto Beach.

"Where is Edisto Beach?" he asked.

Ace scratched the back of his head. "Edisto?" he asked. "Never heard of it."

"It's about an hour's drive north of here," Katie replied, approaching the desk. "Tiny community, pretty isolated from everything else."

The redneck raised an eyebrow. "How in the hell do you know that?" he asked.

"They did a big art show a couple months back that my station covered," she explained. "Well, big for the town, that is."

Ace shook his head. "Must have been a slow news day," he quipped.

"You're not kidding," Katie replied. "Drove an hour just to see twelve booths with collections of lighthouse paintings."

Dante continued reading the notes on the computer. *Begin troop deployments immediately,* he read, and then noticed the time stamp of 3:42 AM.

"If it's as small as you say," he piped up, "then why would the military be ordered to deploy there at three forty-two in the morning?"

Ace joined Katie, and the two looked over the report, just as confused as he was.

"Maybe they knew of an outbreak and were ordered to beat it down?" Ace suggested.

Katie shook her head as she read the memo header, noting that it was from the office of General Adams, head of the Joint Chiefs. "If that's the case, then why is it coming directly from General Adams up in D.C.?" she asked. "Unless he was personally vacationing there at the time, I doubt that he knew of anything going on there."

"Then what the hell is it?" Ace wondered.

Dante stood up straight. "Maybe there's something in the General's office that can fill us in," he suggested.

The trio got moving, finding the stairs to work their way up to the second floor. Just like the ground floor, it looked like everyone inside had simply vanished. The offices were empty and abandoned, and there were no signs of struggle, however most of the doors were wide open.

"Where's the office?" Dante asked.

Katie pointed. "Last one on the left."

They moved down the hall, and he stopped for a beat in front of the General's office, where the door was closed. He inclined his head to Ace, who readied his knife just in case.

Dante pushed the large wooden door open, and the three of them froze at the sight. Katie gagged and turned away from the sight of General Whitley, sitting back in his chair, the window behind him cracked from a bullet exiting his brain.

Dante approached the dead man, shaking his head. He spotted a handgun on the floor, and picked it up, shoving it into the back waistband of his pants.

"That's not exactly an uplifting sign there," Ace muttered, sheathing his knife. He glanced at Katie, still with her back turned, covering her mouth, face pale. He glanced at the coat rack in the corner and snatched a jacket off of it, holding it out to Dante. "Hey, would you do the honors?" he asked.

Dante looked back at Katie's quivering shoulders, and he took the jacket, covering up the dead General and then rolling the chair over to the far corner of the office. After a beat, she straightened, composing herself before turning around and approaching the desk.

"Sorry," she said hoarsely. "Bad enough to see this… worse when it's somebody I know."

Dante nodded. "No apologies necessary," he assured her.

Ace leaned over the desk that was strewn with papers, and picked up a folder, flipping through it to try to find something useful. Dante started scrolling through the reports still open on the computer screen, finding his way back to the main email menu.

He found one report labeled *Evacuation Point – TOP PRIORITY*, with a timestamp of 3:38 AM. He clicked on it and started reading.

"Might have something here," he said. "This came in a few minutes before the Edisto Beach one. Also from the office of General Adams." He scanned the document before clearing his throat. "Okay, it's short and to the point… There is an unprecedented event happening, one that threatens the stability of the nation as a whole. In response, all base commanders are to prepare for an immediate evacuation. There will be an exception in rare cases, and if this impacts your base, you will receive a followup immediately after this." He scanned further down a little more, muttering to himself until he found the next important bit. "Anyone with A-type blood needs to be immediately quarantined. This is to be done without exception. Explanation will follow shortly."

"Are you fucking serious right now?!" Ace cried, slamming the folder he'd been holding down on the table. "The military just up and abandoned us? What the *fuck* man?!"

Dante shook his head. "Looks like we're on our own," he murmured.

Katie swallowed hard, and an envelope on the desk caught her eye. She picked it up and realized the label was in Whitley's handwriting. *General Whitley, Final Words,* it said, and her breath hitched as she opened the envelope, pulling out a single sheet of paper.

Her eyes widened as she started reading, and then Ace cleared his throat.

"You going to share with the rest of the class?" he asked.

She blinked at him and then nodded
when it registered what he was asking.
"It's General Whitley's suicide note," she
explained. "I'll start from the top." She
took a deep breath. "To the survivors. It
pains me to write this, as it feels like I
have betrayed my oath to protect this
nation. In the face of grave danger, my
final official act as commander of this
base was to order the evacuation of every
healthy soldier under my command. Instead
of rushing headlong into battle to protect
innocent life, we are retreating, leaving
those who need us most to fend for
themselves in this time of grave danger."
She paused, putting a hand to her chest as
she continued, "While I am not privy to
the rationale behind this decision, my
only solace is knowing that I won't have
to live with the knowledge of this
betrayal long. I don't know how, but I
have become infected with the virus that
threatens our nation, our way of life,
which leaves me only one option. May god
forgive me for what I have done, and what
I am about to do. Signed, General
Whitley."

The room was silent, soaking in the
words and implications of the letter. The
military had abandoned them. The situation
really was dire.

"Goddamn, that is a rough way to go,"
Ace groaned.

Dante cocked his head. "Single shot
to the head?" he asked. "Seems like it
would be pretty quick and painless."

"No, I mean knowing what he knew
before pulling the trigger," Ace amended,
waving his hands in front of his face.
"It's one thing to just keel over after
being sick, it's another thing entirely to
know you're on the clock and that the
timer is almost zero."

Dante nodded, and Katie stared at the
letter for another moment before setting
it back down on the table, her hand
shaking.

"So what do we do now?" Ace asked
with a sigh.

Dante held up a hand. "First things
first, we gotta get the hell out of here,"
he said. "The military might be gone, but
QXR might still be here."

"I was talking about long-term
planning," Ace admitted, "but I like your
idea better."

"Oh, shit," Katie breathed, looking
out the window, and the boys turned just
in time to see a single military jeep
coming up the main path towards the
building.

Ace groaned. "I'm going to go out on a limb and assume that's QXR and not a welcoming committee," he said.

"Stay calm," Dante said, "maybe they're just on patrol. They don't know we're here."

The trio stood tense as they watched the vehicle driving by each of the buildings to their left, slowly and scanning for god knew what.

"Fuck my life man," Ace groaned as the jeep parked in front of the building they were in. "Just fuck fuck fuck!"

Dante turned away from the window. "We got this."

"They're fucking mercenaries, man!" Ace cried. "We should hide!"

Katie raised a hand. "I agree," she said.

"If we don't fight our way out of here, we may never leave," Dante countered, shaking his head.

"I really think we should hide," Ace replied, though his voice was less forceful.

Katie took a deep breath. "Why don't we do both?" she asked. "We'll hide in here and fight if we need to. Maybe they're just going to peek in and keep moving."

They stared down at the vehicle and watched three mercenaries get out. The men took a moment to stretch and appeared to be talking between themselves.

"Okay, we're going with Katie's plan," Dante said, and pulled out the handgun he'd taken from the floor, checking to make sure there was still ammo in it. "You know how to use one of these?" he asked, holding the gun out to Katie.

She shook her head. "Not really."

"Then here's hoping we're just being overly cautious," he replied. "I want you to keep this out of sight until you absolutely need it. Understand?"

She reluctantly took the weapon, turning it over in her hand.

"So what's the plan?" Ace asked, putting his hands on his hips.

Dante pursed his lips as he gazed back out the window at the trio approaching the building. "Looks like you get to hide after all," he said.

CHAPTER FIVE

Katie stood nervously in front of General Whitley's desk, looking directly at the door. Her hands were on the desk, just a few inches from the handgun that was positioned behind her. She strained her ears as the voices downstairs laughed and carried on, the sounds of glass shattering in between.

They're breaking stuff, she thought, imagining a couple of boisterous guys tossing computer monitors around the office. *Maybe this isn't an official patrol, just some guys blowing off steam. We might be okay.*

Her wishful thinking vanished as she heard the echoes of footsteps in the stairwell at the end of the hall. In the empty building, the sound easily carried. The voices got louder as they opened the door, heading up the hall.

Katie tensed, every muscle in her body on edge. She knew they'd be found. She clenched her jaw as they came down the hall, footsteps getting louder and louder. Occasionally there was a boom of a door being kicked in as they checked the offices along the way.

"And now, gentlemen, let me introduce you to a coward who took the easy way out!" one of the men bellowed, and kicked in the General's door.

Three large men stood there with assault rifles, stopping short at the sight of Katie standing there. The leader immediately leered at her, sauntering into the room.

"Well, look what we have here," he drawled, licking his lips. "Now what's a pretty young thing like yourself doing up here all alone?"

"I think she could use some company, don't you?" the second guy drawled as he slid into the room.

The third smirked and chuckled. "Oh yeah," he added, "lots of company."

Katie's heart hammered as they approached her, three predators with their sights set on her.

Two handgun hammers clicked, and Ace and Dante stepped out from the corners flanking the door.

"The lady has all the company she needs," Dante said, voice like ice.

The mercenaries froze in their triangle formation, the first one at the tip glancing over his shoulder. "Looks like we got a tough guy over here," he said as he raised his hands, and then cocked a brow at Dante's face. "Whoa there brother, and I thought *I* was having a bad day. You let us go, and I can have the doc take a look at your face."

"I'm good, thanks," Dante replied.

One of the guys in the back scowled, keeping his hands high. "You guys have any idea who the fuck we are?" he demanded.

"Nothing but a bunch of hired goons," Ace declared.

The scowling mercenary glared at the short redneck. "Better than being a punk-ass bitch like you," he said with a sneer.

Ace growled, and the lead mercenary took a deep breath.

"Let's all settle down now and talk this out," he said firmly. "No reason for anybody to get hurt, or worse."

Dante cocked his head. "Somehow I doubt you're going to just let us go," he said.

"Well whatever fucked up your face didn't fuck up your brain," the mercenary replied. "No, we're not going to let you go."

"Bold statement when we have guns on you," Ace declared.

The sneering mercenary in the back ran his tongue over his teeth. "Boy, you ain't gonna be hot shit in a minute when I have you bent over that desk," he warned.

Ace clenched his jaw.

"As I was saying," the leader continued, rolling his eyes. "No, we aren't going to let you go. However, we can bring you into the fold, give you protection."

"Just like you're giving protection to those on Hilton Head Island?" Dante snarled.

The mercenary chuckled, shaking his head. "You're the jumper, aren't you?" he asked, amused.

Dante blinked at him in surprise.

"Don't look so shocked," the man continued, "that little maneuver has been quite the story floating around base. Not every day a man does a high dive from a bridge and survives. Looks like I owe Marcus five bucks."

Dante smirked. "I would say I'm sorry for costing you money," he drawled, "but kind of your fault for doubting me."

"No apology necessary," the mercenary replied. "Not like that money is good for anything these days anyway. More of a pride thing really. But now that I know who you are, I'm pretty sure I can get you a job if you want one."

The guy in the back winked at Ace. "And don't worry cupcake, I got a job for you too," he said, blowing the redneck a little kiss.

"You listen here, motherfucker," Ace snarled, and walked right up to the guy, pressing the gun against his temple.

Before Dante could protest, the mercenary reacted immediately, spinning around and smacking Ace's arm out of the way, causing him to pull the trigger.

The shot was deafening in the small office, startling everyone. The mercenary took advantage of the distraction and struck Ace, causing him to drop the weapon to the ground. The redneck fought back, delivering a couple of blows to the side of the mercenary's head. Despite his smaller wiry frame, he managed to get force behind his hits.

The lead mercenary hit the floor as Dante opened fire. His first shots missed, but he quickly turned his attention to the third guy who raised his assault rifle. Dante managed to hit him in the chest with three rounds rapidly, dropping him.

The leader stayed low as he lunged for Dante, tackling him. They slammed into a bookcase, the impact causing Dante to drop his gun.

Ace continued fighting with all he was worth, but his opponent managed to deflect and block every blow. The mercenary sneered as he batted his arm away.

"Man, I thought I was going to have to make you my bitch," he taunted, "had no idea you were already one."

Ace grunted as he swung again. "Fuck you, motherfucker," he snarled. "I'm going to tea bag your corpse."

The mercenary chuckled, and attempted to block, but in his laughter he left the smallest opening for the redneck to land a shot. Ace's fist connected with his nose, staggering him back a couple of steps.

The mercenary wiped at his nose, smiling through the blood. "Hope you enjoyed that," he spat, "because that's the last one you're getting."

As they re-engaged in their fight, Dante exchanged blows with his opponent. The mercenary delivered a straight punch that he deftly dodged, causing his attacker to crack his hand into the wooden bookcase. As he recoiled in pain, Dante used the opportunity to grab his wrist, wrenching it around and down, forcing the mercenary to double over.

As he let out a yelp, Dante gave his elbow a vicious palm strike to the elbow while pulling back his wrist, snapping his arm in two. His opponent let out a blood-curdling scream, drawing his knife with his other arm and swinging it around in an attempt to gut him.

Dante hopped back, narrowly avoiding being stabbed, which allowed the mercenary enough time to get back to his feet, holding out the blade.

"You're one tough son of a bitch," he snarled, "I'll give you that."

"Thought the bridge dive would have taught you that," Dante snapped.

The mercenary grinned and lunged, but Dante smacked his hand to the side, forcing him to retreat. They did the same dance again, and then the mercenary regrouped and tried again, putting a considerable amount of thrust in his attack.

This time, Dante snatched his wrist and pulled him forward, using the momentum to slam him into the bookcase. As the mercenary's head smacked into the thick bookcase, the knife fell to the floor. Dante slammed his skull into the shelves a couple more times and then put him in a chokehold.

He wrestled his opponent to the floor, wrapping his leg up and pulling tight as the mercenary struggled, swinging his good arm around frantically as he struggled to breathe. He tried to pull the arm away, but that didn't work, so he tried to reach back for Dante's face, but he couldn't reach.

He jabbed back with his elbow into his attacker's ribs, and Dante hissed with the pain, but didn't let go. If anything it gave him the drive to pull tighter. The blows started to weaken as the light drained out of the mercenary, and Dante squeezed as hard as he could, taking the last bit of air.

When his opponent went limp, he held on for several more seconds just to make sure he was dead. He finally relaxed, shoving the body off of him and regaining his breath as he rubbed at his ribs.

Ace tried to throw a punch, but his opponent smacked it aside and punched him in the stomach, knocking the air from his lungs and causing him to drop to one knee.

"All right bitch," he declared, "I'm done playing with you. Time to put you out of your misery." He pulled out his knife, raising it up as if he were about to impale it into the top of the redneck's head.

A single shot rang out, and one of the paintings on the wall exploded as the bullet whizzed by his ear. The mercenary startled, and glanced back at Katie, standing there shaking as she held up the gun.

The anger in his eyes caused her to lower her arms in fear, and he pointed the knife at her. "Oh don't worry sweetheart," he cooed, "I got something for you too."

Ace pulled his own knife and stabbed up from a kneeling position, burying it into the mercenary's gut all the way to the hilt. Giving it all he had, the blade tore up several inches of the man's torso.

The mercenary dropped his knife and fell to his knees, mouth open in shock. Ace stood up, tearing his blade out and then immediately slicing the asshole's throat before kicking him in the chest and crumpling him to the ground.

And then, as promised, he stood right over the mercenary's face and bobbed his crotch up and down. "Yeah, who's the bitch now, motherfucker?" he growled.

"Ace!" Dante snapped as he got up from the ground, glaring at him.

The redneck straightened up and stared down at the corpse as the light disappeared from its eyes. He haucked a massive loogie across the mercenary's face. "Bitch." He turned back to Dante, raising an eyebrow. "You okay, Scarface?" he asked.

Dante grabbed him by the shirt, jerking him close and speaking an inch away from his face. "When you have a gun on someone, you do *not* get within five feet of them," he said firmly, "do you understand me?"

Ace's eyes widened, fear evident in his face at the cold hardness of his companion.

Dante let go of him, taking it as acquiescence and stepping back. "Come on, we gotta get the hell outta here," he said. "Get their guns and ammo, and move."

He gave Ace a supportive smack on the back, and the redneck breathed a sigh of relief before joining him in looting the dead.

Dante turned to Katie as he slung an assault rifle strap over his shoulder, noticing that she hadn't moved an inch since firing her one shot. He stepped over and gently pried the gun from her hand, shoving it into the back of his pants.

"We gotta go," he said quietly. "Come on."

She nodded, snapping out of it, and took a deep breath, following the duo out of the office. They thundered down the stairs and burst outside, looking around to make sure nobody else was around.

"Guess nobody heard the shot," Dante said.

Ace jogged over to the jeep that the mercenaries had arrived in.

"What are you doing, man?" Dante demanded.

Ace didn't answer, and simply got into the driver's seat, finding the keys still in the ignition. He started it up and drove around to the back of the building, parking it by the fence. As he jogged back out to where Katie and Dante stood in the open, the latter spread his arms.

"What the hell?" he asked.

Ace shrugged. "Figure it someone comes looking for them, they won't immediately know this is where they are," he explained.

"Good work," Dante agreed, nodding. "Now let's get to the truck."

When they reached the truck, they threw the guns onto the floorboards and squeezed into the cab. Ace fired up the vehicle and pulled off of the curb, moving at a steady but not overly fast pace, so they wouldn't attract too much attention to themselves.

When they reached the turnoff, he stopped at the intersection, looking both ways. Thankfully there were no other vehicles around, and he pulled out, heading away from the base. The tension in the cab was palpable, the trio still on edge from the encounter.

Dante looked over his shoulder, almost completely sideways in the seat to watch behind them for anyone following. As they drove, he didn't see a single vehicle, only the occasional pack of roaming zombies, a few attempting to follow but falling behind.

"Anything?" Ace asked.

He shook his head, finally turning around to face the front. "Looks like we're in the clear," he said.

"Man, I'm so sorry about fucking up back there," the redneck moaned, rubbing his cheek with one hand.

"Don't worry about it," Dante replied.

Ace shook his head. "No, I'm serious man, I could have gotten us all killed," he insisted. "Lucky for us, you were there to handle things. Where the hell did you learn all that stuff, anyway?"

"Spend a few years doing MMA training," his companion replied.

"Like that pay-per-view cage fighting stuff?" Ace let out a low whistle. "Oh hell yeah. That shit is almost as good as wrastlin!"

Katie rolled her eyes. "You know wrestling is fake, right?" she piped up.

Ace slammed on the brakes, lurching them all forward.

Katie braced herself on the dashboard, staring at him with wide eyes. "Okay, okay, I'm sorry, it's real," she said quickly. "Just please, keep driving!"

"No, it's not that," Ace said, putting up a finger, "although, when we get back, I'm going to show you that Hell in a Cell match when Mankind gets thrown off the top and ends up with a tooth shoved up his nose. Then we'll see if you still think it's fake."

She raised an eyebrow. "Then why did you stop then?"

Ace pointed to the grocery store that they'd passed on the way in. There were still a dozen zombies in the parking lot, though none of them had noticed the truck yet.

"Are you crazy?" Katie blurted. "We gotta get out of here!"

"Scarface, are you positive you haven't seen anybody following us?" Ace asked.

Dante shook his head. "Just some zombies, but we lost them a mile back," he replied.

Ace turned to Katie. "We need food, badly," he said quietly.

"Then we'll go somewhere else!" she insisted.

The redneck looked to Dante, a pleading expression on his face.

His companion pursed his lips, contemplating for a moment. "Park around back," he finally said.

Ace cut the wheel hard and headed into the parking lot, smacking into several zombies as he headed to the back of the store. Katie chewed her lip, wringing her hands in front of her with white knuckles.

"Ace is right, we need food," Dante said gently. "Chances are, they're going to have this whole area on lockdown once they find their men. Same with the Hilton Head area. We might not have another chance to get food for a while."

She swallowed hard, giving a begrudging nod.

Ace smacked into a few more ghouls as he pulled up against the back of the store, parking between two large transfer trucks that were backed into loading docks. Dante quickly hopped out of the truck and used the rear tire to vault himself up into the bed.

Katie shuffled across the seat, but Ace reached out and put a hand on her arm. "Give him a minute," he said. He reached behind the seat and pulled out the crowbar, opening the back window to pass it through to Dante.

Katie turned and watched as the large man readied himself for the zombies that were closing in. Just like before, he smacked them down quickly, clearing the way with a pile of corpses.

"Come on, let's get in and out quickly," he said, and jumped down from the bed to the pavement. Ace and Katie got out, and Dante reached into the cab to grab an assault rifle and lead the charge to the back door.

He pulled on it, surprised that it was unlocked. "Guess they got hit while unloading," he muttered, and readied the crowbar.

Ace kept his assault rifle at the ready, and the trio headed into the loading dock. There was blood everywhere, with multiple signs of struggles around overturned furniture and busted shelves. They were about three feet inside when Dante stopped them.

He knelt down and smacked the crowbar several times on the concrete floor, sending a loud clang throughout the cavernous room. A few seconds later, four zombies rushed towards them.

"Hit 'em," he declared.

Ace flicked off the safety and squeezed off several rounds, clipping a few ghouls in the head. Two continued to race towards them, and Dante lunged forward, braining one with the crowbar as Ace took the other one out with a bullet.

With the room seemingly clear, Dante banged the crowbar on the ground again, waiting for a response. Moans and crashes erupted from the retail area, and he moved forward to the swinging double doors that led to the store.

A zombie wandered by, looking around frantically for the source of the sound. As soon as it cleared the opening, Dante held up a finger to signal to the other two to stay put. He gripped the crowbar tightly, gently opening the door and slipping out into the store.

He moved slowly towards the ghoul, sneaking up behind it as it looked around for a target. Before it could swing around to see him, he smacked it in the side of the head, sending it to the ground. It twitched around, so he stabbed the tip into its skull, ending it.

He moved up one of the aisles to the main portion of the store, a big aisle near the registers. He spotted five more zombies by the front doors, but nothing else. When he turned to go back to the doors, he saw Ace had moved in, standing at the far end of the aisle.

Dante motioned for him to stay put, then used some hand signals to let him know there were five zombies ahead, and he was going to lead them his way. Ace raised his rifle into firing position.

Dante smacked the crowbar on the ground, which immediately gained the attention of all five zombies. They screeched and raced towards him, and he whipped around and ran, staying to the right side of the moderately sized aisle to give Ace a lane to shoot.

As he grew close, the redneck unloaded.

By the time Dante reached his side and turned around, all but two of the ghouls were gone, and they were within ten yards. Ace lowered his gun and drew his knife, and he and Dante lunged forward in

unison with well-timed melee strikes to
the head, dropping them both.

"See, guns work at a distance," Dante
teased as he sheathed his blade. "They're
not like knives."

Ace rolled his eyes. "You're an
asshole, you know that?" he asked
playfully.

"So I've been told," Dante replied,
smirking as he clapped him on the back.
"Come on, let's get shopping."

They headed back to the loading dock
where Katie emerged with three shopping
carts.

"Found these in the back," she said,
separating them. "Should help us get
loaded up."

"Focus on non-perishable goods,"
Dante instructed as he took his cart. "Dry
pasta, ramen, canned goods."

Ace chuckled as he took his. "So
basically we're shopping like a broke
bitch on W.I.C.?"

Katie gaped at him, shaking her head.
"My, my," she breathed, "aren't we the
offensive one?"

"Oh honey, I'm like an offensive
onion," Ace declared, puffing out his
chest. "There are many layers to peel
back."

She rolled her eyes and shook her
head.

"Good to know we all have something to look forward to," Dante said dryly. "Now come on, let's stock up."

The trio broke apart, each taking an aisle to throw various goods into their carts, moving with haste. The quicker they got out, the better."

The shopping spree has been going on for ten minutes or so, with the back of the truck being loaded down with goods. Dante headed out of the back door with another cart load, rolling down the stairs and putting the cart next to the truck.

Ace finished up with his and glanced down into Dante's haul, raising his eyebrow. "What in the hell is that?" he demanded, pointing to all the flour and masa.

"You've never baked stuff from scratch before?" Dante replied with a shrug.

The redneck wrinkled his nose. "I mean, I've punched holes in the top of the plastic on my hungry man dinners," he drawled, "but I'm guessing that don't count?"

Dante chuckled as he started hucking bags of flour into the bed of the truck. Ace grabbed a pack of masa and studied it curiously.

"Makes great homemade tortillas," Dante explained.

Ace put up a hand. "So wait," he said, "you know how to cook, too?"

"Well, with my obvious setbacks, I have to make up for it in other areas," his companion winked his one eye.

Ace chuckled. "Shit man, Lily is gonna be all over you," he said.

"Man, you've known me less than twenty-four hours and you're ready to hitch us together," Dante said, grunting as he heaved another giant bag of flour into the truck. "Are pickings really that slim around these parts?"

The redneck shuddered. "Yeah, you should see some of the losers she's dated," he said. "If some of them had washed up on that island instead of you, they would have fed her to those things just to save themselves. You didn't even know her and you fought for her. That's good enough in my book."

"Fair enough," Dante admitted, and hefted the last bag in. He gave it a hearty smack. "Unless we're strapping stuff to the hood, I think we're full," he declared.

"Let's get Katie and get the hell out of here," Ace said.

All of a sudden there was a roar of an engine out front of the store. Both men tensed before grabbing their assault rifles and rushing back inside. They tore through the loading dock, stopping at the swinging doors.

"Head that way," Dante instructed. "You do one pass, down and back. If you find her, great. If you don't, then you get back to the truck."

Ace nodded. "What about you?" he asked.

"I'm going to have to do the same," he said, swallowing hard. "We have a lot more people relying on us than just her. They need that food."

Ace shook her head, but he knew that his companion was right. Neither of them wanted to have to leave someone behind, but there was more at stake here.

The two of them broke apart and picked a direction. Ace was almost at a dead spring, pausing only briefly at the aisles to look up them. He grew more and more frustrated with every step.

Come on girl, where the hell are you? He thought, panic rising.

When he reached the end, he still didn't see her. He hesitated at the row, spotting the fresh produce section at the top of the aisle.

Fuck, you're totally the type of girl who's all healthy, he thought, and against his better judgement, ran up the aisle, hoping she was there.

Sure enough, when he got to the end, he spotted her with her back to him, picking through the apples. At the far end of the store, the doors wedged open, and he darted for Katie. He put his hand over her mouth and dragged her down to the ground behind a center display section holding vegetables.

She struggled and panicked, protesting against his palm.

Ace held her tight and whispered in her ear, "It's me, we're in trouble. Stay quiet."

That was enough to get her to calm down, and she stopped struggling before patting him on the leg gently to remove his hand from her mouth.

They peeked out from behind their cover, down the front of the store towards the door. A moment later, half a dozen armed men entered, one barking out orders they couldn't quite make out.

"They found us," Katie hissed, eyes wide.

Ace shook his head. "They're not here for us," he whispered, pointing to one of the men grabbing some shopping carts. "They're here for food."

She nodded and turned back to him. "Well, let's not give them a reason to look for us," she whispered. She maneuvered to the other side of the display, and without warning, darted from cover, running to the far aisle.

Ace gaped at how quick she was, but then froze at the sound of a mercenary yelling, "We got contact!"

The redneck peeked out, seeing one of the men raise his assault rifle and move swiftly but carefully towards the aisle. He watched Katie get to the end of it, and take cover behind the end.

Ace readied his rifle in case the mercenary continued his pursuit, watching him reach the end of the aisle and walk slowly down it, gun raised. He checked the others, who were going about their business, but on guard.

"Report!" the man in command barked.

The mercenary in the aisle called over his shoulder, "Got a live one."

"Well put 'em down quick," the commanding officer yelled, "we got a lot of work to do!"

Ace watched the mercenary raise his weapon, taking aim at the end of the aisle. He wasn't sure if Katie was still there or not, but given the kill order he couldn't take chances, so he broke from cover.

He quickly darted across, but caught the eye of someone that yelled "Hostile!"

His target heard it and turned around just in time for Ace to shoot him in the face.

"Contact, contact!" the commanding officer screamed. "Put 'em down!"

Ace practically flew down the aisle just as another mercenary reached the top of it. His attacker started shooting immediately, forcing Ace to slide on the floor just as he got to the end. As he did, Katie reached out and grabbed his arm, pulling him behind the end cap.

He didn't speak, simply rolling over and aiming his gun, firing off several times towards the top of the aisle. He missed badly, but forced his enemy behind cover.

"Move!" Ace cried, and scrambled to his feet, taking Katie with him. They got about four aisles down when a shot ripped up the back of the store, forcing him to shove her ahead and hit the deck.

Amazingly, neither of them were hit, and he scrambled to his knees to fire up the aisle, forcing the enemy behind the other end cap. He adjusted his aim towards the first one, who had now made his way to the back aisle.

Ace managed to get off a lucky shot that hit the mercenary in the arm, causing him to drop his weapon. The redneck fired a few more times up the aisle, keeping their other attacker at bay.

"The doors to the back are just up ahead. Go!" he cried, giving her a shove before turning to keep up the suppressing fire. Eight bullets later, the gun clicked empty. "Fuck!"

He tossed the rifle down in frustration and then ran as hard as he could for the back door. He made the turn just as a mercenary in the second aisle reached the back, firing a couple of shots at him and hitting the door frame.

Ace dove through the swinging doors, hitting the ground hard before scrambling to his feet and pinning himself against the wall. He frantically pulled out his knife, sucking in deep breaths as he heard footsteps racing towards him. He took a few steps to the side to make sure that he wasn't in the way of the doors.

A moment later, a mercenary kicked his way in, and Ace swung his arm back, not getting a good look at the target, just a general idea of where he was. The blade came to an abrupt halt as it hit his enemy in the throat.

The mercenary struggled to stay on his feet as he gurgled, dropping his weapon before falling to the floor.

Ace was stunned for a second, and then snapped out of it, pulling his knife and grabbing the gun. He tore for the back door, looking down at the truck just as Katie was throwing open the passenger door.

"Is Dante there?!" Ace cried.

Katie shook her head. "No."

He hesitated, chewing his lip for a moment. He knew he needed to get the food back to the people, but he couldn't just leave Dante behind. He gripped his rifle tightly and headed back inside.

"Where are you going?" Katie called after him, but he didn't turn back or answer.

Ace moved with purpose, reaching the double doors and peeking out. He didn't see any mercenaries, so he slipped out quietly, getting across the back aisle and moving cautiously towards the front of the store.

As he grew closer, he heard several boisterous men.

"Man, check out the mug on this motherfucker," one bellowed. "You ever seen someone so ugly?"

"Not since you picked up that dude in Bangkok," another drawled.

"You know good goddamn well that was a woman," the first one snapped.

"Shit man, that's even worse!" another cried, and a chorus of laughter erupted from the half-dozen men standing around Dante.

"Now, you want to explain to me why you thought it was a good idea to shoot my men?" The commanding officer asked firmly, and Ace's eyes widened at the sight of Dant on his knees.

"I didn't start anything," Dante replied coolly. "Just finished it."

The officer shook his head, laughing. "Impressive," he admitted. "Most men in your position would be begging for their lives, not making defiant statements like that."

"Do I look like the type of person who begs for anything?" Dante asked dryly.

"With a face like that, you probably have to beg for pussy from a prostitute," one of the mercenaries said with a sneer.

Dante cocked his head. "Nah, a fiver usually does it," he replied. "Oh, and your mom says hi by the way."

The rest of the mercenaries burst into laughter at the expense of their insulted comrade.

He didn't find it so funny. "You motherfucker," he snarled, and lunged forward, landing a punch across Dante's face before his commanding officer pulled him back.

"That's enough," his superior declared. He glanced at the front door, seeing the crowd of zombies smacking against it, attracted by the gunfire. He pointed to the offended mercenary and the one next to him. "You two, go make sure that door is secure," he barked.

The duo begrudgingly walked towards the door, leaving just the officer and

three of his lackeys standing by Dante.
Ace knew he had to act fast, or else his
friend wouldn't make it out of this alive.

He looked down at his rifle, seeing a
switch on the side to change it to full
auto. He grinned and carefully moved the
selector down to it, making sure not to
make any noise.

"While I appreciate your attitude,"
the commanding officer was saying,
spreading his arms, "unfortunately my
orders are to put down any and all
resistance, so I'm afraid this will have
to be goodbye." He reached for his
holster, but before he could even pull the
gun out, Ace fired, letting out a primal
yell as he sprayed bullets.

The mercenaries didn't even know what
hit them as the bullets shredded the three
men flew backwards, made into swiss
cheese. Ace turned towards the front door,
firing at the two others, and they ducked,
sending the bullets right into the glass.

The redneck realized his mistake too
late, and the glass shattered everywhere,
quickly opening it up for the zombies to
rush through. The two mercenaries
attempted to panic fire, but were quickly
swarmed, their screams filling the room as
the creatures ripped the flesh from their
bones.

The officer whipped around and aimed his handgun at the front entrance as several ghouls bypassed the two fallen men and went straight for him. His shots were erratic, hitting torsos and little else. A couple of the creatures broke off pursuit, latching onto one of the men on the ground who was still moving.

The officer took careful aim and hit one in the head, but Dante shoved him from behind, sending the asshole face first onto the ground. Three zombies immediately leapt onto him, tearing into his body hungrily.

One of the ghouls lunged for Dante, and he used its momentum to shove it past him, getting behind it and driving it down an aisle as it thrashed about. As he passed a shelf of glass soda bottles, he grabbed one and slammed the base of it into the zombie's temple. It took a few blows before the creature clumped down, lifeless.

He paused for a moment before Ace whistled at him from the back of the aisle.

"What are you watching for, Scarface?!" he barked. "Fucking move, man!"

Dante tore for him, and the two of them raced out the back of the store. They blew out the loading down and scrambled into the truck.

"My god, what happened?" Katie gushed as Ace turned the truck on, peeling out backwards.

Dante looked down and saw the blood coating the front of him. "Don't worry, it's not mine," he replied.

Relief crossed her face, but her brow was still furrowed in concern.

Ace let out a crazed grunt as he sped along behind the store, before turning up the road. "Well, if those fuckers wasn't going to close off this area before," he declared, "they sure as shit are going to do it now."

"You realize you just took down an entire squad of highly trained mercenaries?" Dante asked wryly."

Ace laughed. "Amazing what you can do when you realize guns can fire from a distance," he retorted.

Dante patted him on the back and then turned to watch behind them as they drove over the wrong side of the bridge to avoid the pileup and get out of Beaufort. He let out a deep sigh of relief that nobody was following them.

Ace pulled into his driveway, and the rest of the group poured out of the front door to greet them. Bailey held her sisters' hands, a huge grin on her face, her mother standing behind them. Cam and Phillip turned from boarding up the last window, and Lily flew down the stairs to the truck.

"Well it's about time you boys got back," she said, crossing her arms and jutting out her hip. Her demeanor fell when she realized how defeated they looked. "What's wrong?"

Dante shook his head. "Military is gone," he said.

"Gone?" She gaped at him. "What? How?"

Katie jumped down next to Ace and ran a hand through her hair. "They were ordered to retreat," she explained. "We're on out own."

"Fuck," Lily declared. "Can't believe the base was empty."

Ace tilted his head back and forth. "Not exactly empty…"

"Yeah, some of those QXR mercenaries were there," Dante admitted, absently rubbing at his bruised ribs. "Had a bit of an issue with them."

She skirted the hood of the truck to get to him, batting his hand away to look at his side.

"Easy now," he hissed as he pressed a little too hard.

She jerked her hand back. "Sorry," she blurted, checking him over.

"It's all right," Dante assured her. "I'm all right."

She nodded, stepping back with relief.

"Wow, look at all this food!" Bailey exclaimed as she peered into the back of the truck. "You guys found a lot more stuff than we did today!"

Dante inclined his head to Cam and Phillip. "Slim pickings at the gas station?"

"Pretty much just what was on the shelves," Cam replied. "That back room was so empty they could have rented it out as an apartment."

Dante leaned on the truck. "Well, we got enough here that should hold us over for a while." He waved his hand. "Come on, let's get it all inside."

Everyone pitched in and unloaded the truck, stacking the goods in the spare room in the house. After they got everything situated, the group slowly filed into the living room.

"Now, I'm a firm believer in being up front with everyone," Dante said as he stood facing the couch. "It doesn't do anybody any good to be in the dark about our situation, regardless of how bad it is."

"Hey, if it's okay," Cam said from the doorway, "I'm going to get the girls set up in the back bedroom with a movie." He waved around a DVD. "They probably don't need to hear this."

Bailey nodded and smiled. "That's a good idea," she said.

"Hey buddy, bring that over here, will you?" Ace asked, his brow furrowing.

Cam headed over, holding out the disk. "Hope you don't mind," he said. "I saw a stack of DVDs and looked through it. Thought the kids might like to watch Snow White."

"You might be right on that," the redneck drawled, "but you really need to double check the full titles of the movies in this house." He handed it back, and Cam pursed his lips, squinting and reading *Snow White and the Seven Loads.*

He blinked at it. "Oh… I… Um…" he stammered. "I'm so sorry."

"Yeah, pretty safe bet that if it's in this house, it isn't going to be appropriate for kids," Lily said, rolling her eyes.

Ace jerked a thumb over his shoulder. "Don't worry, one of the houses down the street had some kids," he said. "After we talk, we'll run down there and find something good for the tykes."

"Girls, why don't you go back into that back bedroom and play together for a few minutes?" Abigail suggested. "Don't touch any of Mr. Ace's things."

The girls nodded and obediently left, heading down the hallway.

"Okay, to put it bluntly," Dante said, clearing his throat once the girls were gone, "we're in trouble. The military is gone, they evacuated to somewhere that isn't here, and mercenaries have taken over. Both Hilton Head and Beaufort and under their control."

Lily raised a finger. "Which eliminates Bluffton as well, since it's right on the other side of the bridge from Hilton Head."

"That puts us behind the eight ball, because we need supplies," Dante continued. "Not just food and water, but we need to start fortifying this town, not just the house. Sooner or later a pack of those things, or unfriendly people, are going to come through here. We have to be prepared for that."

Ace clucked his tongue. "More than likely we're gonna have to pull from homes instead of stores," he suggested. "Lot of small towns nearby, but nothing like Bluffton or Beaufort. I mean, Savannah is an hour away, but it has to be a grade-A shitshow by this point."

"We gotta stay small," Dante agreed. "Which makes this next task even more difficult. We have to find a sustainable source of food and water. The supplies we got from the store will buy us a few weeks, and I'm assuming we're going to find stuff in nearby houses, but it's not going to sustain us very long."

Lily raised an eyebrow. "So, what, you want us to be farmers now?" she asked.

"If that's the case, then we're all in trouble," Ace declared. "Lily's thumb is so brown that she kills plastic plants."

"As if you're any better," she shot back.

Dante shook his head. "Well, if that's the case, then we'd better ad library to the list of targets, because we need someone who knows how to grow things," he said.

"Grow things…" Ace trailed off and then blinked as if he'd had a lightbulb moment. "Holy shit, I got it!"

Lily's eyes widened. "No. Just… fuck... NO." She waved her hands back and forth in front of her face.

Ace shot her an apologetic look, but nodded.

"Who is it?" Dante asked.

Lily buried her face in her hands. "My ex," she mumbled through her fingers.

"Oh," Dante replied lamely.

Ace kicked up his feet, crossing them at the ankles on the coffee table. "Maddox, owner of the biggest indoor pot farm in Hardeeville, South Carolina," he announced.

"Probably the only indoor pot farm in Hardeeville," Lily muttered, lowering her hands.

Dante sighed. "I'm sorry, but if he knows how to grow things," he said gently, "we're going to need him if we're going to survive."

"Yeah, I know," she replied, grunting with frustration. "Just… he's a fucking douchebag. Ten minutes ago, I would be cheering the thought of him being gnawed on by zombies, and now we gotta go beg for his help."

Ace winked at her. "Don't worry Lil," he drawled, "you got a big strong man over there to protect you from him."

"Protect me?" she snapped. "Hell, I could kick Maddox's ass six ways from Sunday. Now, if someone can make me deaf so I don't have to listen to his dumb ass, *that* would be helpful."

Dante stifled a laugh. "How far away is Hardeeville?" he asked.

"About half an hour south of here," Lily replied.

He checked his watch. "It's getting a little late to be venturing out," he said.

"And I think we've seen enough chaos and death for one day," Katie added.

He nodded. "Ace, what do you say we go clear out one of your neighbor's houses, and see what they got?" he asked.

"Momma, you wanna help me in the kitchen?" Bailey asked, getting to her feet. "We'll get something cooked up for everyone."

"Look for the blue cooler in there," Katie piped up. "I know we were supposed to focus on dry goods, but I figured some steaks wouldn't hurt."

Ace pointed at her, staring at Dante. "I like this one," he whispered loudly as he joined him. Lily trotted after them, pushing through to lead the way across the neighbor's yard.

"So, you dated a drug dealer, huh?" Dante asked, unable to keep a straight face.

Ace snorted. "I told you man, string of losers," he drawled.

Lily nodded, but then it dawned on her that he was referring to her boyfriends. "You told him *what*?" she demanded, shoving his shoulder. "Have you been talking about my dating life?" She looked to Dante, who put up his palms.

"He brought it up unprovoked," he assured her.

Ace opened his mouth, but Lily smacked him, and he squealed before playfully running away. "Hope you like the violent type, Scarface!" he bellowed.

"I'm gonna kick your ass!" Lily shrieked, chasing him around in the grass.

Dante watched them, laughing, enjoying the much-needed lighthearted way to finish the day.

END

Up Next: With the realization that they are truly on their own setting in, Dante and the others venture out in hopes of making contact with other survivors in Lowcountry pt. 4

DEAD AMERICA

LOWCOUNTRY

PART 4

BY DEREK SLATON

© 2021

CHAPTER ONE

Day Zero +3

The sun barely peeked over the horizon when the noise began. Dante opened his eye, waiting a moment for it to adjust to the dim light. He couldn't quite make out the sound… it was almost as if someone was moving in another part of the house.

He looked around, doing a quick head count of his companions. Cam and Phillip slept by the TV. Bailey was on the couch, and Lily sprawled across the floor beside Katie, who was clustered up against the stove to avoid the splayed limbs.

Dante listened hard, straining his ears, but didn't hear Abigail or her girls moving. And while he had only known Ace for a couple of days, he couldn't imagine the redneck had ever been this quiet in his life.

The noise persisted, a shuffling combined with light tapping. He jumped at a loud *BANG* and sat up straight. The others stirred in the living room, but he hopped up, rushing past them to the window. He peered through the gaps in the wood that Cam and Phillip had put up the day before. The sun was up just enough that he could see movement by Ace's window.

Two zombies stood there, smacking on the wood blocking Ace's bedroom. Dante sighed with relief. It was only two, and the boys had done a good job of securing the outside of the house.

Movement tickled his periphery and his relief quickly flew from him as three more ghouls raced out from behind the trees at the edge of the yard. They ran straight for their brethren, joining in on the banging on the side of the house.

The impact roused everyone that had still been sleeping in the living room. Dante's brow furrowed at another zombie, moving much slower than the others instead of at a dead sprint.

"What's going on?" Cam asked groggily.

Dante turned away from the window. "Unwanted visitors."

"Just tell them to come back later," Cam moaned, throwing an arm over his face, and then sat up straight, fear in his eyes as it clicked that they were in the middle of a zombie apocalypse, and the people outside weren't salesmen. He shook Phillip. "Get up man, get up!" he urged.

His companion rolled towards him, propping his arm up on his elbows. "Dude, are you kidding me right now?" he whined.

The pounding on the side of the house intensified, and Cam shook his head.

"Dante, what is it?" Lily asked, rubbing sleep from her eyes as she emerged from the kitchen.

"Ace's room," Dante replied.

She looked around, grabbing a big butcher knife from the counter and heading down the hall with him to her cousin's room. As they moved down the hallway, Abigail opened the spare room's door.

"Is everything okay?" she asked.

Dante nodded. "Everything's fine," he replied gently, "just some early morning visitors. Just stay in your room for a bit while we handle it."

Abigail nodded and Bailey approached, slipping inside and kneeling next to her sisters' cot.

"Don't worry," she said firmly to the terrified girls, "Dante's going to protect us."

The kids looked up at him and he gave them a nod, and then Abigail shut the door.

Dante paused at Ace's door and side-glanced his companion. "Do we knock, or what?" he asked.

"Depends," Lily replied with a smirk, "does Ace strike you as the type of person you want to just walk in on unannounced?"

Dante immediately shook his head. "I've seen enough horror for the last few days," he declared. "Let's give him a few minutes to cover up."

Lily laughed and banged her fist on the door. "Get your ass up boy, we got a situation!" she barked. There was no sound from the room other than the consistent smacking of the zombies. She furrowed her brow and pounded again. "Ace, open up, cuz!" she yelled.

There was still no answer, and they shared a concerned glance, and Dante slowly turned the doorknob. He pushed it open, the door creaking as he carefully revealed whatever sight awaited them inside.

The duo recoiled at the sight of Ace sprawled on the bed, stretching over the entirety of the queen-sized mattress, wearing only a tattered pair of tighty whities. He wore a large set of headphones, a long cord connecting them to a CD player on the side table.

The banging on the window was loud, but they could hear the music blaring from the headphones over it.

"It's a wonder he's not deaf," Dante muttered, looking away from the scantily clad redneck.

Lily rolled her eyes. "You check our guests," she said, "I'll awaken sleeping beauty."

"Good luck," he said wryly, and headed for the window. He peered through the slats, seeing the five zombies right outside. Four of them were right up against the window, banging away, while the fifth slow one was just reaching the group.

Lily grabbed Ace's leg with both hands, and gave it a good shake, acting like it was a zombie clutching him just before biting.

The sensation startled Ace awake, who began flailing about in a panic. He screamed and tore the headphones from his head, scrabbling to the head of the bed, eyes wide.

"What in the holy motherfucking shitballs are you doing, woman?!" he cried when he realized it was just his cousin. "I thought I was getting eaten!"

She wrinkled her nose. "With the way your tighty-whities are stained, they'd really have to be slumming it," she said, clucking her tongue.

He looked down, realizing how exposed he was, and hopped away from the bed to find a pair of jeans on the floor. He threw them on, zipping up as he looked around, confused. "What the hell is that noise?" he asked.

"Zombies," Dante replied.

Ace blinked, just realizing that the bigger man was in the room too, but headed over to the window to survey the situation. He peeked through the slats, scanning the ghouls.

"Holy shit, that's the Robinsons," he muttered, looking over the older couple with three teenagers. Everyone but the woman had visible bite marks on them.

"You know them?" Lily asked, approaching them.

Ace nodded. "Yeah, they had that house at the edge of town," he explained, motioning vaguely. "Built it a few years back."

"Guessing that's not one we cleared?" Dante asked.

The redneck shook his head. "I didn't think we needed to," he admitted. "The morning this all started, I saw a big ole SUV pulling out of the driveway and hauling ass outta town."

"Looks like whoever left, it wasn't them," Lily murmured.

"Well, obviously, Lil," Ace said, rolling his eyes.

Ignoring him, she peered through the wood to get a good look at them. "Judging by the looks of them, the momma keeled over and took the rest of them with her," she said.

"Met Fred there a few times," Ace declared. "He always struck me as a bit of a wuss. No surprise he got eaten up by his wife."

Lily crossed her arms. "Apparently his kids didn't fare much better."

"There any other houses you think are empty but we didn't check?" Dante asked.

Ace shrugged. "Well hell, based on this, I think we need to check the rest of 'em," he suggested. "There's one more beside their house, and two more on the other side of the gas station. I saw 'em leave that morning, but now that I think about it, they could have left someone behind."

Dante nodded in agreement.

"Well, that's going to have to be after breakfast," Lily cut in, still looking out the window. "We gotta figure out what to do about these five first."

Ace cracked a smile and headed for the closet. He rummaged around for a few moments and then returned with a large medieval looking sword.

Dante and Lily blinked at him as he held it up in a victory pose.

"Okay King Arthur," Lily drawled, "what in the hell are you planning on doing with that thing? No. Wait. Scratch that." She held up a finger. "First question. Why in the hell do you have that?"

Ace grinned. "You remember a few years back when I was dating Betty-Sue?" he asked.

"Yeah?" she replied, raising an eyebrow.

"Well, she dragged me to one of those renaissance fairs down near Savannah," he explained, "and let's just say I got caught up in it. Saw this on the way out and just had to have it."

Lily crossed her arms. "Somehow I doubt that a sword from a renaissance fair is going to be a viable weapon," she said dryly.

He pointed it up and touched the tip of his finger to the pointy end, playfully recoiling as if it were incredibly sharp. "I know I'm not going to hack through them," he admitted. "But this thing is solid enough that a direct shot to the face should do some damage."

"It looks thin enough to get through the wooden openings," Dante added. "Can't hurt to try."

Lily stared at him, eyebrows raised, disbelieving that the tall man would buy into her cousin's ridiculousness. Dante just smiled and shrugged.

"Yeah, I know, I'm just as shocked as you are," he admitted.

She shook her head and chuckled, turning towards the window and sliding it open. The noise intensified as she did so, the zombies' moaning accompanying the loud banging. Their thrashing grew more excited when they realized they were so close to a fresh meal.

"Well, let's see if this works," Ace said, and put the tip of the sword on one of the wooden boards, lining up his shot with a face. One of the teenage zombies had pushed its way to the front of the pack, its face missing a good chunk of flesh from the cheek.

Ace readied himself, getting into position, and then thrusting forward. The sword slid perfectly through the opening, the tip of the blade piercing the zombie's rheumy eye.

The creature convulsed for a moment before sliding off of the blade and down to the ground, only to be immediately replaced by one of its family members.

Ace pulled the gooey sword back inside, shooting his cousin a triumphant smile. "Ren fair for the win, what what?!" he declared.

She rolled her eyes, leaning against the wall. "Yeah, yeah," she said flippantly.

He lined up another shot, this time on the ghoul that used to be Fred

Robinson. "All right, time to put you out of your misery," he cooed, and then thrust again.

The blade cracked through the bridge of the zombie's nose, entering into its skull. As the heavier ghoul fell limp, it didn't dislodge from the sword, and when Ace tried to pull on it, he couldn't get it back out.

"Son of a bitch, let go Fred!" Ace bellowed.

The remaining zombies outside thrashed about, putting weight on Fred as they tried to get at the source of the noise. One of them pushed down, causing the sword to bend. It didn't take much more pressure for the blade to snap in two, leaving the broadsword a short sword.

Ace pulled the busted hilt back inside and stared at it for a moment before tossing it over his shoulder back towards the closet.

"Well, got my money's worth out of it at least," he drawled. "Well… technically I got my money's worth out of it after the ren fair because Betty-Sue was all into that medieval shit. That night we—"

"Stop talking," Lily cut in, putting up a hand. "I just watched you impale two zombies, but if you finish your thought, I'm going to throw up."

Ace chuckled and turned to Dante. "What do you say," he said, "you wanna go finish them off outside so we can have some breakfast in peace?"

"Lead the way," Dante replied, motioning for the door.

The redneck nodded. "We'll head out the back and stop by the shed," he said. "Got another idea of something I've always wanted to try."

"Three of us should be able to take them out pretty easily," Lily added.

Dante cocked his head. "Actually, I'd like you to stay here."

"Don't go getting all protective on me now," she replied with a pout.

He raised his hands. "I would never dream of it," he promised. "But they're fixated on us right now. I just want you to hold their attention while we come around behind them."

She smirked and gave him a playful punch on the arm. "Just giving you a hard time," she replied. "I'll keep them occupied." She winked at him and then stood in front of the window, making silly faces at the zombies clamoring to eat her through the wood.

Ace led Dante out through the living room, where the other three were perched on the couch, looking nervously all around.

"Is everything okay?" Katie asked.

Dante nodded. "Yeah, just a few of the neighbors paying a visit," he said. "We should only be a couple minutes, so you guys hang tight."

The trio nodded, and the two men headed through the kitchen. Dante grabbed a handgun from the counter as they went, pausing at the back door to make sure there weren't any more unwanted guests. Ace peered around too, and thankfully the backyard was empty.

Dante inclined his head towards the small wooden tool shed at the back. "So, you got something useful in there?" he asked.

"Oh yeah, and better than that, I already have an idea!" Ace declared.

His companion raised his eyebrow. "Color me impressed," he admitted, "and terrified."

Ace laughed and opened the door. The two of them darted over to the shed, the redneck slipping inside while Dante kept watch. There was a clamor in the shed before Ace emerged, holding a giant pitchfork and a sledgehammer.

Dante stared at him for a moment. "Really?" he finally asked.

"Oh yeah, really!" Ace replied with a huge grin on his face. He held up the pitchfork, which had foot-long spikes at the end. He handed over the sledgehammer.

Dante took it and tested its considerable weight in his hand. "So what's the plan?" he asked.

"Those things are pressed up against the wall, right?" the redneck asked. "Well, I figure if I get up a head of steam, I should be able to punch through them with this and hold them in place while you go all Gallagher on them."

Dante chuckled. "Little early for a Sledge-O-Matic reference, but we'll roll with it," he said.

Ace gave him a little salute and then took a wide turn around the house, Dante close behind. They went out to the far edge of the grass, a good thirty yards away from the zombies that were still stacked at the window.

Ace moved forward, but Dante grabbed his arm, holding him back.

"What's up?" the redneck whispered. "You see something?"

Dante shook his head. "I don't know," he murmured.

"Okay?" Ace asked.

His companion sighed. "Sorry," he whispered. "Just, when they were running up, the girl zombie on the right side there was moving slow."

"How slow?" Ace asked.

Dante tilted his head back and forth. "I mean, faster than I would have liked," he admitted, "but about half the speed as the others." He watched closely, staring at the ghoul, seeing it was even hitting the window a bit slower than the others who were still at full speed.

"I mean, I got a video camera in the house if you want me to run and get it," Ace teased quietly.

Dante shook his head. "No, I'm good."

"Okay, with the way they're stacked up, I should be able to pin two of them together," the redneck whispered, miming the motion with the pitchfork. "I'll hold them in place while you deal with the third. Sound good?"

Dante nodded. "Lead the way," he said.

The two of them broke out and raced towards the zombies. The grass softened their footsteps, and Lily started to yell as they approached to muffle their noise even more.

"Yeah, you want a piece of this, you limp-dicked dead fucks?!" she bellowed.

Ace held the pitchfork out like it was a jousting lance, picking up speed and aiming it for the torso of the teenage zombie in the back. There were two of them stacked up perfectly behind one another, while the slower ghoul was to the right.

Ace let out a scream as he thrust, jamming the business end of his weapon through the back of the rear zombie so hard that it went all the way through to the front one. They didn't even notice, continuing to focus on Lily's taunting.

The slow zombie *did* notice them, however, and turned to the redneck. Before it could fully lean towards Ace, Dante grabbed the back of its shirt and took several steps away from the window before throwing the corpse into the yard.

"What the hell are you doing?" Ace cried.

"Get them on the ground!" Dante barked.

The redneck shook his head and pulled the ghouls away from the window. He wrenched the pitchfork to the side, causing them to tumble onto the grass. He leaned forward, skewering them into the grass.

Dante swung the hammer down forcefully, driving the weighted end through the back of the top zombie's skull and right into the second one. The single blow was enough to kill both, and the two corpses twitched before falling limp.

As soon as they stopped moving, Ace jerked the pitchfork free and swung around to face the third zombie. He relaxed and furrowed his brow when he saw that not only was it not running towards him, it was struggling to even get to its feet.

Dante rested the blood-soaked sledgehammer over his shoulder, cocking his head. "Good to see I'm not crazy."

"Motherfucker, you crazy as hell!" Ace declared. "Just throwing that thing down behind us on a hunch?"

His companion shrugged. "Figure it was worth the risk," he said.

"How the hell do you figure?" the redneck challenged.

Dante motioned to the zombie. "If these things are slowing down, don't you think that would be useful information to have?" he asked.

Ace wrinkled his nose, but finally nodded. "How do you know she didn't just break her leg or some shit?" he muttered petulantly.

"That's why we gotta watch," Dante replied, "and see what we see."

They stared at it, watching as it finally got its legs under it and shambled in their direction. It seemed to be a half-hearted speedwalk, and they studied its legs, seeing no bones sticking out or anything looking out of place.

"You see anything?" Dante asked.

Ace shook his head. "Just a fucked-up bitch who needs her head caved in."

His companion nodded in agreement and stepped closer to the zombie. He used the top of the sledgehammer to smash her in the chest, sending her tumbling back to the grass. He raised the hammer high and brought it down on her skull with a wet *squelch*.

"What the hell was that all about?" Lily screeched through the slats in the window.

Ace jerked his thumb over his shoulder. "Ask your man there," he drawled.

Dante knelt down, looking over the dead ghoul to see if there was any special damage that could have caused it to be slow.

"What's going on?" Lily called. "What do you see?"

He stood up, shaking his head, and simply said, "Hope."

The group clustered around in the living room, mowing down on pancakes and scrambled eggs. Abigail emerged from the kitchen with a steaming hot pan.

"Who needs more eggs?" she asked.

Ace and Bailey both held out their empty plates, and she dished out heaps of eggs before turning and dumping the rest onto Lily's plate.

She nodded and offered the older woman a smile. "Thank you."

"You're welcome, dear," Abigail replied and headed back into the kitchen, getting rid of her pan and re-entering with a plate for herself.

"So, are you still dead set on going to see Maddox today?" Lily asked, scooping up a forkful of egg.

Her cousin nodded. "Yeah, Dante was right about the food situation," he said through a mouthful of pancakes, spitting crumbs everywhere, much to Bailey's disgust. "So unless you magically learned how to be a farmer last night, we're going to need someone who knows how to grow."

Lily shook her head, letting out an exasperated sigh.

"If you don't want to go," Dante piped up as he studied the sullen expression on her face, "Ace and I can handle it."

She wrinkled her nose. "Thanks, but…" She sighed again. "If that slimy-ass fucker is still alive, I'm going to have to deal with him sooner or later. Might as well get it over with."

"Do you want Phillip and me to tag along today?" Cam asked, holding up a hand.

Ace shook his head. "Nope, you boys got some chores to do in our absence," he declared.

Phillip groaned. "Chores?" he asked. "Really?"

"You can call it whatever you want," the redneck replied. "But shit needs to get done around here."

Dante leaned forward, setting down his fork. "You two did a great job fortifying the house, but now we need you to do it to some of the neighbor's houses as well," he explained. "As much as I like you people, having six of us in the living room isn't exactly a long term sleeping solution."

The boys nodded begrudgingly.

"But what about zombies?" Phillip asked. "Didn't you say those ones you killed this morning were your neighbors?"

Ace jerked a thumb over his shoulder. "We'll handle that before we go," he explained. "While Miss Abigail was cooking, I checked the remaining houses. Only one on the other side of the gas station had some in there. Once we get that cleared, this town is ours."

"So which house do we start at?" Cam asked.

Ace and Dante shared a quick glance, and the redneck shrugged.

"The house across the street has a fence," Dante suggested. "It's a small chain link one, but it's better than nothing. Get that boarded up and see if you can't get something to block off the road and yards up to Ace's. If we have any more visitors, it would be nice to have them waiting on the perimeter instead of knocking on our bedroom windows."

The redneck nodded. "A-fucking-men to that," he drawled.

They finished up their breakfast and set their plates down. Lily started shoveling her food into her mouth to catch up.

"Take your time," Dante assured her with a smile, and she nodded in thanks.

"From best I can tell, there was just one of those things in the last house," Ace piped up. "Scarface and I can handle it. You just be ready to go when we get back. Bit of a haul down to Hardeeville."

She nodded and gave Dante's arm a small squeeze before he passed her.

The duo grabbed their farm tool weapons from the porch and headed to the road, walking towards their target house. The morning had turned out fairly nice, a bit cool with the breeze, with the sun warming their faces.

"Fucking zombies, man," Ace declared.

Dante raised his eyebrow. "Is that in general, or do you have something specific to curse them about?" he asked.

"Football, man," the redneck whined. "Perfect weather for grilling in the backyard before the games started. Then sitting on my ass for twelve straight hours with the case of beer by my side, stuffing my face while watching grown men give each other concussions. It is a bonafide tragedy that I'm not going to be able to do that this season…" His eyes widened and his face went pale. "Or *any* season." He scrubbed his hands down his face. "Fuck, it's really gone, isn't it?"

Dante nodded solemnly. "Afraid it is, buddy," he replied. "Afraid it is."

"You a big football fan?" Ace asked, taking a deep breath in his misery. "Seattle has a hell of a team."

His companion shook his head. "I would watch a bit whenever Grace was over," he replied. "She was a die hard fan, never missed a game. I was kind of indifferent."

"So your sister's a fan, huh?" the redneck asked, cocking a brow. "She ever drag you to a game so you could tailgate?"

Dante chuckled. "We talked about it a few times," he admitted, "but Grace isn't what you'd call a morning person."

"Oh man, you are missing out!" Ace moaned. "Well, just like I'm being your wingman for Lil, I'm going to help you out here, too." He ignored Dante's snort and continued, "I still got a couple of games on the DVR, so tomorrow morning, I'm gonna get up early and we're gonna do a proper tailgate. We're gonna grill whatever we can find, drink a few beers before breakfast, and then sit down and watch us a football game. Gotta take advantage of that shit while we can."

His companion chuckled and nodded. "I appreciate that, man," he replied. "And you're right, we gotta get in that TV watching while we still have power."

"Fucking fuck," Ace stammered, smacking his thigh. "I didn't even think about the power. I was talking about the beer running out."

Dante shrugged. "Unless there's a direct attack, the power plant should be okay for a few more days," he said. "Maybe even a week on its own. Of course, we might actually have power for a while, thanks to the QXR guys. They probably got people addressing that as we speak."

"Here's hoping," Ace said. "I think one of my neighbors has a generator or two, and the gas station got refueled a few weeks back. It would get us through in a pinch, but it would be loud as hell." They reached the target house, and he held his pitchfork high. "But, one problem at a time."

"This the house?" Dante asked.

The redneck nodded. "Yep."

Dante took a deep breath. "So, how do you want to do this?"

"I looked in through the front window and saw it wandering around the living room," Ace replied. "Checked the other windows and didn't see anything, so this is probably it."

Dante studied the front door, noting that it was elevated at the top of four brick steps. He cracked a smile. "You like physical comedy?" he asked.

"Physical comedy?" Ace blinked at him. "Oh, you mean like when people fall down and shit? Hell yeah, I do!"

His companion motioned for him to stay put. "I got an idea," he said.

They reached the front door, and Dante reached for the knob, but then stopped. He bent over and pulled up the welcome mat, finding a key beneath.

"Gotta love small towns," he murmured, and slid it into the lock as quietly as he could. He turned the bolt softly, and then wrapped his hand around the knob, glancing at Ace.

The redneck stood several feet away from the stairs, pitchfork at the ready. Dante nodded and then threw open the door.

"Knock, knock!" he yelled.

A zombie moaned and tore for him, arms outstretched. He jumped out of the way at the last section, and it ran straight ahead, not comprehending the stairs, immediately falling down onto its face.

Before it could scramble to its feet, Ace drove the pitchfork into its back, pinning it to the ground. It writhed and flailed and tried to squirm away, but Dante was quick with the sledgehammer, bringing it down hard to crush its skull.

As soon as the corpse fell limp, both men dissolved into laughter.

"That is one dumb son of a bitch," Ace declared through his gasps. "Of course he wasn't that bright when he was alive, either."

Dante waved for him to follow. "Let's clear the house just to be safe," he suggested.

The duo headed inside, moving swiftly through the rooms, knocking on any closed doors and listening for sound. A moment later they rejoined each other in the front hall, finding nothing else.

Ace led them into the kitchen, opening up the fridge and finding a case of beer. "Good news, we're set up to tailgate tomorrow," he said, pulling out the case with a flourish.

"Well, let's get this meet and greet with Maddox out of the way so we can start prepping," Dante said, and they sauntered outside, heading back to collect Lily.

Ace, Dante, and Lily piled into the truck, the latter in the middle. The rest of the group stood on the porch, watching them.

"Get what you can done today," Dante called through the open passenger window. "If there's any trouble, you get in the house and stay there. We'll handle it when we get back. Everybody good on that?"

There were nods all around, and Ace fired up the truck, waving. He did a burnout as he pulled out of the yard, fishtailing a bit on the road as he headed for the highway, making the turn south.

"So how far is this place again?" Dante asked.

Ace tilted his head back and forth. "Should take half an hour to get there," he replied. "Hardeeville is only about fifteen miles or so, but Maddox has himself a little hideaway down by the river. Got to do a bit of off-roading to get to his place."

"If he's that far off the grid, there's a good chance he's still alive," Dante said.

Lily scoffed. "He's a cockroach in human form," she drawled, "that's how he's still alive."

"Guessing things didn't end amicably?" Dante asked, avoiding her gaze.

There was a long pause, and Ace finally chuckled.

"You can tell him Lil," he assured her. "I don't think he's gonna run away."

Dante raised his eyebrow. "That bad, huh?"

"Yeah," she replied with a sigh, "I caught him in bed with my cousin."

Dante wrinkled his nose. "Yikes."

"Oh, that's not all," she replied with a dark laugh. "I grabbed a knife from the kitchen and proceeded to chase his naked ass down the street, yelling that I would cut it off and feed it to him if I ever saw him again."

Dante blinked at her, and then a smile broke out on his face. "So what you're saying is, I should do the talking when we get there?" he asked.

"Unless he's uncooperative," she amended, crossing her arms, "at which point, I can jump in."

"Good to know we have a negotiator with us," Dante declared, and the trio erupted into laughter.

The road was nearly empty towards Hardeeville, save for a single overturned car a few miles outside of town.

"How big is this town, anyway?" Dante asked.

Ace shrugged. "Just a few thousand, and it's spread out pretty good," he replied. "Still, we're not going to chance it. I know the back roads good enough to get us there without going near the center of town."

He pulled off of the highway onto a country road, driving for a few miles before hitting the river. The view was beautiful, with tall grass complimenting the water and blowing in the breeze.

"A shame we didn't bring our fishing poles," Dante said. "Looks like a nice day for it."

"Well, if we get Maddox on our side, I'm sure he has a private spot for you to get your fishing fix," Ace replied. "If you think I'm a country boy, *whooo*, you ain't seen nothing yet."

He drove along a small road running near the river for a few miles. Dante soaked in the beauty, which he knew was going to be in short supply that day, or really for the foreseeable future. Eventually, the truck slowed to a crawl in the middle of the road.

"It's still a little further up," Lily said.

Her cousin shook his head. "Nah, we're close, Lil," he insisted.

"I'm telling you, the turnoff is still a ways up," she snapped.

Ace rolled his eyes. "And *I'm* telling *you* that ever since you threatened to feed his foot long to him, that he put in a new entrance," he replied.

She scoffed again. "Foot long?" She clucked her tongue. "That thing barely qualified as a lil' smokie."

Dante chuckled under his breath.

"There it is!" Ace cried, and turned off of the road, rolling through a narrow ditch through a small opening in the trees. As soon as they cleared it, they found themselves on a dirt road that wove its way through the forest.

"Pretty impressive for a small town drug dealer," Dante said. "If you didn't know what you were looking for you'd drive right past it."

Lily nodded. "My guess is, that was his brother's doing," she said. "Tate ain't a lot of things, but he has their security on lockdown."

"Yeah, no shit," Ace agreed, pointing up ahead at an eight-foot tall fence with barbed wire coming across the road and weaving into the woods. There was a call box by the entrance.

Lily's eyebrows raised as she appraised the setup. "Looks like they've really upgraded their operation," she said.

"Either that or Maddox is extremely protective of his…" Dante paused and smirked. "Ahem. Goods."

Lily laughed as Ace pulled up to the call box. He reached out and hit the button, and it ran a few times before a hoarse voice floated through the speaker.

"Sorry, but we're not entertaining company at the moment," somebody said in a slow, lazy drawl. "However, if you're a customer, please note that we now only accept canned goods and nudie magazines. Tell me what you got, and I'll tell you what you can get."

Ace furrowed his brow. "Who in the hell is this?" he demanded

"This is Henry man," the guy said brightly. "Now what can I get you?"

"You can get me Maddox," the redneck said firmly. "That's what you can get."

There was a sigh through the speaker. "Aw man," Henry whined, "he's like, in the other room and stuff."

"Then go get him," Ace demanded.

"Well, I… uh…" Henry stammered.

"Now!" Ace yelled.

"All right, all right," the stoner drawled with another sigh. "Just chill, man. Who should I say is calling?"

The redneck leaned his head against the headrest. "Tell him it's Ace."

Henry snorted. "You're named after a playing card."

Ace put a hand to his forehead, shaking his head. He was just about to yell again when the line clicked off. After half a minute, he grunted in frustration.

"That dumbass has about ten seconds before I drive on through this fence and whoop his ass," he growled.

Dante chuckled. "Might need to give him a little more time than that," he suggested. "He didn't sound like he could find the couch he was lying on."

"Maddox's stuff isn't for the faint of heart, that's for damn sure," Ace muttered.

Finally the call box clicked on, and an irritated voice came through. "Who in the hell is this?" Maddox snapped. "I just wanna know whose ass to whoop next time I see 'em."

"Boy, you've been trying since eighth grade to get the best of me," Ace said playfully. "Didn't happen then, ain't gonna happen today."

"Holy shit, is that Ace?" came the surprised reply.

The redneck rolled his eyes. "Who the fuck else would be coming to see your dumb ass in the middle of a zombie apocalypse?" he asked.

"Zombie *what*?" Maddox said with a laugh. "Shit man, I was gonna offer you something to smoke, but it sounds like you've been toking it up already."

Ace shook his head. "I wish," he replied. "So, you gonna let me in so I can tell you what's going on?"

"Yeah, come on up, brother," the dealer replied, and the call box buzzed as the gate slowly moved open.

Ace hit the gas when the door was clear and sped down the dirt road towards the house. They came around a bend into a clearing with a double-wide trailer sitting about fifty yards away from the river. To one side was a large greenhouse that was twice the size of the trailer.

Off to the side facing the water were three large solar panel arrays with cables leading to the buildings.

Dante blinked, reluctantly impressed. "The weed business must be booming for him to be able to afford all that," he said.

"Living in the middle of nowhere it's either pot or meth," Ace explained, "and luckily there's a lot of health conscious people in town."

Lily nodded. "There's also an art school up the road in Savannah," she added, "which doesn't hurt sales either."

The trio got out of the truck, and she hung back a bit, walking behind them as Maddox stepped out of the trailer, flanked by two men and a woman.

"It's been a while, brother," Maddox said, spreading his arms.

Ace shrugged. "Yeah, it's been a minute."

"Now, why you been treating me like a stranger, huh?" the dealer asked.

Lily stepped out from behind Dante, crossing her arms and raising an eyebrow.

Maddox's smile dropped from his face immediately. "Oh. Yeah."

"Really?" she asked. "That's all you have to say?"

"You better check your attitude, skank!" the woman next to Maddox stepped forward, pointing a finger as her disheveled hair poofed around her head.

Lily tongued her cheek. "Excuse the fuck outta me, Miss Trailer Park Queen," she snapped.

"Bitch, what you just call me?!" the woman shrieked, and took another step forward.

Maddox grabbed her around the waist, and Lily moved towards her too, but Ace caught her wrist to stop her.

"Ladies, as much as my redneck heart would love to see a full-on catfight," Ace drawled, "we have a situation on our hands."

The dealer pulled his pouting woman against him, brushing her bangs off of her forehead. "He's right baby," he cooed. "Why don't you go smoke a bowl and calm down?"

She glared at Lily before snaking her arms around Maddox's neck, practically devouring his mouth in a show of possessiveness before flouncing off into the trailer, slamming the door behind her.

"Still slumming it, I see," Lily said dryly.

Ace pinched her shoulder, shaking his head. She rolled her eyes, but kept her mouth shut.

One of the pie-eyed guys, presumably Henry, stared wide-eyed at Dante's face, and Tate smacked him in the back of the head.

"Boy, it ain't polite to be starin'!" he hissed. "Man's been through some shit, just let him be with it." He looked apologetically at Dante, who responded with a nod.

"I'm…" Henry stammered, shaking his head and looking at the ground. "I'm sorry, sir."

Dante smiled softly. "It's all right."

"Who's your new friend here, Ace?" Maddox asked.

"Oh, him?" the redneck motioned to his large friend. "This is Dante. He's a big ole badass who found his way to my doorstep."

Maddox stepped up, cocking his head. "Big ole badass, huh?" he asked. "So what makes you so big and bad?"

"I'm humble," Dante replied with a smirk, "so you'll just have to stick around and watch me in action."

The dealer chuckled. "Okay, come on now, I'm gonna need more than that," he drawled. "Like what would you do if I grabbed your—" He snatched a fistful of Dante's shirt, and the bigger man smacked his arm away, catching him around the throat with his free hand.

Maddox blinked up at him in shock and then grinned.

Tate rubbed his forehead, shaking his head.

"Yep," Maddox choked out, "pretty good."

"I think my dumbass brother gets the point," Tate suggested, scratching the back of his head.

Dante smirked and let go.

Maddox sucked in a lungful and coughed before giving him a thumbs up. "I like him," he said hoarsely, and then cleared his throat. "Okay. So, you wanna tell me what you're doing down here? I'm guessing with your zombie comment it's not because you need drugs."

"We've just been referring to them as zombies since it's as good an explanation as any," Ace explained.

Tate cocked his head. "What makes you say that?" he asked.

"Have you not been paying attention to what's going on out there?" Lily demanded, motioning over her shoulder.

Henry shook his head slowly. "Not since the news went dead a couple days ago, man," he drawled. "We've been locked up tight here ever since."

"So you don't know about the bites?" she asked, furrowing her brow.

Maddox shrugged. "I mean, we know those things try to bite," he replied. "But what about 'em?"

"The people who get bitten are infected," Dante explained. "When they die, they come back."

"Hence, zombie," Ace added.

Maddox wrinkled his nose. "Good thing we didn't let ole Chucky bite us, then," he said.

"Who's Chucky?" Dante asked.

Maddox and his brother shared a look, and Tate nodded.

"Come on," the dealer said, motioning for them to follow, "there's something you need to see."

He led the group down a trail through the woods. They walked a couple hundred yards until they reached a shack that was no bigger than ten by ten yards squared. There were a couple of windows that were closed, and the door had been boarded up.

"Our uncle used to live here back in the eighties," Tate explained. "Went abandoned for quite a while after his death. Then we started using it before upgrading our digs."

Lily rolled her eyes. "Impressive," she mocked. "So why did you bring us down here?"

Maddox opened his mouth, giving her the side-eye, but Tate spoke up, pointing.

"Look in the window," he said.

The three stepped up to the window, peering into the dim ransacked space.

"Looks about how I would expect Maddox to live," Lily muttered.

He pursed his lips, ignoring her, and knocked on the glass. A second later, a zombie emerged from the shadows, shambling towards the window. It didn't have any visible bite marks and looked clean save for the decaying skin.

"Is there anything wrong with him?" Dante asked.

Maddox raised an eyebrow. "You mean, besides being dead as fuck?"

"I mean with his legs," Dante replied, pointing. "Could he run before?"

The dealer nodded emphatically. "Oh hell yeah," he replied. "A couple days ago he said he wasn't feeling well and asked if he could crash out in the cabin. We came down a few hours later to check on him and he ran like a fucking Olympic sprinter, smacking into the windows."

"We got bored and started having fun with him," Tate added, "baiting him to keep running around the cabin like a crazy person."

Dante cocked his head. "When did he slow down?" he asked.

"Started getting gimpy yesterday, and frankly just took all the fun out of it," Maddox said with a sigh.

Dante and Ace shared a pointed look.

"Hey now, don't go getting all judgy on us now," Tate drawled, pointing a finger at the visiting redneck. "Especially with all the shit you've pulled over the years."

Ace shook his head. "Nah, it's not that," he said, waving a hand. "We think they're slowing down."

The stoners looked at each other, confused.

"Okay, you guys are going to have to start from the beginning," Maddox piped up. "Because it feels like we're coming in halfway through."

Henry slowly raised his hand, looking nervous. Nobody knew quite how to react until Dante finally pointed at him.

"Um... yes?" he asked.

The stoner chewed his lip for a moment, with his hand still in the air. "Why don't we go smoke a bowl?" he asked. "And let them fill us in."

"Well hot damn, there it is," Maddox declared, clapping his hands together. "His one good idea this week. Come on, let's go have us a chat in comfort."

CHAPTER FOUR

The four rednecks sat there, dumbfounded, staring at the trio after the long tale they'd just been told. Maddox reached over and grabbed the bong from Henry, taking a long hoot and holding it in for half a minute before exhaling a massive cloud of smoke towards the ceiling.

"Jesus fucking christ," he groaned, "no military, mercenaries have taken over, and there are flesh-eating zombies rampaging everywhere."

Tate buried his head in his hands. "So we're really on our own?" he asked.

Dante nodded. "Yep," he replied. "Military just up and abandoned us."

"So what are you wanting us to do about it?" Maddox asked, throwing up his hands.

Ace jerked his thumb in the direction of his companion. "Dante here had the bright idea of starting to grow our own food."

Maddox burst out laughing, his bloodshot eyes filled with mirth. "Ole McMaddox had a farm, E-I-E-I-O!" he sang, and Henry guffawed, joined in by Maddox's girlfriend, who's name had turned out to be Teagan.

Tate, however, sat in contemplative silence, rubbing his chin.

When Maddox realized his brother wasn't laughing, he calmed down, pushing against his shoulder. "Come on, you aren't taking that seriously, are you?" he asked.

His brother shrugged. "If those mercenaries are killing people in broad daylight, and the military is gone…" Tate trailed off and then shook his head. "We have to assume this situation is far worse than we can imagine."

Maddox chewed his lip, glancing over at Teagan and Henry, who were still singing Ole McMaddox and laughing. "You two knock it off," he snapped.

Henry clamped his mouth shut, and Teagan pouted.

"You're really gonna talk to me that way?" she whined.

"Yes," he replied. "And if you ever want to smoke any of my shit again, you're gonna be quiet."

She crossed her arms and flopped back against the couch, screwing her face into a comically dramatic scowl.

Maddox contemplated for a moment and then leaned forward. "Man, I'm not even sure where to begin," he groaned. "Henry, what do you think?"

"What the hell are you asking that teenage burnout for?" Lily blurted, motioning to the red-eyed redneck.

Tate pursed his lips. "Because he's our plant specialist," he said.

Henry sighed, rubbing his eyes before blinking rapidly. "How much food we talking?"

"Assuming we add more to the group," Dante paused, thinking for a moment, "revolving food supply for twenty people."

Henry pulled a phone out of his back pocket and started hammering away at the calculator. He twisted his lips as he ran some numbers and then shook his head.

"Well, for starters," he said, "we're going to need a much larger setup than we have here."

Maddox cocked his head. "How big are we talking?"

"School gymnasium size," Henry replied.

Ace threw up his hands. "Where the hell are we supposed to find *that*?" he asked.

"How about we just take over a school gymnasium?" Tate suggested.

Dante shook his head. "Even if we could take one over," he replied, "it would be a huge target if QXR gets this far out."

"That's the beauty of it," Tate declared with a smile. "This school is abandoned. Has been since the nineties."

Maddox nodded, snapping his fingers and pointing at his brother. "And it's isolated," he added, "a couple miles outside the city. They built it out in the country since a lot of the smaller towns fed into it. Then, in the late nineties, the town decided to build one closer to downtown."

"We still have extra solar panels, right?" Henry asked.

Maddox jerked a thumb over his shoulder. "Yeah, I got a few I haven't broken out yet," he confirmed. "Hardware store guy couldn't pay his bill, so he gave me solar panels instead. Best deal I've made in a while."

"You tell us what we need, and we'll get it for you," Dante said.

Maddox shook his head. "Shit man, what we really need is Francis," he said.

"You ain't kidding," Tate agreed. "He'd be loving this right now."

"Who in the hell is Francis?" Ace asked.

"Our cousin from Florida," Tate explained. "He moved up here a few months back, been helping out with things around here."

Maddox clasped his hands together. "We really should go get him," he said slowly.

"That's gonna be a hell of a job," Tate reminded him, letting out a deep *whoosh* of breath.

"It's okay," his brother declared, motioning to Dante. "We have a big badass over here, ain't that right?"

Dante raised his eyebrow, chuckling. "We can certainly add Francis to the list," he agreed. "But we really need to get the food going."

"Francis needs to come first," Maddox insisted. "Because as luck would have it, he's on the clock, so to speak."

Ace furrowed his brow. "Where is he that he's on a clock?"

"County jail up in Ridgeland," Tate replied.

Lily gaped at him. "You want us to break into a *jail* for one of your lackeys?"

"He's much more than a lackey, sweetheart," Maddox said, and she grimaced at the endearment. Teagan scoffed with disapproval, but simmered down at her boyfriend's icy stare.

"And knowing those boys up at the jail," Tate continued, "they probably bailed out at the first sign of trouble.

Which means he hasn't had food or water in a few days."

Ace shook his head. "Man, that is one hell of a risk," he said. "Do you really think he's worth it?"

Maddox bristled, but Tate leaned forward to defuse the situation.

"Before he moved up here, he would get work every Halloween as a celebrity impersonator," he said.

Ace raised an eyebrow. "Oh yeah?" he asked. "Who was he impersonating?"

"Andre the Giant," Tate declared.

Ace let out a low whistle and then slapped his knees. "Okay, I'll get the truck," he said. "We got a jail to break into."

"Before we do that," Dante said, holding up a hand, "we're going to need a plan. I imagine breaking into a jail, even a county one, isn't going to be all that easy."

Maddox jerked his thumb over his shoulder. "We got a welding torch in the cabin," he said. "We'll just have to deal with ole Chucky to get it."

"That's not a problem," Dante said.

"Torch should get us inside without issues," Maddox continued. "Same with the cell. Last time I was there, they were still using the old school locks with the oversized keys."

Dante nodded slowly. "Sounds like a secure facility, there," he said.

"It's a county jail in a small town," Tate drawled. "Ninety-nine percent of the people in there got popped for DUI or drugs."

Dante cocked his head. "And what did Francis do to get in that one percent?"

Maddox chuckled. "He body-slammed two people at a bar," he replied. "At the same time."

"Liking this guy already," Ace said with a grin.

Henry tore a sheet of notebook paper from the pad he'd been writing on and handed it over to Maddox.

"What the hell is this?" the dealer asked, brow furrowing.

"It's a shopping list," Henry explained. "There's a great little farming supply store in Ridgeland that should have everything on that list."

Maddox crossed his arms. "The fuck I look like, your mom?" he snapped. "Get off your lazy ass and get ready to go to the store."

"Question," Lily piped up, holding up her palm. "Does anybody else besides Henry know how to grow food?"

Nobody moved or said anything.

She raised her eyebrows. "Didn't think so," she said firmly. "That makes

Henry the most important member of this group. So he's not going anywhere."

"I'm important too," Teagan piped up. "So I shouldn't have to go out there."

Lily rolled her eyes. "Sucking lil' smokies ain't important," she muttered under her breath.

"What did you say?" the other woman snarled.

"She was just reminding me to ask if you guys had more weapons," Dante said quickly.

Ace nodded, stifling a smile. "Yeah, our supply is limited," he added, "to say the least."

"Tate and I got handguns," Maddox replied. "That's about it."

"Some drug kingpin you are," Lily scoffed.

He glared at her. "The fuck I look like, the head of the Rivas Cartel?" he snapped. "I'm a small town weed-slinger, I don't have any need for heavy artillery."

Before she could argue, Dante patted her leg and got to his feet.

"Well, if you know any place to get heavy artillery," he said, "if QXR comes a knocking, we could use it."

Maddox and Tate shared a look, and the latter shrugged.

"We might know of a place," he said. "But first things first. It's time for a jailbreak."

CHAPTER FIVE

The drive to Ridgeland was mostly quiet, with only the occasional zombie sighting on the side of the road. A side street sometimes came into view within sight of the interstate, which was devoid of life.

No cars, no zombies, no nothing.

"It's like the world just stopped on a dime," Dante mused. "Don't think I've ever seen an interstate that empty."

Lily shook her head. "No real reason for people to be on the road, even on a good day outside of going between Savannah and Charleston," she explained. "Outside of transport trucks, that is."

"Port of Savannah, right?" he asked.

"Yeah, it's a trip going over that bridge into town," she replied with a nod. "Gotta be tall enough for those ships to squeeze under. Really gets you up there."

Ace barked a laugh. "Hell, it took me til I was twenty-two before I owned a car with a good enough engine to make it up that incline," he added.

"Well, if these zombies keep slowing down, we might have to pay Savannah a visit," Dante suggested. "Could be some useful stuff in those shipping containers."

The three of them thought about it for a few moments as they reached the town line. Ridgeland, much like Hardeeville, was a small town of a few thousand people. The jail was just a few blocks north of the farming supply store, which meant they had to venture into the heart of town.

Maddox slowed his truck to a stop ahead of them, reaching his arm out the window to motion for them to pull up beside. "What do y'all wanna hit first?" he asked as Dante unrolled his window.

"I think it's going to be smarter to hit the farm supply store first," he replied. "That said, how close in the jail to the store?"

"Less than a mile," Maddox replied.

Dante nodded thoughtfully. "I think we should do a drive-by of the jail," he suggested, "just to see what we're up against."

"It's a fucking jail," Maddox drawled. "I mean, what are you expecting us to be up against?"

Dante cocked his head. "Well, we had a crowd of zombies around the TV station when we went," he explained. "These things have a tendency to congregate around buildings if they think there are people in it. If we're going to have substantial company, it might be good to know, don't you think?"

Maddox glanced at his brother in the passenger seat.

Tate shrugged. "Man's got a point," he said.

"Yeah yeah, all right," Maddox said with a sigh. "Ace, I'm gonna be hauling ass, so you stay on my bumper."

"Lead the way, brother," Ace called.

Maddox smacked the side of his truck to fire himself up before slamming on the gas. Ace hit his, easily catching up to him.

They cut straight through the center of town, moving at a fast clip. As they went by the streets, Dante and Lily peered down to see what was going on.

"Focus on the left," he instructed, "I'll cover the right."

As they flew by the side streets, they looked down them for zombies. While there weren't any major congregations of them, there were still several packs numbering as high as what looked to be two dozen in a single group.

Dante furrowed his brow with worry. If they weren't careful, they could have a horde fairly easily.

"There's the supply store," he said as he spotted it down one of the empty streets. "We're looking good down there, at least for now."

"Let's hope it stays that way," Ace replied.

They came out of the downtown area into a residential community, which was a lot quieter than downtown. There were still a few packs of ghouls roaming about, including one or two that ran out in front of Maddox's truck.

He plowed right into them, crushing them under his tires as he didn't even let up on the gas. Each time, he'd pump his fist out of the driver's side window.

"Enthusiastic, isn't he?" Dante asked dryly.

Lily rolled her eyes. "That's an understatement," she replied. "No matter how trivial the accomplishment, he'll let you know how awesome he was."

"I can see why you dumped him," he said with a chuckle. "That sounds exhausting."

"You have no idea," Lily drawled.

Ace slammed on the brakes, lurching everyone forward and barely missing Maddox's rear bumper in the process. Muttering obscenities, Ace curled the wheel and backed up, driving around to come up alongside the other vehicle.

"What the hell, man?" he demanded.

Maddox pointed in the direction of the jail.

The trio stared front and froze at
the sight of two dozen ghouls clustered by
the front entrance.

"Well, ain't that a kick in the
dick," Ace breathed.

Maddox nodded sheepishly. "Yeah,
hoping you boys got an idea of how to get
past them," he said. "Because that front
entrance is the only one there is."

"Let's get back to the farming supply
store," Dante suggested. "Maybe we can
find something in there."

The two trucks pulled up outside of the small farming supply store a block off of the main road in a row of shops. They quickly hopped out, looking around for any ghouls that were wandering around, luckily finding none.

Maddox immediately headed for the front entrance, but Dante held out an arm to stop him.

"Hold up there, bud," he said. "We have to be prepared for anything in there."

Maddox stopped in his tracks, nodding and taking a step back. Ace approached, holding out to Dante.

"You wait here for a moment," the larger man said, and approached the front door, peering in through the large glass panel. He didn't see any movement, so he jammed the tip of the crowbar into the door latch to pop it free with a single push.

As soon as he breached the store, he heard shuffling and moaning, followed by multiple sets of feet rushing towards him. He stood his ground in the doorway, watching intently in the dimly lit store.

A moment later, a zombie tore around the corner, almost running completely past him before spotting him and adjusting course. As it whirled, Dante cracked it in the head with a horizontal swing, sending it flying face first into the ground.

The second ghoul tore up the aisle directly in front of him, moving considerably slower than the other one, though still faster than a shambler.

As he waited for it to reach him, the rest of the group clustered around his back, watching it.

"Please tell me that's going to happen to all of them," Lily breathed.

"One can only hope, Lil," Ace said, shaking his head. "One can only hope."

"Goddamn, what the fuck happened to it?" Maddox moaned, staring wide-eyed at the multiple bite marks across the zombie's body.

"That's what those things do to you," Lily replied. "They rip you up."

He didn't respond, simply watching in horror as the ghoul grew close enough for Dante to impale it with the crowbar. With its skull crushed, the corpse crumpled to the floor.

Once it was down, there was silence. Just to be sure, Dante leaned down and smacked the floor a couple of times with the metal, but there was no response.

"Let's get what we need and get moving," he instructed, leading the way inside. As he secured the door behind them, he pointed to his companions as he spoke. "Lily, Ace, start pulling everything we need for the farm. Just stage it by the door, and we'll load everything up at the end. You two, let's figure out how to get past those zombies at the jail."

Everyone leapt into action, Lily and Ace rushing off with the list to pull things from the shelves.

Dante and the brothers headed over to the closest checkout counter to game plan.

"Okay, I'm open to ideas," Dante declared.

Tate shrugged. "In my experience," he said, "a propane tank and a flare seems to work pretty well in clearing a crowd."

"And leveling the front half of the building," Maddox added dryly.

Dante shook his head. "Not to mention attracting every zombie in a two-mile radius," he replied. "We need something smaller."

"There are probably some smaller propane canisters for torches and stuff," Tate suggested. "That could work."

Maddox raised an eyebrow. "That ain't gonna pack enough punch, is it?"

"We'd have to get several of them, that's a given," his brother confirmed.

"Is it going to create enough shrapnel?" Dante mused. "These things

aren't going to be hurt by the concussion
blast."

Tate shook his head, pursing his lips
in thought.

Lily passed by with an armload of
seed packets and dumped them into a
shopping basket by the cash. "Why not just
make some potato cannons?" she asked.

"You want to attack these things with
potatoes?" Maddox drawled, rolling his
eyes.

"No, dumbass," she snapped, "I said a
potato cannon. You do realize you can fire
anything out of those, don't you? Just has
to be packed tightly."

He sneered at her. "Potato, rock,
whatever," he said dismissively. "It's
still not going to take out the horde."

She shook her head, pointing to a
display against the wall behind them. The
three men turned and spotted the nuts and
bolts section, filled with thousands of
small metal objects.

"You're a genius," Dante breathed,
nodding in approval.

She smirked. "Just motivated to get
you boys done with your planning, so you
can help us carry this shit," she said
flippantly. "But thank you." She winked at
him and hefted a bag of potting soil over
her shoulder and strolled over to the
door.

"I've never made a potato cannon before," Dante admitted to the guys, "is it difficult?"

Tate shook his head. "Nah, just need some PVC pipe, a drill, and some sort of flammable agent," he explained. "Shouldn't be difficult to find here. However, they aren't very durable, might only get a shot or two out of them before they risk shattering, especially with the velocity we're going to need. So we're going to need to make a few."

"What about the tightly packed object?" Dante asked, studying the wall. "Can we get the bolts tight enough?"

Tate approached the display and looked for a moment, hand over his chin. Finally he found a plastic bag dispenser, and tore one off, pouring a couple handfuls of bolts before wrapping up tight. He tossed it over to Dante, who inspected it with a smile.

"I'd say that works," he said. "Let's get to building."

Tate nodded. "If you want to start bagging these up, Maddox and I will start building the cannons," he suggested. "Get 'em about halfway full and set 'em to the side. We'll adjust the size when we get 'em assembled."

Dante nodded and headed for the display, but as he reached for a bag, Ace yelled from the front door.

"We got company!" he barked.

Everyone tensed, drawing their guns and ducking.

"What do you see?" Dante called.

Ace peered out from behind the wall. "Car load of people, three… no, four, just got out," he said. "They're walking this way."

"QXR?" Dante demanded.

"No, civilians," Ace replied.

"Armed?"

"Yeah."

Dante took a deep breath. "Stay low, I got this," he declared, and then turned to Tate. "Let's flank them. I do the talking and don't fire unless I do. Good?"

Tate nodded and moved down a few aisles before heading towards the front of the store. Dante moved down the aisle one over and crouched down by the side.

The front door opened, and somebody said, "I don't know about this," in a worried voice. "There are trucks out here."

"We need ammunition, and this is the only place in town to get it," somebody else said. "We'll be in and out quick, I promise. These trucks are probably abandoned anyway, like all the others we passed."

Dante emerged to face two men and two women, varying in ages between thirty and fifty. "Sorry to disappoint you, but those trucks aren't abandoned," he said.

The oldest man's eyes widened, and he raised his hands. The other three immediately raised their hands too, one of them holding a shotgun by the barrel, arm shaking.

"Now, we're not going to hurt you, but I'm going to need you to put that shotgun on the ground, slowly," Dante instructed.

The man nodded and slowly placed the weapon on the ground. As soon as it was town, Tate emerged from behind them, grabbing the weapon and stepping back into the main aisle, out of their reach.

"Now, what are you doing here?" Dante asked, crossing his arms.

The man shook his head. "We don't want any trouble," he said shakily.

"I appreciate that, but that's not what I asked," Dante said firmly. "What are you doing here?"

"We're getting out of town," the man explained, "but we used up most of our bullets just getting out of our house. We came here to restock before hitting the road."

"Road to where?" Tate asked.

"My brother has a farm a couple hours north of here, near Kingstree," the man said, and the woman behind him tugged on his shirt in a panic. "Oh, relax woman, if they wanted us dead they'd shoot us here, they aren't going to track us to Kingstree."

Tate cocked his head. "City life ain't cutting it for you anymore?" he asked, lowering his gun.

Dante motioned for the group to put their hands down, and everyone relaxed.

"Not after what we heard about Beaufort," the oldest man replied.

"Beaufort, huh?" Tate asked. "What did you hear?"

The man turned to his companion. "Billy, you want to tell them?" he asked.

"My girl and I live in Beaufort… at least we did until this morning," the younger man next to him said. "A bunch of men with guns started going through neighborhoods, shooting those things, but also pulling people out of their homes. Not a lot mind you, but a fair number of people that were just holed up hoping for rescue. We were like that too, until we saw them roughing them up and throwing them into the back of a truck." He winced, swallowing and shaking his head. "We got in the car and took off."

Dante cocked his head. "How did you get across the bridge?" he asked.

"Dumb luck, really," Billy replied. "They were just pulling up to block it off when we sped by them. They fired a couple of shots, but didn't follow us. We didn't know what to do, so we came here to her Uncle Jack's place."

The older man, apparently Jack, nodded. "And when they told me all that, I loaded them up in the car and we came here," he added. "I don't know who those boys are, and I get the sense I don't want to know 'em. I'm too old to be fighting."

"They're mercenaries from the QXR group, and you're right, you don't want to know them," Dante said.

Jack raised an eyebrow. "Sounds like you know that firsthand," he said.

"Wish I could say otherwise," Dante replied.

Tate inclined his head towards the group. "You said you came here for ammunition?" he asked. "Didn't know they had that here."

"There's not much, mind you, but they got a cage in the back room," Jack explained. "Come on, I'll show you." He stepped forward slowly, and Dante motioned for him to lead the way.

Jack reached underneath the counter behind the register, pulling out a set of keys. He led them into the back room, which was a small storage area. There was a four-foot tall metal cage with a swinging gate, and he unlocked it, opening it up.

"Well I'll be damned," Tate breathed as he looked over the forty boxes of ammunition. "I had no idea this was back here."

Dante cocked his head. "So what do you need, old timer?"

"Could use a couple boxes of twelve gauge," Jack replied. "Maybe a couple of nine mil, if you can spare it. If you're sticking around here, you're going to need more bullets than we're going to."

Dante and Tate shared a look, nodding in agreement.

"Go ahead and take you a couple boxes of each," Tate said. "We'll manage."

Jack nodded in appreciation and grabbed four boxes. He shifted from foot to foot and then lowered his voice. "For the love of god, don't tell my wife what I'm about to tell you," he said quietly. "She's not really the trusting type, and there's already enough things out there trying to kill me."

"We got your back," Dante assured him, chuckling.

Jack took a deep breath. "My brother's arm is isolated, and mostly automated, so he's going to have food," he whispered. "Has a whole processing set up right on site. If this thing stretches on like I think it will, and you boys get hungry, you come see us up in Kingstree. I'll leave a map to the farm in the Kingstree post office, under the register."

The boys nodded, and Dante shook his hand. "Very kind of you, sir."

"We do appreciate it," Tate added as he shook his hand as well.

"I fear hard times are ahead of us," Jack said, shaking his head. "Good people are going to be harder and harder to come by. The fact you didn't put us down and take our stuff shows me you're better than most."

They headed out of the back room, and then Dante clapped the older man on the back. "Hey, before you go, I think I saw some jerky by the counter," he suggested. "Can't have a road trip without snacks."

"Billy, why don't you get us something for the road?" Jack asked, and Billy broke away from the door to load up on jerky.

The group congregated by the door, and Jack poked his head out to make sure the coast was clear.

"You boys be safe out there," he said. "And remember my offer."

"We will, sir," Dante said. "And you be safe, so that your offer can stand."

Tate nodded in agreement and handed the shotgun back over to him as they bustled outside to their car. Once they fired it up and headed off, Dante nodded and secured the door.

"All right, let's get back to work," he declared as Maddox emerged from hiding. "We have us a jailbreak to get to."

CHAPTER SEVEN

The two trucks pulled up within a block of the jail, stopping next to each other.

"All right badass," Maddox drawled, "how do you want to do this?"

Dante nodded. "We got three guns total," he said. "Ace will drive us to the other side of the lot, which should attract a good number of them. Lily and I will take out as many as we can with our shots. You block off the other side of the lot and do what damage you can."

"And what if there are some still standing after we hit 'em hard?" Tate asked.

"They can't climb," Dante explained, "so just hang out in the truck and beat them down."

Maddox furrowed his brow. "Well, why in the hell didn't we just do that in the first place?" he demanded.

"Because dumbass," Lily piped up, "you get enough of those things, and they can tip over a truck."

He thought about it for a moment and then shook his head. "So we doing this, or what?" he urged.

Lily and Dante climbed up into the back of the truck, sitting against the cab, their potato cannons beside them.

They sat on top of several bags of soil
and other goods for the farm, which made a
decent seat.

When they were in position, Lily
pulled out a can of compressed cleaning
solvent, spraying a generous amount into
the firing chamber of the cannon.

"That looks like a lot," Dante
commented.

She nodded. "Oh, it is," she agreed.
"But it needs to be. We need this stuff to
hit hard, right?"

Dante smiled and nodded as she primed
his cannon as well. She banged on the back
of the truck, prompting Ace to start
driving.

"Y'all hang on," he said through the
back window, "this might get bumpy."

His passengers in the back braced
themselves as Ace sped through the parking
lot of the jail, hitting a speed bump and
sending them up off of their seats a bit.
When he reached the other side, he slammed
on the brakes.

"You're good!" he bellowed.

Dante and Lily stood up, racing over
to the edge of the truck and setting up
their potato cannon barrel on the truck
gate. They looked out and saw about
fifteen or so zombies racing towards them,
about twenty yards away.

"Wait until they're close," Lily instructed.

He nodded, following her lead since he wasn't sure exactly what the cannons were going to do. She stared down the ghouls, spread out a couple yards apart from each other, but still fairly tightly packed.

"Hit 'em!" she cried, and both sparked up their lighters, pressing a flame to the firing chamber. A moment later, there was a significant *BOOM* as both cannons fired.

The result was a blunderbuss, sending shrapnel flying through the air at high velocity. The nuts and bolts smacked into zombie skulls, dropping half of them in a single shot. Their heads exploded in a spectacular display of red goo.

Even with the success, eight or so were still racing towards the truck.

"Reload!" Dante yelled.

Lily took a knee as he grabbed his crowbar, awaiting the coming enemies. The first corpse hit the side of the truck and he gave it a forceful strike to the top of the head, slumping it over. Before he could strike again, seven more slapped into the vehicle, causing it to rock a bit.

Arms flailed, reaching over the end gate at them. He swung down again, but the constant movement of the truck wobbling made it difficult for him to aim properly, and his blow landed on a shoulder. He grunted and pulled back, striking again, this time hitting a head.

"Reloaded!" Lily yelled, and he turned to help aim the makeshift cannon as she lit it.

The force of the blast at point blank range eviscerated the zombie heads, sending skull and brain fragments flying several yards behind them. The shot was so good that only one ghoul remained, and Dante quickly smacked it down.

"Nice shooting," he declared as he stood back up.

Lily brushed off her shoulder playfully. "What can I say?" she asked, batting her eyelashes. "You don't grow up in a rural town and not know how to shoot one of these."

A moment later there was another *boom* from the front of the jail. They looked over, and saw that Tate had taken down most of his pack, leaving only a couple that he took out from the back of the truck with a baseball bat.

Lily smacked the roof. "Back it up, they're good!" she called out. She and Dante knelt down as Ace swung the vehicle around, bringing them back up to the entrance.

Maddox jumped out of his truck, carrying a small hand-held welding torch. "Cover me, I'll get the door," he said.

The group formed a semi-circle around him, looking out across the road, hoping that their potato cannons hadn't attracted any more company.

Maddox fired up the torch, going straight to work on the locking mechanism. It didn't take long for the flame to burn bright, and the metal began to melt away. A few moments later, the door fell open.

"We're in," he said, hooking the torch to his belt as the other readied their weapons, preparing to go inside.

Dante entered first, gun aimed high. He quickly swept the small lobby area, finding not much of anything. There was an overturned chair, and some magazines strewn about.

"Not sure if a fight took place here, or they're just really messy," Ace said, looking around.

Dante tongued his cheek. "Let's assume the former," he said.

Maddox pushed the door closed behind him, and grabbed the overturned chair, dragging it over to wedge it under the handle. "This ain't gonna do much if a bunch of those things show up," he said, "but at least with it closed, they might just walk by it."

Dante nodded. "So where's Francis going to be at?" he asked.

"Probably the main holding cells in the back," Maddox replied, and led them over to a door that led to a long hallway that cut through the entire building straight to the back. As soon as he got through, there was an office on the left that he stopped at.

He tried the doorknob, but it was locked, so he used his gun to smash open the glass, reaching in to unlock it.

They entered the room, and it was a small guard post. There were several monitors in there that showed various parts of the jail, and what they could see wasn't very encouraging.

Several packs of zombies roamed about. Ten, maybe fifteen total across the main hallways. They found a monitor showing the main holding cells, and there were half a dozen ghouls in there, all congregating around one cell.

"That's gotta be Francis," Tate hissed.

Maddox looked around the room, finding a microphone. He went over to it and checked the buttons, finally flipping a switch. "Yo Francis," he said into the mic, and his voice echoed throughout the hallways on every speaker. "It's your cousin Maddox. If you're in that cell, give us a sign."

They watched the monitor, and one of the zombies' heads disappeared between the bars. A moment later, the body convulsed and fell backwards, missing its head.

"Oh yeah, that's him all right," Tate declared.

Dante took a deep breath. "Now we just gotta figure out how to get to him," he said.

"My potato cannon should be good for another shot," Tate said.

Lily nodded. "We have one shot left too," she added. "Mine is starting to crack after that second but, and I'd rather not blow my hand off if I can help it."

"I'll go grab 'em," Tate offered.

"I'll come with," she said. "Going alone isn't exactly advised these days."

As they turned to leave, a walkie talkie on the far end of the table clicked on.

"All right there Maddox," a firm aged male voice came through, "why don't you pick up the radio so we can have ourselves a chat before you go and do something stupid?"

Maddox froze, eyes wide and unsure.

"Maddox, you dumb son of a bitch," the man growled, "you just announced you

were here over the loudspeaker, so I know
you're in the office and can hear me. Now
pick up the damn radio."

He sighed and picked it up, clicking
the button and raising it to his lips.
"Judging by your friendly tone," he
drawled, "I'm going to guess this is
Sheriff Brandt."

"Congrats on solving one mystery
there," the Sheriff replied. "Now maybe
you can solve one for me. I seem to recall
that the last time we met I said in no
uncertain terms, if you ever came into my
county I was going to put you in solitary
confinement and lose the key. Now you want
to explain to me just what in the hell
you're doing here?"

Maddox sighed. "Not sure if you
noticed or not Sheriff, but the world has
kinda gone to shit," he said forcefully.
"So my friends and I came up here to get
Francis out before he starves to death.
Because judging by the monitor, nobody has
been in to see him for a while."

"Now you sure this is Maddox?" the
Sheriff drawled. "Because that sounds way
more selfless than I would have thought
you could muster up. Now if you were
smart, you'd go ahead and walk right back
out that front door and never look back,
because if you try to break him out, I'm
going to beat you down and lock you up

with him. Once Francis is done serving his time, he'll be released."

Maddox growled, but before he could respond, Dante let out a whistle and waved him over. He pointed to a pack of zombies eight strong that congregated around an office door on the other side of the building.

The redneck grinned. "I know full well you think I'm a moron," he said into the walkie talkie. "And chances are, you can find some people who would agree with you." Lily gave an enthusiastic thumbs up from across the room and he flipped her off. "However, I'm smart enough to pick my friends right, and they've figured out that you're trapped like a rat in the east wing office."

There was a long pause, and he smirked at the silence.

"Judging by your silence, I'm going to guess I'm right," Maddox continued. "So if that's all, we'll be on our way."

He set down the radio, and they began to leave the room. Before they reached the door, the walkie talkie crackled to life.

"Hope you weren't planning on cutting him out of the cell with one of those little propane cutters," the Sheriff said, a note of teasing in his voice.

Maddox froze, glancing at Dante and then rushing back to the table to pick up

the radio. "And what if I am?" he
demanded.

"Then you're exactly the dumbass I
thought you were," came the pert reply.
"We installed steel doors earlier this
year."

Maddox threw down the radio and
clenched his fists. "Fuck, fuck,
motherfucking fuck," he snarled.

"Calm down," Dante said, holding up a
hand. "What is it?"

Maddox motioned to the torch attached
to his belt. "This thing doesn't get hot
enough to cut through steel."

"Shit," Dante replied.

"Judging by your silence, I'm
guessing I was right," the Sheriff echoed
Maddox's earlier words with a mocking
tone. "How about we work out a deal?"

The group looked around at each
other.

"Let's hear him out," Tate suggested,
and there were nods all around.

Maddox raised the walkie talkie to
his lips. "Okay, we're listening," he
said.

"Go over to the control pad by the
monitors," the Sheriff instructed. "Punch
in twenty-three then the pound sign."

Dante did so, and it changed one of
the screens to an office. Sheriff Brandt
stood in there with two other officers.

"Yeah, we see you and your friends," Maddox said into the radio.

"Good," came the reply. "This is what I propose. You and your friends get us out of here, and I'll give you the key."

The redneck rolled his eyes. "So we're just supposed to take your word that you have the keys on you?"

Brandt set down the radio and walked closer to the camera, pulling out a set of keys from his belt. He held up the ring, showing off a large key that looked like it was for a jail cell.

"Shit," Maddox said, shaking his head. "What do you guys think?"

Dante shrugged. "It's risky, but I don't see another way," he admitted.

"Tate?" Maddox asked.

His brother nodded. "I agree with our new friend here," he said.

Maddox took a deep breath and raised the radio to his mouth once again. "Okay, Sheriff, you got a deal," he said. "But when we get you out, you and your boys just walk on out of here and leave us be. If you think it's bad in here, you ain't seen nothing yet. The whole world has gone to shit and getting out is the best thing for you."

There was a long pause, and then Brandt finally said, "Deal. Now come get us."

Maddox tossed the walkie talkie down on the desk in disgust. "Can't believe I have to help that motherfucker," he snarled.

"Guessing we can't trust him to keep his word," Dante said.

"Oh fuck no, he's a lying sack of shit," the redneck replied. "Vindictive, too. One of his underlings made the mistake of treating me with some respect, joking around with me one day. He not only berated that officer in front of everyone, but demoted him to the overnight shift."

Tate crossed his arms. 'You think he's going to screw us?"

"I think it's hella possible," Maddox confirmed.

"We'll cross that bridge when we come to it," Dante piped up. "In the meantime, we have to worry about those zombies."

Lily smacked Tate on the arm. "Come on, let's get those potato guns," she said.

The two rushed outside, and Ace smacked Maddox on the arm.

"There any other place in here that could have some useful stuff?" he asked.

The dealer thought for a moment before responding. "Couldn't hurt to look in the chow hall," he replied. "Weapons are going to be minimal, but there should be some rolling carts."

Dante nodded. "We can use that," he said, and then glanced at the monitor. "You two grab what you can and get back. Doesn't look like any of those things are near the cafeteria. Just stay quiet."

"What are you going to do?" Ace asked.

"Figure out how we're doing this," Dante replied.

The redneck nodded, and the duo rushed out of the room.

Dante moved back to the monitors, focusing on the office with the zombies around it. He thought hard, running through a variety of plans in his head… none of which sounded particularly good.

CHAPTER EIGHT

The five of them stood in the small office at the front, going over the plan. There was a single pushcart in front of them that normally held lunch trays, and two potato guns laying on it.

"Okay, we know how many they have, but they don't know about us," Dante said. "I think it's in our best interest to keep it that way."

Maddox nodded. "Agreed," he said.

"He's going to be expecting you," Dante continued, pointing at him. "I think Ace and Tate should go with you. At least have the numbers even, which will hopefully deter them from doing something stupid."

Tate raised his hand. "And if they *do* decide to do something stupid?" he asked.

"If you can safely take them down, do it," Dante replied, "but don't risk it. Lily and I will have your backs."

Maddox shot Lily a suspicious glare, and she rolled her eyes.

"Don't worry dumbass, if anybody is going to kill you, it's going to be me," she drawled. "And it ain't gonna be today."

He nodded, somehow comforted, and went back to focusing on the mission at hand.

Tate picked up one of the potato launchers as the three men shoved handguns in the back of their pants. They left the other cannon in the office, but brought a cart along with them.

"We'll keep watch at the monitors," Dante said. "Good luck."

The three men set out down the hallway, weaving through the maze-like halls towards the office near the back. They stayed silent, not wanting to attract attention to themselves, even the wheels squeaking along the floor, feeling too loud.

When they reached the corner that led to the office, Tate peeked around it, seeing eight zombies by the door. The hallway was fairly wide, about ten feet across. He ducked back behind cover, leaning in to speak quietly.

"Okay, I'm going to blast them with this thing, then get back behind cover," he whispered. "Whatever doesn't drop is going to be hauling ass after me. Maddox, I want you to use this cart to knock 'em on their ass. Ace, we aren't going to fuck around with 'em either, pick your shot and pop it in the head. Hopefully letting these asshole cops know we have guns will keep 'em calm."

The other two nodded in agreement as Tate picked up the potato cannon. He checked to make sure the nuts and bolts were packed in tightly and then took a deep breath. He stepped back several yards away from the corner, and used the compressed lubricant to fill the firing chamber, hoping the sound was muffled enough not to alert the ghouls.

Ready to strike, he walked back to the corner, peeking around to make sure they were still occupied with the door. He stepped around, walking halfway down the hall as noiselessly and slowly as he could, stopping about ten yards away before lighting it up.

The boom was deafening, the sound bouncing off of the walls, but the impact was excellent. The metal shrapnel ripped through the horde, shredding several of them. Four of them dropped to the ground with significant head wounds.

Those corpses fell into the others, knocking over two more. The final two let out loud moans and sprinted towards him.

Tate immediately backtracked, tearing around the corner, and Maddox appeared with the cart, holding it tightly as the zombies got close. He rushed up and rammed into one creature, sending it tumbling down to the concrete. The other was several steps behind, but Ace aimed and fired, hitting it in the head.

As the one on the floor tried to get back up, Tate circled around Maddox and shot it in the face. The other two knocked down ghouls by the door found their footing and rushed the trio. Both Ace and Tate had time to line up their shots, firing a couple of times each to drop them.

In the aftermath, the three men stood stock still, listening hard to wait for more zombies to appear. Much to their surprise, nothing else emerged in any direction.

"Come on, let's get these assholes out," Tate muttered.

Maddox approached the door, kicking a couple of the downed ghouls to make sure they were dead for good, and there was no movement. He smacked the door a few times with his open palm.

"All right Brandt, you're good to go," he bellowed. "Time to honor your half of the deal!"

A moment passed, and then the deadbolt clicked. The door opened, and the Sheriff stood there, looking smug. His two officers sat on a desk in the back of the room.

"Well well, you actually did it," he drawled.

Maddox nodded sharply. "Yeah we did it," he replied, "now give me the key and get the hell outta here."

"They're on the desk over there," Brandt jerked a thumb over his shoulder. "Let me go grab 'em."

Maddox followed him inside, and as soon as he crossed the threshold, there was the sharp *click* of a shotgun cocking.

"Fuck my life," he muttered, glancing over at the corner. There was another officer standing right under the camera, wielding a shotgun.

The Sheriff casually walked over to the desk, picking up the keys and clipping them to his belt. "You didn't actually think I would be stupid enough to tip my hand, now did you?" he drawled, hooking a thumb into the top of his pants.

"Apparently we did," Maddox growled.

Brandt waved a hand. "Okay boys, you have until the count of three to get in here, or ole Maddox here is going to be missing a head," he drawled. "One…"

"Calm your tits, Sheriff," Tate said, and he walked in with Ace, both men's hands high in the air.

"Oh, it's you two, why does this not surprise me?" Brandt shook his head. "Well, I stand corrected, it does surprise me a bit that you three have managed to survive whatever this is as long as you have. Y'all saw the world ending, and you just had to pay me another visit, is that it?" He sneered. "Or did you just miss this place?"

Ace raised an eyebrow. "I've never been in here," he pointed out.

"Not for lack of trying," the Sheriff said. "I know you've started shit in my county, yet somehow always slipped away. That isn't happening this time." He motioned to the officers behind him. "Boys, get their guns if you don't mind."

One of them grinned as they stood up. "With pleasure," he said. Once they'd collected the weapons, he asked, "So, what do you want to do with them now?"

"Well, they came in here to be with their giant-ass cousin," Brandt said with a smirk. "I say we take 'em there. Plenty of cages they can get comfortable in."

CHAPTER NINE

Dante and Lily watched on the monitor as the Sheriff and his three men captured their companions.

"Fuck," she muttered.

He shook his head. "Don't worry, we'll get them out," he assured her.

"Oh, I know," Lily replied. "I'm just upset that I have to save his dumb ass."

Dante smirked as he picked up the potato gun, holding it out to her. "Come on, let's go get 'em."

They headed out of the office, walking down the hallway. Rather than go for a straight assault, they went towards the holding cells in the back, ducking into a small office a few doors before the main gate to the cell.

"You know what we're doing, right?" Dante whispered.

She nodded. "Yep."

They laid in wait for the seven men to come closer. There was a glass panel on the door, which Dante positioned himself to see through while remaining behind cover. He watched as their friends walked by first, followed by Brandt, and then the shotgun officer and two others.

Dante nodded to Lily, and she returned it, ready to roll. He peered out towards the gate, watching as Brandt unlocked it. As soon as it was open, Dante motioned to Lily, and she opened the door.

He moved swiftly, stepping out into the hallway and firing twice, hitting the two officers in the back, striking their vests and knocking them to the ground. The shotgun-toting officer turned and fired, prompting Dante to keep rushing across the hall and crashing through the door.

He hit the ground hard, forcing the gun out of his hand. He scrambled to get it, but the light darkened behind him as the shotgun-wielding officer stood in the light.

"You just fucked up, buddy," he declared, and raised his weapon.

Dante took a deep breath as he stared down the barrel, but then the officer's face exploded, and he slumped to the floor. Lily stood behind him, holding her handgun.

"Get 'em!" Brandt screamed, and a few bullets hit the doorframe, forcing Lily into the room.

Dante scrambled across the floor, grabbing his gun, and ducking out the door at the wounded officers approaching the door.

They retreated, firing blindly, forcing Dante to slide to cover across the hall.

"I don't know who you are, but I'm assuming you're with these three assholes!" Brandt screeched down the hallway. "You have five seconds to throw out your guns, or else I'm going to blast a hole through this motherfucker's head!" He cocked back the hammer on his revolver and pressed it against Maddox's head.

The redneck chuckled at the massive size of the weapon. "Compensating for something?" he drawled.

The Sheriff shoved it into his temple even harder with a growl. "One. Two… three…"

"Okay, we're sliding out the weapons," Dante called, shoving both handguns out the door.

The two officers, still nursing the bruising they'd taken when they were shot in their vests, moved up at the motion from the Sheriff.

They moved cautiously, together. The first one reached the door and turned towards Dante's room. "Let me see your hands," he demanded, finding Dante sitting up against a desk casually. "Let me see your hands!"

The large man casually raised his arms, looking past the officer for his friend to make the turn into Lily's room. As soon as he did, Dante curled his hands around, giving two middle fingers to his attacker.

"Motherfu-" the officer cried, but was cut off by the blast of Lily's potato cannon. The officer at her door fell as the shrapnel ripped through his face, the rest smacking into the back of Dante's officer.

Dante didn't waste time as his attacker doubled over in pain and rushed him. The officer tried to recover and raise his weapon, but Dante grabbed his wrist and pushed it down, sending a bullet into the floor.

He delivered a sharp uppercut, catching the officer under the chin and stunning him. He reached back, grabbing him by the back of the head and pulling him close, sending a headbutt to the bridge of his nose, the impact causing his attacker to drop his gun.

Staggered, the officer was helpless as Dante choke slammed him into the floor, his head smacking against the cement and knocking him woozy.

As this happened, the other three in the hallway took on Brandt. The blast startled him, giving Tate an opening to shove his arm away from Maddox's head. Maddox ducked as well, but Brandt still pulled the trigger, missing but partially deafening his captive.

Tate held the gun arm in place, and Ace wrapped his arms around the Sheriff's neck, cutting off his air supply.

"Let go of the gun," he snarled, "and I let go of you."

Brandt struggled to hold on, but finally relented, dropping the revolver. Ace held on for another few seconds, just to prove a point, before finally letting go. Tate shoved the Sheriff against the wall, holding him in place by the throat.

"You move, I squeeze," he said firmly. "And I'm not as nice as Ace here. I won't let go."

The sheriff nodded jerkily.

"Jesus motherfucking tap-fucking-dancing christ that hurt!" Maddox bellowed, rubbing at his ear viciously. "I think my eardrum is gone!"

Tate rolled his eyes. "Suck it up, brother," he drawled, "one less ear to hear that nagging girlfriend of yours with." He spotted Dante emerging from his room, and called, "You two all right?"

Dante ignored him, focusing on Lily as he walked across the hall to her. She sat against the far wall, staring off into space in shock.

"Are you okay?" he asked gently, kneeling down in front of her. When she didn't respond, he put his hand on her shoulder. "Lily, you did good," he said. "We're safe now."

She looked up at him and then wrapped her arms around his shoulders for a beat, taking in a deep breath before getting emotional. "I'm good, I'm good," she assured him, and looked past him at the mess in the hallway.

"You saved my life back there," Dante said, snapping her away from looking at the dead bodies. "Twice."

She smiled. "I figured if you were going to make me save that asshat, I was going to save you as well," she said. "Give me some good memory of today."

He chuckled, and she joined in, dissolving the tension in the room.

"Hey, are you two all right?" Tate called again.

"Come on, we're not done yet," Dante said, standing and holding out a hand to her.

Lily took it, getting to her feet, and they headed out towards the others.

"We're good," Dante called to the others, "you boys okay?"

"Yeah," Tate replied. "We're gonna have to listen to this one whine all the way home, but other than that we're golden." He inclined his head towards Maddox, who was still rubbing his ear and moaning.

Dante looked at the ground, picking up the shotgun and his handgun before grabbing the other woozy officer and shoving him down the hallway towards Brandt. Lily collected the rest of the weapons from the dead bodies.

"What do you say we go get Francis?" Dante asked.

The group walked down the hall to another gate, and Tate forced the Sheriff to open it. Around the next corner was the cell block, and Francis sat inside, six heads stacked up nearly in the corner. Six headless zombie corpses lay in the hallway.

"It's a good thing we risked our lives to come rescue him," Ace drawled. "He might not have been okay otherwise!"

Lily rolled her eyes. "He still needed to get out of the cell," she said, poking him in the ribs.

"Hell at this point, I'm kinda surprised he didn't bend the bars," her cousin shot back.

"Get his keys," Tate said.

Maddox ripped the keyring from Brandt's belt and opened the cell next to Francis. "In you go, Sheriff douchebag," he said with a flourish.

Tate shoved him in, and Dante guided the still wobbly officer in after him.

Maddox slammed the cell shut and locked it.

"You're making a huge mistake there, buddy boy," the Sheriff growled.

Maddox smirked. "Oh, am I now?" he asked. "Doesn't look like it from my perspective."

Brandt leaned on the cell door, staring menacingly through the bars. "You should know my officers are out there, and they're going to come find me," he hissed. "And when they do, I'm going to hunt you down, find the deepest hole in all of the Lowcountry, and throw you in it."

Maddox made a puppet out of his hand, pretending to mouth along. "Blah blah blah," he mocked. "And how many days have you been thinking that while locked in that little office, huh? Do you have even the foggiest idea of what's going on out there?" He leaned in, smirking. "Nobody is coming for you. Any officers you have out there are probably already dead, and if by some miracle they aren't, they sure as shit aren't risking their lives coming to rescue your ass. The world outside is dead, and the people who are still alive couldn't give two shits if you ever get out of that cell."

The Sheriff clenched his jaw, eyes finally showing a flicker of fear. "So you're just going to let us die in here?"

he asked. "Lock us up like animals to
starve to death?"

"Yup," Maddox replied brightly.
"That's what you were going to do to us.
That's what you were doing to Francis. Why
should you be any different?" He hocked a
big loogie into the Sheriff's face.
"That's for breaking our deal, asshole."
He headed off towards Francis.

Brandt reached through the bars
towards Dante, eyes wide. "You're not a
part of their group," he pleaded, "don't
throw your life away, son."

Dante stared down his nose at him.
"If you do get out of here," he said in a
level tone, "hopefully you'll have learned
your lesson and will honor future deals."
He headed off, Lily beside him, raising
her hand to flip off Brandt as they moved
away.

Maddox unlocked Francis' cell door,
throwing it open.

The beastly man sat on the edge of
his bed, which was barely enough to
accommodate even half of him. He was
leaning forward, elbows on his knees, in
such a casual pose Dante almost wanted to
laugh.

"You ready to blow this joint?"
Maddox asked.

Francis cracked a smile and stood up,
joining the group. Dante, Lily and Ace

stood in awe, even the tallest barely coming up to his pecs.

"Good to see you, cousins," Francis said, his voice a deep rumble. "And new friends."

Tate motioned to the others. "This is Dante, Ace, and Lily," he said.

The trio nodded politely and said hello in unison.

"Is it true what you told the Sheriff?" Francis asked, turning to Maddox. "Is it really that bad out there?"

The redneck nodded. "It's actually a whole lot worse," he admitted. "So I hope you're ready to bust some heads."

"Oh, I'm ready," Francis replied, cracking his knuckles. He glared at Brandt. "And if we don't leave now, I'm going to get started."

Tate clapped him on the back. "Let's get going, then."

The group headed off, and Maddox hung back, dangling the keys in the air in front of the Sheriff. He turned and shot them like a basketball into the cell across from them, grinning as they splashed into the toilet.

"Always thought I could have gone pro," he quipped, punching a victory fist into the air. "Well, enjoy starving to death, asshole," he declared, and then glanced at the officer who had finally sat down on the bed. "Oh, and if I were you, I'd make the first move. Because this dick is totally going to kill you in your sleep and cannibalize you."

The officer's eyes widened, and Maddox laughed, sauntering off. Brandt kicked the bars and screamed curses, but they fell on deaf ears.

CHAPTER TEN

The trucks pulled up to the school outside of Hardeeville, and it looked like it had been abandoned for ages. The grounds were overgrown with tall grass and weeds, the front door completely ripped off, and graffiti covering just about every square inch of the building.

The group hopped out of the trucks, standing in front in a line to appraise the situation.

"Looks like a grade-A shithole," Ace drawled.

Maddox grinned. "Yeah, but it's *our* grade-A shithole," he said, smacking the other man on the shoulder.

"There any signs of civilization around here?" Dante asked.

Tate shrugged. "Couple of mid-sized neighborhoods about half a mile away," he replied. "Other than that, there's not much."

Dante nodded. "I think we should proceed like those people evacuated and took refuge in the school," he suggested. "Come too far to get caught off-guard now."

They nodded and collected their weapons from the vehicles.

"Well come on," Ace finally said as he handed Dante the crowbar, "let's go check out the farm."

They walked up to the school, staying cautious as they approached the door. Both Dante and Tate took the lead, heading in first to aim their guns down the hallway as soon as they entered.

The environment hadn't been kind to the building, with all sorts of dead grass and leaves as well as trash blowing down the long corridor. There were lockers running along both sides of the hall, the ones closest to the door showing signs of significant rusting as they were close enough to get rain when the wind was blowing.

As they walked, they made sure to check every classroom, most of which were empty, however some desks remained. There was graffiti on most of the walls, and signs of squatters and drug usage littered about.

"Looks like quite the party spot for the local teenagers," Lily said dryly.

Maddox shook his head. "Doesn't surprise me," he replied. "Cops don't give a shit about this place. Came out here a few times when I was in school. Hell, pretty sure some of this graffiti is mine."

Lily looked to her left and found a large painting boasting *Iron Maiden Rules!* with a crude drawing of their mascot. "This can't be yours," she drawled. "Not only is everything spelled correctly, but it's also great taste in music."

He opened his mouth to retort, but there was a loud moan. Everyone froze at the noise, except for Francis, who stepped forward and smacked a locker with his open palm. The thin metal crushed inwards, sending a loud echo down the hallway. The moan intensified, followed by footsteps pounding the floor.

A moment later, a zombie tore out of a nearby classroom, heading straight for them. Francis stepped a few yards away from the group, readying himself as the others watched, transfixed.

The ghoul raced straight towards him, and he reached out with his large hand, grabbing the creature by the throat. He picked it up off of the ground, its limbs flailing about, before grabbing its waist and pile-driving it straight into the ground.

The zombie's head completely vanished, shattering into a thousand pieces, coating the floor with blood and brain. The giant straightened up, swiping his massive palms against each other, a smug smile on his face.

"Told you he was worth rescuing," Maddox declared.

Ace nodded, eyes wide. "You weren't fucking kidding, brother."

They continued to the end of the hall where the gymnasium was. They looked through the windows into the darkened room, with some stay beams of sunlight piercing through the skylights.

"So much for natural sunlight," Maddox muttered.

Ace grinned. "Maybe we can have big fella here punch some holes in the wall."

Francis glared at him, and the redneck shrank away.

"I'm sorry," he stammered, holding up his hands.

The giant smirked and clapped him on the back, shaking his head.

"Well, let's go check it out," Maddox said, and pushed open the door. As soon as the door scraped across the dirty floor, moans and a chorus of footsteps echoed towards him.

"Shut the door, shut the door!" Tate screamed.

Maddox quickly pulled the door shut, and a few seconds later, a dozen or so creatures crashed into them.

"Jesus, where the hell did they come from?" he gasped.

Dante peered over their heads, spotting an exterior door that was slightly ajar, held together with a chain. "Look like the back door," he said. "They got in a chained it shut."

"And what, they just sat in the dark?" Maddox asked, throwing up his hands.

Tate shook his head. "Probably had a camping light or something," he replied, but then waved his hands in front of his face. "Doesn't really matter, though. We just gotta figure out how to clear 'em out."

"I'm sure as hell not opening the door again," Maddox replied. "As soon as they get a handhold, they're gonna throw it open."

Dante tilted his head back and forth. "Just getting it open a little would be good enough, though," he said. "We have the ammo, so we could shoot through the cracks and take them out one by one."

"I don't know about you, but I don't want to get that close to the door and have them be able to grab me," Maddox replied. "Or hell, pull me ion."

Ace shrugged. "Why don't we just shoot through the glass at them?" he asked.

Tate leaned in, looking close and knocking on the pane a few times. "Safety stuff," he said sullenly, shaking his head. "It would take a lot to punch through it, then we have the problem of getting them to line up in front of them. With the door open, they'll be trying to get in, but we could be waiting a while."

As they talked, Lily looked around, spotting an exterior door about fifteen yards away, with a long chain wrapped around it to keep the swinging doors locked together. She politely tapped Francis on the shoulder, and he looked down at her, following her, pointing to the chain.

He smiled and nodded before walking over to it. The others trailed off from their conversation as they watched him grab onto the chain, putting his foot on the door and pulling hard. It took a few moments, but finally the release bar on the door cracked, breaking away, and then it snapped completely free.

"Which door do you want?" he asked as he approached.

Dante nodded. "Middle?" he asked.

Francis nodded and put the chain through the metal release bar on the door, stretching it several yards back and wrapping it around his wrists, holding tight.

Bracing himself, he gave Dante a nod. "Whenever you're ready," he said in his gruff voice.

Dante pulled out his handgun and walked to the door. "Here we go," he said, thankful for the awesome giant on their side. He hit the release, and Francis let a little give on the chain so the door could open a few feet.

As soon as the zombie arms jetted through the opening, he tightened his hold to make sure that the door held fast. Dante lined up his shot, popping off one by one.

For each zombie that hit the ground, another one rushed in to take its place. Dante took his time, selecting his shots and hitting each one, all while the door stayed fast thanks to Francis and his strong arms.

This went on for several minutes, until finally the last ghoul dropped. Just to be sure, Dante smacked on the door a few times, listening to the sound echo in the gym. There were no returning moans or footsteps.

"I think we're clear," he said.

Francis cocked his head. "Are you sure?" he asked.

"Yes, thank you," Dante said, and the giant let go of the chain. The door didn't

move at all with the mountain of dead
bodies clustered around it.

The group stepped over the corpses,
filing into the gym.

"I'll get us some light," Dante said,
and jogged over to the far end to the
exterior doors. He peered through them to
make sure there were no other surprises
and then pushed them open.

The sun-drenched the dust-covered
floor, revealing a few small tents and
camping equipment, as well as several
pools of blood.

"Guess they didn't know about the
bites," Ace muttered.

Maddox shook his head. "That's gotta
suck, thinking you've survived and that
you're safe, only to have your friend or
mother wake up and start ripping your
throat out," he said.

"Is this going to be big enough?"
Dante asked as he walked back over.

Ace shrugged. "Damn well better be,"
he said.

Tate nodded. "I think if we can find
enough lights, we can branch out into the
classrooms if we need to."

"I tell you what," Maddox said, "why
don't I go get our boy Henry and he can
tell us what he thinks?"

"I could use a nap on a real bed,
too," Francis piped up.

Maddox grinned. "Don't worry big man, I'll hook you up."

The giant approached Lily, Dante, and Ace, extending his massive hand to shake them all in turn. "Thank you for coming to rescue me," he said sincerely. "You didn't have to risk your life for me, yet you did. I will do my best to make sure I live long enough to repay you for your kindness."

"You keep cracking skulls like you're doing, and we'll call it good," Ace declared with a grin.

Lily rolled her eyes. "What my cousin here means, is that there's no repayment necessary," she said.

"Go get some rest," Dante said. "We have a lot of work ahead of us."

Francis smiled and nodded, before heading off with Maddox.

"Yo bro, you coming?" the latter called.

Tate glanced at Dante, who had a concerned look on his face. "Nah, you go ahead," he replied. "We got some stuff to handle here."

"Suit yourself," Maddox said, waving him off. "I'll bring you back something to eat."

As the duo disappeared, Tate approached Dante, crossing his arms. "I can see if on your face," he accused. "Spit it out."

"If this many people came from the nearby neighborhoods," Dante said slowly, "we could have a whole lot of trouble waiting in the wings for us."

Tate nodded, taking a deep breath. "I was kind of thinking the same thing," he said.

"You want to do a quick tour?" Dante asked.

Tate motioned to the door with a flourish. "After you," he said.

"Ace, do you and Lily feel comfortable staying here?" Dante asked. "We need to make sure this place is locked down tight."

Lily smiled at him. "We'll take care of it."

Ace took his keys out of his pocket and tossed them over to Dante. "Just don't ding up my truck," he warned.

Dante chuckled and led Tate outside.

Dante drove with Tate in the passenger seat, and they drove around a small neighborhood half a mile from the school. So far there had only been a couple of zombies that had run up to them, and Tate put them down with a precise shot to the head.

The neighborhood was part tranquil, part war zone, just depending on which house they went by. From the looks of it, several families had been able to leave, but others weren't so lucky.

"Three streets down," Tate said, "one more to go."

Dante turned onto the next street, stopping short when they spotted a pack of ten zombies in the road. They hadn't noticed the vehicle yet, milling around each other.

"What do you think?" Tate asked.

Dante cocked his head. "You don't happen to know a good auto body repair shop, do you?" he asked dryly.

Tate chuckled. "Maddox and I have been restoring a sixty-seven Impala," he offered.

"Good enough for me," Dante said, and then floored it, picking up speed. The roar of the engine attracted the ghouls, and they immediately sprinted for them.

The truck hit sixty when the first zombie impacted the front bumper, completely demolishing it. The ghouls behind it bounced away, flying in various directions.

A second later, Dante slammed on the brakes when they cleared the mini-horde, looking back and seeing a lot of devastation in his wake. Three zombies still stood, unscathed.

"Three coming up," he said, and both men readied their handguns, waiting for the ghouls to reach them.

As soon as the corpses came up alongside the truck, each man popped off shots at near point blank range, dropping them.

"Should we inspect the damage?" Dante asked.

Tate nodded. "Just make sure you clear the truck when you get out," he said.

They made sure to jump away from the vehicle, which ended up being a good plan, as there was movement beneath. One of the ghouls crawled out from underneath it towards Dante, squirming and writhing with busted legs.

Tate shook his head as he came around to look at it. "These things just keep coming, don't they?" he asked.

"Yeah," Dante replied, and fired, putting the zombie down. The duo walked around to the front of the truck.

The front end was beat up a bit, covered in blood. Tate let out a low whistle.

"Ace ain't going to be happy with you," he drawled.

Dante crossed his arms. "We totally got surrounded, right?" he asked.

"Oh, without a fucking doubt," Tate replied, and they cracked up together.

As they headed back inside, Dante shook his head. "You know, I'm not a fan of how that thing got underneath the truck like that," he admitted.

"You and me both," Tate agreed. "Would be way too easy for one of those things to get tangled up in the axel, or even in the engine."

Dante sighed. "There goes my big dream of doing donuts to take out big crowds."

"Nah man, you can dream big," the redneck assured him. "Just means we gotta find you a monster truck."

Dante's eyes widened. "You can find those around here?" he asked.

Tate chuckled. "You ain't from around here, are you?"

His companion shook his head. "Seattle."

"Shit man, we're going to add a trip to the dirt track to our list," the redneck replied with a grin. "I'm gonna make you a country boy yet."

CHAPTER TWELVE

Dante and Tate pulled up to the school gym, seeing one of the sets of doors propped open. Ace emerged from inside, putting his hands to his forehead.

"What happened to my truck, man?!" he cried.

Tate shook his head sadly as they exited the vehicle. "We were fucking surrounded man, zombies everywhere," he said. "Dante had to punch it or we were done for."

Ace nodded, though sadness still covered his face. "Well, as long as y'all are safe, man," he said.

Dante glanced at his partner-in-crime, receiving a wink.

"And don't worry," Tate continued, clapping Ace on the back, "we'll get it fixed up for you."

Lily came outside, swiping her palms together. "How did the neighborhoods look' she asked?

"Clear now, so we should be good out here," Dante replied. "At least from hordes."

"We should still have someone keep watch for stragglers," Tate suggested.

Dante motioned to the building. "How are we looking in there?" he asked.

"Henry is still looking around," Lily replied.

A few moments later, Henry came outside, flanked by Maddox with Teagan hanging off of his arm. She stroked his chest, glaring at Lily.

"So what's the verdict?" Tate asked.

Henry shrugged. "I can make this work," he replied, "but we're going to need lights to make the indoors work."

"That's going to take some time to get," Ace said.

"Time we don't really have," Tate added.

Henry nodded. "Which is why our main focus is going to be the football field," he said, and waved for them to follow him. They headed around the gym to the field, which was overgrown, but had a fence around it. "It's not too late in the season, so if we can get this cleared and plowed in the next week or so, I can still get some stuff planted."

"What kind of stuff are we talking?" Maddox asked.

Henry tilted his head back and forth. "Beets, lettuce, maybe some spinach if we can find it."

"Ugh, that does not sound appetizing," Teagan whined.

"Sounds better than starving to death," Lily snapped.

Dante sighed. "How long is that going to take before we can eat it?" he asked.

"Six to eight weeks," Henry replied, "which is why we're going to have to stagger everything when we plant it. Doesn't do us much good to have an entire field's worth of food ready at the same time when we won't be able to eat all of it."

Tate pursed his lips. "No way to store it?" he asked.

"We can try canning, but it's going to be limited," Henry said. "Not exactly a huge supply of the raw materials we'd need."

Dante cocked his head. "Still… if you can make us a list of what to look for, we'll do our best," he suggested.

"I can do that," Henry replied, nodding. "But in the meantime, I think we've done all we can do today. The sun is starting to get low, and this place is nowhere near ready to be staying at."

"Yeah, I'd rather not be out on the road at night, either," Ace agreed.

Maddox nodded. "So are y'all gonna come back down tomorrow to do some shopping?' he asked.

Ace glanced at Dante, who nodded in agreement.

"Yeah, I think this takes priority over everything else, don't you?" he asked.

Maddox nodded. "Agreed."

"You drive safe," Tate said, and headed over, shaking everyone's hand. Maddox approached and did the same, but Lily simply glared at him, arms crossed.

"For what it's worth, you did good today," he said gently.

She jutted out her chin but nodded in acknowledgement. As they headed off, they heard Teagan laying into him. The words were unintelligible, but they could tell she was pissed.

"Giving praise to an ex in front of your girlfriend," Ace drawled. "That's a man sleeping on the couch tonight."

"Told you he was a dumbass," Lily muttered.

Dante chuckled. "I can see why you left him."

They clambered into the truck, and Ace fired it up, rolling down the window to hang his arm out. Dante turned and watched Lily as they drove away, and she was blankly staring ahead, not really looking like she was staring at anything at all.

"You okay?" he asked softly.

She nodded. "Yeah, I'm good," she replied with a smile. "I worked customer

service before all of this, so I'm used to
dealing with dumbasses."

"That's not what I mean," he replied.

She paused and swallowed hard,
staring straight ahead. Her jaw was tight,
and it looked like she was fighting tears.

Dante reached out and grabbed her
hand, and she squeezed back.

"I'm rattled a bit," she admitted,
"but I'll be okay."

They shared a small smile and
continued holding hands as they headed for
home.

END

Up Next: With zombies on the island
still being a major threat, Grace, Troy
and the other members of the QXR civilian
squad are sent on another dangerous
mission in Lowcountry - Pt. 5

DEAD AMERICA
LOWCOUNTRY
PART 5
BY DEREK SLATON
© 2021

CHAPTER ONE

"Morning, Princess," Troy drawled as Grace stretched, groaning as her back crackled.

She wasn't quite awake enough to level him with a proper glare, so instead she twisted back and forth, relishing in the crackles of her spine. A ragged yawn overtook her, and she rubbed her eyes.

"Needs her sleep after yesterday's badassery," Hawk said, his deep voice echoing through the cells. "I'll be honest, girl, I didn't think you'd be so good at this."

She wrinkled her nose and pulled out her saggy ponytail. "Killing zombies?" she asked dryly. "Or trying to survive under threat of getting eaten or killed by a group of insane assholes?"

Hawk chuckled, shaking his head. "All of the above," he admitted. "No offense, but you don't look like much in a fight at first glance."

"You know, when somebody starts a sentence with 'no offense', it's usually offensive," she said as she wound her unruly hair back up into a messy bun.

He shook his head. "Just being honest," he said. "I mean granted, you survived this long, but seeing you in action yesterday was surprising."

"Can't say the same about the others they had with us," Eddie muttered, stretching his lean frame down to touch his toes. He was a stark contrast to Hawk, who was a beast of a man, but despite his wiry body, he was ruthless out in the field.

"Yeah," Troy agreed, shaking his head as he lounged back on his bed. "Those poor suckers didn't know what hit 'em. It was almost more of a liability having to deal with them then an asset having extra bodies to help out."

Grace sighed. "They're fucked either way," she mused. "Either they're useful and they try to help and die, or they refuse and QXR kills them."

"What else are any of us supposed to do?" Troy asked, though he wasn't speaking to anyone in particular. "We have to do as they say, with who they say."

She grabbed a water bottle from beside her bed from the night before and took a long swig.

Troy shrugged. "At least we've got a warm bed and food and drink," he amended.

"I'd rather have to find that shit myself and be free," she replied.

"We'd be fighting zombies either way," he said.

She shook her head. "On *our* terms, though. Everything we do right now isn't

for us. It's so that QXR can solidify
their own position of power."

"What do you think they'll do with us
once the island is clear?" Hawk asked, and
the insinuation hung in the air.

Grace took another long swig and
swallowed slowly. "I don't think we have
to worry about that anytime soon," she
replied. "Seems like the clearing is
endless."

"Except it's not endless," Eddie cut
in as he stretched to the side. "It's
going to run out. You think they'll carve
out a little community for us to just
chill in?"

Troy snorted. "Not likely," he said,
and crossed his feet at the ankles, making
the most of their relax time. "Though I
don't think we'll be useless. There'll be
floors to sweep and dishes to do."

"I guess it's better than being
shot," Hawk muttered.

Eddie rolled his eyes as he twisted
his torso back and forth, hopping from
foot to foot. "Not by much," he retorted.
"But the fact still stands that we need to
make sure that we're as useful to them as
we can be. It's not like this is going to
be a vacation spot for us once all the
zombies are cleared out."

Grace leaned forward, resting her
arms on her knees. "Maybe for them."

"Rise and shine, pissants!" Mosley declared as he descended the steps to their cell block, clapping his hands loudly. "Oh, you're already awake. Such excited puppies, ready for their next playdate."

Grace clenched her jaw, resisting the urge to glare at him. How she hated this man.

"Get some good rest?" he asked with a sneer. "What about you, city boy?" He tapped on the bars to Troy's cell and clicked his tongue. "Accommodations up to snuff for you?"

"Oh yeah, five stars," the New Yorker drawled, not sitting up.

Mosley glanced over the crew, making sure they were paying attention. "You fuckers get to go clear the mall today!" he said brightly, spreading his arms. When there was no response, he looked back and forth, eyebrows raising. "What, no cheers? You should be fucking ecstatic that you get to go out and do this instead of taking a bullet to the head, no?"

"We're already doing all your grunt work," Eddie declared, leaning on the bars. "Is it a requirement to be happy about it, too?"

"Gratitude would be nice," Mosley snapped, narrowing his eyes. "I could kill all of you."

Grace finally looked up at him, feigning surprise and putting a hand to her chest. "But then who would do all your dirty work?" she asked, fluttering her eyelashes. "You're clearly incapable of doing it yourself."

"Bitch, I have no problem showing you exactly what I'm capable of doing," he growled, drawing his lower lip between his teeth.

She forced herself not to wither under his leer, but her skin crawled at the insinuation. If he made a move on her, she knew she could probably hold her own in fighting him off, but that would likely mean death. But the other option—just laying down and taking it—was just *not* an option.

"What do you say, hm?" he asked, voice sickly sweet. "You need me to show you what real dirty work is like?"

"Go fuck yourself," she snapped.

He growled, taking a step towards her cell.

"That's enough," No Name declared, entering the hallway from the stairwell. He carried a tray of steaming bowls and set it down on a small table next to the door.

Mosley scowled at him, eyes narrowing. "I'm busy," he snapped.

"So am I," No Name replied, crossing his arms and straightening his broad shoulders. "These four have a big job today and I need to get them to it, so get lost."

Mosley snarled, stalking up to him. "You don't get to tell *me* what to do," he said petulantly, but there was a hint of a quiver in his voice.

No Name glared down at him. "You want to put your fists behind that?"

The shorter man shriveled and threw a glance back at Grace before heading up the stairs in a huff. No Name shook his head with disgust and then began doling out the bowls, shoving them one by one into the cells.

"I'd say thank you for getting rid of that creep," Grace said dryly as she picked up her bowl, "but you're also keeping me in a cell and forcing labor, so… not exactly much to be thankful for."

He didn't respond, simply finished handing out breakfast, which turned out to be bowls of scrambled eggs and ground meat.

"No hot sauce?" Hawk muttered. "Terrorists." He scooped a forkful into his mouth.

"Today's target is the mall," No Name announced once everyone was eating, leaning against the wall and crossing his arms. "It was an impromptu rescue shelter when everything started to go to shit. We were able to lock it up tight day one, but it's full to the brim."

Eddie raised an eyebrow. "A *mall*? Full to the brim?" He shook his head. "How the hell are we going to deal with *that*?" he asked, flabbergasted.

"That'll be for you to figure out," No Name replied. "It's going to be a major operation, and you'll have to get a lay of the land. You'll be going in with four other civilians."

"Wait, only eight of us for the whole mall?" Troy exclaimed. "No backup from your trigger-happy mercenary buddies?"

Hawk and Eddie both opened their mouths, and No Name raised his hands.

"I know," he said loudly to shut them up, "I know. If it were up to me, I'd be going in there too. This is too big. But orders are orders, and orders are to send the eight of you in to do this."

"Why?" Grace demanded. "I get that we're expendable to you assholes, but this is just inefficient for your timeframe."

No Name shrugged, shaking his head. "I don't know. I just get my orders."

"Woof woof," Hawk muttered. "Follow blindly, little doggy."

Their captor glared at him, but had
no rebuttal. "Eat your breakfast," he
said. "We're moving out in five."

Grace sat in the passenger's seat as No Name drove them out to the mall, the men in the back. She stared out the window, but didn't really see the landscape passing her by. Her time in the cell was spent thinking of her brother, hoping he was okay, torn between wanting him to mount some kind of rescue and wanting him to just stay away, stay safe.

There was no way out of this for her, or at least it didn't feel like it in the near future. She would do everything she could to survive, and that was all she could do. There was no real standing up to these men. At least if she was really good at what they were sending her to do, she could prove useful for after.

After. What came after? These thoughts plagued her in her cell as well, in the quiet, when she struggled to sleep. Her body was exhausted after missions, but her mind reeled. These days were nothing but determination and fear and survival, the nights terrible simply for not knowing what the next would bring.

She spotted a line of civilians being offloaded into a processing area, and her gaze perked up, focusing on the here and now. "Where did they come from?" she asked.

No Name glanced over. "We've been finding quite a few survivors in Bluffton. They're transporting them all here."

"What happens to them all?" Hawk piped up from the backseat. "The ones who don't get sent off to die clearing out zombies?"

No Name shook his head, and Grace noticed the tight line of his jaw, as if he were reluctant to answer. He didn't say anything, and that was answer enough. She studied him as he drove, glaring daggers into the side of his head. She wasn't naïve enough to think that she could gain his sympathy, but there was definitely something about him that was different from the others. He didn't seem to take pleasure in tormenting them. He didn't seem to take pleasure in really anything he was doing to them. And by the tense muscles in his upper body at Hawk's question, she didn't think he took much pleasure in the whole slavery thing.

But he was still doing his job, still following orders. And that meant he was not her friend, and likely never would be. If he cared about the civilians more than his own livelihood, then he would have done something about it before now, instead of just falling in line.

Woof woof, Hawk had said. *Woof woof, indeed,* Grace thought bitterly, and turned back to the window.

They reached the mall, seeing several mercenaries standing guard around it and on top of it. She assumed that it was to make sure that the ghouls didn't figure out how to escape. It boiled her guts to think that they were allowed to just stand outside in the safety, while sending untrained civilians inside to do their dirty work.

No Name pulled up near the front entrance, and a mercenary approached, slinging his gun over his shoulder as they all piled out of the van.

"I've done some recon on the roof," he said, pulling a sheet of paper from his pocket and unfolding it. He held it out so they could all see as they clustered around. "There's hundreds of those things in there, but the majority of them are in the big department store, here." He pointed to the giant square on the far side of his crudely drawn map.

Grace pursed her lips. "What are the chances it's sealed off from the rest of the mall?" she asked.

The mercenary shook his head. "It's not," he replied. "The main floor is closed, but the second floor doors are open. They must have been opening those up

for employees to get in when everything
went to shit."

"If you want to stand even a slim
chance of surviving this, you're going to
have to get those doors closed," No Name
said.

Grace glared daggers at him. *No shit,*
she thought, but held her tongue. She took
the map and studied it. Crude as it was,
it was fairly detailed, with all of the
entrances marked clearly.

"There's a service entrance on the
first floor that seems to stay pretty
quiet, so you can get in safely," the
mercenary said, pointing to one of the
marked entrances. "You should be able to
fight your way up to the second floor
easily from there, with that escalator.
Once the doors are shut, and you thin out
some of the horde, you're to make a call
to No Name here so we can take out the
rest of those things."

Grace pursed her lips in thought.
"What's this big store here?" she asked,
pointing to one just beside the department
store doors.

"It's a sporting goods store," the
mercenary explained.

She nodded. "Probably our best bet is
to get up there, close the doors, and then
hide out in there for a few minutes to

take the heat off of our initial run, and
get a lay of the land," she suggested.

"Are you going to be coming in after
us?" Troy asked, crossing his arms.

"Once the main mall is clear, your
job will be to bang on the doors to draw
those things in the department store
towards the access panels above," the
mercenary said. "We'll kill them all from
above."

Grace continued staring at the map
and then looked up as No Name held a
walkie talkie in front of her face.

"Call me when you're ready," he said
gruffly.

She snatched it out of his hand and
shoved it into her back pocket. "Not if
we're in trouble?" she asked dryly. "Guess
there's nobody coming in to help us if we
get cornered, huh?"

He shook his head, not meeting her
gaze. Another van pulled up, and the
sliding door opened, four civilians
reluctantly getting out.

"Oh, fuck no," Hawk muttered at the
sight of Aaron, a middle-aged man that had
nearly gotten them killed the day before.
"No way we're taking him in with us."

Aaron scowled at him as they
approached. "I don't wanna go in there any
more than you do," he snapped.

"You should stay out here then, since you can't follow directions and you only care about your own ass," Hawk shot back.

No Name held up his hands. "The eight of you are going in. You need all the hands you can get." He reached into his holster and grabbed his handgun, holding it out to Grace. "She's in charge. Listen to her if you want to live through this."

"No pressure," she muttered, and shoved the gun in the back of her pants. The weight of it was like a ton of bricks. Eight, *eight* of them to get through this. She took a deep breath. "I think our best bet is to split into groups. One group to cause a diversion, one to secure the sporting goods store, and one to get those doors closed."

The mercenary returned with a plastic bin full of melee weapons, crowbars and tire irons and the like.

"How come *she* gets a gun?" one of the new civilians whined.

Grace took a deep breath. "Because I'm getting us through this, if you listen to me," she said firmly. "This isn't my first rodeo here, and if you complain too much, these guys will shoot you, so stay focused."

Her speech had the intended effect, and the group stood there, staring at her expectantly, clutching their weapons.

"You and you, what are your names?" she asked, pointing at two of the newcomers.

"I'm Aly, and this is Joseph," a middle-aged woman said. They both looked like they hadn't seen a lot of action in their lives, but at least seemed in good enough shape to run and swing a crowbar. Joseph's forehead shone with a thick sheen of sweat, fear written all over his face. But who wasn't afraid these days?

"Okay, you and Hawk are with me," Grace continued. "We're going to secure the doors. Then we'll need two groups of two, one to cause a distraction to clear the area, and another to clear the sporting goods store so we have a safe place to regroup."

"I'll take the distraction team," Eddie said, raising his hand.

Troy glanced at Grace, and she shot him a knowing look, hoping he understood that she wanted a person she trusted on each team.

"Yeah, I'll do the sporting goods store," he said with a sigh, and smacked Aaron on the shoulder. "You ready for a proper mission, following orders?"

The older man glowered at him, but nodded, gripping his crowbar tightly.

"Guess you're with me," Eddie said brightly, turning to the final man, a wiry guy that looked like he'd sat in front of a computer his whole life. "What's your name?"

"Leo," he said, taking a deep breath. "You?"

"Eddie," came the reply, and they shook hands.

Grace nodded and pointed to a section of the map. "We'll have to get a lay of the land once we're in there, and think on our feet," she said. "But I'm thinking probably over here would be a good place to make a ruckus. It's far enough that it shouldn't draw too many from the department store, but enough to thin it out a bit where we're working."

Eddie nodded. "You got it."

"We'll go up the escalator as a group, and then split up at the top to do our jobs," she continued, looking around the group. "That make sense?" There were nods all around, and then she turned to No Name. "I guess that means we're ready. Are we free to go, or does somebody need to intimidate us first?"

He pressed his lips into a thin line and shook his head, not saying a word.

Grace took a deep breath and folded up the paper, shoving it into the pocket of her jeans. She grabbed a crowbar from the bin and gripped it tightly. "Okay, let's go."

Grace reached the service entrance and motioned for Troy to come forward as she stepped to the side with her crowbar raised. "Open it just a little and then be ready in case there's pushback."

He nodded, and Hawk sidled up next to him to help brace the door. Troy took a deep breath, and then turned the handle, pressing his shoulder against the door and inching it open. He grunted as a body slammed into the door, a bloody arm flailing out of the gap.

Grace took her time lining up her jab, as Troy and Hawk had a fairly good brace on the door. When she managed to get a good look at a snarling face, she lunged forward, avoiding the arm to stab the creature in the head.

The corpse fell, the rotted limb still hanging out of the bottom of the door, and Troy waited a moment before pulling it a little further.

Footfalls echoed in the hallway, and Hawk dropped his stance, really digging in his feet as the door shuddered from the force of bodies slamming into it.

"Jesus Jesus Jesus," Joseph moaned, clutching his tire iron to his heart with white knuckles, and backing up a few steps.

Eddie threw himself between Hawk and Troy, the latter ducking down as a flailing arm whizzed past his face. Grace brought the crowbar down on the limb, snapping it at the elbow so that it dangled harmlessly. The upper arm continued to bob about, the corpse unperturbed that it had lost functionality of its claws.

She managed to stab the zombie in the face, right through the eye socket, and it slid down a little, revealing two more scrambling to get past it. "You need to open the door a bit," she said, widening her stance.

"What?" Troy huffed as he struggled.

"I can't reach the heads," she explained impatiently. "I need them to be able to get partway out the door."

He grunted and turned to Eddie. "Let's slide back a bit, so I'm out of the swipe zone."

Eddie and Hawk nodded, then moved back towards the hinges to give him room to slide. As the trio eased towards the wall, the door opened another inch, and three ghouls wormed their way into the opening, snarling and snapping at Grace.

She timed a jab, going high and stabbing into the forehead of the top zombie. It flopped back as the other two writhed around, one of them snatching her arm in its dead hand. She wrenched her arm away, but the death grip on those things was intense, and she couldn't shake it.

Troy stared at her, wide-eyed, and she put a foot against the brick wall to hold her flesh away from the snapping jaws.

She noticed with a sour taste on her tongue than none of their other four teammates were coming to her aid. The door men wouldn't be able to leave their posts, otherwise they'd have all the maintenance hallway monsters pouring out and overrunning them.

She wrestled her crowbar into her free hand, smashing it down on the hard-gripping arm as hard as she could. There was a sickening crack, but the fingers didn't let up. These things had no chill—all they wanted was to feed, and nothing but a direct blow to the brain would stop them.

Aly screamed from behind her and lunged forward, swinging her tire iron hard into the gap in the door. Something crunched, and then the arm holding Grace dropped, taking her wrist with it. She pried the fingers off as Aly continued to flail away, smashing the tire iron with abandon.

Grace ducked to avoid one of the back swings, and then another head shimmied through the corpses on the bottom, managing to wriggle its torso out through the widening gap. She stabbed it in the top of the head, and soon the pile of corpses was still.

Aly continued to smash the zombies, despite them not moving, and Troy stepped away from the door, pushing her arm down. It was gentle but firm at the same time, as if he were trying to avoid getting smashed himself.

"Thank you," Grace said, chest heaving, as Aly backed up, eyes wide.

The woman swallowed hard and nodded jerkily, quivering.

Grace glanced over her shoulder at the other three men, still rooted to the spot. She was starting to feel like Hawk was right, and this team wasn't going to be good for them. But it wasn't like they could change it, or do anything about it. She just had to hope to hell that having someone she trusted on each team would be enough to get them through this.

"Ease up on the door," she said, and Eddie and Hawk leaned forward, letting it open another few inches.

Grace poked her head in and strained her ears, listening for any more movement down the maintenance tunnel. She spotted the door at the end, blessedly closed, with no more bodies moving about. She grabbed the brown collar of one of the corpses and hauled it out of the way of the door.

"Help me," she said, inclining her head to Troy. "I don't want to leave any doors open if I don't have to."

He nodded and reached down, and between the two of them, they dragged all the fallen zombies from the doorway, leaving them on the asphalt.

Once clear, Grace led the way into the tunnel. There was only one other door on the way to the mall proper, but it was locked tight with a warning sticker on it, likely electronics or water heaters or the like.

When she reached the door leading to the mall, she and Troy sidled up next to each other, peering out into the open area.

"What a shitshow," Troy muttered, and her stomach sank.

She agreed with him. They were looking at an open area, the broken down escalators about fifty yards away. But there were zombies everywhere on the main floor, and they could see lots on the top floor balcony as well.

"This isn't going to be easy," she mused, and then stepped back to face the group. "Everyone take turns having a look, make sure you get a lay of the land."

The group moved up two-by-two, all coming away from the window with concerned, pale faces.

"What's the play here?" Eddie asked, voice tight.

Grace took a deep breath. "Same as we said outside," she replied firmly. "We're gonna fight our way across to the escalator, and then at the top, my team will go right towards the department store along with the sporting goods store team, and the decoy team will go left. I can't see far enough that way, but you should be able to find somewhere to make enough noise and fall back somewhere safe."

"*Should,*" Eddie replied dryly.

She shrugged. "You volunteered for that job," she replied, waving a hand at him. "I know you'll be able to figure it out."

"Thanks," he quipped.

"But there are so many of those… so many of those…" Joseph stammered, pointing shakily at the door. "How are we going to get even to the escalator?"

Grace took a deep breath. "They're fairly spread out, and not in bigger groups than two or three." She held up her crowbar. "Your best weapon is fists and shoulders. If you can't knock them aside, barrel 'em over. Don't stop moving, or you're dead. Don't even go for kill shots,

just focus on making a path for yourself.
Hawk and I will take the lead, and we'll
try to move in a train, two by two, with
the decoy team bringing up the rear.
Questions?"

Aly raised her hand with the tire
iron. "What if we trip or fall?"

"Get back up fast," Troy replied
dryly.

Grace nodded. What else was she
supposed to say? "Let's go," she said, and
turned towards the door.

CHAPTER FOUR

Grace waited until the door was clear about ten yards on either side, and inched it open, slipping through. She held it until Hawk passed it off, and then darted forward, stabbing a ghoul in the face as the others bustled out into the mall.

She knew she was breaking her own rule of not going for kill shots, but she was confident that she could take the time as she waited for the group to catch up. The door clicking shut and the sound of the corpse falling alerted some of the nearby ghouls to their presence, and then the chase was on.

Grace and Hawk moved forward side by side, stabbing and shoving zombies as they went. Sounds of struggles and grunts echoed behind them, but she couldn't afford to look back to see how her team was faring. They had their instructions, and they had to follow them—she needed to focus on moving forward.

Halfway to the escalator, a pack of four ghouls tore towards them, with a fifth straggling behind, a lot slower than the rest. She didn't have time to ruminate on how No Name had reported that some of the zombies were slowing down, and that if that was the case, why not just wait for them *all* to slow down?

She and Hawk moved as one, lowering their shoulders to barrel into the first two ghouls to get close. They drove back the duo into their brethren, tripping them all up.

Grace did glance over her shoulder this time, unsure if they should leave the ghouls here for their friends or not. Aly screamed as she kicked a zombie in the chest, and Joseph cowered behind her, waving his tire iron wildly at another.

Grace grunted and knelt, stabbing efficiently at the fallen zombies. Hawk shook his head and took one out too, and then leapt up at the fifth shambling ghoul, giving it a hearty shove back into a few runners to slow their progress.

Grace darted for the escalators, finally seeing a clear path, and skidded to a stop at the bottom, whipping around to defend the area until the rest of the group could catch up. Troy, Eddie, and Aaron reached her first, and they formed a perimeter around the foot of the escalators.

Aly and Joseph tore over, hot on Hawk's heels, while Leo smacked down a few ghouls and sprinted to catch up.

Grace turned and spotted some zombies staggering down the escalator towards them, on the left side. "Stay right!" she cried and began the charge up the stairs.

The zombies weren't very steady on their feet, and began to fall, all flailing limbs and snarling mouths as they tumbled down the stairs.

One managed to grasp on to the center median, slowing its descent, and swiped at her. She smashed down on its skull as she went by, and though she wasn't sure she killed it, at least it was out of the way.

A few steps from the top, a zombie tore into view, launching itself off of the second floor towards her. She lashed out, holding her crowbar with both hands to push it back, grappling with it as she braced the bar across its putrid throat. She wrestled it to the side, trying to throw it over, but it was too strong, and had the high ground.

Hawk reached over her shoulder and smacked it in the head, and though he didn't drop it, it faltered enough that she was able to shove it over the side, plummeting to the first floor below.

Grace took the last few steps quickly, emerging onto the second floor. She immediately dashed to the right, lowering her shoulder and barreling into a zombie right by the balcony railing.

"This way, fuckers!" Eddie whooped, and his weapon echoed as he smacked it along the railing.

Grace didn't look back as ghouls converged, tearing towards them from the department store. She trusted Eddie to do his job, and she needed to focus on the doors.

Hawk was next to her then, swinging and smacking. It seemed easiest to shove as many as they could towards the railing, and that way the fallen bodies were out of the way. Plus, if they landed on their heads and happened to break their necks, then that was more dead corpses that wouldn't get back up again.

The sporting goods store came into view, and Grace turned to Troy, who waved back at her. He tugged Aaron after him, and they moved to the left side of the corridor, knocking over a few ghouls to tear for the store.

Eddie hollered some more in the distance, Leo whooping as well, though not quite as loud and proud.

Grace and Hawk each grabbed an arm of a particularly thick ghoul, running like defensemen together and slamming it into the railing, sending it toppling over to the first floor. Aly and Joseph clustered behind them.

"I thought we were supposed to just run!" he cried.

"We gotta clear a path to the doors!" Grace hissed. "Hopefully the decoy team can keep the rest away, but the ones between here and the doors won't just run past us. If you can get to the doors first, start working on them, but we gotta kill what we can."

The rest of them nodded, but didn't have time to strategize any further, because three more ghouls tore for them from the department store.

Gotta think on our feet, remember? Grace thought bitterly and swung her crowbar for a mighty kill shot.

Troy burst into the sporting goods store, the metal chain doors only half-closed. It was probable that they were either just opening the store, or just trying to protect themselves with locking up, when things went from bad to worse.

There were five zombies inside, and they perked up as soon as Troy and Aaron crossed the threshold.

"Get this closed!" Troy barked, banging on the metal barrier, and his partner began to struggle with it, dragging it along the track as quickly as he could.

Troy sprinted across the three waist-high aisles of various equipment, a ghoul in each, three in the far end. He snatched a hockey stick from the wall display and thrust it out lengthwise, attempting to use the business end to hold the oncoming ghoul at bay. Instead, it sank into the rotted corpse's chest cavity, sticking inside.

Troy fought back a gag, and swung the zombie back and forth, using it as a shield to bonk back its brethren. He changed tactics and began to use it as an undead battering ram, consistently shoving them back.

His reasoning was to keep them busy while Aaron dealt with the other two, but that seemed to be taking longer than he'd anticipated. He chanced glancing over his shoulder, and saw Aaron just locking the metal barrier, and leaping back as a bunch of zombies in the mall hallway smacked into it.

He raised his weapon, as if to jab it through the holes.

"Leave them!" Troy barked. "There's two more in here!"

Aaron whipped around just in time to see the two ghouls heading up the aisles, and he darted around to Troy's aisle, wide-eyed.

"Fuck," Troy muttered under his breath. He'd misplaced his hope, but at least the guy had managed to get the barrier locked. They had to get these zombies taken care of, though, before the others came back to hunker down in the store.

Aaron at least had the forethought to grab a hockey stick, and huddled up behind Troy, holding it in his opposite hand to the tire iron with white knuckles. The ghouls came around the end of the aisle, about to box in the duo.

"Once they get close, we're gonna hop the shelves," Troy said. "Ready?"

Aaron nodded, eyes wide.

"Now!" Troy cried, and shoved his ghouls back before throwing himself over the shoe shelves, rolling over into the clear aisle. Aaron followed, but he was a bit slower, and one of the zombies grabbed his ankle on his way over.

He screamed, swinging the hockey stick wildly, so hard that Troy had to duck, unable to get close enough to help him. The heavy shelves managed to keep the ghouls at bay for the most part, though he had to back up to avoid their grasping arms.

He jumped to his feet, stabbing his trio in quick succession, and then finally lashed out to grab Aaron's flailing stick, wrenching it out of his hands. He brought it down hard on the zombie's neck, cutting into it slightly. Aaron kicked up with his free leg at the rotted arm, finally dislodging it, and Troy lunged with the crowbar, catching it in the temple with the curved end.

He jerked downwards, tearing the front of the zombie's skull clean off, leaving only one ghoul to deal with.

It shrieked as it clawed at him, mouth open, bloody drool flying everywhere as it gnashed its teeth together trying to snap at him.

Troy sneered at it, and then jabbed forward with the tip of the crowbar, burying it into the monster's eye socket. As it fell, he stepped back, chest heaving. He looked down at Aaron, who was still on the floor on his back, covering his face with his arms.

"Thanks for the help," Troy muttered, and poked Aaron's shoulder with his shoe. "Come on, we gotta check the back and make sure it's clear."

The prone man swallowed hard and got up, picking up his tire iron and following Troy to the cash counter. There was a rack of baseball bats off to the side, and Troy dropped his hockey stick to grab one of them, sliding the crowbar into his belt loop. He gave the heavy wood an experimental swing, and then approached the back room, peering through the glass window.

A zombie in a striped umpire's outfit smacked into it, and Troy jumped, his muscles relaxing a bit at the fact that the door was shut tight. He reached out and gave it a push just to make sure and then turned back to his partner.

"We need to get back to the front of the store, see what's going on," he instructed. "And unlock the door if the others are coming back." He swallowed hard. "*When* the others are coming back."

He stalked to the front of the store, Aaron scurrying after him. The metal clanked and jangled as ghouls wrestled with it, their nasty fingers curled in through the holes. Troy stared at them for a moment and then set the baseball bat against a shelf of rock-climbing gear.

He pulled his crowbar again, and lined it up with one of the holes, waiting for the right moment to jam it through into a face. He hit his target, and one of the corpses fell. He glanced over at his reluctant partner.

"That tire iron isn't going to do it," Troy said, motioning behind him. "Find something sharp and get stabbing."

Aaron clenched his jaw for a moment. "Isn't the decoy team supposed to be drawing them away?"

"They might be too far away, now," Troy snapped, rolling his eyes. "We might as well do our part. No use sitting in here cowering when we can be thinning the herd."

His partner chewed his lip, eyes wide, but looked around for something to use.

Troy stabbed another one and then inclined his head towards the back. "Check behind the register, maybe they have a box cutter or something."

Aaron nodded and scurried off, not as quickly as he could have, and Troy rolled his eyes again, assuming that the man was stalling for time. Really, of all the ways they could be fighting zombies, safely from behind a metal barrier was one of the best ways to get to do it.

After stabbing two more ghouls, he was just about to bark at his partner to hurry up when a loud noise echoed out through the mall. It almost sounded like… an electric guitar?

Troy laughed at the sound of some crunchy distorted power chords began to fill the air, and the zombies immediately dispersed, taking off towards the direction the decoy team had gone.

He shook his head, smiling. "Rock'n'roll."

CHAPTER SIX

As Eddie broke away from the group at the top of the escalator, his heart hammered even faster in his chest. There were zombies everywhere, and they were going to be on top of them fast. He hoped Leo was keeping pace with him okay, because he didn't have time to glance back over his shoulder.

He tried to stay in the center to avoid getting boxed in, as most of the stores were closed up tight. He shoved through the ghouls he could, toppling those close to the railing over to the floor below.

At the huffing behind him, he was comforted that Leo was keeping pace. They reached a bit of a lull, and he slammed his metal weapon down on the railing, echoing a loud clang.

"This way, fuckers!" he bellowed, looking back towards the department store. There was a plethora of ghouls all over the place down there, and though Grace and Hawk were holding their own, they needed the door clear if they had any hope of getting them shut.

He kept hooting and hollering, turning towards the direction they needed to go, and soon enough, Leo joined in, although without as much vigor. Eddie knew

the man was scared—hell, they were all
scared—but he was going to have to pull
his weight if they were going to get out
of this.

They tore across the gap of hallway,
and out into a more open area of the
second floor. The outer shops were all
fancy boutique stores, high-end jewelry
shops and the like. And the whole area was
full of zombies.

"Oh, fuck," Eddie breathed.

Quick on our feet, he thought, trying
not to panic. *Need to think quick!*

They had to make noise, but they also
had to not die, so he looked around
frantically for somewhere they could do
that.

"They're coming!" Leo cried, looking
behind them, and Eddie grabbed his wrist.

"There!" he yelled. "The music
store!" He pointed and began to run,
tugging the middle-aged man behind him.
Leo almost stumbled, but thankfully caught
his footing, because the yelling caused
every single ghoul in the area to turn
towards them.

He ran with everything he had,
pumping his legs until they screamed, and
he was moving so fast that he realized too
late that zombies were coming out of the
music shop towards them.

Just run, just go, he thought, and lowered his shoulder, knocking between two of the ghouls and tearing into the shop proper. He could hear the thundering footsteps behind them and had to make a quick decision. They couldn't change course now, or they'd be overrun.

"Into the back!" he yelled, though he was still dragging Leo behind him like a running rag doll.

He skirted the counter and burst into the backroom, Leo stumbling in behind him, and slammed the door, locking it with the deadbolt. Soon a wall of zombies smacked into it, some getting caught on the cashier's desk, others flying over it into the door and falling to the floor. But soon, they converged on it, and the whole window was just a pile of rotting flesh and gnashing teeth.

Leo cried out, and Eddie whipped around, crowbar held high. The older man grappled with a zombie with blood-matted dreadlocks down to its waist. They toppled over into a drum set, cymbals clashing loudly as Leo shrieked in fear, trying to hold the ghoul's mouth away from his own face.

Eddie waffled, trying to line up his shot but afraid to accidentally hit Leo.

"Get it already!" Leo grunted, and gave a great push, shoving the zombie up as far as he could.

Eddie reacted, stabbing it in the temple, dropping it on top of his partner.

Leo immediately shoved the corpse off of him, backing up along the floor like a crab, and pressing himself against the far wall. "Are there any more?" he gasped.

Eddie shook his head, looking around the open store room. It looked more like a jam room, a place where music lessons took place. Off to the side was a desk, with a pretty impressive soundboard. Ignoring the pounding on the door for the time being, he approached the mixer, noting it was hooked up to a stereo.

He cocked a brow and hit the power button on the stereo. Some soft crooning piano music waved throughout the store, and he looked out at all the speakers lining the ceiling.

"That's not gonna do it," he murmured, and looked around for a stack of CDs or something. When he noticed a patch cord running from the mixer to a large amplifier, his eyebrows hit his hairline, and he grinned.

"What are we gonna do? What are we gonna do?" Leo moaned, pressing his hands to his head. "We're stuck in here!"

Eddie shook his head. "Our job is distraction, so distraction is what we're going to do," he explained as he picked up a bright red electric guitar and slung the strap over his shoulder. "Once they're done their job, they'll come get us."

"Are you sure?" Leo babbled. "What if the others die, and they just leave us in here?"

Eddie shrugged as he plugged the patch cord into the guitar, pushing up the main slider on the mixer. "Then we're going down rockin'."

Grace reached the department store first, and her heart leapt into her throat at the sheer number of zombies inside. Even on the second floor, the place was packed. Why were there this many people in the mall before things were even open?

Hawk slid up next to her, and they slid one of the doors closed, clicking the floor bolt down into place. This sent the ghouls into a frenzy, and they thundered towards them at full tilt.

"Hurry!" Grace screamed, and Hawk pulled on the second half of their door, managing to get it shut just in time. She looked over at the second set of doors, expecting Aly and Joseph to be there, doing their job, but they were still catching up.

Fuck fuck fuck, Grace thought, and tore for the other set of doors. The ghouls followed her, and Aly reached them just as she did, managing to throw both of their bodies into the doors just as the zombies crashed into them.

"I can't!" Joseph blubbered, and quickly turned tail, hurrying off towards the escalator.

"Get back here!" Hawk cried as he pushed in next to Grace, trying to dig in his heels. Their shoes squeaked against the smooth tile floors, and the three of them breathed heavily, grunting as they tried to close the doors.

"It's not working!" Aly shrieked, her eyes wide with horror.

A loud squeal echoed from the far side of the mall, followed by a series of rapid distorted power chords.

"We're not going to get these closed," Grace said, shaking her head. "We're going to have to make a run for it."

Hawk swallowed hard as he tried to dig in harder, fingers starting to wiggle through the gap in the doors. "We won't make it to the sporting store before they overwhelm us," he replied.

"If we go the opposite way, maybe they'll run towards the guitar noise and we can hunker down and wait for them to be clear so we can close these doors," Grace suggested.

"That's a big maybe," Hawk groaned.

Aly whimpered as her feet slid. "Make a decision!" she urged.

"On the count of three, we let go and run for that cafe over there," Grace blurted quickly. "Ready? One, two… three!"

The trio pushed off all at the same time, diving towards the little cafe at the end of the second-floor balcony. If they couldn't make it in, there was

nowhere to go but down. It wasn't the best
tactical decision, but it was a gamble
they had to take, better than being
trampled by zombies.

As the doors flew open and ghouls
poured out of the department store, some
of them moved towards the guitar solo, but
a good number of them took off after the
fresh meal.

Aly tripped over her own feet and
fell face-first onto the floor, smacking
her face into the tiles. She screamed, and
Hawk looked over his shoulder as zombies
piled on top of her. Grace's blood ran
cold at the sound of tearing flesh, but it
didn't slow her down. The woman was gone,
done like dinner. Literally.

As morbid as it was, Aly's gurgling
body slowed down the bulk of the zombies
chasing them, and they managed to skid
into the empty cafe, dragging the
Plexiglas divider across its track and
locking it. It bowed a bit as a quartet of
creatures crashed into it, but held.

"Fuck," Hawk cursed, bringing a hand
to his forehead.

"We need to clear the back," Grace
said, voice thick. She hadn't known Aly
for very long, but it was still a tragedy
when anyone died because of these stupid
missions they were forced to complete.
However, there was no time to mourn, they

had to do their jobs so they could survive.

Hawk nodded grimly, and they gripped their weapons, miraculously having held on to them during their battle with the doors. "I don't hear anything," he said, but they stayed cautious as they approached the counter.

"Me either," she replied, and when they reached the curtain for the back room, she strained her ears before hooking her finger in the edge of the fabric and pulling it aside.

The back area was a small prep room, with two ovens built into the wall. A tray of muffins sat on the prep table, and Troy approached them, relaxing once realizing they were truly alone. He poked one of the muffins, and then knocked on top of it.

"Hard as a rock," he lamented, wrinkling his nose.

Grace took a deep breath and pulled the walkie-talkie from her pocket, raising it to her lips. "No Name, are you there?" she asked, and turned around, heading back out into the cafe proper to keep an eye on the front.

Hawk followed her out and poked around behind the counter. He pulled a few levers and discovered the machine that spit out hot water, muttering under his breath as he pulled a few mugs down from one of the shelves.

"Copy, what's your status?" No Name's voice came through the radio.

Grace leaned on the counter as Hawk puttered around behind it and held the speaker to her mouth. "We couldn't get the doors closed," she reported. "Hawk and I are holed up in a cafe past the department store. I think Troy and Aaron are in the sporting goods store, and somebody from the decoy team is playing the electric guitar somewhere down the way. We can still hear it."

"That is not good," No Name said dryly. "What about the other two civilians that were with you?"

Grace rubbed her forehead. "Aly's dead, Joseph ran away as soon as we got to the doors." She sighed. "I don't know if he's alive or not. He ran towards the decoy team."

No Name grunted on the other end with dissatisfaction. "So the doors are still open, and all of you are trapped?" he asked. "Is that what you're telling me?"

"Maybe if we had proper preparation, and a team that was actually trained to do this kind of shit, then I wouldn't have to tell you shit like this," she snarled. "Or, you know, maybe if we weren't slaves to a—"

"That's enough," No Name cut in sharply. "Let me talk to some of the guys on the roof and we'll see what we can do."

CHAPTER EIGHT

"Hey!" Troy cried as Joseph ran towards them, pumping his legs hard with what looked like a lot of effort. "Hey!" He fumbled with the lock on the metal gate, hoping he could get it open in time so that the man could come inside to safety.

Joseph completely ignored them, spurred by fear, and ran past them towards the decoy team.

"Is he stupid?!" Aaron blurted, pressing his hands to his head. "The noise is where the zombies are gonna be!"

"Asshole coward," Troy snapped, shaking his head. "I'm not going out there and risking my neck to get him back."

He turned to stare at the department store, where the others were struggling to hold the second set of doors shut. Before he could unlatch the grate to go and help them, they dove out of the way, letting the floodgates open.

"Get back!" he hissed as the department store zombies tore towards them. He shoved Aaron around the corner from the metal gate, pressing them both against the wall. The ghouls thundered past, towards the still-wailing guitar, and Troy peeked out, trying to see what was happening at the store.

A woman's scream pierced the air, and he winced, spotting a cluster of ghouls bearing down on the floor. Guilt twisted his guts when relief washed over him that it was Aly and not Grace who'd fallen. The latter running for the cafe on the other side with Hawk.

"Who was that?" Aaron moaned, sounding near tears. "What's going on out there?"

"Shh," Troy replied. He wanted to make sure that the zombies eating Aly were going to steer clear of them. When they finished their meal, they took off towards the cafe instead of the guitar, slamming into the plexiglass barrier protecting Grace and Hawk.

He sighed heavily at the sight of the department store door still open. Every once in a while a zombie would come tearing out, catching wind of noise from the mall. The zombies banging on the cafe were loud enough that two more headed that way, including Aly as she reanimated, peeling her half-eaten corpse from the floor.

"Aly's dead," he murmured, and Aaron took in a ragged breath behind them. "Hawk and Grace are trapped in the cafe."

"We're fucked," he groaned. "What are we going to do now? They're just going to let us die in here, QXR bastards!"

Troy shook his head. "Just stay quiet," he instructed. "If we get an opening, we can go close the doors and then kill the zombies outside of the cafe."

"No way, no way we're going to do that," Aaron argued shrilly. "They said there are hundreds of those things in that store! Our job was to secure this spot, and we did it, and that's all we're doing!"

Troy turned to him, eyes blazing. "How do you go from crying about us being left to die in here, to standing by our *job*?" he hissed. "Clearly the plan didn't work, so we have to change it. Grace and Hawk aren't going to be able to get out of there by themselves, and we don't know how long Eddie and Leo are going to be able to keep up the distraction down there. Not to mention how screwed we'll be if all of the hundreds of those things get into the mall and are drawn to that noise. If they get too packed in here, we'll really be trapped. We need to get those doors closed."

"I'm staying right here," Aaron said, swallowing hard.

"You realize if those of us that are useful die in here, and you're the only one left, they're just going to leave you in here, right?" Troy asked, voice low and menacing. "You realize that Grace is the only one who can get us out of this alive, *right*? No Name gave *her* a gun. You want to stick with her."

"She wasn't able to do her job!" Aaron protested. "They're trapped too! What we should do is get down the escalator and back to the exit while all of the zombies are distracted!"

Troy rolled his eyes. "Oh yeah, and those guys won't just shoot us as soon as we come out, huh?" he asked, poking the man in the chest. "If we walk out that door, tell them that we abandoned what we were supposed to do and left four able-bodied slaves in here to die instead of completing the mission, they're not going to put bullets right into our foreheads."

Aaron's resolve seemed to be slipping, but it was being quickly replaced by blind fear, and Troy was seriously starting to think there was no saving his team. He looked back towards the doors, trying to work out if he would be able to get there and shut them on his own.

He figured he probably could, and get them shut, but he wouldn't be able to take out the ghouls at the cafe by himself. He'd have to run back to the sporting goods store and hunker down and regroup. But he wasn't sure if Aaron was the type of guy that would be so overcome with fear that he'd lock him out. Especially if he had any zombies on his tail.

He chewed his lip. If only he could talk to Grace, try to figure out the best course of action. If he could plan with her from the outside, so that they could help from the inside, they could probably take out the zombies outside of the cafe without Aaron's help. He grunted in frustration, ducking out of sight again as another pack of ghouls poured out of the store.

There were too many *ifs*, and not enough solutions.

"Doesn't she have a radio?" Aaron suddenly said. "She's supposed to call for help once it's done, right? She's probably figuring something out right now."

Troy hated to admit it, but he had a sinking feeling that Aaron was right. She likely was relaying the information to No Name and figuring out what to do next. If he tried to play hero, which he *really* didn't want to do, then he might throw a wrench into whatever plan they'd have going on.

He kept his eyes firmly locked on the cafe, waiting for some kind of signal, some kind of instructions. *Come on girl, give us a sign…*

CHAPTER NINE

"Grace, do you copy?" No Name asked through the radio.

She and Hawk sat at the cafe bar, sipping some surprisingly delicious coffee he'd managed to make with one of the pour-over stations.

"I'm here," she said. "What have you got?"

"We've done some recon from the skylights on the roof," he replied. "There's a couple hundred zombies throughout the mall, with dozens still in the department store."

Grace took a long, thoughtful sip of her hot brew. "Wonderful," she said dryly. "So what's the plan?"

"We have the opposite problem now, where the bulk of the zombies are in the mall instead of the store," No Name explained. "So same plan, but I'll need you on the other side of the locked doors, inside the store. You clear out in there, and then we'll do the fish-in-a-barrel routine from the other side."

Hawk took a sip of his coffee, and then motioned to the barrier, where there were now nine zombies—Aly included—pawing at the plexiglass. "What about them?"

Grace nodded, bringing the radio to her lips again. "We've got nine of those things boxing us in here," she explained. "They don't seem to care about the decoy team's noise."

"There's an access panel just outside of the department store," No Name replied. "I'll get one of my men to shoot something loud to draw them away from you, so you can get into the store."

She pursed her lips for a moment. "How close to the doors?" she asked. "What if it draws a bunch of those things out to us?"

"Pick your moment," he replied. "There's nothing else close enough that it would make a difference."

Hawk scoffed. "No, of course not, you know there aren't a bunch of dudes with guns outside that could come in through the same door we did and *help* us or anything," he muttered.

"We'll try," Grace replied simply. "I supposed there's no place near wherever the decoy team is to shoot out the horde?"

"Negative," No Name replied. "That would be the easiest option, but there's no roof access there."

"Of course there isn't," Hawk said, shaking his head and downing the rest of his coffee.

Grace sighed. "Okay," she said into the walkie-talkie, "I'll report back soon, one way or the other." She clicked off the radio before any reply, not wanting to hear his voice anymore. Regardless of him seeming more sympathetic than his comrades, he was still putting them through this, and she was sick of listening to his voice.

"So, this is fun," Hawk said, voice high in sarcasm.

Grace nodded and drank the rest of the mug, smacking her lips together. "At least the brew was good," she said. "Thank you."

"Anytime," he replied, and then got down from their stools.

They approached the barrier slowly, sticking to the shadows.

"I don't even know why they're still here," she whispered. "You'd think that after no movement for a while, they'd have gone after the noise."

Hawk shrugged. "Maybe they can smell us in here," he suggested. "It's hard to imagine they have any kind of memory with dead brains… like do they remember that we came in here and have the mental capacity to know that we're trapped?"

"Don't know," she replied, and shook her head. It was unsettling to think about these things having any kind of thought process. But there wasn't any use ruminating on it. They were stuck in here, and nine corpses needed to get out of their way before they could make a run for the doors.

She wished they'd have been able to communicate with Troy. She could see the sporting goods store, and wondered if they were close enough that if they made a bunch of noise, the zombies would go their way.

But again, these types of thought trains were useless. All she could do was hope that maybe he was watching, and would come out if they got into a grapple.

There was the crack of gunfire and the ghouls snapped around, all save for one. Eight of them took off, and Grace didn't waste any time.

She threw the bolt and opened the barrier, lunging forward and swinging at the remaining zombie, dropping it to the floor. She took off for the doors, but the zombies were already disinterested in the gunfire.

She'd been hoping that they would get all the way under that panel so the mercenary above could take them out, but no such luck as they reared on her and Hawk.

He nearly smashed into the back of her as she stopped short, preparing to sprint back to the coffee shop.

"Heyooo!" somebody bellowed, and there was a clatter of metal as Troy darted out from the sporting goods store, a baseball bat in his hand.

The zombies seemed confused for a moment, looking back and forth as if unsure which human would taste the best, and Grace took advantage of the situation. She lunged and stabbed at one that had its back turned closest to her and then leapt back as the noise drew the attention of its partner.

Hawk took care of that one, smashing it in the side of the skull with his weapon, and Troy let out another holler as he neared them.

The five still standing ran for him, and Grace and Hawk tore after them, swinging hard.

Troy's baseball bat connected with one's face, sending the body staggering back into its friends, and the back two fell with wet *crunches* as metal crushed their skulls. The final ghoul flailed around as the others fell on top of it, and Grace leaned forward, stabbing it in the face before it could get free.

Aaron skidded up to them, clutching his tire iron with wide eyes.

"Oh, you decided to join us?" Troy drawled.

"We have to get into the store!" Grace urged, and took off for the doors, three teammates in tow.

"Wait, inside?!" Troy cried, though he followed her in.

She and Hawk closed the doors, bolting them down, and then turned around to face the horde of hungry ghouls turning around to face them.

Grace dove to the right, slamming into a ghoul in a department store uniform, sending it over the railing to the first floor below. They were on a mezzanine, a store escalator in the center next to an elevator in a glass tube.

The first floor crawled with zombies, but there were enough up where they were to be deadly.

"We need to block the escalator!" she cried, and it was true, but they were going to have to fight their way there.

Hawk grabbed a rolling rack of clothes, swinging it around and letting it go to smack into a group of zombies running at him. They got tangled up and fell in a heap, the hangers clattering to the floor as the rack fell over.

Troy followed his lead, and thrust a second rack at Aaron, who was simply standing open-mouthed in fear.

"Get your shit together!" he barked. "We've got to fight!"

Grace flew past them to the wall, wrapping her fingers around a sturdy-looking shoe shelf. It was fastened to the wall, so she climbed it like a ladder until she balanced on top of it, pressed back against the wall. She pulled the handgun from the back of her pants, took aim at one of the ghouls closest to Hawk, and fired.

The bullet hit its mark, and the noise caught the attention of the bulk of the creatures. They ran towards her, their fingertips just brushing the tops of the shelf. Shoes fell everywhere as they flailed for her, but she focused on the ones still unperturbed by her.

The trio of ghouls stuck under Hawk's rolling rack found their footing and launched towards Aaron. Grace fired three times, taking out two with headshots and hitting the third in the shoulder. The cluster around her grew, drawing most of the zombies to the noise of the gun.

"Block the escalator!" she screamed, as she spotted some ghouls attempting to get up the frozen stairs below. Despite their clumsiness, with enough flailing and determination, she didn't want to bank on them not being able to get up.

Hawk and Troy brained two more ghouls near them, and then grabbed their rolling racks of doom, pulling them towards the escalators. Aaron staggered over to the railing, looking down to the floor, and Grace's blood boiled. She couldn't help but imagine what it would be like to put a bullet in his head, put him out of his misery.

But she wasn't a murderer. Killing zombies was one thing… killing a human was another. Of course, if he kept up this level of uselessness, it likely wouldn't be long before he *was* a zombie, and she'd have to put him down anyway. But they'd cross that bridge if and when they came to it.

Hawk and Troy shoved rack after rack down the stairs, and the noise began to draw the back of Grace's group, easily now at twenty or so.

She took aim and fired at one that was closest to the boys, dropping it and putting the heat back on her. A particularly tall zombie clawed at the tip of her shoe, and she grunted, kicking out and steadying her balance before swinging down with her crowbar to take it out.

When the escalator was sufficiently full of metal and clothing, creating the most effective barrier they could build, Hawk and Troy turned back to her.

"If you try to get them from the back, I'll keep drawing them back to me with the gun," Grace called, and they both nodded.

Troy glanced over at Aaron, who was still clutching the railing, looking down at the sea of angry ghouls below. He stalked over and grabbed the man by the arm.

"Get your ass in gear or I'll throw you over myself," he snapped.

Aaron clenched his jaw, defiance in his gaze, but it was laced in stone fear at the threat. He nodded jerkily, and they came to stand with Hawk.

Grace fired again, at a zombie in the middle of the horde to make sure the falling body wouldn't draw attention to the back, and then the three men went to work.

They darted forward, each smacking down a skull. Hawk managed to stab a second ghoul before jumping back, and Aaron and Troy retreated immediately as creatures whipped around.

Grace was ready and aiming, and popped off three quick shots in succession, dropping three distracted zombies in the back. Another hand brushed her shoe, and she swung with her crowbar again.

She overestimated her balance and had a moment of panic where she thought she might topple right into the mini-horde. She windmilled her arms and pressed up on the balls of her feet, and her heart hammered in her chest as she regained her balance, pressing her back against the wall and breathing heavy.

She steadied herself and watched Hawk, Troy, and Aaron lunge forward again, each taking down another ghoul. Once they leapt back into the clear, she popped off a few more shots, keeping her other hand firmly against the wall to keep herself grounded. Her aim was off a touch, and only two of the ghouls fell, but they were thinning the herd nicely.

When they were down to five, she holstered her gun, hoping that she hadn't wasted too many bullets that they'd need later. Hawk stabbed a ghoul in the face and then used the corpse to bowl over two other zombies.

Grace shimmied until she was above him and then dropped down behind him, darting around to lunge at one of the ghouls trying to get the drop on Troy. Aaron swung wildly at his zombie, but his blow glanced off of its neck, and it latched onto his arm. He screamed as it bit into his tricep, and tried to wrench his arm out of its teeth, to no avail.

Grace moved towards him, but the zombies Hawk was wrestling with pulled away and tore for the easy meal. Between the three of them, they tackled Aaron to the floor, and his screams quickly turned to gurgles.

"While they're distracted!" Grace hissed, though her blood ran cold at the thought of it. Hadn't she thought about shooting Aaron? Hadn't she thought he wouldn't survive? And here he was, on the ground, being feasted on, the perfect distraction for destroying the threat. Her mouth tasted like bile.

They rushed over, each stabbing down at a ghoul, and the bodies fell limp on top of Aaron. He was barely alive, his eyes rolling as his head lolled back and forth, blood pouring from his mouth and throat.

Grace swallowed hard. "Sorry," she whispered, and then stabbed him in the eye socket with her crowbar.

The trio stepped back, tentatively relieved they'd survived this leg of the battle. The moans and groans and snarls echoing up from the first floor didn't do anything to comfort them, however, because the battle was far from over.

"We need to clear this floor," Grace said, checking to make sure her gun and walkie-talkie were still there.

Hawk nodded. "I don't think there's anything else, considering all the noise we made," he pointed out, "but a sweep would be best."

They readied their weapons and headed past the escalator, glancing down to make sure that the pileup of clothing racks were still doing their job. A few had dislodged at the bottom, but the ghouls hadn't made it even a quarter of the way up, so they were okay for now.

They wove their way through housewares and linens, making sure there were no more zombies hiding anywhere, which there didn't seem to be. When they came out the other side, they looked down off of the mezzanine to the terror below.

There was a clatter as some of the rabid creatures pulled down a few more clothing racks, struggling beneath them but freeing up half of the escalators.

"How many bullets do you have left?" Troy asked, though his tone betrayed that he knew the answer already.

Grace shook her head. She didn't even need to look. "Not enough," she replied dryly.

Hawk chewed his lip for a moment. "That's not going to hold forever," he said. "What are we going to do, here?"

"No chance our buddies outside can come in and mop this up?" Troy asked, wrinkling his nose.

"Nope," Grace replied, shaking her head. "We gotta clear in here and then draw the mall zombies to us. Somehow." She sighed. "But that's later. What are we going to do *now*?"

Hawk rubbed his forehead. "I have an idea…" he drawled, trailing off. "But I don't really like it."

"Spit it out," Troy said, waving a hand at him.

Hawk motioned to the elevator. "We've still got power. We could take the elevator down."

"They'd be on us as soon as the doors open," Grace replied, brow furrowing. "We'd be stuck."

"Not if we ride on the top of the car," he replied, and then winced. "See? Don't like it."

But she had a thoughtful expression on her face. "It would work."

"That's not a very big elevator shaft," Troy mused.

She nodded. "That's why you're going to stay up here," she said. "You stay at the top of the escalator, make sure that the barricade holds, and Hawk and I will ride down and kill whatever ends up attracted by the doors opening. Once it's clear, we'll play cat and mouse like we did up here."

He gaped at her. "Except with a lot more of those things," he protested.

"And you'll have to make noise without a gun," she replied. "I think we might need it more downstairs, just in case."

Troy shook his head. "Okay, girl, I don't have any other ideas," he admitted.

"I'll get prying on the ceiling panel," Hawk said, holding up his crowbar.

The trio headed for the elevator, and Grace clapped Troy on the back as they passed by it to the escalators. "Cause enough of a ruckus and we should be able to just take them all out from behind," she said.

"I don't know, that's quite a group," he replied, shaking his head. "What do I do if they start getting too far up?"

She glanced over her shoulder at a few shoe displays. "Toss whatever you can on top of them," she instructed. "Just try not to hit us." She cracked a small smile.

"I'll do my best," he said, putting a hand on his chest.

Grace jogged back over to Hawk, who was just pulling the ceiling door of the elevator open. The sliding doors began to close automatically, and she stuck out a hand to push them back.

"Got it?" she asked, and he nodded.

"Yep, come here, I'll give you a boost," he replied, lacing his fingers together to make a step out of his hands.

She shook her head. "How about I give you a boost?" she asked. "I think you can probably pull me up through that hole better than I can pull you."

"Fair enough," he replied, and moved over to the door open button, mashing on it as she took a position beneath the trapdoor. She laced her fingers together and then gave him a nod.

Hawk stepped forward and put a foot in her hand, pushing off of the ground. Grace hauled up as hard as she could, and he reached up into the hole, grabbing the sides and pulling himself up.

She darted over to the door and hit the button again to keep the doors open just as they started to close, and then smashed the first floor button before darting back underneath the hole. Hawk's arm hung through, waiting, and she crouched as low as she could, leaping into the air. She managed to grasp his wrist, and he pulled her up enough with a grunt so she could grab the side of the hole, pulling herself up just as the doors gave a *ding* and closed, beginning the descent.

"How are we going to do this?" Hawk asked. "I know it was my idea, but depending on how many get in…"

Grace shrugged. "We can try to stab them, and if that doesn't work I'll shoot them until I run out of bullets," she replied. "Hopefully I don't have to do that, and Troy and draw enough of them to the escalators."

"Guess we didn't think that far," Hawk muttered. "If they swarm over here, we're stuck in this elevator shaft."

She shook her head. "We can either climb, or Troy can push the button for us," she replied, as the elevator reached the bottom floor. "But one thing at a time."

The doors gave a *ding* and slid open. They watched through the glass shaft as three zombies tore towards them, slamming into the elevator, looking around, confused.

Troy began to smack the metal racks with his crowbar, making a ruckus, and one of the ghouls took off, the rest on the bottom floor converging on the escalators. The two in the elevator seemed at a loss, bumping into each other, and then bouncing off the walls of the small elevator.

Grace pursed her lips. She didn't think she'd be able to reach low enough with her weapon to stab one, so they had to hope they'd just leave. After what felt like forever, the two zombies managed to bonk their way out the door, shoving each other to tear towards the escalator.

"We've got to hurry," Hawk murmured, motioning.

The sheer amount of zombies tangled in the clothing racks was easily thirty, and the flailing bodies continued to dislodge the haphazard barricade.

Grace nodded and hung her legs into the hole, taking a deep breath before dropping down. She immediately ducked out of the way, pressing her back against the button panel, out of sight of the horde. Hawk came next, and did the same, across the way on the other side of the elevator car.

She pointed to him and then motioned to a makeup kiosk on his side of the store. He peered out and nodded, and she

jerked her thumb over her shoulder, to
signal that she would go the other way.

They made sure the coast was clear,
and then darted out of the elevator, each
running off in their own direction.

As soon as Grace cleared the elevator
shaft, a duo of zombies appeared from
behind a magazine display, surprising her.
She ducked her shoulder and slammed into
one, sending it flying backwards. She
swung around immediately, burying her
crowbar into the temple of the other one,
and stopped long enough to stab the fallen
ghoul before sprinting behind a larger
shelf of magazines and stationery
supplies.

Chest heaving, she took stock of her
surroundings, making sure there would be
no surprises, and when she was sure her
area was clear, she moved over to the
other side so she could get a better view
of the escalators.

The zombies had managed to traverse
about two-thirds of the stairs, and Troy
was just toppling a large shelf over the
top rack. It bounced off of a few ghouls
and flattened a few more, skidding to a
stop about three-quarters of the way down.

Grace reached up and wiggled the
shelf she stood behind, finding it flimsy
and not bolted down. She took a deep
breath and then let out a sharp whistle.

As soon as a pack of zombies came
running her way, she disappeared behind
the shelf, and then gave it a shove,
clambering up onto a foothold and holding
on. The unit toppled forward, her body
weight on top of it as it flattened a few
bodies.

She ran forward, light on her feet,
keeping the unit pinning the ghouls
beneath her. Two that were just out of the
way when it fell lunged for her, and she
stabbed one, using it as a battering ram
to shove the other back. As it fell
beneath its friend, she jumped down and
stabbed it through the eye before whipping
around to deal with the pinned zombies.

One head stuck out from beneath the
shelf, so she got rid of it fast, but the
others were writhing arms and legs, so she
left them for the moment. A few more
ghouls were hot on her tail, so she took
off to dive behind another bookshelf.
These deeper for full novels instead of
magazines, running down one aisle, ducked
down to stay out of sight.

Troy banged his crowbar again,
yelling and whooping, hopefully drawing
the bulk of the ghouls back towards him.
She wasn't sure how Hawk was faring, but
she had to trust that he was pulling his
weight. They needed to be a team here.

Footsteps echoed behind her and she whipped around, bringing her crowbar down on top of a zombie skull. It stumbled, and she smacked it again, cracking it this time, and as the corpse fell, another launched at her from right behind it. She kicked it in the chest, sending it back away from her, and then stabbed forward, killing it with an eye shot.

When she emerged from the other side of the shelf, Troy was just sending another shoe rack downrange, and it flattened a few more ghouls on the stairs on the left side. Grace crept along behind another bookshelf, and then soundlessly darted out to the back of the far left of the horde.

She stabbed one in the very back and then jumped back. Troy's voice was growing hoarse, but still loud enough to hold their attention and drown out the sound of falling bodies, so she lunged forward for another, picking off the zombies at the back.

By the makeup counter, Hawk leapt over a pile of bodies he'd amassed in front of it, and crept quietly behind the horde on the right side. Between him and Grace, they began to fell corpses, and Troy upped his noise game to keep them as focused on him as he could.

"Yeah, fuck you, fuck you, and *especially* fuck you!" he bellowed, brandishing a metal post from one of the racks as well as his crowbar. He started to play a drum beat on one of the racks, and although he didn't have much rhythm, it was loud and did the trick.

A zombie spun around and threw itself at Grace, and she instinctively ducked, sending it tripping over her and flopping to the floor. She dove to the side in case any of its friends decided to join it and then circled around to stab it before it could get up.

Before long, Hawk and Grace had taken care of all of the standing zombies, leaving only the ones crushed by racks and shelves.

"Hang tight up there," she called to Troy, who gave her a little salute. "I need help with the magazine rack," she said to Hawk, motioning back towards the ghouls trying to slither out from beneath her fallen shelf.

"Nice one," Hawk commended, and they strolled over to the rack, still running on adrenaline. One ghoul had managed to wriggle its way half out, and he dispatched it before kicking a leg sticking out beside it. "I pull, you stab?" he asked, and Grace nodded.

He wrapped his hands around the flailing ankles and jerked, pulling the zombie clear. Grace stabbed it quickly, and then they turned back to the escalator, where a few pissed-off ghouls thrashed, tangled up in equipment.

"Think it's safer to disentangle them, or climb up and stab through the racks?" Grace asked, and Hawk shrugged.

"Either or is plenty unsafe," he replied, and she couldn't help but laugh.

This was life, now.

She nodded and moved forward, climbing up onto the center median and shimmying up the escalator. She jabbed a few times through metal posts and clothes hangers, eventually catching the last animated zombie in the skull, ending the threat.

Or at least, the immediate threat of the department store.

"That went a lot better than I thought it was gonna," Troy called from the top, pressing a hand to his forehead.

Grace nodded, letting out a deep breath. "Me too," she admitted. She slid down the median and hit the floor, waving for Hawk to follow her to the elevator. "Let's do a sweep and go back upstairs," she instructed, pulling the walkie-talkie from her pocket. "Job isn't over yet."

"Department store is secure," Grace said into the radio as she and Hawk stepped out of the elevator.

There was a moment of silence before No Name came back, "Good. We have some fenangling to do."

"Fenangling?" she asked, raising an eyebrow.

"The guitar is still going, and we need those zombies to come to the department store side," he explained. "So we're going to cut the power to that end of the mall, and when it stops you can draw them all to your end so we can shoot them from the access panels."

She took a deep breath. "Okay," she replied. "And what about the zombies on the bottom floor?"

"We'll mop those up after we deal with the second floor," No Name replied.

"And go and get Eddie and Leo, right?" Grace asked firmly. "They're probably pretty pinned down over there."

"Yes, once we finish off the ones you can draw to you, we'll come in and take care of whatever is left on their end," No Name said.

She nodded. "Okay, we'll cause a ruckus over here, just make sure your guys are ready."

"Done," came the reply, and then she shoved the walkie-talkie back in her pocket, leaving the volume up in case he needed to get back to her.

Hawk swiped his palms together and slicked his sweaty hair back, having slid his crowbar into his belt loop once again. "Being stuck in the cafe was nicer, at least we had coffee," he said.

"You guys got *coffee*?" Troy asked, throwing his hands up. "I miss all the best shit."

"It was really good coffee, too," Grace teased. "Freshly brewed dark roast."

"Stop, girl, you're making my mouth water," Troy replied, waving her off as they headed for the doors.

She sighed. "I mean, I would much rather go for a latte, but it is what it is," she said wistfully.

"Triple-shot mochaccino," Troy moaned, licking his lips.

Hawk rolled his eyes. "Listen to you both with your hipster drinks," he drawled. "Black coffee, strong as hell, that's all you need."

"Pumpkin spice with almond milk, extra foamy," Grace continued, ignoring him.

"Short espresso with whipped cream on top," Troy added.

She nodded emphatically. "Yeah, what's that called, a con panna?" she asked, pointing at him. "So good!"

"Disgusting," Hawk muttered.

As they reached the doors, enjoying their tiny bit of levity in a terrible situation, they could hear the guitar muffled in the distance.

"I don't know if that's Eddie or Leo, but their fingers must be bleeding by now," Troy said.

Hawk shook his head. "Nah, that's some pro playing there. If they're that good, they've got calluses on their fingers the size of this mall," he pointed out.

All of a sudden, the music stopped, and the lights down the hallway went out.

"Make some noise," No Name's voice came through the radio, and the trio nodded at each other.

"Makes sense to open the doors and yell until they get close enough, right?" Grace asked, and though the others looked reluctant to break their safe barrier, they knew she was right.

Troy put a hand. "Let's all do one set, though, just in case," he suggested.

"Good call," Hawk agreed, and they moved to the right set of double doors. "You take one, I'll take the other, and Grace you're on locking duty?"

She nodded and knelt down, pulling up the deadbolts from the floor. "Ready," she said, and they pushed open the doors.

The boys began to holler, and Grace pulled her lip between her teeth, letting out one of her sharp whistles. She could see a square of light on the floor with a silhouette in it and assumed it was one of the mercenaries up top at an access panel. Another square of light appeared next to it, and a second silhouette, which was comforting. At least they were there, ready. She just hoped the plan would work.

Soon, the footsteps thundered towards them, and they could see a horde tearing up the balcony towards the doors. They hollered until the zombies reached the sporting goods store, and then Hawk and Troy pulled the doors closed, and Grace locked them tightly. She grabbed the radio.

"Get ready!" she barked into it, but the guys up top had already opened fire.

Bullets sprayed the horde in full automatic fire, peppering their bodies into swiss cheese. Those that didn't get hit in the head still fell backwards from the momentum of the shots, and the horde began to fall, bodies piling up and causing the ones behind to trip in a stumbling mass of death.

"Is that...?" Grace asked, squinting, staring out at a particular zombie flopping and twitching just on the other side of the doors.

"It's Joseph," Hawk replied, shaking his head.

She wanted to say *he shouldn't have run,* but it didn't need to be said. They'd lost three today, and hopefully they wouldn't lose a fourth. Or a fifth. Or a sixth…

It didn't take long for the mercenaries to plow through the mass of corpses, and soon there was nothing left but limp, bullet-ridden bodies in a heap.

"If they have this much ammo, *why* do they insist on sending us into buildings with crowbars?" Troy snapped, throwing his hands up. "This is fucking absurd!"

Grace shook her head. There was no time for this type of thinking. They had to get through this job.

"It's a power trip," Hawk said, drawing his bottom lip between his teeth. "That's all it is."

Grace lifted the radio to her lips. "Looks good, what now?" she asked.

"We're going to come in from one of the roof access stairwells and go clean up wherever the decoy team is," No Name replied. "I'll need you three to come out and watch the escalator, make sure nothing is making its way up from the bottom floor."

She nodded. "Got it," she said, and pocketed the radio again. "Crowbars ready," she instructed. "I don't trust that all of these things are all dead."

Hawk opened the door, weapon tightly in hand, and they carefully picked over the mountain of corpses, making sure nothing was still moving or moaning. Troy found one, stabbing it despite it being pinned by a ton of its brethren, but the rest were all still.

The trio converged at the top of the escalator, and there were a few ghouls milling about at the bottom, but no other corpses to be seen from their vantage point. As gunfire echoed at the far end of the mall, Grace assumed the ones on the bottom floor were probably hanging out over there.

"So, we just wait?" Troy asked. "I like this."

Hawk rolled his eyes. "Don't get too comfortable."

CHAPTER THIRTEEN

As Eddie continued to shred the guitar, playing a crunchy rendition of one of his favourite classic rock tunes, two things happened at once.

One, the power went out, killing his wicked solo, and the second was the distinct sound of shattering glass.

"Stay clear of the door!" he yelled, assuming that the glass breaking was the door window. The louder moans and snarls solidified this theory.

"I can't see the door!" Leo cried from somewhere behind him.

"Then stay away from the sounds!" Eddie called back, frantically scrambling for his crowbar. He didn't think any of the zombies could get in, especially through an opening so high off of the ground, but he didn't want to take chances. He needed to kill as many as he could to plug the hole in the door.

"What are you doing?!" Leo yelled as Eddie dropped the guitar with a crash.

"I need to kill enough of these fuckers to barricade the door!" he called back.

"But how can you *see* what you're killing?!" came the shrill question. "If you get bit and turn into one of those things, I'm boned!"

Yeah, only you'd be boned, Eddie thought bitterly, but chose not to argue. His hand finally clasped around the crowbar, and he stood up, listening hard, willing his eyes to adjust to the darkness. But there was no adjusting to this. If the power was out, then the only light in the mall was from the sparse skylights in the center over the main walkway, not close to this store. Between the shadow of the deep store, and the horde of zombies blocking the door, it was completely devoid of sight in there.

He strained his ears as he moved, and then tripped over one of the fallen drums, cursing as he fell to his knees. However, it gave him an idea, and he picked up what felt like a snare drum on a stand. He grabbed the metal base and then held it straight out in front of him, testing the darkness.

It finally hit the wall, and didn't move, which meant he wasn't poking the door. He moved to the left, where he could hear the moans, and finally slid the drum over the seam of the doorframe. Something grabbed onto the side of the drum, and it vibrated as hands smacked into it.

He shoved it over a little more, lowering it until it felt like the ghouls were pushing down on it, instead of the side. He braced his torso into the bottom of the stand and readied his crowbar.

Do I go with a swing or a jab? Eddie thought and then shook his head. Probably a jab would be best, hoping he hit a head.

"What are you doing?" Leo asked, closer now. "Don't get bit, man."

"Shut up, I'm concentrating," Eddie muttered, and then froze at the sound of muffled gunfire. "What the hell?"

Zombies shrieked from outside, and some pulled away from the window, casting a tiny bit of light on the situation. Eddie stepped back, lowering the drum. The gunfire was louder now that the window wasn't full of rotted flesh, and he moved out of the way to avoid catching a stray bullet.

"Looks like the cavalry has arrived," he muttered, and if he were being honest, he hadn't expected it. He'd been certain that the QXR were going to leave him and Leo in this room to die. Hell, maybe they still would, and were just clearing out the last of the zombies.

When the window was clear and the shots ceased, he carefully moved into the center of the room to peer out through the darkness.

"You alive in there?" somebody barked.

Eddie's shoulders sagged with relief. "Yeah, we're alive," he called. "Can we come out now?"

"Come on out," the man replied, "slowly."

"Slowly?" he muttered under his breath. "Like we're robbing a bank or something."

Leo grabbed his arm. "I can't go out there," he hissed.

"What?" Eddie replied, shaking his head. "We have to go out there. We don't have anywhere else to go, man."

The man shook his head rapidly. "I can't."

"Why the hell not? I know it sucks man, but we've got to go back to our cells now," Eddie said. "Grab some food, get some sleep, and then do all this shit again tomorrow."

Leo blinked rapidly, and then rolled up the sleeve of his plaid shirt, revealing a crimson bite in his forearm.

"What the fuck?!" Eddie blurted, eyes narrowing. "You had that this whole time? When the hell were you going to tell me? And you were all pissed about me getting too close to the door, *why*?"

"It happened when that thing had me in the drums," Leo hissed.

"Get out here!" the mercenary outside bellowed. "We've got shit to do!"

"Stay in here, then," Eddie replied. "I don't know what you want me to do about it."

His partner shook his head rapidly. "They're going to kill me!"

"You're going to die anyway," Eddie shot back, and though his chest tightened in a mixture of sympathy and pity, he didn't know what he could possibly do about this situation. "It's your choice whether you want to die slowly in here, alone, or quick from a bullet. I can't make that choice for you, and I don't know what else you want me to say. I'm not going to stay in here and get eaten."

Leo backed away from him, shaking. "Just tell them I'm already dead."

"And risk them finding out I lied?" Eddie shook his head. "You know I can't do that, man. I know it sucks, but you have to own up to this."

His partner crossed his arms. "I'm not going out there."

"Hey!" the mercenary yelled, all semblance of patience gone.

Eddie shrugged and headed for the door, opening it slowly. He raised his hands, still holding his crowbar, and moved out into the store. Three mercenaries stood by the entrance, guns trained on him.

"Where's the other guy?" one of them asked.

Eddie glanced over his shoulder, not seeing Leo following him. "He doesn't want to come out," he replied.

"Does he need us to drag him out?" the mercenary snarled. "You ain't gonna like that, boy!"

For a second, Eddie wished that Leo was closer to death, so he could send these assholes into the room for a nasty surprise. But he shook it off. Nothing about this situation was good. He didn't want an innocent man to die because of these guys. He didn't want to be complicit in outing him for being bit. But the fact of the matter was, if they left him there, he was a danger to other innocents that would potentially be inhabiting this mall.

"He's bit," he finally said, and two of the mercenaries immediately stormed forward, brushing past him into the back room.

"No, no!" Leo screamed, and then two gunshots silenced him.

Eddie's gut clenched hard, and he hung his head. He didn't feel good about this at all. Any elation he'd felt from his revisit to his guitar heyday evaporated. He also felt guilty for being so angry that the man hadn't said anything, and could have turned at any

time while they were stuck in that room,
killing them both.

"You're clear?" one of the
mercenaries asked him, eyeing him
carefully.

"Did you even check him before you
shot him?" Eddie ashed through clenched
teeth.

The mercenary sneered at him. "He was
holding up his bitten arm," he said,
tapping the flashlight on the top of his
gun. "Do I need to strip you to check?"

"No, you can just take a look at me,
asshole," Eddie muttered, holding up his
hands higher so they could see his intact
clothing.

"He's clean," the other mercenary
said, and then they ushered him out of the
store. No Name approached them, pointing
to a few off to the side and motioning for
them to head back towards the department
store.

"Where's your teammate?" he asked.

Eddie clenched his jaw. "He was
bitten," he said.

"We took care of it, sir," one of the
mercenaries added, and No Name nodded, for
a moment looking just exhausted.

"Where are the others?" Eddie asked,
tucking his crowbar into his belt buckle.
"Are they okay?"

"Your shipmates are the only ones to survive," No Name replied flatly. "Come on, we still have to clear out the main floor."

Grace straightened as No Name approached with Eddie in tow, but not Leo. Mercenaries lined the railing, firing sporadically down at the ghouls wandering around on the main floor. Thankfully, none of the ghouls had attempted to get up the escalator, so the trio had finally had a well-deserved break of it.

"Leo didn't make it?" Troy asked, voice tired.

Eddie simply shook his head as he joined them. "I see you guys fared just as well," he replied.

"That was some kick-ass guitar playing, my man," Hawk piped up.

"Saved my ass," Troy added. "Thanks."

Eddie shrugged. "Saw an opportunity."

"Stay sharp," No Name cut into their reunion, motioning to the ground floor.

Grace rolled her eyes. The zombies didn't stand a chance against the mercenaries' guns, and they were easily taking out the few stragglers.

The stragglers from the hundreds that we dealt with for you, she thought bitterly, shaking her head. The quartet stayed quiet, standing vigil as the gunmen took out the last of the ghouls.

"Sweep the mall," No Name barked, and men jogged towards him, heading down the escalator in a single file.

"Are we done, then?" Troy drawled. "Or do we get to lead the men with assault rifles on their sweep, carrying crowbars?" He held up his weapon to accentuate his point.

No Name didn't meet his gaze, his jaw clenched hard. Grace watched him, noting his discomfort and his tired eyes. She knew it was dangerous to wonder if he would break and go against his masters, but she couldn't help it. Especially after such a long, draining day. It was difficult not to give into such hopes.

As the last of the men headed downstairs, No Name motioned for them to go. "Let's get back outside, through that maintenance tunnel," he said. "I'll drive us back to the ship."

They filed downstairs like good little lemmings, and out into the fresh air. The mall had a stench to it, the stench of death. Grace wondered if any of these buildings would ever *not* smell like death, ever again. After being packed full of corpses and blood… could it ever really wash away?

They dumped their weapons into the bin by the van, and Grace reluctantly pulled out the gun and walkie-talkie, handing them back over to No Name. He checked the chamber and popped out the mag, blinking down at it in surprise.

"Bullets to spare," he said. "I'm impressed."

She shrugged. "I didn't want to waste any resources," she replied. "Only used it when I needed to."

He nodded and opened the passenger door, motioning for her to climb up.

Grace wrinkled her nose, not exactly excited about his act of chivalry, but decided she was too tired to argue, and climbed up into the passenger seat. He shut the door as the others got into the back of the van and skirted the hood to come around to the driver's seat.

They rode in silence, and Grace couldn't help but ruminate on how, after such a short time, they'd already been trained like dogs. They did their job, gave their equipment back at the end of the day, and then rode back to their cells. Just that morning they'd accused their captors of being QXR canines, but here they were.

She held on top the hope that it was okay for them, because they had no choice. She side-glanced No Name. Did he really have a choice, either? She knew it was dangerous thinking, and mentally chastised herself, but it was possible that No Name,

and maybe other mercenaries that were in
the group, were just as much prisoners as
they were.

She shook her head. She didn't need
to worry about anybody other than herself.
She was the bottom of the food chain, and
she needed to survive. For Dante.

When they got back to the ship, they
filed inside, feet dragging as the
exhaustion really began to overtake them.
No Name locked them up, and then
disappeared as they got comfortable,
returning in a few moments with a tray of
food.

"Mac and cheese?" Troy raised an
eyebrow as he took his bowl. "What are we,
college students?"

No Name glared at him. "Would you
rather have nothing?"

"No sir, enroll me in a local class,"
Troy quipped, and took his bowl, digging
in with fervor as he sat on his bed.

"Yet another delicacy that could be
improved with hot sauce," Eddie declared
as he took his bowl, and No Name took a
step back to regard the quartet as they
ate their meals.

"You four did a really great job
today," he said.

Grace couldn't hold in her scoff.

"Got something to say?" he asked.

She licked her lips, setting down her fork. "It was a shitshow in there," she said. "We were under prepared, and only half of our team survived."

"That's why I said *you* four did a great job," No Name explained. "I appreciate it."

Hawk scowled. "Yeah, we really live for your appreciation."

"My appreciation keeps you alive another day," No Name snapped, but the words didn't hold as much venom as they could. He sighed. "Rest up. Don't know where you'll be posted tomorrow." He turned around and left through the stairwell before any of them could retort back at him.

"That guy gives me a rash," Eddie said through a mouthful of cheesy noodles.

Hawk nodded. "He's better than Mosley at least," he replied.

"Amen to that," Troy agreed, raising his fork in solidarity.

Grace stayed quiet, chewing slowly, enjoying every bite of the boxed mac and cheese. It had been a favourite of hers when she was a little kid, and Dante made it for her often. At the time she hadn't realized it was because it was cheap and they didn't have a lot of money—she just thought he was doing it because she liked it.

Her heart clenched at the thought of him scraping pennies together to take care of her, so young. She couldn't help but wish for a world where he didn't have to take care of her anymore. Where he could just move on and live his own life, a happy life.

"So, where'd you learn to shred the guitar like that?" Hawk finally asked, regarding Eddie.

The smaller man laughed, shaking his head. "Used to play in a punk band when I was a teenager," he said. "*Twisted Carnage*, we called ourselves. We were fucking terrible."

The others laughed, even Grace, who couldn't suppress a chuckle.

"It was me and five guys, and all of us still lived with our parents," Eddie continued. "Thing was, none of our parents wanted to listen to us making noise, so practicing in anyone's garage was out. We worked shitty fast-food jobs and pooled our cash to rent out a storage container where we'd go to shred. Though I use the term 'practice' loosely… really we just got stoned and made a ton of noise."

"Did you play gigs?" Troy asked.

"There was one bar that used to hire us, and it was grungy as all hell," Eddie replied, chuckling and shaking his head. "They had all the random shitty punk bands all the time, and the place was always full of a bunch of teens and early twenty-somethings slamming into each other and busting the place up. I can't believe that place didn't get shut down for selling to minors."

"How long has it been since you've played?" Hawk asked. "If it's been that long, your hands must be killing you shredding for so long in that store."

"Oh, I still play," Eddie said, and then lowered his gaze. "At least, I did, before the world went to shit. Had a nice setup in my basement at home. Just to jam out after a hard day's work."

"What did you do?" Grace asked, finding her voice. It felt good to talk about normal things, instead of strategizing how to not die.

"Factory dog," Eddie declared proudly. "Camshafts." He waggled his eyebrows, and she rolled her eyes. "What about you?" he asked.

"Crossfit instructor," she replied, smirking.

"Well that explains a lot," Hawk said, cocking a smile.

"And what about you?" Grace asked, motioning to him. "You a firefighter or something?"

He barked a laugh, shaking his head. "No, little lady, I am most definitely not a firefighter," he replied. "I was between jobs when this all went down, but before that I was doing some carpentry work."

"Nothing like the apocalypse to save us from unemployment," Eddie quipped as he polished off the rest of his food. "What about you, Troy? You look like you were a stockbroker or something."

Grace laughed, shaking her head.

"Investment banker, thank you," Troy replied haughtily.

Eddie blinked at him. "Isn't that… that's the same thing, right?" he asked, looking between the other two.

"Not the same thing at all," Troy said, stabbing at his pasta with more force than was necessary.

"Okay, fancy pants," Eddie drawled, and set his bowl by the cell door, for whoever was going to pick it up later.

Grace did the same, and soon all of them were finished, thoughtfully sipping on their water bottles.

"What do you think they'll have us doing tomorrow?" Eddie asked as he stretched out on his bed. "Maybe we'll get lucky and get to clear out a strip club."

"Zombie strippers, man?" Hawk asked, shaking his head. "You are damaged."

Eddie shrugged. "Just want to see all there is to see in this new world," he replied. "Might as well take in all the local flavor."

Grace shook her head as quiet fell over the group, and curled up under her blankets, picking up the fluffy romance novel she'd grabbed from the basket in the corner. It was a ridiculous tale of a damsel in distress and the handsome duke that saved her, but it was escapism, and that was what she needed, now more than ever.

END

Up Next: When a squad of QXR mercenaries stumble across their location, Dante and Ace must take drastic measures to protect the others in Lowcountry - Pt. 6

CHAPTER ONE

Day Zero +4

The sun peeked through the blinds, shining right onto Dante's face as he laid on the couch. His first instinct was to pull the covers over his head and roll over, but he quickly succumbed to the inevitability of being awake. He sat up slightly, looking around the empty room.

Ever since they'd cleared out the house across the street, there was a lot more room to move about. No more cramped sleeping quarters, no more piles of sleeping bodies, although there weren't quite enough beds to go around yet.

As he lamented the discomfort of the couch, he took pause, and pressed his palms to his head. *Be thankful you have this,* he thought to himself. *Grace could be sleeping on a whole lot worse.*

He took a deep breath, not wanting to imagine the horrors she could be going through. She might not even be sleeping at all.

She's a tough girl, he thought firmly, shutting down that thought process. *She'll be okay.*

The sound of coffee mugs clanking together perked him up, and he sat up. He slipped off of the couch and approached the kitchen, peeking in to see Lily standing in front of the coffee maker, tapping her foot impatiently. The little appliance seemed to be struggling, pumping out a tiny trickle of the black gold.

She grunted in frustration as the machine sputtered.

"Having some issues this morning?" Dante asked, and she squeaked, leaping off of the ground as she whipped around to face him.

She put a hand over her heart. "Jesus tap-dancing Christ Dante," she breathed.

He cracked a smile, and she returned it, lowering her hand and shaking her head.

"Sorry, I didn't mean to startle you, there," he said, chuckling.

Her smile widened, and she waved him off. "It's okay," she said, and then turned back to the coffee maker, smacking the side of it before unplugging the cord. "On the plus side, I don't need this to wake up, now."

Ace wandered into the kitchen in just his boxers, rubbing his eyes with his fists and yawning. "Well some of us do, Lil," he groaned, scrubbing his hands down his face. "Especially when they are woken up at the ass crack of dawn by a couple of knuckleheads in the kitchen."

Said knuckleheads shared an apologetic glance.

"Sorry cuz," Lily said.

"Maybe they have some across the street," Dante suggested.

Ace ran his hands through his hair. "Well, why don't y'all go check," he said thickly, stifling another yawn. "I'll stay here and try to figure out what the fuck I'm doing."

"Well, there goes his morning," Lily quipped, and led Dante out of the kitchen away from her pasty scantily clad cousin.

There was a clear path leading from Ace's front door to the house across the street. On either side of the yard was a stretch of cars and other debris, creating a makeshift barricade. It wasn't much, and wouldn't protect them from a horde of any significant size, but it would buy them a bit of time should problems arise. At least problems with the undead.

As they walked towards the other house, they spotted Cam and Phillip standing guard, looking down the street towards the gas station, only occasionally looking back in the other direction.

"Come on man, Jason Voorhees is *way* more of a bad guy than Michael Myers," Cam was saying, and the argument already sounded heated, as if it had been going on for a while. "He's got a higher body count and is more indiscriminate with his kills."

Phillip threw his hands up. "Michael Myers killed his teenage sister!"

"So?" Cam scoffed. "Jason has killed enough teenagers to fill a high school football stadium."

Phillip cocked his head. "Yeah?" he asked and then pointed a finger at his partner. "Well, Michael spent an entire movie trying to kill his ten year old niece! Jason never tried to kill kids, now did he?"

"Part six!" Cam shot back. "He broke into the bunks and scared those kids."

Phillip shook his head. "But he didn't try to *kill* them, now did he?" he asked.

His friend thought for a moment, his excitement fading, but then his eyes widened as another thought dawned on him. "Oh, oh, oh!" he exclaimed. "But in that Nintendo game, he totally killed the kids!"

"Really?" Phillip rolled his eyes. "We're bringing video games into this now?"

Cam sneered. "You're just mad because you lost the debate," he accused.

"Two things," his friend said flatly, holding up his pointer and middle fingers. "One, the kids die off screen, so it doesn't count. Two, Michael Myers actually kills a kid on-screen in his game."

Cam scowled. "When the hell was there a Halloween video game?" he demanded.

"Atari 2600, my friend," Phillip declared, puffing out his chest.

His companion rolled his eyes. "Oh yeah, the system with games featuring square tanks, square bullets, and square circles," he drawled, sarcasm heavy in his tone. "I'm sure the deaths were all kinds of realistic."

"Had blood and everything," Phillip argued, "so realistic enough to piss off parents back in the day."

Cam shook his head emphatically. "Man, how in the hell do you know so much about the ancient times?" he asked.

"Well, you never know when you might have to converse with someone who is ancient," his friend explained with a laugh.

"Morning guys," Dante said as they reached them. "Sounds like you have a hell of a debate going on here."

"Case in point?" Phillip asked, jerking a thumb towards Dante. The boys chuckled, the two newcomers shaking their heads in confusion.

"Come on, let's leave Beavis and Butthead here to do their thing," Lily said, rolling her eyes.

Phillip held up a hand. "No, no, wait," he said. "We could actually use your help."

"Okay, shoot," Dante replied, crossing his arms.

"Well, we're trying to say who the most evil villain in film history is," Cam explained. "I say it's Jason Voorhees, and he says it's Michael Myers."

Phillip nodded. "So who do you think it is?"

Dante contemplated for a moment, and glanced over at Lily, who shot him an amused smirk and playfully motioned for him to share his thoughts.

"Well, as fate would have it," Dante began, "I actually know a little about this topic. Out of the two, I would have to say Michael Myers is the more evil of the two."

"Boom!" Phillip cried, raising both his hands in a faux explosion.

Cam gaped at him, shaking his head. "How, man?!" he blurted. "Jason has a much higher body count than Michael does!"

"It's not about the number of kills," Dante replied, "but *where* he killed them."

The younger man raised an eyebrow. "I don't follow."

"Of course you don't," Lily drawled, "because you're an idiot."

"I mean, it's pretty simple when you think about it, really," Dante continued. "Crystal Lake is his home, and outside of killing Alice at the beginning of the second movie, pretty much every single one of his kills has been people who came to Crystal Lake. Or, in his mind, people who were invading his home. Granted, that case isn't as airtight as say, Leatherface's, but it excuses a lot of the murders when compared with Michael, who just hunts and kills all over town."

The boys looked at each other and shrugged, finally nodding at the answer.

"What are y'all talking about?" Ace asked as he sauntered up behind them, finally fully clothed.

Dante chuckled. "They were having a debate on who the most evil movie character was," he explained.

"Oh yeah?" Ace asked. "Who won?"

Phillip puffed out his chest. "My pick, Michael Myers," he declared.

"Eh, not a bad choice," Ace said, tilting his head back and forth. "A hundred percent wrong, but not a bad choice."

The younger man raised an eyebrow. "Oh yeah?" he challenged. "Who is your pick?"

"Oh, that's easy," Ace drawled. "It's Jenny from Forrest Gump."

Everyone froze and stared at him with blank expressions.

"I'm… almost afraid to ask," Lily said slowly, closing her eyes. "But why is Jenny the biggest movie villain?"

Ace balked at her. "Are you serious?" he asked. "She raped a mental midget who she knew was in love with her, completely abandoned him afterwards, then showed back up years later to dump an AIDS baby in his lap and then took advantage of him yet again, so she'd have someone to take care of her as she died." He took a breath, having spouted all the information without breathing. "That's way more evil than a few dumb sex-crazed teenagers meeting the business end of a machete."

Lily facepalmed so hard she was sure she'd given herself a minor concussion. The rest of the group was speechless.

"Based on your reactions," Ace drawled, "I'd say I won that round."

His cousin sighed. "More like you killed so many of our brain cells that we lack the ability to respond," she said.

"Before he shares more film history thoughts," Dante cut in, "do you boys have any coffee?"

They shook their heads in tandem.

"Only thing they had in the house was decaf," Cam replied.

Lily grimaced. "Now *that's* evil," she said.

"Come on, we'll get some at the gas station," Ace suggested. "Need to fill up that dirt bike with gas anyway."

His cousin furrowed her brow. "When did you get a dirt bike?" she asked.

"Found it yesterday, going through that last house's garage," he explained, jerking a thumb over his shoulder. "Doesn't look like it's been run in a while, so I need to put it through its paces so it doesn't break down."

"If you want to grab that," Dante said, "I'll grab my handgun and we'll start walking."

Ace nodded. "Yeah, good call," he agreed. "Grab my knife if you don't mind. Can't be too careful these days."

As the trio headed off, Cam stepped forward.

"Hey, will you bring us back a cup, too?" he asked.

Dante paused, glancing over his shoulder. "How do you take it?"

Cam smirked. "I take my coffee like I take my women," he said, waggling his eyebrows.

"Then you already have it, since the only women you take are imaginary," Lily quipped.

He opened his mouth, but then just hung his head, prompting laughter from everyone, especially Phillip, who bumped his shoulder in his mirth.

The trio walked up the street, Dante and Lily up ahead as Ace pushed his shiny new dirt bike a few yards behind them. They walked quietly, just enjoying the peacefulness of the morning.

Dante glanced over at Lily, unable to keep his eyes off of her, and she side-glanced him back, the two blushing a bit and immediately averting their eyes.

Ace saw the exchange and rolled his eyes, speeding up to a jog to catch up to them. "It's the apocalypse, this ain't the time to slow play it," he quipped.

Both of them started to argue as he jogged by them, pushing the bike, but clamped their mouths shut to avoid further embarrassment.

He looked back over his shoulder as he jogged ahead. "You know I'm right," he called in a singsong voice, "which is why neither of you are saying anything. Now would one of you make your damn move already, so we can get on with our day?"

He turned his back to them and rushed off towards the gas station.

When he was out of earshot, Dante scratched the back of his head nervously. "I… I know it's only been a few days since we met," he began, avoiding looking at her. "But I do kind of like you."

She chuckled, unable to hold in her smile. "I know it's only been a few days," she echoed, "but I kinda like you too."

He smiled down at her, reaching out and grabbing her hand, and she laced her fingers into his. They walked along, enjoying the human contact and the peaceful morning for a few moments.

"Just so you know," Dante finally said playfully, "I don't put out on the first date."

Lily winked. "Just so *you* know," she replied, "I do."

They shared a laugh and were still chuckling when they reached the gas station.

Ace spotted them from his perch next to the bike, the gas pump firmly lodged in the tank. "Well, it's about damn time," he drawled, throwing his hand up dramatically.

"I'll get the coffee going," Lily said, shooting Dante a smile as she pulled away from him, lingering her fingers on his as long as possible before letting go.

He watched her sashay off into the gas station and took a deep breath. "Some solid wingman work there," he commended as he stepped closer to Ace.

"Well, one of us needs to be decisive," the redneck quipped, and finished topping off the tank, replacing the nozzle on the pump. "You know anything about dirt bikes?" he asked.

Dante shook his head. "Not really," he admitted. "Wasn't great with machines growing up. My father was a graphic designer, so there wasn't any of that learning at my father's knee stuff as he fixed the car. Now, if you need me to drive it down to the mechanic to have the oil changed, I can handle that for you."

Ace laughed as he pushed the bike towards the store. "Well come on, I'll give you a quick run through on this bad boy, so you'll at least know what the working parts are." He held up a finger. "Now just so we're clear, Lily's my cousin, so I can't show you how *that* works."

Dante barked a laugh. "Don't worry," he said, "I've got that one covered. Believe it or not, I didn't always look this pretty." He motioned to his face.

Ace stopped short, brow furrowing, face a rare expression of seriousness. "Hey man, you know Lily don't care about that," he said. "I mean hell, you met Maddox, so it's pretty obvious she ain't about looks."

Dante chuckled and patted his friend on the back. "Come on, let's check out this bike."

CHAPTER TWO

The bike stood on its kickstand by the front counter. Ace knelt down on one knee, pointing out some things on the engine as Dante looked over his shoulder. He nodded along with everything the redneck said, intently focused on it even though much of what he was saying went over his head.

"Coffee's on, boys," Lily declared, and both men looked up as she held out two tall cups of liquid gold. "Savor it, because in another week or so we're going to be out of the light roast," she added, as they both nodded and thanked her for the brew.

"Looks like we have something to add to the shopping list," Ace said.

Dante raised his eyebrow. "You mean it wasn't already?" he asked.

They chuckled before turning back to their engine lesson, sipping the steaming brew.

Lily walked back to the coffee maker, pouring herself a nice tall cup, mixing in a couple packets of the powdered creamer. She took a deep sniff of it, enjoying the steamy scent of fresh brew. She walked over to the front door, enjoying the peace and quiet as the sun crested the horizon.

The view from the front window of the store wasn't too impressive—at least on a normal day. But with the sun creeping up over the trees in the distance, and no flesh-eating monsters in sight, it was beautiful enough for her to enjoy it.

The beauty was short-lived, however.

Lily froze at the sight of two large SUVs in the distance. She opened her mouth, but her voice came out in a quiet squeak.

"Dante…" she rasped, and then finally found her voice. "Dante!"

The boys raced over to her, concerned.

"What is it?" he asked.

She motioned to the vehicles. "Down the road," she gushed.

They squinted and quickly realized that the SUVs were similar to the ones QXR had on the marine base when they were there a few days ago.

"Fuck man, how in the hell did they find us?" Ace breathed, pressing his hand to his forehead.

Dante shook his head. "I don't think they have found us," he replied, "or they don't know that they have. Look."

The trio watched as the vehicles stopped a hundred yards away at the first set of houses on either side of the road. Eight men got out, standing around for a moment before seven of them headed off to investigate various houses.

"They're just doing a sweep," Lily said, relief in her tone.

Ace nodded. "Well, let's get the fuck outta here," he said.

"How?" she asked, shaking her head. "As soon as we start up the truck, they're going to be on us. We don't have the firepower to take them on!"

Her cousin crossed his arms. "Well what do you propose?"

"We gotta pull them away from here," Dante cut in firmly.

"What?" both cousins exclaimed at the same time.

He held up his hands. "If we don't pull them away, they'll just follow us down to the school," he explained.

Ace swallowed hard as the insinuation sunk in. The last thing they needed was QXR finding their farming operation.

"Well, how in the hell are we gonna do that?" he asked.

Dante motioned to the dirt bike.

Ace shook his head. "You wanna outrun a bunch of mercs on a dirt bike?" he demanded. "And go where?"

"We head back towards the prison where we broke Francis out," Dante explained. "Lose 'em in the town and hightail it back down south."

"We?" Ace asked, raising an eyebrow.

Dante nodded. "Yeah, *we*," he confirmed. "I'm assuming you know how to drive that thing?"

"Been riding since I was four," the redneck replied proudly.

"You good enough to have a passenger on the back?" Dante asked.

Ace smirked. "You saying you wanna ride bitch?" he asked.

The taller man drew his handgun. "I'm saying I want to do a drive by, and I need you to drive," he replied. "You think you can handle it?"

"Let's do it," Ace agreed.

"As soon as you get clear, I'll get everybody to safety," Lily cut in.

Dante nodded. "Thanks," he said.

"And Dante…" she added, and when he looked over, she grabbed the front of his shirt and pulled him in for a searing kiss that left him light-headed. When she pulled away, she smirked up at him. "We've been a couple for all of ten minutes now," she said. "Don't go making me single again, you hear?"

He brushed a stray hair from her face. "I'll see you for dinner, hon," he promised.

He broke away from her and headed over to the bike, where Ace was already sitting in the seat.

The redneck patted the seat behind him. "Hop on there, cowboy," he drawled. "You about to get way closer to me than you ever wanted to."

Dante got on and Ace flicked the switches on the handles. He readied himself to kick-start it and then glanced over at his cousin.

"As soon as I get this thing fired up, you push open that door and then stay outta sight," he instructed. "You got it?"

Lily nodded and got into position as the boys got situated on the bike. Dante gripped the gun tightly in his hand, psyching himself up to strike.

"You hit that throttle and never let up on it," he said. "Doesn't matter if I hit them or not, we just need them to follow."

Ace chuckled. "Well, there's eight of them and we have one handgun," he drawled, "so if you could hit at least one of 'em that would help us out."

"I'll do my best," Dante replied.

"Hold on to your ass," Ace declared, and then hit the kick-start. As soon as the engine roared to life, he slammed the accelerator and picked up speed, bursting out of the gas station as Lily pushed open the door.

They tore out of the parking lot and onto the road, racing towards the two

SUVs. The one remaining mercenary guard, who was relaxing against the driver's side door of the front vehicle, perked up at the noise.

He walked around in front of the hood, clutching his assault rifle, trying to get his bearings on the noise. When the dirt bike came into view, he raised his gun.

"Contact, contact!" he screamed, and took aim.

Dante aimed over Ace's shoulder and fired, his bullet missing side and punching through the windshield of the vehicle. It had the intended effect, and the mercenary dropped to one knee, giving them another second to fire again.

The second bullet hit the guard in the throat, and he fell to the ground, gripping his neck as he rolled back and forth gasping for air.

The bike blew past the vehicles as the other mercenaries poured out into the road, firing wildly after the duo. Ace didn't let up despite the bullets whizzing by them, keeping up his speed and putting distance between them. Luckily they were moving fast enough that the retaliatory shots missed them by enough of a safe margin.

Dante glanced back and saw the guards leaping into their vehicles, slamming the doors and spinning the SUVs around to give chase.

"Did it work?" Ace yelled.

"Yeah, and you need to get a move on," Dante yelled back. He looked over his shoulder again, keeping watch as the vehicles gained speed, slowly but surely closing the gap. He started to worry as they came within fifty yards, and mercenaries began to hang out of the windows, rifles in hand.

"We need a turnoff!" Dante cried.

"Interstate is another mile up!" Ace called back.

Dante looked again, noting the SUVs only forty yards behind now. "We don't have that long!" he warned.

"Fuck, hold on!" Ace bellowed and veered to the left, nearly toppling them right off with the sharp turn. They bumbled through a shallow ditch, getting settled in the grass, and then gaining traction up the other side to hit a small dirt road through the countryside.

Ace rose back up to top speed as the tires gripped the dirt, and Dante looked back over his shoulder again. The SUVs spun out for a moment in the ditch before gaining traction, giving them a chance to gain more distance again.

"How we looking?" Ace asked.

"Bought us a few seconds, but that's it!" Dante replied.

"Dammit!" the redneck barked.

They raced down the dirt road as the SUVs started gaining again. They could hear the faint sound of rifle rounds firing, even over the high-pitched whine of the engine.

There was another dirt road a few hundred yards up on the right. Both men kept their heads down as bullets whizzed by them, hoping to make it to the turnoff in time. Dante looked back, and the vehicles were gaining again, so he aimed and fired his gun as best he could on the bumpy terrain.

The bullets pinged off of the front end of the lead SUV, causing no damage but forcing the gunmen to duck back inside for cover.

Ace made another dramatic turn, nearly losing it on the loose gravel, but correcting at the right second and managing to keep them upright. As soon as they made the turn, they nearly crashed into a cow, but he managed to deftly swing around it.

Up the road a bit, a fence portion had broken loose, allowing for dozens of cattle to escape their enclosure. They dotted the road, most of them off to the side to feast on the grass, but several in the road.

Ace wove in and out between them, putting them at a safer distance from the pursuing vehicles. Dante turned and looked, watching the SUVs swerve and smack into a cow, knocking it down and denting their hood in the process. It slowed them down a bit, but they were still managing to cut a path through the obstacle course.

"This helps, but now what?" Dante asked. "We're still miles away from Ridgeland."

"I got an idea, but you're not going to like it," Ace called back.

His passenger took a deep breath. "Seems to be the way the day is going," he muttered. "Do it!"

Ace sped up again, keeping the distance but not getting so far ahead that the SUVs wouldn't be able to see them. The whole point was to lure them away, so if they lost them they might head back to the gas station and spot Lily's escape with the others.

At the end of the dirt road, they hit a paved two-lane road. Across the street there was a sign to the left reading *Ridgeland – 3 miles*. A small orange and white sign sat beside it, pointing to the right that said, *Detour*.

"Ace?" Dante asked, voice skeptical.

The redneck shook his head. "Told you that you weren't going to like it," he drawled.

Dante held on tight to his friend's waist as Ace made the turn and picked up speed again. He glanced over his shoulder, though stayed low, and spotted the SUVs gaining rapidly on the pavement.

They raced towards Ridgeland, a long country road with vast fields on either side. Less than a mile up ahead, there was some major construction equipment blocking their path.

Bullets started flying again as they reached the construction zone. Ace pushed the bike as fast as it could go, narrowly avoiding one of the big machines as he darted in between them.

Dante looked back, seeing the vehicles slowing down in order to weave their way through the large machines. Even with the obstacles in the road, they remained close enough to keep the bike in view.

The construction zone ran for a solid mile, with a lot of road work being done. Giant dirt and gravel piles dotted the area, work half-finished and not completed due to the end of the world. Ace slowed down near the end of it, making sure that their pursuers wouldn't give up on them.

"Two mile sprint to Ridgeland," Dante said, "do you think we can make it?"

"This thing has enough juice to get us there," Ace replied, "but I have no idea what we're going to do once we're there."

"Find some zombies and head towards them," Dante said.

The redneck froze. "Are you out of your fucking mind?" he cried. "You want me to go *towards* those things?"

"I have seven shots left, and somehow I doubt I'm going to be able to go seven for seven on headshots against these guys," Dante explained. "We need to get them off our tail once we get there, so unless you got a better idea…"

"Yeah yeah," Ace drawled, though he didn't sound happy about it. "I hear ya." He shook his head as he revved the engine.

They looked back and saw the vehicles getting close enough to them, so they took off. As they moved, the gunmen began firing again, narrowly missing them as they picked up speed.

The road was mostly straight, allowing them to remain within sight of the mercenaries, which were quickly gaining once again. They were able to put enough distance between them to reach the town before lethal firing range, however.

Ace sped down the main road through town, looking frantically for a horde of zombies. Finally, on the third cross street, he spotted a pack of a few hundred at the far end of the next block. He screeched around the turn and accelerated towards the hungry ghouls.

"Hang on!" he cried, and Dante braced himself as they reached thirty yards away from the mass of rotting flesh.

When they first started, it had appeared as though they had a path to roll through them, but the engine noise attracted more ghouls, closing that off.

Ace slammed on the brakes about twenty yards from the horde. "We ain't getting through that!" he yelled.

Dante looked back just as the SUVs made the turn towards them. He frantically looked around the store-lined road, one long building on each side with different shops sectioned off from one another.

"Clothing store, go!" he urged, motioning wildly.

The duo leapt from the bike, leaving it to crash to the ground as they raced towards the store on foot. Gunfire from the mercenaries peppered the road, bullets whizzing by their heads and hitting the zombies that were now trying to converge on them.

Dante raised his gun and fired a few times, shattering the front window of the store. They leapt through the opening as the SUVs pulled up outside, the seven pissed-off mercenaries bustling out.

"You two, buy us some time!" one of them barked, and two of the men broke off and set up a firing line, popping zombies in the head as they got close. Most of the ghouls seemed to be moving slower than normal, but still at a dangerous clip. They concentrated their fire on the fastest moving ones.

"Cover in the rear," the leader continued, pointing at a lone soldier. "Rest of you, push in!"

Ace and Dante reached the back of the store, hiding behind the cash register. They could barely hear what the leader was saying at that point, but they heard enough to know they were in trouble.

"What now?" Ace whispered.

Dante looked around. "We gotta get out the back," he replied quietly.

Ace nodded, and they stayed low, creeping towards the back door as quietly as possible. At the sound of boots on broken glass, they knew the mercenaries were entering the store, and they reached the end of the counter, stopping at a gap of five yards of open space between their cover and the door.

"I'm going to fire," Dante murmured, "and when I do, you run like hell."

Ace nodded and readied himself.

Dante took a deep breath and then popped up over the counter just enough to catch a glimpse of his enemies. He pulled the trigger rapidly, firing off three shots in quick succession.

One of the bullets managed to hit a mercenary in the vest, sending him tumbling to the ground. The other three next to him adjusted their aim and opened fire, sending three-round bursts towards the direction of the gunfire.

As soon as Dante pulled the trigger, Ace darted out from cover, racing to the back storage room door. He smashed through it and slid inside, leaving it open for Dante, who was right behind him.

Bullets peppered the wall, sending shards of wood and mannequins flying everywhere. Dante dove head first, sliding along the floor until he reached the door. Ace reached out and pulled him in before slamming the door shut.

Bullets shredded the cheap wood and continued to fly through the wall as they rapidly crawled across to the back door.

"Go!" Dante hissed. "I'll buy us a second!"

Ace scrambled to his feet, racing towards the back door a few yards from him. Dante rolled over onto his back, firing the remaining three shots from his handgun blindly through the door, hoping to hit something. The gunfire stopped for a second, assumedly so the mercenaries could take cover.

Ace burst out the door, and a mercenary in the alley grabbed him by the throat and shoved him against the brick wall of the adjacent building.

"Got you, motherfucker," the beast of a man snarled, squeezing the redneck's throat tightly.

Ace thrashed about, flailing his arms in a vain attempt to break free.

Dante burst out of the door, lowering his shoulder and crashing into the mercenary's back. The impact sent the large man hurtling face first into the wall, smashing his nose into the brick and allowing Ace to wriggle free.

Dante didn't let up, not wanting his enemy to regain any composure, immediately going on the attack. He delivered a few forceful strikes to the side of the large warrior's head, stunning him. The mercenary whipped around and threw a hook that Dante was able to block, though he stumbled to the side a few steps.

As they fought, Ace gasped for air, finally regaining his breath. He leapt to his feet and slammed the large metal door shut, throwing the thick latch down to lock it from the outside. There was a place for a padlock, but no lock to be found, so he snatched a chunk of metal from the ground and shoved it through the loop to reinforce it.

Dante exchanged blows with the large mercenary, finally landing one on the man's nose, shattering it and sending blood down his face.

The man staggered back, rage in his eyes. "I'm gonna rip the pretty side of your face clean off, motherfucker," he snarled.

"You're welcome to try," Dante replied with a smirk.

His opponent let out a grunt and lunged forward, throwing a forceful straight punch. Dante ducked to the side and managed to catch his wrist, pulling it and using the momentum to fling him into the wall.

As soon as he hit, Dante shoved his forearm into the back of the guy's neck, wrenching his arm behind his back.

Ace darted forward with his pocket knife, rushing over and stabbing the mercenary in the side like a prisoner shanking a rival, in short fast strikes.

Their opponent screamed in pain, bracing his foot against the wall and shoving back. His weight was too much for

Dante, and he staggered backwards onto his ass. The mercenary drew his handgun and turned towards the fallen man, holding his side with his free hand.

Before he could aim, Ace leapt onto his back, stabbing him in the throat. The mercenary threw an elbow, hitting the redneck in the side of the head and sending him to the ground. The knife stuck straight out of his neck, blood pouring out around the blade.

He put one hand to the wound, and raised his gun towards Ace, who reached out and grabbed his wrist, forcing the gun high. The bullets just missed the redneck's head, and in the confusion, Dante rushed forward and gave the hilt of the pocket knife a forceful palm strike, driving it deep into the mercenary's throat.

Blood spurted everywhere, and the large man staggered back, firing one more shot before collapsing to the ground.

The back door of the store began to shake violently as the men inside struggled to break out.

"We gotta get out of here," Dante said.

Ace grabbed the fallen man's handgun and shoved it in the waistband of his pants before grabbing the assault rifle and trying to get it off. It was clipped to the man's vest, however, and he couldn't disengage it.

"Leave it!" Dante barked, spotting a few zombies heading towards them from one end of the alley. He started moving in that direction, and Ace stood up, eyes wide.

"Where the hell are you going?" he blurted.

"We still need cover," his companion replied, waving for him to follow.

They broke out into a sprint, pumping their legs hard, and Dante psyched himself up as he neared the trio of zombies in the mouth of the alley. He smacked into the first one, a smaller teenage ghoul, and picked it up by the shirt and belt, driving it back into the others. His momentum and added weight allowed him to push through to the open road.

He tossed the corpse on top of the others, looking both ways quickly. To the left was mostly clear road, and to the right was the back end of the horde that was headed towards the still-firing mercenaries. A handful of creatures turned and spotted them, moving their way.

"Come on, we have to get a few more blocks away," Dante urged.

The duo tore as hard as they could away from the horde, and due to the slower gait of the zombies, they were able to pull away.

They made it up a block before cutting over, darting past ghouls as they went, none of which posed a significant threat to them.

Finally, after getting halfway across town, they ducked inside a store that had an open front door. They quickly swept the room, finding that it was empty before they ducked down behind the counter to regroup.

"Well, that was a whole lotta fun," Ace huffed, sarcastic even through his exhaustion. "Can't wait to do that again."

Dante shook his head. "That's good, because we're not out of this yet," he said.

"Pretty sure we've bought Lily and the others enough time, don't you?" the redneck asked.

His companion nodded. "Yeah, but we still have to get out of here without them seeing us," he replied. "And at the moment, we don't have a vehicle."

"There are some neighborhoods nearby," Ace said, waving a hand above his head. "We can try and find us a ride there."

Dante shook his head. "Would take too much time," he said. "Even if we find a car, we'd have to find the keys to it, and there's no guarantee they're going to be in the house."

"So what the hell you wanna do?" Ace asked, letting out a deep breath.

Dante contemplated for a moment, and then finally shook his head again. "Well, I got an idea," he said, and smirked before repeating Ace's words back to him, "but you aren't going to like it."

CHAPTER THREE

"You gotta be fucking shitting me, dude," Ace blurted, staring wide-eyed at the police station across the street.

They knelt under cover, staying out of sight just in case the QXR guys came rolling by.

"Look at the parking lot," Dante said quietly. "Plenty of police cars, and chances are they're going to have the keys locked up in there. Plus, they might have some weapons, which we could really use right now."

Ace scrubbed his hands down his face. "Yeah, all right," he finally agreed. "Let's get this over with."

They looked both ways and then broke from cover, rushing across the street to the station. They paused at the front, looking through the swinging doors that were unlocked. There were some dried bloodstains on the window.

"I don't remember that from before," Ace muttered.

Dante chewed his lip. "Me either," he agreed.

They slipped inside, on guard in case of an attack. They reached the front lobby before working their way back to the control room just off of the main area.

Dante checked the monitors, seeing the cells where Brandt and the other officer had been locked up. Dante shook his head at the sight of a dozen zombies crowded around it.

"Didn't take those things very long to find 'em," Dante muttered.

"Good, that son of a bitch deserves to feel scared," Ace declared.

Dante looked over the monitors, checking all of the hallways and finding them clear, with all the zombie activity in the back cell area. "You have any idea where the weapon lockup is?" he asked.

Ace shook his head before looking on the wall by the desk. There was a printout of a map of the building, though there wasn't a listing for an armory.

"Gotta be the supply room, don't it?" the redneck asked, tapping his finger over the listing for a supply room.

"Even if it isn't, can't hurt to check it out," Dante replied with a shrug. "Come on."

They headed down the hallway towards the storage room, taking special care at every intersection and office door to make sure there weren't any stragglers hanging about.

Finally they made it to the back hallway that led to the storage area, finding one lone zombie lingering towards the back. Not wanting the noise of firing a gun, Dante looked around, spotting a fire extinguisher on the wall.

He removed it from the moorings and readied it, and he and Ace shared a nod before creeping forward.

The zombie was transfixed on its reflection in the storage room glass, occasionally attacking it like a confused cat when it moved. The duo moved quietly and were able to get right close to it without the ghoul knowing they were there.

Dante smacked it in the side of the head with the extinguisher, sending it to the ground in a heap. He slammed the heavy unit down into its head a few more times, just to be sure.

As he did so, Ace kept his gun aimed, watching down the hallway just to make sure they didn't attract any attention. Nothing appeared, and he relaxed.

"We're good," he said, lowering his gun.

Dante nodded, setting down the extinguisher. "Then let's get our stuff and get on our way," he said, and reached for the door handle. He pushed it down and pulled, but the door was locked. He tried a few more times and then grunted in frustration when he realized there was an electronic keypad next to the door.

"Damn," he said.

Ace grinned and knocked on the glass panel of the door. "Don't worry, I'm pretty sure we can get in," he said.

Dante shook his head. "You can try, but I doubt it," he replied.

Ace smirked as he picked up the bloody fire extinguisher. He readied it before slamming the big red metal container into the glass. It reverberated up his arms, and he poured every bit of power he had into it. He smacked it a few more times before stopping, bewildered.

"Well, shit," he muttered.

Dante pressed his face against the glass, straining to see what was inside. The light was off, but there was a small skylight at the top of the wall, illuminating the room just enough to show off some SWAT type equipment.

"Looks like it's the room we need," he said, "which explains why that glass is going to be unbreakable with what we have."

Ace sighed. "Well, what the fuck are we gonna do, then?" he asked.

Dante took a deep breath and then fixed the redneck with a look that spoke volumes. That look said *I'm sorry,* and *we don't have a choice.*

Ace groaned, shoulder slumping. "Goddammit, we gotta go save that asshole Brandt, don't we?" he whined.

"If anybody is going to know how to get in there, it's going to be him," Dante said.

"Well, I've already lost my new dirt bike, so this is par for the course today," Ace grumbled. "Come on, let's do it."

The duo headed down the hallway towards the cells and paused at the supply room doors where they'd been ambushed by Brandt and his men a few days prior. Dante headed into one, rummaging around for anything that could be useful against an army of zombies. Nothing in the room was going to help them out in any significant way, as it was all office type stuff.

"Well, maybe we could paper cut 'em to death?" Ace joked, picking up a stack of printer paper.

Dante didn't respond, still looking around and spotting a wooden-handled mop in the corner. He walked over to it and gave it a forceful kick, snapping it in two. He tossed the new spear over to Ace.

"You think you can take those things out with that?" he asked.

The redneck inspected it for a moment before nodding. "Yeah, maybe one, before they tackle me."

Dante headed back to the corner and broke two more handles, tossing them over as well.

Ace rolled his eyes after catching them all. "Great, now I can kill one of them three times before I get tackled," he drawled.

Dante patted him on the shoulder as he passed by. "You aren't going to have to worry about that," he said, and leaned over to grab the dead officer from the center of the hall, dragging him along.

"No, that's not concerning at all," Ace muttered, confused as he followed.

Dante led them down the hallway to where the cells were, stopping at the door leading towards them. He got a good grip on the corpse and lifted it up, pressing it against the door before letting out a yell.

The zombies by the cell mostly broke away, rushing for Dante. They hit the corpse hard, but he was able to hold them in place.

Ace gaped at the scene, and his companion grunted, inclining his head towards him.

"Start stabbing!" Dante barked.

The redneck shook himself back into the moment and started attacking. He aimed and thrust one of the spears into an eye socket, dropping the ghoul to the ground. Before he could ready another strike, another zombie was there.

He stabbed again, but missed badly, taking the ear off of one of the creatures. Another managed to smack the weapon away, forcing him to grab another one.

This time his aim was on target, dropping another, but the spike lodged itself in its skull.

"Shit, I'm down to one!" Ace cried.

Dante struggled to hold the zombies back, taking a deep breath. "Well make it count!" he instructed through his teeth.

Ace struck a couple more times, taking out two but losing the weapon on the next strike. There were still five zombies trying to force their way past Dante.

"Shit!" the redneck exclaimed, and hesitated, trying to think of what to do next. Finally he pulled out his gun, looking to his companion for guidance.

Dante gave him a nod, ducking his head.

Ace cocked the hammer back and aimed, pulling the trigger only when he was confident of a kill shot. He repeated this multiple times until the threat had been neutralized.

His partner finally dropped the officer corpse, stretching his shoulders to relieve some of the fatigue. As he did, Ace walked into the room and stepped over to the last remaining ghouls still trying to get into the jail cell. He executed them both at point blank range, finally getting rid of the threat altogether.

The duo stood outside of the jail cell, seeing both Brandt and his officer stretched out by the back, sitting on the mattress for a bit of cushion.

"Well, well," the Sheriff drawled, "I was wondering when one of you boys would wise up and come get us."

Ace sneered. "Sorry to disappoint you there, chief," he said, "but we're just here for some supplies."

"Somehow I doubt that," Brandt said with a smirk.

The redneck shrugged. "Doubt it all you want, bubba."

The Sheriff shook his head and stood up, walking over to the bars close to the men. "Nah, if you were here for supplies, you would have just taken them and ran," he said, and then paused for a moment, thinking. "Oh, you're not here for supplies… you're here for *supplies*." He barked a laugh. "Had a little trouble getting into the room, did you?"

"I'm guessing you know how to get us into that room?" Dante asked, crossing his arms.

Brandt nodded. "Oh, that's for sure, but it's gonna cost you," he replied.

"Why does that not surprise me?" Dante asked, rolling his eyes.

The Sheriff crossed his arms, leaning casually on the bars. "Well, for starters, you're going to get me and my friend Officer Henson here out of this hellhole," he said.

"You know how to pick a lock?" Ace asked with a shrug. "Because we don't have keys."

Brandt pointed to the cell across the way from them. "If there's something in the toilet, you can blame your idiot friend Maddox," he drawled. "He's the one who tossed it in there."

Ace and Dante looked at each other, and without saying a word, they both extended their fists and launched into an immediate game of *rock, paper, scissors*. Ace threw rock, and Dante threw paper.

"Damn!" the redneck cried. "Best two out of three?" he asked hopefully.

Dante raised his hands. "I think I'm good, man," he replied.

Ace hung his head before heading into the cell and looking down into the toilet. He let out a deep sigh of relief when he saw only water—or at least what he hoped was water, and reached in. He felt around in the pipe and plucked the keys, shaking them dry before tossing them over to his companion.

Dante caught them, wrinkling his nose when he felt they were still wet. "Thanks for that," he said.

"My pleasure," Ace replied with a grin.

Dante turned to Brandt, who stood on the other side of the bars, putting on a stoic face.

"Here's the deal," Dante said, pointing at him. "I'm going to let you out of here, you're going to get us into the supply room, and we're both going to wake what we need and then go our separate ways."

The Sheriff shook his head. "Sorry, but I'm going to need more than that."

"Afraid we don't have much else to give at this point," Dante replied.

"Oh, you do," Brandt said with a sneer. "You're going to tell me where Maddox is."

Ace stalked towards the cell, fists clenched. "Fuck you, man!" he snarled.

Dante held up his palm to calm down his friend. "Sorry Sheriff, but we have enough people trying to kill us, without adding you to the mix," he said.

"You boys out there making friends, I see," Brandt said tightly.

"Something like that," Dante replied. "So that's off the table, however, I'm willing to honor the deal I offered you."

The Sheriff contemplated for a moment, and then glanced back at Henson, who looked gaunt and a little worse for wear. He gave his superior a weak thumbs up.

"Okay," Brandt said with a sigh, "you have a deal."

CHAPTER FOUR

"So, why did you come back here for all this shit, anyway?" Brandt asked as they headed down the hallway to the supply room.

Dante and Ace, walking behind the officers, shared a glance.

"They're gonna find out anyway," the redneck said.

Dante sighed. "QXR group is in town," he replied. "We led them here to keep them away from where we are holed up, and they're combing the town for us. We're probably going to have to fight our way out."

The Sheriff wrinkled his nose, whirling on them and stopping short. "QXR? Those bad boys are after you?" He smirked.

"Before you even think about it," Dante said, pointing a finger at him, "they're not going to care whether you give us up or not. They'll just kill all four of us, put us down like dogs."

Brandt pursed his lips.

"He ain't jokin'," Ace added. "If you wanna walk out there with your hands up and offer yourself to them, go for it, cuz I would be *happy* to see 'em make you into swiss cheese."

599

Henson paled even further than he already was. "I don't want to get mixed up with those guys," he said hoarsely.

"You either help us get out of town, or you die," Dante said with a shrug. "It's not a threat, it's just the facts."

The Sheriff grunted and turned back towards the supply room, leading them down the hall. When he reached the keypad, he typed in the code quickly and the light on the top went green. When he reached for the handle, Ace smacked his hand away.

"Yeah, I don't think so, we're getting suited up first," the redneck declared.

Brandt clucked his tongue and stepped back, leaning against the wall with Henson as Ace rummaged around in the storage room. He tossed out a vest and a shotgun to Dante, and he geared himself up.

"Can we trust you?" Ace asked as he handed some vests out the door to the Sheriff, and he rolled his eyes.

"I'm here, aren't I?" he drawled. "You don't trust my word, so you're gonna have to decide for yourself."

The redneck clenched his jaw and handed over two shotguns, glaring daggers at him in warning.

"How do I know I can trust *you?*" Brandt shot back as he strapped on the vest. "What if your QXR story is bullshit?"

Ace rolled his eyes. "If it was, we wouldn't have given you any weapons or gear. Your asses would be going right back in that cell," he said, and held up a hand. "As a matter of fact, we wouldn't even *be* here. So I think you can trust that."

Henson took in a ragged breath as he donned his vest. "Do you guys have any food?" he asked hoarsely.

Dante cocked a brow and pulled a granola bar out of his pocket, tossing it over.

Brandt glanced at Ace, but the redneck shook his head.

"Hell no, mine is chocolate-covered, I ain't sharing shit," he drawled.

Henson broke his in half and handed it to the Sheriff, and he wrinkled his nose as he looked it over, then stuffed it into his mouth.

"Let's get this over with," he mumbled through a mouthful of oats, and pushed off of the wall.

The unlikely quartet headed back to the front entrance, and Dante pressed himself against the wall to peek out the window and make sure they were alone. There was no movement outside, not even a

zombie, and the hair on the back of his
neck stood up.

"See anything?" Ace asked.

He shook his head. "No, but I have a
bad feeling," he admitted.

"Let's go!" Brandt demanded. "If they
didn't see you come in, they don't know
you're here, let's get the fuck out so we
can go our own way."

Dante nodded reluctantly, peering
around once again just to be sure. He
opened the door slowly, inch by inch, and
then slipped out, head on a swivel to scan
the area for enemies. But it seemed that
the Sheriff was right for once, and they
were in the clear.

He waved for Ace to follow, and the
other three filed out into the parking
lot. They hadn't gotten three steps before
a gunshot cracked, and a bullet buried
itself into Henson's head, dropping him to
the ground.

The remaining trio dove behind a
police car as bullets pinged off of the
building, and Dante cursed under his
breath.

I fucking told you, he wanted to
scream at the Sheriff. *I told you they'd
kill you on sight, and I told you that I
had a bad feeling!* But it was no use and
wouldn't do any good in their situation.

"Where are they coming from?" Ace asked, as he tried to peer up through a window, but only succeeded in ducking as glass shattered above their heads.

Dante shook his head. "Too far away to take out with a damn shotgun," he said. They looked left and right, hoping that there would be cover to get them to better cover, but the row of cars ended and there was nothing but open parking lot.

The roar of an engine approached, and a black SUV came screaming into the lot, somebody hanging out of the window with an assault rifle.

Dante popped up and fired, ducking back down quickly without waiting to see what he'd hit. By the sound of shattering glass, he'd hit the vehicle, and with no return fire, he hoped that meant that he caught the gunman with the blast.

"What did you morons do to these guys?" Brandt barked.

"Just tried to breathe the same air," Dante grunted, and at the sound of a car door opening, he popped up again. This time, Ace jumped up with him, and they fired quickly on the vehicle.

Somebody screamed, and more glass shattered. Dante reloaded and peered around the hood of their cover car, and spotted a mercenary running over from the trees, skidding behind the SUV. He aimed the shotgun, waiting for a head to pop up, but there was nothing but the sound of low voices hissing.

He fired at the closest tire, blasting it to shreds. A black blur popped up over the hood and fired on him. When his attacker ducked down, they heard footsteps and moans, and Ace cursed under his breath.

"A loud-ass gunfight in the middle of the zombie apocalypse," he muttered. "Great fucking idea."

Dante pulled out his handgun as the footsteps got closer. "This could work to our advantage," he said quietly. "Just have to be careful."

As he'd anticipated, panic fire erupted from behind the SUV, as the remaining mercenaries fired on the approaching zombies.

Dante peeked up over the hood and was simultaneously thankful and filled with dread at the twenty-strong horde descending on their enemies. A few fell, but the rest swarmed a limping soldier, sending the last one tearing off towards down, leaving his brother to die screaming.

He put a finger to his lips, signalling to Ace and Brandt to stay quiet, and thankfully, the ghouls took off

after the other mercenary once they were
done with their meal.

"Let's get the fuck outta here,"
Brandt finally hissed, eyes wide.

Dante shook his head. "No, we need to
take out the rest of these mercs," he
said.

"Fuck that!" the Sheriff growled. "We
need to get away from those things! Who
knows how many are in town?!"

"If they get back to QXR and report
that we're here, this whole area is going
to be crawling with mercenaries," Dante
argued. "We need to take them out."

Brandt shook his head. "Then let's
get out of the area," he snapped.

"And go where?" Ace demanded.

"Survival of this thing is going to
count on sustainability," Dante added. "We
can't just pack up and leave." He took a
deep breath. "Listen, if you stay and help
us, I have a safe place you can go."

Ace opened his mouth to argue, but
Dante put up a hand.

"The family we met at the hardware
store," he said, and the redneck
contemplated a moment, finally nodding.
"We can get him to them, they're out of
the way enough."

Brandt threw his hands up. "What
family? Let's just go there now!"

"I'm not going to tell you where they are until you help us get rid of these assholes," Dante said firmly.

The Sheriff scowled. "Fine," he snapped. "What's the plan, then?"

CHAPTER FIVE

There was a low moan from the road, and Ace dashed out from behind the police car, drawing his pocket knife. Before the dead mercenary could fully reanimate, he stabbed it in the head. He looked around, and his heart pounded at the sound of moans rising up nearby.

Dante was the first to spot them, seeing ghouls come around the corner of the station into the parking lot. Brandt fired at them, and the blast hit a zombie in the chest, shredding it but not slowing it down.

He turned tail and ran, despite Dante's cry of warning, but it didn't matter anyway, because more zombies came around the other side of the building.

"Back inside!" the Sheriff screamed, running for the door.

Ace lashed out, grabbing his arm and stopping him. "If we go in there we're stuck there, they'll swarm the door."

"Safer than out here!" Brandt argued, jerking his arm away.

Dante clambered up onto the hood of one of the cars, making it up onto the roof.

"You can't be fucking serious!" Brandt cried, and Ace shook his head.

"Suit yourself, then, but we're not saving your ass a second time," the redneck drawled, and jumped up on top of his own police car.

The Sheriff waffled for another second, but the zombies were coming fast. Instead of climbing up on a car, he ran for the SUV, diving inside.

"The tires are flat, idiot!" Ace called, but Brandt didn't get into the driver's seat, instead opting to pop up out of the sunroof. He gave Ace the finger, apparently unappreciative of the *idiot* moniker.

Dante drew his knife, stabbing at one of the ghouls smacking the side of the car he stood atop. There were enough zombies that the vehicle wobbled beneath him, but he was confident at least that it wouldn't topple over. He hoped.

"Try not to waste bullets," he called over his shoulder. "We also don't want to make too much noise and attract too many of these things."

Brandt scoffed. "As if there aren't already *too many*?!" he demanded.

"Looks like we'll be saving your ass for a second time," Ace muttered, realizing that if the Sheriff couldn't shoot, he wouldn't be able to reach any heads from the sunroof. Unless he hung out one of the windows, but somehow the redneck didn't foresee that happening. He wasn't even sure if he had a blade, anyway, since they'd only suited up he and Henson with vests and shotguns.

"Should have grabbed Henson's gun," he said, dawning on him they could use the extra weapon.

Dante shook his head as he stabbed another zombie. "We'll get it after," he replied.

"After what?" Ace asked, sighing at the sheer number of ghouls surrounding them. "This is a lot bigger than I thought it would be."

"Me too," Dante admitted. "But we're here now." He continued to stab, as did Ace, but soon another problem arose. As corpses fell around the vehicles, the zombies got taller from being able to stand atop their dead brethren.

"We're gonna have to move," Ace said, pursing his lips as he assessed the situation. The last eye socket he'd buried his knife into had gotten him an arm swipe that was far too close for comfort.

"Any room on the other side to jump down the row of cars?" Dante asked, turning around to face him.

"Gonna have to be," Ace replied, taking a deep breath. He raised his leg and kicked a zombie in the chest, slamming it into a few of its friends. Before he could second-guess himself, he leapt for the next car.

It wasn't a large gap, only a few feet, but from one slick car roof to another, it seemed more precarious than it should be. When he hit the fiberglass on the other side, Ace's life flashed before his eyes as his shoes slid on the smooth rounded surface. He vaguely heard Dante yelling for him, but all he could concentrate on was staying on top of the car, staying alive.

He managed to keep a hold of his knife, miraculously, scrabbling as he slid down the windshield on his belly. A rotted hand grabbed his ankle, and he kicked and flailed, hands squeaking against the car as he struggled to get back up on top.

There was a hard *thump* as Dante landed on the roof, the vehicle bowing under the impact. He grabbed Ace's arm and heaved, dragging his body up on top of the car. The zombie came with him, but at least its mouth wasn't within biting distance, and Dante fired once with his handgun to end the creature.

Ace disengaged the ghoul's grip and got to his feet carefully, the two of them standing back to back on the car.

"We should be able to take the last of 'em out from this one, but if not we'll

make the jump down the next two," Dante
said, and the redneck nodded.

"Thanks, man," he said.

"Anytime," Dante replied, and then
swung down, stabbing a zombie.

Ace followed suit, vigor renewed
after his adrenaline-fueled near death,
and soon there were only three zombies
left, struggling to clamber over their
fallen pack.

Dante bent his knees and then jumped,
his feet hitting the lead one in the
chest, knocking it back into its
companions. Ace slid down the back of the
car and joined him in lunging down to stab
the zombies before they could struggle to
their feet.

Once finished, the two men stood and
admired their pile of bodies, more than a
little shell-shocked at how the whole
thing had gone down.

At the sound of a door slamming, they
turned towards Brandt, who was shaking his
head, face pale. "We gotta get out of
here," he said.

Ace rolled his eyes. "Plans don't
change just cause a few zombies show up,"
he drawled. "We still gotta take out those
QXR assholes."

"Did the one that reanimated have his
gun on him?" Dante asked, inclining his
head to the SUV.

"They took it," Ace replied, shaking his head. "We going back into town, then?"

The larger man nodded. "We'll have to get to the bike, once we take care of these guys," he suggested.

"Good call," Ace agreed, and pocketed his knife, keeping his shotgun at the ready.

As the trio came up to the main road, the sound of squealing tires rose in the air, and they pressed themselves against a building on the corner. A bullet exploded the brick above their heads, and they ducked and dove.

Brandt and Ace lunged behind a dumpster, while Dante darted around the corner. He spotted an SUV skidding out, having spotted him and in the process of turning around. He ran full-tilt across the road and into an alleyway, coming face to face with a pack of five zombies.

They shrieked when they spotted him, but he didn't let it faze him, simply dropped his shoulder and took a run. He slammed into the first ghoul's torso, pushing off of the ground so that it flew back into its brethren. He fired twice, hitting one in the face and another in the throat, and then ran overtop of them, using a chest as a stepping stone to leap clear of the writhing group.

Once on the other side, he tore down the alley and hung a right, skidding at the sight of a thick copse of corpses. He darted to the right and clambered up on top of a closed dumpster, just as more shots rang out.

Can't catch a fuckin' break, he thought as he whipped around, aiming behind him. There was a blur of black as a mercenary ducked behind a building on the far end. Zombies swarmed the dumpster, reaching up and attempting to grab his ankles. He didn't like how out in the open he was, but it couldn't be helped at this point.

If his opponent fired enough times, he hoped that the ghouls would go that way, but he couldn't count on it.

As soon as a head popped out from around the corner, he fired, missing, but sending the mercenary back behind cover. He chanced looking around to find a way out of his predicament and spotted a ladder across the alley that led up to the roof of one of the main road buildings. He glanced back towards the mercenary, waiting for him to come back.

He didn't often commiserate on missing an eye, but this was one of those moments when he wished he had more peripheral vision so he could calculate

the odds of his jump while also keeping
watch on his enemy.

More gunfire echoed from the road,
and he hoped that Ace was okay if he was
fighting the rest of the QXR goons that
had skidded up the main road.

A head popped out from the corner and
he fired again, loathe to waste the
bullets considering the distance, but it
covered him enough that he made the snap
decision to make the jump. He backed up
against the wall and took a deep breath,
running and pushing as hard as he could
off of the edge of the dumpster.

A three-round burst whizzed past him,
one narrowly missing his nose as he flew
through the air. He didn't flinch for fear
of missing the ladder and managed to grab
onto a rung with one hand. He maniacally
shoved his gun in the back of his pants,
next to the shotgun that was slipping down
his pant leg and making it difficult to
climb. He quickly gripped the rungs as
another three-round burst came his way and
hooked a foot up as high as he could.

Something gripped his other ankle,
and he kicked wildly, booting a zombie in
the face.

A few ghouls from the pack tore off
in the direction of the gunman, and the
mercenary focused his fire on them, giving
Dante an opening to try to dislodge his

leg without worrying about being shot. He finally managed to disengage the rotted arm and hauled himself up the ladder as fast as he could.

The zombies quickly lost interest in him as the mercenary continued to fire, and Dante made it to the roof. He ran across as fast as he could, heart pounding at his series of near-deaths, and crouched when he reached the front edge.

There was more gunfire in the street, and he peered over the edge. The SUV had been abandoned, and four mercenaries stalked towards an alley across the street where, presumably, Ace and Brandt were.

Dante took aim with his handgun, carefully focusing on the head of one of the guys in the back of the quartet. He fired, and managed to clip his target in the shoulder, and the entire pack whipped around. Before he could aim again, one of them spotted him.

"The roof!" the mercenary screamed, and all three not injured pointed their assault rifles at him.

He jerked back from the edge as bullets peppered the tip of the building. Hopefully he'd given Ace and Brandt enough of an opening to regroup. He crawled away from the edge and then stood up into a crouch, heading down the row of buildings. The downtown core was a strip of

buildings, so the roofs all connected, and
he was hoping he could find a way down in
a strategic space.

The shotgun wasn't going to do well
at long range—what would be ideal would be
to grab a fallen mercenary's assault
rifle. He skidded to a stop and changed
directions, heading back towards the
building where the soldier had been firing
at him while he was on the dumpster.

He had to hop the alley that he'd run
down when he was outrunning the SUV, but
it wasn't too big of a gap, and then he
crouched, creeping to the edge of the
building. He heard moans, but no gunfire,
and looked down to see them feasting on
the mercenary. While he was happy the
ghouls were doing his job for him, it
would be difficult getting a gun off of a
fresh zombie.

Some of them were slowing down, it
seemed, but the newly reanimated ones were
at full steam. Dante shook his head and
then moved to the front of the building,
taking stock of what the other four were
up to.

Nobody was on the main road, save for
a few ghouls tearing across the street to
the alley the mercenaries had been
fighting with. He looked down at a series
of metal bars holding the sign out front

of the building and spotted a busted sedan beneath it on the sidewalk.

Dante hooked his legs over the side of the roof, balancing on one of the bars and testing its sturdiness. Satisfied, he crouched and wrapped his hands around it, lowering his feet to one of the bottom ones. He managed to climb down and hang, with only a few feet between his boots and the sedan.

He dropped down, but as soon as his boots clanged on the car, moans erupted, and zombies swarmed from around the building.

Dante pushed off of the car, sliding down to the road and pumping his legs. The shotgun clattered to the ground behind him, but he left it, glancing over his shoulder at the horde of ghouls chasing him. He made sure the handgun was secure as he ran, and dove through an open door, pulling it shut behind him. He threw the deadbolt, wincing as the bodies slamming into it on the other side made it groan.

As he turned around to sweep whatever store he'd ended up in, a body slammed into him. It didn't smell like death, only blood, and the angry grunt that came from its mouth told him it was a life human, not a zombie.

"I'm going to skin you alive, pretty boy," the mercenary snarled, his fist connecting with Dante's face.

When he regained himself from the surprise of the attack, Dante wedged his knee up between them, pushing hard against the soldier's gut. He scrambled to draw his knife, but he couldn't reach down, so settled on gripping the man's throat.

They tussled on the ground for a few moments until the mercenary managed to jab Dante into the side enough times to wind him.

His grip loosened on his attacker's neck, allowing an opening for another brutal blow to his face. He swung wildly, and gave a great heave with his knee, managing to connect with his attacker's ear and throw him off.

As he gasped for breath, he managed to draw his knife, backing up enough to regain his senses before they met again.

The mercenary didn't waste time, throwing himself back towards Dante, who raised his blade at just the right time to drive it into flesh. He didn't hit a vital organ, unfortunately, but buried it deep enough into the man's shoulder that it distracted him with a scream of pain.

Dante twisted the knife and then drew it quickly, shoving the mercenary back and then slashing across his throat. As his opponent gurgled and choked, he stabbed him through the eye socket, not wanting to take a chance that he'd been bitten.

The mercenary's lifeless body crumpled, and the door began to buckle beneath the weight of the ghouls outside. Dante rushed for the back of the store, now realizing it was full of candy. He had the vague thought that under different circumstances, he would have loved to collect up some watermelon gummies for Grace, and then marveled at how random his thought process could be in times of stress.

He found the back door just as the front began to crack under the pressure and inched it open. He spotted one lone zombie a few feet away and didn't hear any gunfire. The sound of glass and wood shattering from the front of the store spurred him on, and he burst into the alleyway, lunging to bury his knife into the back of the ghoul's head.

Gunfire cracked in the distance, and he hopped the fallen corpse, running down the alleyway to try to find his companions.

As Dante took off into the town, Ace tried to find the source of their shooter. Gunfire followed Dante, and the redneck smacked Brandt's shoulder.

"Come on, let's go around back to the next alley over and flank 'em," he hissed, and then took off at a run, not waiting to see if the Sheriff followed.

He did, however, and they tore around the back of the building, stopping at the corner to the alley to peek around. He caught sight of the glint of an SUV, and the back of a mercenary's head.

Ace headed down the alleyway, aiming his shotgun as he got closer and closer, hoping to get close enough to fire at a useful range. Halfway down the alley, the mercenary turned around and raised his assault rifle.

Ace fired despite being too far away and then ducked behind a cluster of trash cans to take cover from the return fire.

"Down here!" the mercenary yelled.

Brandt ran towards Ace, eyes panicked, and then did a baseball slide to join him behind the cans. A pack of ghouls was on his tail, pouring into the alley from the back.

"Shit," Ace said brightly. They were boxed in, flesh-eating corpses on one side, a quartet of crazed soldiers on the other. He looked up over the top of the cans, narrowly missing more bullets, and spotted a metal door just on the other side across the alley. "We gotta get in that building," he said.

"How the fuck are we gonna do that?" Brandt barked and fired his shotgun into the oncoming horde. He blew apart the top half of one ghoul, tripping up a few behind it.

Ace popped up as the assault rifle bursts stopped, and fired at the mercenaries, who took cover around the corners of the mouth of the alley. He fired again, darting for the door, and pulled on it, willing it to be unlocked.

Thankfully it was, and he opened it towards the mercenaries, using it as a shield as Brandt ran towards him. They slipped inside just as the zombies reached them, managing to pull it shut just in time.

Moans echoed from behind them in the storeroom they'd entered, and both men whipped around.

"Lock the door!" Ace cried, before blowing a zombie's head off.

Brandt scrambled to lock the door and then grunted as a ghoul lunged for him. They tussled for a moment before he finally kicked the corpse away, raising his shotgun fast enough to blast it in the head, splattering brains everywhere.

Ace, needing to reload but without time, used the butt of his gun to smash a zombie in the face, and then clambered on top of a large wooden crate as the ghoul struggled to get to its feet again.

He pulled out his knife and began to stab down like whack-a-mole, dropping zombies left and right. Soon there was a pile of corpses around the crate, and the Sheriff stood, chest heaving, across the room.

Both men stood there, waiting, listening hard, which was difficult with the banging on the door.

"Front or back?" Brandt asked hoarsely, and Ace jumped down from the crate.

"If they're heading towards the back, I say we go out the front and try to get 'em from behind," the redneck said, and headed for the store. They came out from the back room into a gift shop, wall to wall with kitschy overpriced items. When they reached the front, they peered out of the large glass window, and it immediately shattered with gunfire.

Ace hit the floor, and Brandt rolled around, pressing his back into the wall next to the window frame.

"HEY!" the Sheriff screamed. "I'll
come out! Don't shoot me!"

One of the mercenaries laughed.
"Yeah, come on out, piggy," he called in a
singsong voice, followed by a chorus of
snorting.

"I'm not with these assholes," Brandt
cried, and Ace's gaze darkened. "I'll even
help you take 'em out!"

"Idiot," the redneck muttered under
his breath, staying on the floor as Brandt
stepped into the window.

The mercenaries immediately opened
fire again, and a bullet caught the
Sheriff in the arm. He grunted and dove
back behind cover.

"Goddammit!" he cried, incredulity in
his voice.

Ace was torn between being angry at
him and amused that his selfishness had
gotten him shot. "How many times do we
have to tell you these guys ain't fucking
around before you believe us?" he asked,
shaking his head.

He peeked up a little, seeing all
four mercenaries out front, walking slowly
with their guns aimed towards the store.
He began to crawl along the floor back
towards the storeroom, and Brandt hissed,
but followed him.

"We gotta beat 'em to the back door,"
Ace grunted as he got to his feet. "That

is if you still want to get out of this alive."

The Sheriff simply huffed in response and followed him through the back storeroom. They ran past the side door that still had thumping on it and inched open the back door. The alley was clear, with a pack of thirty or so ghouls headed their way from the far end.

"They're going out the back!" one of the mercenaries cried from inside the store, and Ace leapt into the alley.

Brandt fired towards the inside, backing out next to Ace. "Let's go!" he cried, but the redneck shook his head.

"Let's keep 'em pinned down until those zombies get here," he said, inclining his head towards the oncoming horde. "Find something to jam in the door so they can get in."

"Are you crazy?!" the Sheriff demanded.

Ace simply grinned. "Don't you know that by now?" he asked and motioned to a pile of chunks of wood next to a trash can. He fired his shotgun into the warehouse again and then ducked behind the door to avoid an onslaught of bullets.

"They're outside!" somebody yelled from inside.

"We can't get around back!" somebody else called back.

"That's it," Ace cooed quietly as he reloaded the shotgun. "There's only one way out, and it's through here, boys."

Brandt rushed over, groaning at the pain in his wounded arm as he knelt down to shove a chunk of wood into the seam of the door. Ace let it go, and it closed a bit, staying about a foot open.

"Let's go!" the Sheriff said, hopping from foot to foot as the zombies grew closer.

Ace shook his head. "One more," he said, and fired into the warehouse again to keep the mercenaries pinned and interested.

When the ghouls were about ten yards away, he poked his head into the doorway, and the mercenaries fired, three-round bursts peppering the door. Ace jerked away and tore off with Brandt, leaving the ghouls to pour into the warehouse, drawn by the sound of the gunfire.

Screams erupted from inside, but they didn't look back, running away from the carnage to what they hoped was safety.

Dante peeked around a corner, spotting a lone SUV in the middle of the road. Two mercenaries backed up against it, aiming at a storefront with shattered windows. By the look of the limp corpses hanging over the sills, it looked like they'd just fought their way out of a massacre.

He hoped to hell that Ace wasn't a body in that massacre, but by the way the mercenaries seemed to be on guard, he hoped it was because they were still expecting resistance.

"We should go," one of them said shakily.

The other shook his head. "Bob's got the keys, man," he replied, receiving a grunt of frustration in return. "We just gotta guard the car till he gets back."

"What if he's already dead?" the first one asked.

"I dunno, man," the second one admitted.

Dante quietly checked his mag, sighing when he found only one bullet left. With his knife in his left hand, he used his wrist to steady the gun with his right, taking careful aim at the closest one's head.

After a silent countdown from three, he fired, his bullet finding its mark into the back of the mercenary's head. The other one reacted with shock, but didn't raise his gun fast enough before Dante was on him.

He used his assault rifle to block the knife strike, and they wrestled for a moment before their tussle resulted in both weapons flying to the side and clattering against the ground. Rather than dive for them, Dante launched himself on top of the man, shoving him back into the hood of the SUV.

The soldier managed to get a good hit to his face, but he'd had enough of those that day, and grabbed a fistful of the mercenary's hair, slamming his head down into the hood of the vehicle.

As his skull pinged off of the fiberglass, Dante kneed him in the stomach, knocking the wind out of him.

Before he could lunge down with an elbow strike, the mercenary slammed into him, knocking them both back to the ground. Blows rained down on Dante, and he finally managed to shove him over, rolling them and ending up on top.

He wedged his forearm into the soldier's throat, holding him down and pinning his body. The mercenary gasped for air as Dante crushed his trachea, his arms flailing, but Dante didn't let up, taking every hit as they grew weaker and weaker.

After the soldier fell limp, he got off of him and retrieved the assault rifle and the knife. He switched the gun to single-burst mode and put a bullet in the soldier's head.

Dante wheezed as he looked around, making sure no zombies had come running towards the noise. As he caught his breath, he stabbed each tire of the SUV for good measure, just in case 'Bob' was still alive and coming back with the keys.

Wiping a touch of blood from his face, he took off at a slow jog towards the area where they'd left the bike, hoping that Ace would be there.

When he rounded the corner, the redneck was there, with Brandt, who had a strip of fabric crudely tied around his arm, soaked with blood.

"Dante!" Ace exclaimed, letting out a *whoosh* of breath. "Thank fuck! I was really not looking forward to my sister beating the shit out of me for letting you die."

Dante rolled his eyes. "My life is not in your hands, man," he said, and clapped Ace on the shoulder. "Glad you made it. Any more mercs lurking about, do you think?"

The redneck shrugged. "We trapped four of 'em in a store with a bunch of zombies, so I don't think they'll be making it out."

"Even if they do, I slashed the tires on their last SUV," Dante replied.

Ace nodded. "Good call, good call," he said. "I think we're good. I haven't heard any gunshots in a while. If any of them are still around, I don't think they'll get very far. You look a little worse for wear, man, you okay?"

"I've had worse," Dante said with a half smile. "Not a scratch on you, though."

"Thanks for caring that I've been *shot*," Brandt piped up.

Dante raised his eyebrow. "What happened?" he asked. "Finally piss off Ace enough?"

"He tried to sell me out to QXR," the redneck announced, stifling an amused smile, "but they shot him instead."

Dante shook his head. "Guess that's the price you pay for not listening to us," he said with a shrug. "And after we offered you a safe place, too."

"There's no way you were actually going to bring me to a safe place," the Sheriff snapped, clenching his jaw.

Moans rose in the distance, and Dante looked past him, spotting ghouls down the street, pouring out of an alleyway and heading towards them. Ace lifted the bike, securing his weapons to him and kick starting it.

"We were," Dante said, refocusing on the red-faced Sheriff, "but now you'll never know." He hopped on the back of the bike.

"Wait!" Brandt cried, staggering towards them. "You can't leave me here! Please!"

"Shouldn't have tried to sell me out," Ace snapped, and then hit the throttle, leaving him in a cloud of smoke, unable to aim his shotgun at them.

They sped to the main road, and then the redneck skidded to a stop around the corner. The route they wanted was crawling with zombies, and they all turned at the same time, mouths opening in excitement.

"Fuck," the redneck declared. "Ideas?"

"How much gas we got?" Dante asked.

"Not enough to get to the next station," Ace replied. "I need the one on the other side of that pack."

"Well, let's lead 'em away, then," Dante suggested. "Head the other way."

Ace pulled a u-turn, and as they passed back through the intersection, they spotted Brandt firing into the horde, to no avail as it overwhelmed him.

"Good fucking riddance," Ace muttered, and they sped down the street.

The side streets had packs of zombies down them, clustered enough that they wouldn't be easy to navigate around. He kept going straight, but they were both worried about the gas running out before they could loop back around.

They stopped at another intersection with lights, and the left side was fairly clear. There were two ghouls aimlessly wandering in the distance, easily avoided when the time came. Ace idled for a moment, letting the pursuing zombies catch up a bit so they didn't lose them. They'd need enough time to outrun them and then also fill the gas tank before tearing out of town.

When the front of the horde was about ten yards away, Ace hit the throttle and zoomed for about a quarter mile before the engine sputtered.

"Fuck!" he barked, and they began to slow down.

"Get off and push!" Dante cried, and hopped off of the vehicle. "We're fucked if we leave it behind!"

"No shit!" Ace quipped, and they ran, both hands on the bike as they rolled it along with them.

"Take the next street, not the alley," Dante suggested. "We don't want to get caught in a bottleneck."

The redneck nodded, and they ran at a good clip towards the next road. The zombies kept pace with them, thankfully not as fast as their early days sprinting. However, as they made the turn, the sound of rapid boot falls grew closer.

The duo looked over their shoulders, and Ace rolled his eyes.

"This fucker just won't quit," he muttered.

A zombified Sheriff Brandt, fresh off the zombie press, sprinted towards them, milky eyes and huge chunks of his flesh hanging from his body.

Dante raised the assault rifle as they ran, and when the zombie was a few feet away, he loosed a bullet into its forehead.

"Gone for good this time," he declared.

Ace nodded, smirking. "Francis and Maddox'll be happy with this story," he said.

"Over the moon," Dante agreed, and his legs began to protest as they ran. It had been an exhausting day, and at this point he was running on pure adrenaline. "So… how are we going to fill the gas tank?"

The redneck grimaced. "I was hoping you had some thoughts about that," he huffed, "cause I got nothing."

"Well…" Dante began and then sighed. "I've got this," he said, holding up the assault rifle. "Makes a lot of noise."

Ace raised an eyebrow. "You saying you draw them away while I fill the tank, and then I come and pick you up?" he asked.

"Or you could draw them away while *I* fill the tank," Dante joked. "That would be cool too."

The redneck chuckled through his heavy breaths. "I'm good, man, I'll take one for the team and be the gas bitch."

"Suit yourself," Dante replied. He spotted the building up ahead where he'd climbed down on top of the sedan, and pointed to it. "I'll get up on top of that building and draw the horde back down to the other end of the road from the roof. You gas up and then meet me back under that sign."

"Gotcha," Ace agreed, and they nodded to each other before Dante broke off and ran for the busted car.

He clambered up on top of the roof and crouched, leaping up as high as he could to grab the metal bars. He pulled himself up with a grunt, hooking a leg up on one of the bars to propel himself to the top. The ghouls were almost at his position, and he wanted to make sure he kept their attention so Ace could get away.

As soon as he clambered up onto the roof, he pulled the assault rifle from his pack and fired into the horde. A few zombies fell, and the rest poured towards him, smacking into the building, confused.

"Yeah, come party with me, you dead fucks!" he bellowed, and started walking along the roofs of the stores.

He hopped the first alleyway and then fired again, taking out a few more zombies and drawing the horde after him. He continued to hoot and holler and yell, loosing a few bullets every so often as he walked to the other end.

"Hurry back, Ace," he murmured, hoping that the redneck wouldn't run into any trouble at the gas station.

CHAPTER EIGHT

Ace jogged up to the gas station, pocket knife in his fist, looking around everywhere in case of any friends trying to surprise him and eat his face. If he were being totally honest, he was more worried about stray mercenaries, even though after his mental count he was sure that they'd gotten them all.

He could still hear the crack of Dante's gunfire in the distance, so he was sure that any zombies wandering around would be more apt to go in that direction.

He reached the first pump and hit the kickstand, unscrewing the cap for the tank as fast as he could. He grabbed the pump and stuck it in the tank, and pulled the handle.

Nothing.

"Fuck," he muttered. Was the pump empty? He looked at the screen and saw an error message saying to go speak to an attendant. "An attendant that wants to chew on my brains, great." He looked back and forth and then sprinted for the gas bar. The front door hung open, and he did a quick sweep of the store, finding it empty.

He skirted the counter and checked the panel for the gas pumps, pushing all the buttons until the cash register gave a *ding*. With the lights all green, he assumed that the gas would be flowing, so he burst back outside and sprinted for the bike.

This time when he pulled the handle, gasoline began to pump into the tank, and he let out a sigh of relief.

"At least it didn't want a credit card," he muttered, and then chuckled under his breath, shaking his head.

Once full, he turned and replaced the pump, and then a rotted hand narrowly missed his face.

"Jesus fuck!" he cried, at high enough of a pitch that he was glad nobody was around to hear it. He ducked and dove around the pump, out of the reach of the excited zombie that had come out of nowhere.

He stabbed through the pillars at the pump, but the ghoul was fast enough that it passed his arm, staggering around to get to him. He kicked it in the chest, sending it stumbling back into the windshield washing station, the squeegee knocking loose and splattering brown water everywhere.

Ace took his opening and lunged forward, burying the knife into the zombie's eye socket. As soon as it fell limp, he whipped around. He had to be fast, Dante was waiting on him, but he didn't want to start up the bike and make a bunch of noise.

He quickly replaced the cap on the gas tank and steered the bike around, running as fast as he could with the rolling vehicle alongside him. When he reached the main road, he heard Dante yelling instead of shooting, and assumed he'd either run out of bullets or decided to conserve them.

He spotted his companion on the roof at the end of the row, waving his arms and jumping up and down. It was an almost comical sight, and he filed it away to describe to Lily later.

There were no ghouls in sight, so he chanced walking out into the street with the bike, trying to figure out how he was doing to get Dante's attention without making a sound. Thankfully, his companion seemed to spot him, because he waved.

Now, how to get him over here? Ace wondered, but it seemed Dante had that covered as well. He fired a few times into the crowd and then ducked down, so that he was out of sight. Ace spotted him coming into view on the back side of the row of buildings, running across the roof.

He wheeled the bike over to the broken sedan, and got on it, ready to kick start as soon as Dante was down.

As soon as the man's boots hit the roof of the car, the zombies began to trickle their way.

Ace hit the starter, and Dante jumped onto the back, wrapping an arm around his waist. The redneck chuckled and hit the throttle, speeding them out of town.

Both men seemed afraid to let out sighs of relief, but as they left their harrowing day in the dust, they felt lighter and lighter. There was just the hope that QXR wouldn't come knocking. At least if they did, they'd find them here, and not right on top of Ace's house and the little community they'd begun to build for themselves.

The redneck went straight to Maddox's and punched in the code for the gate.

"Where is everyone?" Dante asked, getting off of the back of the bike, brow furrowed. There were no signs of struggle, but it unsettled him how quiet it was.

Ace hit the kickstand and wandered up to the trailer, finding a little yellow sticky note attached to the door. "Gone to the farm," he read out loud, and shook his head. "You okay riding bitch a little bit longer?"

Dante laughed, shaking his head. "You mean I get the pleasure of hugging you for another leg of the trip?" he pretended to

flip imaginary hair over his shoulder.
"Sign me up!"

CHAPTER NINE

As the bike rumbled up towards the abandoned school, Lily emerged from the gymnasium door, flanked by Cam and Bailey. She put her hands on her hips, giving the men a stern look like an angry mom.

"About time you boys got back," she scolded, but couldn't keep the smile out of her voice.

Ace rolled his eyes. "Don't even pretend like you missed me, Lil," he drawled.

"I didn't miss you at all," she teased, and then her gaze softened when she noticed how rough around the edges Dante looked. "What happened?"

He stepped up to her and brushed some stray hair back from her face, gazing down at her with a smile. "Lots. But I'm fine."

"Well I can see that, you big oaf," she shot back, but her voice lacked any venom as she grinned goofily up at him.

Cam gaped at them, and then turned to Ace, eyes wide.

"About time, right?" the redneck drawled, and clapped the younger man on the back, leading him back inside.

Bailey blushed crimson and trotted after them, brushing past Cam to be first back into the gym.

Dante looped an arm around Lily's shoulders, pressing a soft kiss to the top of her head as they headed inside.

"Fine, but needs his woman to hold him up, I see how it is," she joked as she slid her arm around his waist, and he pretended to lean on her. She poked him in the side and he laughed, easing up on her shoulders.

"I could clean up," he said, looking around.

The gym wasn't exactly a hive of activity, given their low population, but work had definitely been done. There were raised garden beds everywhere, with neat little rows. Henry and Tate sat on the far end at a set of desks someone had pulled together, sharing a giant bong as they leaned over some papers.

"Over here," Lily said, waving for him to come to the right.

There was a long hose coming out of one of the change rooms, and it hung over the side of a large plastic tub. The nozzle attached to it had varying sprays, and there was a stack of towels stacked neatly next to it.

"Need a shower?" she asked with a sly wink, squeezing the handle and spraying in a sprinkler pattern.

He chuckled low in his throat. "Maybe later," he replied, heat blooming in his belly at her insinuation. He stuck his hands in the tub and let her spray him down and then wet a towel to wipe the blood from his face.

"There he is," Lily said as he dried himself off. "Want the grand tour?"

He raised his eyebrow. "Is there more?"

"No," she said and trilled a laugh. "This is it."

"I'm glad you all made it out okay," he said, lowering his head. "Did you run into any trouble at all?"

She shook her head. "No, we had a clean getaway." She crossed her arms. "Now, tell me what happened to you, mister."

"No fucking way!" Maddox exclaimed, his laugh booming across the space as he doubled over.

"I think Ace is already regaling everyone with our tale," Dante said with a chuckle, and took her hand, leading her over to the others clustered near Tate and Henry.

Ace wiped pretend tears from his eyes. "Yes, way!" he said, shaking his head. "He was such a fucking dick, and then he tried to sell me out, so we left his ass."

"That's amazing!" Maddox guffawed, and slapped Francis on the back as the large man walked by, carrying a bucket of soil from outside. "Did you hear that? They left Brandt in the middle of a zombie-infested town!"

"That's not even the best part," Dante cut in with a smirk.

Ace grinned. "He caught up to us later, all zombified."

"No!" Maddox declared, raising his hands. "Tell me you shot that fucker in the face!"

At Ace's nod, the other redneck whooped, doing a little jig. Lily rolled her eyes, glancing over at Abigail and her daughters, who were off to the side, thankfully occupied.

"What were you doing back at the prison, anyway?" Tate piped up, turning towards them with bright red eyes.

Ace shook his head. "We needed wheels, and this guy thought it would be a bright idea to snag a cop car," he said, jerking a thumb at Dante. "Which we weren't even able to get, anyway. We also needed some gear to fight the QXR, but of course the supply room had a keypad with a number code."

"Ugh, of course," Maddox moaned.

"Also thanks for tossing the keys to his cell in the toilet, asshole," Ace added, staring at Maddox with disdain. "I

lost rock paper scissors and had to fish
'em out."

"Ew!" Tate cried, wrinkling his nose.

"Thankfully there was no shit in
there," Ace said, but still glared at
Maddox.

"Y'all are disgusting," Lily quipped,
shaking her head. "Anyway, did you take
out all of those QXR guys, or are we going
to have problems?"

Dante shrugged. "By our count, we're
pretty sure we got them all," he said.
"And we slashed all of their tires, so
even if there are any left, they won't be
going anywhere by car. But we left a lot
of hungry zombies downtown, so it doesn't
look good for any survivors."

"What if somebody comes looking for
their friends?" Henry asked, his words
slow and sluggish. "I mean, won't somebody
come looking for them?"

Dante shrugged again. "Honestly, I
don't know," he admitted. "They don't seem
like the type of guys to really care if
they lose anyone. But they might come
investigating to see if there's resistance
out here other than zombies."

"Not out *here* though," Tate said.
"We're out of the way, and this place
doesn't look like anything."

Ace shook his head. "Probably best to set up a watch, anyway," he suggested. "Just to be on the safe side."

"You two get to sleep tonight," Lily said firmly. "After the exciting day you've had."

Her cousin stretched his arms above his head, cracking his back and shoulders. "And you are right about that, cousin dear," he drawled. "I could use some eats and a nap."

Bailey jerked a thumb over her shoulder. "We've got some stew going in the kitchen," she said. "Come on."

Lily hooked her arm through Dante's, and they followed the young woman down the hallway to the cafeteria.

"You guys got set up nice in here," he said, noting some of the classrooms cleared out with some sleeping bags and amenities set up. "For having to leave so fast."

"Well, we weren't sure how long we were going to have to stay, and we wanted to make sure it was comfortable for the little ones," Lily said. "It's pretty good what we managed to find in here, even with the building so old. I was amazed there was power, at least for the time being. Grabbing some camp stoves or something would be a good idea for the long term."

Dante nodded. "A generator would be ideal," he said, "but I don't know if it would be a good idea to make that much noise. We don't want to attract a whole pile of those things."

"Speaking of, we're going to have to talk about defense," Ace piped up. "It's all well and good to have doors that close, but if a bunch of zombies end up surrounding the building, that's just a pain in the ass."

Lily nodded. "Yes," she agreed, "but first, we eat."

Bailey grabbed the pot from the kitchen and tipped it, pouring the thick stew into some disposable paper bowls. "There's no washable stuff in here," she said. "I found a couple of mugs, but we figured we might as well use these up first."

Dante smiled at her as he took his bowl and grabbed a few plastic spoons from the condiments table. They were in plastic packaging, so thankfully not as covered in dust as the rest of the stuff kicking around the area. The quartet sat down at one of the picnic table style benches, and Dante tossed Ace a spoon.

They dug into their stew like animals, and the girls shared a playfully disgusted look at their vigor. Once their

bowls were clean, they smacked their lips
in satisfaction.

"Hey, didn't you say you had a
chocolate-covered granola bar?" Dante
asked, raising his eyebrow.

Ace crossed his arms. "Hey, just
because you wasted yours on an asshole cop
that died five seconds later, doesn't mean
you're entitled to mine," he said with
playful haughtiness.

"But mine wasn't chocolate-covered,"
Dante shot back. "It wasn't even one with
little marshmallows in it."

"The humanity!" Bailey exclaimed, and
the four of them shared a laugh at her
sarcastic outburst.

Ace rolled his eyes and then pulled
out the granola bar in question, tearing
into it and breaking it in half. He
offered the smaller half to Dante, who
took it with a smile.

They got up and headed back to the
gym where everyone had filtered off to do
their own thing. Abigail waved Bailey
over, and she offered the others a smile
before heading to spend time with her
family.

Dante stared out over the beginnings
of their little farm, but his thoughts
were elsewhere. He thought of his sister,
trapped with those QXR assholes. What were

they doing to her? Or making her do? He clenched his jaw.

He knew that he couldn't have done anything differently. He knew that he couldn't have saved her at the time, that she was too far away from him. He even had overcome his guilt in not staying with her, because he'd managed to get Bailey out. Had he stuck around, she would have been captured as well, and that would have been just one more person he couldn't save.

"Hey," Lily said quietly, and he looked down at her, snapping out of his trance. "You okay?" she asked.

Dante looked to his left and realized that Ace had wandered off to talk to Francis, who was finally relaxing in the corner instead of hauling dirt.

"Just worried about Grace," he said, running a hand over his hair. "I can't stop thinking about what could be happening to her right now."

She squeezed his hand gently. "That's a dangerous path," she said. "You'll just drive yourself crazy with that thought process. Best to think about a plan of action."

He nodded, smiling down at her. "You're right."

"Shit, you're built like a brick house *and* you admit I'm right?" she said,

putting a hand to her chest. "I hit the
jackpot."

He laughed, and it felt good. They
headed for the planning table, surrounded
by their companions that grew stronger by
the day.

At least for now, Dante could have
hope.

END

Coming Soon: The survivors in the
Lowcountry face new threats as they
continue to rebuild after the zombie
apocalypse.

Up Next: The Second Month begins in
the main Dead America series as a zombie
horde a million strong marches towards El
Paso in "Dead America: Creeping Death".

www.ingramcontent.com/pod-product-compliance
Lightning Source LLC
Chambersburg PA
CBHW071418190726
48292CB00001B/28